THIS IS ALL A LIE

THIS IS ALL A LIE

A NOVEL

Thomas Trofimuk

ENFIELD
&WIZENTY

Enfield & Wizenty
(an imprint of Great Plains Publications)
233 Garfield Street
Winnipeg, MB R3G 2M1
www.greatplains.mb.ca

Great Plains Publications gratefully acknowledges the financial support provided for its publishing program by the Government of Canada through the Canada Book Fund; the Canada Council for the Arts; the Province of Manitoba through the Book Publishing Tax Credit and the Book Publisher Marketing Assistance Program; and the Manitoba Arts Council.

Design & Typography by Relish New Brand Experience
Printed in Canada by Friesens

LIBRARY AND ARCHIVES CANADA CATALOGUING IN PUBLICATION

Trofimuk, Thomas, 1958-, author
    This is all a lie / Thomas Trofimuk.

Issued in print and electronic formats.
ISBN 978-1-927855-77-5 (softcover).--ISBN 978-1-927855-78-2 (EPUB).--
ISBN 978-1-927855-79-9 (Kindle)

    1. Title.

PS8589.R644T45 2017   C813'.54   C2017-902012-9
                                     C2017-902013-7

ENVIRONMENTAL BENEFITS STATEMENT

Great Plains Publications saved the following resources by printing the pages of this book on chlorine free paper made with 100% post-consumer waste.

TREES	WATER	ENERGY	SOLID WASTE	GREENHOUSE GASES
11	5,194	5	348	957
FULLY GROWN	GALLONS	MILLION BTUs	POUNDS	POUNDS

Environmental impact estimates were made using the Environmental Paper Network Paper Calculator 3.2. For more information visit www.papercalculator.org.

Canada

FSC
www.fsc.org
MIX
Paper from
responsible sources
FSC® C016245

Perhaps you begin to read this book in a bath. The temperature is perfectly Goldilocks – not too hot, nowhere near tepid, just right. You are more buoyant because you have added mineral salts to the water but you do not notice this buoyancy. The water feels silky – heavier, slower through your fingers. Candles stand guard along the ledge and throw dancing shadows against the tile. You probably used one of the utility lighters you bought last week to light the candles. Of course, there were five of these long-necked lighters in the package, because people always need five lighters all at once. You had to use industrial scissors to open the package. Maybe you have wooden matches and these are what you used to light the candles, so you do not think about the excessive packaging.

It's possible your kids are in bed, asleep, and your husband is watching the hockey game in the basement. Or, perhaps your wife is out with her girlfriends and you read five stories to the kids before they fell asleep, and now this bath is waiting. Maybe your partner is at a yoga class and you've opted out – Yin yoga is too intense for you. Instead, you've carved out this time to be alone. You found this book on your to-read shelf and decided to dive in. You poured yourself a generous glass of wine because you do not want to have to get out of the bath and go downstairs for more, and you do not want to haul the entire bottle upstairs because it will just get warm. You like your white wine so cold it's almost frozen.

Last week, you poured yourself a hefty portion of scotch, crawled into the tub, drank half the whisky and promptly fell asleep. You hope the wine will not have the same effect. You like reading in the bath.

Snow is falling past the window above the bathtub. It has been snowing since 2 p.m. You slide the window open, just a bit, and listen. Silence. You can't even hear the traffic from 97th Street. Your tulips are completely covered by the snow. You hope they will still bloom despite this setback. You dry your hands and light the last two candles. You open the book and flip through the first few pages. You might notice the

Note on the Font and the *Acknowledgements* are at the beginning. While you've never really thought about fonts, you expect there are hundreds, if not thousands of them in the world. You've never paid attention to them. Not really. You do not have a favourite font, nor do you know which ones are easier to read, and more importantly, you don't care.

The first pages in this book bother you. You have questions. Does the author actually want you to read the *Note on the Font* and the *Acknowledgements*? What about the *Epilogue*? Because it's there too. These sections are normally at the back of a book and because of this, they are easy to ignore. Well, you always read epilogues, and prologues for that matter. The prologue is the set-up; the epilogue is the denouement – the exhalation at the end of things. Regardless of your normal reading habits, you know you won't be able to flip past the *Note on the Font* and the *Acknowledgements*. You'll read them. You'll read them because they're out of place. You might peek at the first chapter, which is Chapter 24. This might make you feel even more unsettled. Perhaps the whole book is backwards. It seems everything is flipped around. You might take a big breath and tell yourself – *it's okay, it's fine.* This is the writer trusting the reader to do the right thing.

You look out the window at the falling snow. Except it's not falling anymore – it's rising. The snow is lifting from the ground and drifting silently into the sky. You take a sip of your wine but it's not wine anymore – it's the good scotch your father-in-law gave you for your birthday. And the bathwater is cold. How long have you been in here? You reach with your left foot and nudge the hot water tap, and hot water spreads into the tub. Somewhere down the hall, a baby is crying. Music is playing and you recognize it as Elgar's 2nd Movement, from his *Serenade for Strings*. You do not remember knowing anything about classical music – you've always preferred jazz. This music is so sad. What the hell is going on?

In the beginning movement of the book, you can see there is a chunk of writing – marked with the symbol for 'half' and an ellipsis. It is stranded just before the *Note on the Font* and it's about you. In this section of writing, you're in a bathtub with the water at the perfect temperature and you are starting to read a book in which everything is backwards and nothing is true.

Everything is backwards and nothing is true. Is that right? Is truth the opposite of a lie? Is the world pure black and white with no degrees of grey when it comes to truth? Either you tell the truth, or you lie? You're old enough to recognize this is bullshit. Life is all middle ground. Black is an idea. White is a pretty idea.

You start to take a sip of your drink and you're not sure what to expect. Will it be wine, or whisky – or something else? You might find you are still drinking wine.

Maybe a lie can be a stepping-stone to the truth. Or, is a lie just the red clown nose on the face of truth? Perhaps truth is the adjective, and lying is the verb, and they both modify the colour grey. This book says it is all a lie, but is this title a lie too? Which would mean nothing in the book is a lie? Your head hurts – like when you were in university, in Philosophy 365, studying the relationship between reality and consciousness. You remember late nights in the campus pub talking about Hegel, Marx, Kierkegaard, and Nietzsche with anyone who would engage. You were mesmerized by these ideas. You were just barely smart enough to recognize that while this conversation was not new, it was important. You were trying on new ideas and some of them would stick with you. You probably didn't get laid a lot.

You do not know what's in your glass anymore and you no longer care. Elgar's *Serenade for Strings* seems to have stopped. It's so quiet. You want to check on the snow. You want to see if it's still rising into the sky. Maybe your tulips are uncovered. But no, you place these things aside. You open the book and start to read.

....

Imagine a woman with luxurious brown hair sitting at a desk, marking her students' papers. She has pulled her hair into a sloppy ponytail so it is not in her face and she can focus on her work. The phone might ring and she looks up from her marking and sighs. She will pick it up and say nothing. The woman on the other end hesitates before saying anything, so the brown-haired woman thinks it's a machine trying to sell her something, but then a human voice. The teacher places her red pen aside, and she listens.

"What did you say your name was?"

The woman on the phone tells her, again, and still the teacher is uncertain.

"Okay, look, whatever your fucking name is, you should know, I am too old for jealousy. I've been there and I'm not interested anymore. What do you want?"

"Did you actually hear me? I'm sleeping with your husband."

The teacher swallows. She wills her voice to be unwavering. "So?" she says. "Good for you. I do not own him. He is not my property. If he wants to spend his sex on some twit, I don't care."

"You're not angry? Because I would be beyond pissed off. I would want to rip your fucking head off if you did this to me."

The teacher is beyond angry; she's seething. Just on principle, she's angry, but there's no way she is going to show this woman her anger. Also, this is a surprise and its immediacy stings. She's going to hold it together. "He sleeps with me, honey. He wakes up with me. He has a life with me." The teacher pauses. She holds her breath. She says a little prayer – please, please, please, don't say you're pregnant. That, I couldn't take. Dear God, she thinks. Don't let this woman tell me she's pregnant. Please, God. Please.

"But you're married to him."

"And?" the teacher says. She exhales.

"And when you're married…" But she doesn't finish. Either this woman is truly unaffected by this or she's pretending – and she's an amazing liar. There are rules in marriages, for God's sake. "You're the good wife, aren't you?"

"Well it's better than being an amusement ride, honey. Because that's all you are."

The woman on the phone is silent. The teacher does not feel good about calling this woman an amusement ride. She knows it is hurtful but she is shocked and wounded and off balance. The words just tumbled out. But she is protective now, of her husband. This other woman is trying to hurt him, she's betraying his trust in her, and this pisses her off. She places her anger and hurt aside. She is not surprised her husband had it in him to fool around on her. But the jolt of hearing this woman's voice takes her breath away. The realization that he actually did fool around on her shakes her to the core. But there is also a quiet voice reminding her she is not innocent. A voice that assures her that jealousy would be a meaningless waste. That she has already forgiven her husband for this, because she has no choice but forgiveness. She has no choice.

"Okay," the teacher says. "Are we done here?"

"Don't you want to know how long it's been going on?"

"No..." Hang up, she tells herself. Hang the phone up now. "If my husband wants to relieve himself with some bimbo, I could care less."

"Are you really that much of a heartless bitch?"

"Look, you don't sleep with him. He fucks you – that's all. I know this because I'm the one he sleeps with, wakes up with and has a life with. You're nothing but a fuck. Why don't you go try and ruin someone else's life?"

The teacher puts the phone down. She's done. She does not want to hear any more.

Well, this isn't right – the note on the font is normally at the back of the book, after the acknowledgements. You may wonder what it's doing up here at the beginning, instead of the end. Is the font important? Maybe the font is a key part of the story. You're right to question the placement of this note, but regardless, here it is.

This particular font is Garamond, which comes from the punch-cutter Claude Garamond (Latinised as *garamondus*). Garamond lived, historians believe, from 1480 to 1561. Many Garamond fonts resemble the work of punch-cutter Jean Jannon, or integrate the italic designs from Robert Granjon. However, among present-day typefaces, the Roman versions of Adobe Garamond, Granjon, Sabon, and Stempel Garamond are directly based on Garamond's work.

Garamond's letterforms suggest a sense of grace and constancy. Some unique characteristics in his letters include the small bowl of the "a," the slender eye of the "e," and the soaring upper-case "W," which resembles two superimposed Vs. The lowercase italics z is particularly appealing, with its swooping extender, as in – *zinc, zephyr,* and *azure.* Garamond's long extenders and top serifs have a delightful downward slope. Like all old-style designs, the variation in stroke width is presented in a way that resembles handwriting, creating a design that seems both organic and, for the most part, unembellished. Of course, Garamond's lowercase italics z is the lovely exception.

Garamond is considered one of the most legible and readable serif typefaces when printed on paper. This sounds like one of those "true" things you read on the internet – something like 'eating quinoa every day will add ten years to your life.' Which is an unsubstantiated declaration someone posted years ago and it was re-posted, liked and shared millions of times, until it arrived in your social media feed and it's almost true because it's ubiquitous. Except, it's complete bullshit. Or, that mantra from your mother – every time you talk with her it's "Are you drinking eight cups of water a day, dear?" More bullshit. There is no science to back it up. It's an urban myth. You probably need around six to eight cups per day but this is usually achieved through food, caffeinated beverages and even alcohol. And water, of course. Yup, wine and coffee do not dehydrate you. So you can stop carrying around that water bottle. Just listen to your body, not your mother. Drink water when you're thirsty.

Here's the thing: Garamond actually is a readable font. Test it for yourself. You'll see.

ACKNOWLEDGEMENTS

The author would first like to acknowledge Claude Garamond, the masterful father of the Garamond font, who is most definitely not a character in this book. Good old Claude Garamond is not here – not really. The font you're reading is Garamond, so his work is here, but the guy died in the middle of the sixteenth century. Writing about him would nudge this story toward the genre of historical fiction, and that's not going to happen here. A writer would have to deal with the Protestant Reformation and the corruption of the Catholic Church, the death of Christopher Columbus in 1506 and the ramifications of his explorations – syphilis for one, the explorer Jacques Cartier claiming Quebec for France in 1534, and Copernicus publishing his ridiculous theory that the Earth and the other planets revolved around the Sun in 1543. Three years after old Claude Garamond shuffled off his mortal coil in 1561, William Shakespeare was born. Seriously, this is not historical fiction. You should forget about Claude Garamond now. Bit of a red herring. Sorry about that.

Also, as an equally absurd historical note on this text, there will be no Vikings in this book – not one. You're probably wondering why there would be reference here, in the opening frames of this book, about the absence of Vikings – unless the author is sneakily giving himself permission to write about Vikings at some point in the coming pages. The answer is no. Unequivocally, unquestionably, emphatically no. There will be no Vikings in this book.

Anyway, now that the problems of Claude Garamond and the Vikings are cleared up, you're about to start reading a new book described as 'a novel.' It's right there on the cover. However, you should know this before you begin reading – this probably isn't a novel. Perhaps, if you pick up a book called *This is All a Lie – a novel,* you should not expect it to be a novel, or at least, acknowledge the possibility it might not be a novel at all. The author might say this is a story, and it is populated by deeply flawed characters. Of course, the reviewers will want to call it a novel, because they need categories, and subcategories, genres and – things have to fit somewhere. And what if this writer has a history of writing things called *novels*. You can easily imagine the author, a strikingly handsome man, a witty man, a charming and sensitive man, muttering – in private, and after a couple glasses of wine – "If you're looking for Dickens, or Virginia Woolf, or Brontë, well, read goddamned Dickens, Woolf, or Brontë."

Look, at some point in the next few pages you're probably going to meet a woman named Nancy Petya. Her real name is Nensi Katarina Petya. When she came to North America she changed her name because she grew tired of spelling it for people. She was born in Kursk, in Russia, and in the opening movements of this book, she will be caught inside a terrible moment and it will change everything. She will teeter on the brink and for a while, she won't care which way it goes – she'll be completely free. She will be beyond caring.

Nancy's father was killed in 1989, at the end of the Soviet-Afghan War. He was killed when he stepped on a landmine. There are still over ten million unexploded landmines in Afghanistan. That's what the Kapitán told them when he delivered the news that what remained of her father was in the desert outside Kandahar. Her mother called it the *godforsaken* desert. Nancy is not fond of the country of Afghanistan, nor Afghans, nor anyone who looks like they may be Afghan. She would not like to think she hates anyone, but Afghans, in general, come close. She recognizes the irrational nature of this almost-hatred aimed at a country and its people – the vast majority of whom she has not met. She knows it's absurd, but it's also powerful – sometimes overwhelming. Afghanistan killed her father and therefore she hated Afghanistan. She was eight years old when the news of her father's death marched up to their door. Nancy and her mother were alone in the flat. They were making soup when the door shook. Nancy's siblings were not in the house. Her older brother was fishing, and the twins were playing in the park. "Your father is a hero," the Kapitán said. He did not say 'your father *was* a hero,' as if he were avoiding past tense and purposely keeping his comrade in the present – for the family. "He saved a family caught in a cross-fire. He saved four children and then…" The Kapitán did not finish his sentence. Nancy remembers the Kapitán smelled strongly of cigarettes – he smelled acrid and stale, and his shoes were shined like mirrors. Her mother was struggling to understand – her face contorted in pain. "He was trying to save an Afghan family? I thought we were fighting Afghans."

"Yes, innocents. He saved innocents. He is a hero…" The Kapitán stopped. He took a deep breath. It was as if he realized, finally, his positioning this man as a hero changed nothing for his family. The father, the husband, the soldier and the man were all dead in a pointless war and now the family would have to find a way to survive. This family would have to go on without him. The Kapitán fidgeted with his wristwatch and finally managed to remove it. He bent down with his sad, moustached face and gave the watch to Nensi. "This is for you," he said. Nancy remembers he patted her head, stood up and looked at her mother. "I am sorry for your loss," he said, saluting and turning to leave in one smooth motion.

The Kapitán, whose name was Anatoly Ilia Taras, was well on his way to drinking himself to death. He delivered the news of casualties of war to mothers and fathers, husbands and wives, and to children – and for three-and-a-half years, he held himself together with moderate amounts of vodka. He opened himself to the sadness of what he was doing. He tried to bring a sense of honour and dignity to the reality of so much death. In the third year, with each delivery, he began to drink a little more. When he knocked on Nensi's family's door, his liver was failing and he knew it would be his last assignment. He was at the end of such deliveries. Someone else would have to continue and he knew someone else would always continue.

Anatoly Ilia Taras goes AWOL with a couple crates of vodka. He retreats to a friend's cousin's dacha, a little cottage in a forest near Saint Petersburg. The dacha is not winterized but with the woodstove going almost constantly, the Kapitán makes it work. In almost four years he'd knocked on 512 doors and it was, finally, too much darkness for him. It was as if life and death both dissolved into something awful. Each knock on a door took something essential away from the Kapitán and it was never replaced.

Nensi came to North America wearing Anatoly's wristwatch. She was nineteen years old, and in love with a National Hockey League prospect named Dmitri, who was signed by the Montréal Canadiens.

She managed to stay in the West after he grew tired of her. Honestly, it was Nensi who had grown tired of him. His whining was never-ending. It was always the coach's fault. It was the coach's prejudice against Russian players in Montréal, and in Detroit an assistant coach who believed he was too soft in the corners. Everything was the coach's fault. Nensi believed she understood the game better than he ever would. He was a six-foot-four, 220 pound baby. Dmitri plays for one of the New York teams now, she can't remember which one. He's a third-liner and makes good money. He married a woman with jet-black hair. Nensi's hair is beach blonde, at least that's what the woman who colours it calls it. She says it is sun-streaked, as if it were blown wild by salty ocean breezes. Nensi suspected this woman read this description on a box of hair dye.

On the night they met, Dmitri told Nensi her eyes were ferocious, the colour of blue glass that has fallen on the floor and shattered.

"What does that mean?" she said. "Is there something wrong with my eyes?"

"It means they are intense and beautiful."

"Well, I worked very hard to get them to be that way."

He looked at her and did not understand. He was asking himself if it was possible to work on your own eyes. Was she making fun of him? He knew he was missing something but he didn't know what. He thought he was paying her a compliment. "Are you angry, Nensi? Are you pissed off at me?"

"I will never be pissed off at you, Dmitri," she said, her first lie to him coming so easily.

Nensi was pretty sure she frightened Dmitri most of the time.

A year later, she changed her name to Nancy and took a job working in an art gallery on South Firth Street. This was when she met and married an investment banker who was addicted to working out and to sex. He spent every spare moment working on his body, and he insisted on sex, every day, sometimes more than once – as if he were trying to prove something. Nancy divorced the investment banker three years later after an incident during which he tossed her onto a table at a Thai restaurant and choked her until a group of customers pulled him away. She's not sure if her husband was trying to kill her, or if he just wanted to scare her by choking her. Regardless, she was unconscious when he stopped. The restaurant was packed with witnesses and two people even recorded it on their phones. Nancy refused to press charges, and instead, negotiated a generous divorce settlement that included a condominium, a car, and hefty monthly payments.

Listen, all you need to remember about Nancy, for now, is her father was killed in a war in Afghanistan when she was eight – he marched away and never came home. She has never stopped wearing the gift from the Kapitán – the inelegant *Vostok* military watch with its fading green face. On the back of the watch there is an inscription that reads – *for Anatoly, love papa*. Nancy likes to think the Kapitán's name was Anatoly. It makes her happy to believe this. Also, Nancy has a tattoo of the Russian word for *grace* on her left forearm. She does not believe she has grace. Rather, it is a steady reminder of her intention. She got the tattoo because the investment banker forbade her to get it.

....

So, here's the thing. If you asked a thousand people to define what a novel is, you would likely get two thousand different answers, three thousand different examples, and a lot of flailing and 'um-ing' and 'ah-ing.' Perhaps the author of *This is All a Lie – a novel* would say this is nothing more than a story comprised of moments and characters, and a bit of a case study of how these characters misbehave inside these moments. He might lean back in his chair, cross his left leg over his right, and look at you as if he's waiting for you to say something more.

Of course, this is a book of lies. Lying is something young writers are told to practise – you lie to get at the truth. The facts are irrelevant – you manipulate the facts to find the truth. It sounds psychotic, but in writing, a blatant fabrication can be completely true.

For instance, there could also be a woman named Tulah Roberts in this book and there might be something essential you ought to understand about her – something like the fact she loves snow. It's an irrational love. A kind of ridiculously obsessive love. In fact, if snow were a man, it would have dumped Tulah long ago because she was too in love. Snow would probably have felt overwhelmed by Tulah's love.

When she was fifteen, she started a snow journal in which she decided to record snowstorms, snowfalls, and flurries. When it snows, she goes out into it, lets it touches her, and she touches it. Breathing becomes sanctified because she is aware of each inhalation, each exhalation, the pause at the top, and the pause at the bottom. She is not precious about it. She would not call her ritual holy. For Tulah, it was a simple thing. With snow falling all around, she stops and listens, and watches. She breathes it and each time out she finds the beat of the snow – a sort of silent measure that is about the snow's veracity, and its velocity, and its texture.

When Tulah was twenty, and staying in a cabin on the side of a mountain near Nelson, British Columbia, she went outside and stood naked in a snow storm. She stood on the veranda surrounded by pines and ghost peaks as the snow came down. The man she was dating was in bed, asleep and she'd had enough wine to think being naked in the falling snow was a fabulous idea. She'd stoked the fire in the living room for her return, slipped out of her clothes, and stepped barefoot onto the veranda. She stood still and felt everything. She saw only shades of white shifting through white. The air was cool and clean and she could smell strands of wood smoke. She heard an owl somewhere near the cabin – and then the muffled, folding silence. Even though she was sure she loved the man asleep in the bed under the thick down quilt, and he had spoken his love to her, Tulah felt a deep loneliness. She did not wake him. Something in her wanted to keep this for herself. She didn't want to risk anyone telling her this was silly, or stupid, or ridiculous. She did not know what the sleeping man would have said to her about this naked snow shower she was taking. She was cold, but it was not bitterly cold out. She would have liked to walk into the woods like this – to move under the tall pines away from the cabin as the snow twisted through boughs but there were no stairs to the forest. It was just an inexplicable yearning to move through the forest – to become even more vulnerable – to let the snow swallow her.

There are 487 entries in her snow journal. She knows this because she numbered them. Some were long reflections on the particular snow, and some had a brief description of the snow and a long reflection on her life. This one was number seventy-nine and it was dated November 3, 1995, two days after her twentieth birthday.

....

You might know people who would be bothered by the placement of the acknowledgements at the beginning of this book. You might be the kind of person who likes the acknowledgements at the back of the book where they belong – right beside the note of the font and a picture of the author. Mea culpa. Mea culpa.

Here is another possible lie: you will be introduced to a character in the chapter immediately following these acknowledgements. His name is Raymond Daniels but nobody calls him Raymond except for an aunt in Billings, Montana, who owns seventeen cats and, as Ray's mom used to say, *really enjoys the wine*. Ray works as an arborist with the city, and sometimes he talks to trees. He will be up in a bucket, suspended within the high branches of a poplar, or an elm, or a conifer and he will have an impulse to talk with the tree. Sometimes, Ray Daniels surrenders to the impulse.

It's tempting to show Ray having a conversation with a tree here, but to really understand him there is a moment three months after his mom dies that is perhaps more illuminating. His mom's house has been sold, and the new owners will take possession in a couple weeks. For the previous three weekends, he and Tulah and the girls have been clearing out the contents of his mom's life. For the girls, it was fun for the first hour, then just hard work and boring. After two hours, Tulah drove the girls to her mom's house.

This weekend, Ray has been working alone, going through the boxes of her life, and boxes of his life. It is an overwhelming exercise. It's all minutiae and sorting and deciding about importance. There are hundreds of pictures in boxes – pictures of people he does not know, and whom he doubts his mother knew, pictures of him as a child that he'd not seen before, and pictures of a person he thinks might be his biological dad. He keeps six pictures – three of his mother, two of himself, and one, a black-and-white photo of a woman feeding a bear cub in the mountains. This idiot woman is not his mother. She is a stranger, a mystery woman who thinks it's perfectly fine to feed bears in national parks. There is something wide-eyed and innocent about this woman. Ray decides to keep this image of her – to move her forward in time.

On this particular Sunday night, when the final dumpster has been hauled away, and the three boxes he could not look at yet had been loaded into his trunk, he pauses at the back entrance.

It's all done. The house has been cleaned. It's ready for its new owners. It smells faintly of cleaning product. He'd walked through the hollowed out rooms and hallways one last time.

He is tired and numbed by the previous weeks of clearing. He is no longer sentimental about the house. He's worn down by it. After the first weekend, he came home stunned by grief and shocked by the realization that an entire life came down to a bunch of stuff that could be thrown away so easily. His mother had jewelry, and a new television, which Ray had bought for her. Everything else was going to Good Will, or into a dumpster. It made him look around at his own stuff. His stuff was newer, but it was equally dismissible.

A week before, sitting on the front porch with his wife, Ray looked at her and sighed. "All the things we think are important – all the things we cling to, all the shit we carry around – it's all just meaningless stuff," he said. "So, what remains of us? What do we leave behind of value? What's the point of all this running around to get money to acquire more stuff?"

"Yup," his wife said. "What's important? What has value? And why? And to whom?"

The problem for Ray was, he wasn't sure. It was as if someone came in the middle of the night and poured grease on all the floors. His world was slippery and uncertain.

Ray is standing at the back door, ready to leave. He is halfway out the door, ready to pull it shut but he can't. He can't shut the door yet. In the kitchen, he sits on the grey tiled floor, his back against the wall, and remembers his mother sitting at the kitchen table on a Christmas Eve, drinking coffee. He is lying on his stomach in his bedroom, down the hall, his head sticking out just enough to see. She is playing one side of an album that has the song *Silent Night* on it, and she is playing it over and over. It's Bing Crosby. The record starts with *Silent Night* and ends with *I'll be Home for Christmas*.

She will get up and walk into the living room and play the same side over and over. Ray thinks perhaps she was not drinking coffee – that there was something stronger in her mug. He wonders about who she is remembering, or if she is remembering anyone. But she is definitely filled with sadness about something. He remembers his mother's sadness and also feeling helpless to do anything about it. He could not offer comfort because he did not fully understand what he was seeing.

Bugger. Bugger. Maybe showing Ray up in the branches having a conversation with a tree is a better way to get to know him. There are elms all over this city, thousands of them, and Ray is particularly fond of elms. Perhaps when he talks with trees it is a way for him to sort things out. He is not a crazy person standing and having heated arguments with inanimate objects. His conversations are quiet and private, more a muttering than anything.

"Well, tree," he will say to an elm on Savoy Avenue. "I'm worried about this branch. It's not as strong as it should be."

Ray will imagine his voice vibrating through the leaves and into the trunk and down into the roots. He imagines the tree hears him.

"You see where it forks, there is weakness. I'm not going to try and correct this problem but I want you to know I'll be watching it." He will make a note in his log, and sometimes draw a little picture. Every boulevard tree and every tree in a public space is identified and logged on an interactive website. There's a public page and then there's the page Ray uses, which has room for his sketches. He has an assistant named Clara who thinks his sketches are "little works of art" and uploads them to the site as if she's performing a sacred ritual.

Ray will find a damaged branch and wonder if trees have memories.

"Something must have happened," he will say. "Maybe you remember? An infestation? A drought? A severe windstorm? Yes? Do you remember a spring snow storm with the weight of the snow breaking branches?"

Ray wonders if it is the wind, or if the tree is answering *yes* to his question. Because the tree will seem to be nodding.

He spies a branch that has been rubbing against another, lower branch, and he smiles. "This, I can fix for you, and it will feel better, tree." He removes the upper branch, which had been threatening to rub a wound into the lower one – a wound through which insects and disease could enter. He uses his Japanese pruning saw, which is perfect for tight spaces and small cuts like this one.

There are days when Ray doesn't want to come down – days in which he would rather be in the high branches of a tree than anywhere else. Even though the trees never say anything, he feels they listen, and that his words are safe. He feels safe when he is with his trees.

....

Normally, authors thank a group of people in their lives in the acknowledgements – the people who helped them endure, or abide the long, disappeared days of writing. First, if you want to do this right, you might thank your publisher, who forked over a hefty sum of money for this book and as a result, felt emboldened and cocky enough to try and change the title. And secondly, an editor or two who had their hands on your baby, and then you should thank all the people in your life who helped you be a writer – which is just about everyone you've ever met – and a much shorter list of all the people who protected you while you wrote, who tolerated your sometimes whimsical, flighty nature. And to your charming agent, and to your wife, and to that woman at *Bistro Four* who over-pours your wine – you know the one, the brunette with the tortoise-shell glasses and the colourful bras under her white blouses. And you should give a nod to your hard-edged, demanding fantasy – the woman who lives at the periphery of what you can barely admit to yourself. Can you see her? She's full-figured – which is a nice way of saying she has terrific breasts and curves, and her eyes are green and needy. She will do the unimaginable things with you – the things that sit uneasily at the periphery of decency.

Finally, acknowledgements sometimes have something eccentric, or heartfelt, or kind. You'll probably do none of the above, and instead, you'll write out some Buddhist blessing because of that yoga teacher at the 97th Street studio who has the most exhilarating body odour – the one with the tattoo of a Fibonacci curve on her forearm. She teaches hot yin and about halfway through her class, when she comes to you, to make an adjustment, you shiver inside her scent, an elemental smell that cuts through any walls, or barriers. You want her to stay near you.

She offers a blessing at the end of her class: "May you be filled with loving kindness. May you be well. May you be peaceful and at ease. May you be happy." Of course, she finishes this off with a deep bow and a beautiful Namaste. You believe she is sincere beyond sincere and you love her a bit in that moment. Her voice is deeper than you expected – it's almost husky. Truthfully, she could have said 'go screw yourself,' and you would still be a little in love with her.

This would have been a sweet place to stop these so-called "acknowledgements" – with a prayer, and an admission of a naïve, embryonic love based on the body odour of a yoga instructor. But you can't stop thinking about Claude Garamond, who probably stunk to high heaven because, well, everyone stunk to high heaven in the 1500s. You might wonder if the father of the Garamond font could have been a guy who talked with trees. You look at the careful and eloquent beauty of the Garamond letterforms and you wonder about whether or not its inventor might have been obsessive. It's possible, even though the term 'obsessive compulsive' didn't exist in the sixteenth century – maybe they pointed and said things like, 'Oh, Claude Garamond? He's really detail-oriented.' There is no way to know much about him but look at this font. It's elegant and concise and could have been designed by a guy who was borderline obsessive compulsive. A guy who had to wash his hands for two full rounds of Happy Birthday, or some other song, as Happy Birthday did not exist in the 1500s. Easy to imagine him as a man who locked the door three times every night – back and forth, back and forth, and back and forth. Or a guy who kissed his wife four times on each of her nipples before bed. It was something she asked him to do five years ago on a whim, and he continues to do it. She did not say, *Claude, I want you to kiss my nipples, four times each.* No, it was not like that. He kissed her breast one night and she said, "Yes, again, and this one too, please." He has not missed a kiss in five years, and because he is a bit compulsive, he knows the sum of these kisses is 14,468. But forget about kissing nipples.

Think about old Claude Garamond hunched over his work desk, creating and recreating the same simple letter, trying it on, again, and again, and again – looking for perfection. Maybe there's a cat perched on a shelf overlooking his work. The cat knows better than to interfere. It waits until Garamond pushes away from his desk and stretches, then, purring, the cat will jump to the floor and self-rub along his leg. Normally, Garamond will bend down and pet the cat. But this morning, he has been working on the letter 'g.' He has been sketching ideas and refining the bottom bowl for weeks. Just now, he has finished cutting the letter into a punch. He pushes it into an open flame until its surface is covered by soot – and then presses it into a sheet of paper. He looks at it and smiles. He thinks he has landed on something that is both readable and beautiful. He is excited about this and so ignores the cat, picks up the page and trundles across the courtyard to show his wife, Marie Isabelle. This is not the final 'g.' He will struggle on-and-off with this letter for two more years. Other letters – the letter 'f,' and its elegant and simple italics sister '*f,*' for example – will come more easily.

It has been raining and there are puddles of reflected sky in the courtyard but he splashes through the puddles. The cat follows, tip-toeing around the puddles. Garamond pushes the door open, stomps his shoes, and before he is fully inside he is shouting and waving the sheet of paper: "G! I have the g. It's a fine letter g!"

"What?" Marie Isabelle says.

"Where are you? I have the g…"

Marie Isabelle is in the pantry, plucking a chicken – feathers float-ing in the air. "You have to pee? Is that what you're going on about?" Why is he telling her this instead of just going ahead and doing it?

"No. The letter g. It's the letter g! Where are you?"

"I'm in the pantry," she says, pushing a loose strand of hair behind her ear. "Come and show me your g." He is a bit like a child in his enthusiasm for these letters but Marie Isabelle finds this to be charm-ing. There were many gentlemen who came to court her but of all the men, only Garamond brought a passion for books and type, which she found fascinating. She never felt stupid when he talked about his work. He took the time to explain and always assumed she was intelligent. He was excited about his work, which was creating text, designing let-ters, and working with publishers. The printing press was changing everything. Claude told her the printing press and movable type meant everyone would be able to own and read books. Up until the later 1400s, it was only monasteries and universities that owned books, and the very rich. She already knew this, of course. While her family was not considered wealthy, Marie Isabelle could read and write, and this set her apart. Her father insisted a woman's capacity for intelligence was no different than a man's.

Garamond was the only one who made her laugh. He was the only one who brought her poetry. It was her grandmother who said, 'Enough! This is the man you will marry.' And Marie Isabelle did not argue.

When Garamond started out, he was an apprentice with the publisher and punch cutter, Antoine Augereau, a man who was eventually implicated in the 1534 *Affair of the Placards* – during which anti-Catholic tracts were posted in the major cities of France. On Sunday, the 18th of October, Parisians on their way to Mass were outraged to discover Protestant placards attacking the doctrine of the Mass had been put up in various public places overnight. Rumours swirled about one of these a placards being nailed to the King's bedchamber door.

Augereau was arrested, hanged and burned at the stake, along with dozens of other suspects. Garamond had already left his master behind, but still, he thought it would be prudent to put distance between themselves and Paris. If this could happen to Antoine Augereau, it could happen to them.

Less than a month after the day of the placards, the King's police chief arrested and tortured a known Protestant, who eventually identified other Protestants in the city. He did this by halting an elaborate procession of the Corpus Christi outside supposedly Protestant houses. Once the procession was stopped, the occupants of the house were arrested and trundled off to prison for trial and execution. The executions were held all over Paris and the burnings took place more or less daily for several weeks. This wholesale vengeance for simply posting a placard caused an exodus among the citizens of Paris. Craftsmen and traders, goldsmiths, engravers, lawyers, even some priests and monks, and particularly printers and bookbinders, fled the city. Many publishers and punch cutters moved away from Paris, to Switzerland and beyond, so they could publish what they wanted without fear of persecution.

....

On their last day in Paris, Garamond came to Marie Isabelle before breakfast and told her they would be leaving at sunset.

"Pardon me?" she said. "What do you mean leaving?" She has never liked being told what to do. Surely he's making a joke.

"Leaving, and not coming back for a while."

"But why are we leaving?"

"Can you please not fight me on this?"

"I am not fighting you, Claude. I am not leaving. There is Sophie Marot's dinner party next week, and my mother is ailing, and our friends…"

"…Paris has become too dangerous." Garamond did not want to tell her everything.

"So we are in danger?"

He nodded, slowly.

Marie Isabelle looked at her husband. Garamond looked scared. His eyes were frightened and she knew he did not scare easily. He did not back away from a challenge. He was not irrational, nor impulsive.

"Pack light," he said. "We'll replace what we leave behind."

"Very well, Claude. I trust you."

"It must not look like we're moving," he said. "But we are. We won't be coming back for a long time."

This was too much for her. Now he was saying they were being watched? And what does he mean by a 'long time'? "What have you heard, Claude? Tell me. I am not some sort of delicate creature who is prone to fainting."

"Rumours," he said. "But it is a fact they are marching their Corpus Christi processional around the streets of Paris and when they stop…"

"Merde!"

"There are executions every day and it seems the trials are routinely quick, which makes me wonder about how just they are."

Marie Isabelle knew, of course, about her husband's association with Antoine Augereau but that was so long ago.

As if he could read her mind, Garamond smiled and nodded. "Poor Antoine. He had no idea what was coming. This is a broad Catholic brush," he said. "I do not think this is about justice, or truth, but rather, atonement and fear. It is about the piousness of the Roman Catholic Church. I think it may be the beginning of something bigger."

"All this because of a few placards?"

"Yes," he said. "Placards that were written and printed. Placards that deeply insulted the Roman Catholic Church."

"The power of a few words?"

"The power of words," he said. "And ideas. And the freedom to distribute those words."

"And what do you believe, Claude?"

He smiled. "You mean the matter of St. Paul and whether or not he says, *eat the body of Jesus Christ*, or just *eat this bread, it's a symbol of the body of Christ*?"

"Yes," Marie Isabelle said. "That question. Transubstantiation."

"That question is not worth dying for," Garamond said. "This is why we are leaving."

"Oh Claude. I know you know this but let me speak it out loud so we have a shared understanding; the question of the right and proper place of the Holy Eucharist is, for most Catholics, entirely worth dying for."

When she had packed her bags with essentials, Marie Isabelle sat down and wrote a letter to her mother. Garamond told her they would be travelling south so she told her mother they were going to Austria. *Things have finally calmed down in Austria,* she wrote. *And you know how Claude loves the mountains.* She did not hesitate to mislead her mother, and anyone else who might read her letter. Away is away is away, she thought, and the destination did not matter.

....

There – an imagined picture of Claude Garamond and his wife is in the book, and what was the first line in these acknowledgements? That's right: "The author would first like to acknowledge Claude Garamond, the masterful father of the Garamond font, who is most definitely not a character in this book."

See? This is all a lie.

EPILOGUE

Imagine this: *A man wearing a dark winter coat with the collar turned up walks along the edge of the river. The river is not yet frozen but he imagines it as sluggish. It does not appear to be slower but he can picture the molecules of water decelerating and perhaps yearning to become crystalline. Maybe it's this longing that slows the river, and a desperate wanting that freezes it.*

He's wearing a black, over-sized beret and his hands are shoved deep into his pockets. Snowflakes dust the beret. He has left his scarf in the car.

The man does not meander. He knows exactly where he's going. He is carrying a bouquet of flowers under his arm. The flowers are wrapped in a funnel of paper, which is scant protection but enough for today. He bought yellow. He always buys freesia. Not because of what it was, but rather because of what it was not. It looked nothing like a daisy. The woman in the flower shop never made assumptions about his purchase, even though she could have. She waited for him to ask about the freesia: "How is the freesia today, Mrs. Ralston?" And she would reply: "The white is fresher than the yellow — it came in yesterday." It would be a derivation of this conversation every time. Sometimes the purple was better. Sometimes it would be the yellow. Sometimes, if a new shipment had just arrived and the flowers were exceptional, Mrs. Ralston would mention the tulips, or the daffodils, or the roses, and this would not annoy the man. He listened with respect, pretended to consider her offering, and then asked for freesia.

He dusts the snow from his shoulders and quickens his pace.

Under the walnut tree, the man pauses and takes a deep breath. At least it's not bitterly cold. He smiles. He could have driven all of this. There was a road that would take him to within a few metres of his destination. But walking gave him time to frame what he was doing, and it allowed for a contemplative honour to form. He needed the walk to find the place in his heart. He'd like to think this will be the last time he'll make this journey but he knows this is nonsense. He stomps the snow from his shoes and begins to walk again.

The clock is ticking

Chapter 24? What just happened? Did you have a stroke and misplace the first twenty-three chapters in your head? That would be awful. Don't you remember reading this story? No? Seriously, you're fine. You haven't read this book yet. You're okay.

This is actually the beginning of a story. This is not the end. The end is not near. This is Chapter 24 and next up is Chapter 23, and so on. Do you want to flip through the book to the end of Chapter 1 and look for the dedication, and some sort of clever epigraph? Go ahead. It's probably a Zen saying – something like: *"Before enlightenment, chop wood, carry water – after enlightenment, chop wood, carry water."* And under that, there is a quote from Ken Robinson that reads: *"What we do know is, if you're not prepared to be wrong, you'll never come up with anything original."* Did you look? If you did, you know the epigraph is not a Zen saying. Nor is it a quote from Ken Robinson. It's something else.

Admittedly, nobody puts an epilogue at the front of a book. But here's the thing – this particular epilogue could be inserted anywhere in the book. It's the kind of epilogue that is loaded up with mystery. It's a massive, undulating question mark.

Maybe, at this point, you don't know who to trust. What does all this counting chapters backwards nonsense mean? Well, it could be as simple as an extension of the idea behind the title of the book – the order of the chapter numbers is a lie. The structure is a big, fat, bald-faced lie but the narrative is the right way 'round – for the most part. You might ask yourself how these backwards chapter numbers make you feel. Could it be the author's intention to make the reader feel a little anxious or uneasy? Maybe the author is unnerved about what's going on in this story and the backwards chapters are a coping mechanism. Regardless, we read from left to right – unless we're reading Arabic, or Japanese – and we always read from start to finish, regardless of the numbers. Right? We push through. We keep moving. On the other hand, it does seem like a bit of a countdown. But a count-down to what, exactly?

Let's review. There are three characters – four if you count the lie of Claude Garamond – Tulah Roberts, Nancy Petya, and Ray Daniels. The chapter numbers are presented backwards but the narrative moves forward. You may, or may not be…wait. Did you skip the acknow-ledgements? Really? After all that encouragement? So you have no idea what this is all about. Sigh… If you go back and read the acknowledge-ments you'll know what's going on. And while you're there, maybe take a look-see at the *Note on the Font*. Then you will be completely up to speed. If you already read these important sections – Bravo! or Brava! Good for you, and carry on.

. . . .

Okay, so there are three characters in this story, five if you count Claude Garamond and his lovely wife. You know a little bit about each of these people. Tulah writes a snow journal. Nancy's father was killed in Afghanistan. Ray Daniels talks to trees. Claude Garamond is working on the letter 'g,' and his wife, Marie Isabelle, is unhappy about living in the country. Is any of this true? Yes. Emphatically yes! Is it factual? Why would you care?

You think of them as people now, partly because, well, they're as real as that guy your Uncle Frank talks about at family get-togethers after he's had too much to drink – the guy who saved his life on the side of a mountain in Switzerland in 1953. You remember that story? Well, this story is like that story, except the writer isn't drunk, for the most part, and there are no Swiss mountain guides.

There must be a rule of writing that states, never mess with the order of your chapters – always make them go from chapter one, to chapter two, and so on. Hmmm. And there has to be a rule that says never start a book with a *Note on the Font*, and do not, under any circumstance, ever follow the *Note on the Font* with a blatantly self-con-scious list of *Acknowledgements*. Hmmm. The celebrated writer Michael Ondaatje once said – *"Never start a book with anyone in a bathtub, no matter how beautiful or heart-breaking. Unless it's a nun. Nuns in bath-tubs are fine."* In 1976, at a literary event in Seattle, Washington, the outspoken writer Margaret Atwood said it was preferable if readers began reading her books while they were in the bath. The American writer John Irving said: "*I don't like taking baths.*"

Speaking of rules for writing, the late, great American writer Kurt Vonnegut once said stories should always start as close to the end as possible. Well, you're reading the acknowledgements, which are normally at the end of a book. He also said writers should make their characters want something, even if it's as simple as a glass of water.

Maybe the two characters you're about to meet want different things. Maybe the wife wants to know she's loved but she doesn't know how to ask for it. She wants to know, unequivocally, that she is loved. She thinks her husband might roll his eyes and say something simple like – 'well of course, I love you. I have always loved you.' And, she is afraid he will say all the right things and she won't believe him. She wants to feel grounded with him – not this dull ache of uncertainty.

Maybe the husband wants to live more truthfully, because over the past couple years he's been living so far away from truth it pains him to think about it. Most of the time, he feels like one of Peter Pan's Lost Boys. He wonders what would happen if he spoke the truth. He's not sure he trusts his wife enough to tell her the truth about what he feels. He's afraid she'll bolt. He wants to feel more safe and found, and not so bloody lost all the time. And he wants to make love with his wife.

Inside this moment, maybe they both just want another bottle of wine, because it's pleasant to sit and talk with someone – even if there are unasked questions, and apprehension, and insecurity.

Right now, the husband and wife are in a restaurant on North 104 Street. This particular street is brimming with bistros, and wine bars, and cafés. The husband picked this restaurant because of the piano player, who wheeled through a list of jazz classics and started every night with 'I'm in Love Again.' He can't explain why he loves this song so much. When they leave here, the man and his wife, Tulah, will likely go to the Marc for a drink before calling a taxi. They hesitate to even think of it as a nightcap because that's too old-fashioned. But it will be a nightcap.

The man just ordered the Rouleaux de Printemps – a goat's cheese spring roll, pistachio beetroot hummus, sautéed kale, mustard greens, with sweet espelette dressing. His wife orders the marinated flank steak, new potatoes, wilted spinach, smoked red pepper aioli. She asks for her steak to be medium rare. The waiter smiles and says, "Of course, Madame." The husband nods his head. He knows perfectly well this chef would not cook a steak to anything other than medium rare.

They are drinking a bottle of *Jackpot Petit Verdot* from a vineyard in the Southern Okanagan called *Road 13*. It was one of Tulah's favourites. She loves the black current flavours that persisted beyond expectation. At least that's what she said. Ray thought it was a nice, chunky red.

Tulah Roberts and Ray Daniels have been married for eighteen years and they haven't made love for two years and three months. They both try to think of this as not a big deal. They lower their expectations of marriage, of each other and their life together. And there was the story in *The Guardian*, about thousands upon thousands of married people who go without sex. It's no big deal.

Tulah kept her name when they married. Neither of them liked hyphenation – they thought it was goofy and a bit ostentatious, as if all the hyphenated couples in the world were trying too hard to prove how enlightened they were. And then, of course, Tulah and Ray did it to their girls. They were Sarah and Patience Roberts-Daniels.

Ray looks at his wife. The colour of her hair has always stopped him, the severe chestnut tones, and the way it falls across one eye and flows like water to her shoulders. She says if she stops colouring it, it will be grey, and she's not ready for that.

Tulah teaches grade 10 English and Science at Strathmore Senior High School. Even though she will often rail against the curriculum, she loves teaching, and has her own set of fixes that sometimes cause her students to sit up straight. For instance, in her English class, there are no set rules around the interpretation of literature – if a student's thinking is sound, or original, or even analytical, Tulah is fine with moving away from the accepted analysis. However, in her Science classes, Tulah is firm. The school is in a bit of a Bible belt, so in her first class each term, she explains right up front that in their discussion of the origins of man and the Earth, there will be no mention of creation. She makes it clear her class is a science class, not a theology class. Some students take this announcement in stride; others are wide-eyed and astounded.

⋯⋯

They've been talking about a book over dinner. They are both reading a small novel by the Italian writer, Alessandro Baricco, called *Mr. Gwyn*. Ray believes the two parts are absolutely linked – they were simply two parts of one novel. Tulah thinks they are separate and distinct novellas.

"Even the publisher says these are two novellas. It's on the front of the book. It says *two novellas*."

"The publisher is all about positioning the book to sell. It's a sales pitch, and this time, an inaccurate one. Besides, publishers are never authorities on the book." He's grasping and he knows it. At best, he thinks, there could have been some confusion as the book was translated from Italian.

"Books," she says, smiling and hissing the 's.' She takes a sip of her wine. "Two novellas. One physical book."

The waiter is there, silently and efficiently pouring wine. When he leaves, Tulah leans toward Ray over the table and whispers, "For a hundred dollars I'll let you fuck me up the ass."

They've both been drinking, but Ray is thinking this is way beyond wine. This is quite different. This is not something his wife would say. Nor is it something she would normally do. It's true they've been struggling with sex. The spontaneous, wild and exploratory sex of the early years is a distant memory and they have been at a loss about how to move forward. They are at the point now where neither of them knows where to begin. A first touch, a first kiss – it seems as if there are so many barriers to getting there. Each time is awkward and uncomfortable, because they know it shouldn't be this awkward and uncomfortable.

Ray smiles at his wife. "I'm sorry?" he says.

"You heard me." She does not smile. As if this is serious business and she is focused on making the deal. As if this type of negotiation is something she does all the time, or that the details of this are beneath her.

Ray's heart is pounding. He's excited by her offer. He's not obsessed with the idea of sex. That's not why he's excited. Not exactly. He likes it that Tulah has surprised him. He is pleased that after being with her for twenty-two years, he still gets turned on when she talks dirty, and she can still surprise him.

"If I give you a hundred dollars, you'll do that?" He wonders if his wife has been looking at porn.

"That? That?" She sighs as if she is impatient, or pretending to be impatient. "Yes. I will do that, but I want my money first."

"But we're in a restaurant."

"Oh, you want the logistics spelled out for you? Okay." She leans back and looks around the room. "In the bathroom, right now."

Ray was not even close to thinking about the logistics of his wife's proposal. This was so out of character for her. He's in shock. He knows for a fact there are sodomy laws in this country and they definitely apply to anal intercourse in public. His wife is a fervent follower of rules, laws, and her own self-designed lists. It would be natural to not believe her. But, he was considering the erotic notion of it, and listening to her voice, and enjoying the view of her body. He leans forward and whispers. "You want to have sex in the bathroom of this restaurant?"

"No," she says. "You do. That's why you're going to pay me a hundred dollars and meet me in the women's bathroom."

"You're serious?"

"Yes. I'm serious." She stands up, places her napkin on the table, and looks at him with such knowing and intention.

....

There is different moment that might be more appropriate for the opening scenes of a book called *This is All a Lie*. This 'other' moment unfolded three days before Ray and Tulah had a conversation about having sex in the women's bathroom in the basement of a restaurant on North 104 Street.

Imagine a man standing on an expansive balcony, thirty-nine floors in the air, and he's holding a square, crystal glass containing a few ounces of eighteen-year-old whisky. The name of the whisky doesn't matter. This man might be wearing a black polo shirt and khaki trousers but what does it matter what anyone is wearing? The glass is heavy – it's chunky and yet he takes care with it, protects it. This glass cost

$120. There used to be two of them but he dropped one about a month ago. He'd gone online and tried to replace it. With shipping, it was $270 for two glasses. They came as a set. Buying one was not an option.

There is a woman slouched in a chair beneath a massive painting of a yellow horse. On the tile floor beside her chair, there are two books – both by the Russian poet Anna Akhmatova. The woman's name is Nancy Petya. When Nancy says her name, Ray hears Nincy. Her pronunciation is heavily accented and he finds this to be both charming and amusing.

He might take a sip of the whisky and then try to do the math on how old he was when this whisky first went into the cask. He'd like to say he was eighteen when this eighteen-year-old whisky started its journey, but he knows better than to lie about his age – especially to himself.

Nancy turns toward him, places her tea on the floor beside her chair. "I want you more than you want me," she says. "I want all of you."

"You know that's not realistic…" He looks at her, notices the rip in her nylon. He chastises himself for noticing such an insignificant thing. What does it matter? But it's not like Nancy to have a rip in her stockings. He can't take his eyes away from the rip.

"…I don't care about realistic. I want the banalities, the lists of things to do, shopping trips to Costco, a glass of wine after work. A vacation together."

"You have a rip in your stocking," he says, and instantly regrets saying it.

"Are you even listening to me?"

"Yes, I'm listening to you."

"Because I was telling you that I want more from you and you're telling me I have a goddamned rip."

"I heard you, it's just, for some reason I noticed the rip in your stocking."

"You're an asshole, Ray," she says.

He looks at her and weighs her words against her voice and the view of her body. He measures the sting of her words against the truth.

"Surely you know you're a bit of an ass."

"Do I?" This hurts. It pushes against his admittedly self-delusional belief that he's a fairly decent guy who is just a little damaged.

"It's not a bad thing, or a good thing. It's just a thing. But let's not do any judging. We're beyond judging, yes?"

"Look," he says. "I'd like us to be more real too."

Her face becomes a study in sadness. "But that's not going to happen is it?" She covers her body with her robe. "I might want babies, Ray. What about that?"

"Babies?" Something in him is panicked by this word. It would complicate things immeasurably if Nancy were pregnant.

"Yes. What if I want to have a child?"

"Do you want to have a child?" Why is she talking about babies? This has never been about babies.

"I don't know. I'm uncertain, but this could change. Tomorrow, I might wake up and want to have children. The clock is ticking, Ray. My clock is ticking and it's getting louder."

"I don't know how I can give you more."

"Yes you do."

He grunts his acknowledgement of this truth. "Yes, I do," he says.

Ray takes a couple sips of his whisky and Nancy looks into the depths of her tea. They are silent for a few minutes.

"You would be a wonderful mother," Ray says, finally.

"What?"

"I said you would make a great mother."

"But why would you say that?"

"Because I can imagine you as a mother."

"Trust me, I'm not mother material…"

"…but you just said…"

"…I said I can feel my biological clock ticking when I close my eyes at night. You piss me off when you don't listen."

"Still. I think you would make a great mother."

Her voice is a straight and narrow line. "Oh, God, you really do not know me."

"I know what I know," he says.

Even though she realizes he's likely referring to knowledge he's gained by having children with his wife, she feels oddly complimented. She lets her robe fall open again. "That's sweet of you to say, but I just want more right now. I want something normal for us."

"But not babies?"

"I would have a baby with you. You should know that. Do you know that?"

"Okay," he says.

"Okay?"

"Yes, I heard what you said." He takes a sip of his whisky.

"Good," she says. "Right now, I just want something not hidden. Just one normal thing."

Even though he knew this was coming, Ray feels backed against a wall – pushed into a corner, claustrophobic. These are reasonable requests. He has enjoyed getting to know this woman. She is clever, and kind, and she has been nothing but understanding. Well, she's been complicit in an affair, but he pushed her into this complicity – complicity and a complex dishonesty and any other number of words that mean dishonest and secretive.

It's clear now. He can see the line of them, stretched out over an impossible thirteen months of desire. He wonders if desire of this sort always ends with a simple and reasonable request for something normal. One request for something not secretive, and that's the end of it. This is the end of his desire and Ray can imagine himself smashing into a brick wall. The second it gets complicated, it's over.

"Okay," he says.

But this 'okay' is not an affirmation. He is not agreeing to anything. He is saying yes to a completely different thing. He is saying yes to a decision only he knows about.

Nancy watches as he carefully places the square whisky glass on the edge of the balcony railing and turns around. "Okay?" she says.

She's slouched in the chair, her bathrobe fallen open, the swatch of darkness between her legs, the fullness of her breasts. The body he knows so well, the curves and scars and skin – everything – is just there, waiting for him, if only he can say the correct words. He knows the right words but he's already bashed face-first into the brick wall and there's no recovering. He wonders if she's done this on purpose – positioned herself to be so salacious. Her hips lifted and turned out slightly, her soft body, there in the chair, poised at the corner of need and want. He wonders if she knows about the brick wall, if she knows how hard it has become for him to push away his life to have a fragment of something with her. And now she wanted more.

He leans over and kisses the top of her head. "Goodbye, Nancy," he says.

She looks up at him with her slow, sad eyes. "Will I see you Tuesday?" "No," he says. He crosses the room and closes the door softly, as if he is trying to erase the fact he was ever there.

The elevator arrives quickly and he hopes for a swift, uninterrupted ride to the ground. He watches the numbers as they flash down. He thinks only about the numbers. He counts them off in his head, like a shifting mantra.

....

In the elevator, Ray is thinking about the appeal of newness, and being in love, and its inevitable unsustainability. Nothing remains new. No one stays 'in-love' forever. He does not know one person in his life who has managed to stay *in-love* with their partner. 'In-love' is the force that bangs people together. It is the doorway to something deeper and more sustaining, and surprisingly, freeing. Nancy wanted to step through that doorway into love. But that sort of love is nested inside a long conversation between friends, and an abiding respect. This, and a willingness to work at it when things threaten to go off the rails. Of course, he is a bad example of these concepts. He was willing to work at his marriage only after he strayed into a wild affair. He was not about to confess to Tulah – to fall on the ground in a heap of remorse and beg forgiveness. He could punish himself better than she ever could. He knows this about himself, and keeps his self-loathing in a room with a good sturdy lock on it. He places his guilt in the same room.

Ray is confused about why he feels he's lost something. Nancy was an illusion of something real. Can you miss an illusion?

He's feeling twitchy because he just walked away from her. He dumped her and he has no idea what she'll do now. Does she keep the secret of them, or does she lash out and spill everything? Ray is counting on her discretion – a sort of honour among adulterers. But she could do anything. She's Russian and she has a temper. The elevator slows around 20 and stops at 18. The doors slide open and a tall woman wearing a low-cut cocktail dress and a grey, sequined scarf wrapped three times around her neck, steps carefully over the crack with her high heels and looks at him. Her face scrunches into a question. "Are you okay?" she says.

"What?" Ray can smell lavender, and sandalwood, and pine. And somewhere in that mix, a heady body odour. This combination of scents makes him dizzy with memory.

"Are you okay? You look pale." Her smile is crooked – it rises up more on one side than the other. It's charming, and disarming.

"Oh. I'm fine," Ray says. "I just don't like elevators."

She looks at him hard, as if he's naked and can do nothing about her gaze. "Well, that's not really true is it? You're perfectly fine with elevators. But you're not fine in your life. Not by a longshot."

Ray steps back. He lines his spine up against the side wall of the elevator. "What?"

"I said elevators are quite safe. I dated a guy once who was an inspector with the government. He said they're very safe."

"I was in an elevator that stopped for two hours once," Ray says. He's never been stopped in an elevator for more than a few panicky seconds.

"More bullshit," she says, her voice a pleasant flat line. "I don't understand why you feel compelled to lie to a complete stranger." She smiles again. "You're not flirting with me are you?"

"Flirting? I'm...No. I'm not flirting."

"I think you are. You're flirting with me, despite being married and I am thinking you probably have children."

"What?" He has no idea what this is, or who this woman is, but she makes him uncomfortable. As much as he enjoys awkward conversations, it's manufacturing the awkwardness that he likes the most. He's okay with awkwardness so long as he created it. This is a few big steps beyond awkward.

"Oh, I'm not dangerous," she says. "Unless the truth can hurt you." She turns toward the mirrored wall of the elevator and makes a small letter 'o' with her lips – she applies red lipstick and puckers. "You don't live in this building. I would know. Are you messing around on your wife? Is that why you're here? She lives in this building? Your mistress?"

"Who are you?"

"I am called Amitiel, but how is this relevant?" She lifts her right arm, sniffs at her armpit, and frowns. "Seriously. How is my name relevant?"

"It's not," he says. "I just thought…" He thought her name would help him remember if he'd met her before. He didn't quite catch her name. He thought he heard 'animal.' "Okay, lady. Have we met before? I would remember meeting someone like you but…"

Amitiel smiles and shakes her head. "…Oh my dear Lord. You want me don't you? Look at you. You're drooling. You have no clue about your own heart – you don't know who, or what, you love. You have no idea about your own capacity to love and still you manage to want me. Remarkable." She pulls at her scarf, adjusts it. "I would ruin you. You have no idea who I am, or what I am."

Ray is stunned. He looks at the flowery tattoos on her arm – the twisting vines and a melded garden – soft blues, orange and green. They're moving. They seem to be moving. He starts to feel lightheaded. "What? No," he says. "I don't know you. I…Who are you?" He's thinking – what the hell is this? Yes, of course. What man wouldn't want her? He wonders if this is some sort of prank. There must be a camera somewhere.

"That's it, Ray. Stay in character. Stay true to form. Lie to yourself and everyone in your life. Don't change."

He did not tell her his name. "I didn't tell you my name," he says. "Who are you, really? Did someone put you up to this? What's going on?" He thinks about Nancy but she didn't have time to set this up, and besides, Ray doubts she knows what's going on yet.

Ray looks at the buttons on the elevator panel. He leans over and presses "G" again, to make sure this is where they're going – to be certain there is a destination, and against logic, to speed the descent.

"My, aren't you full of questions. At least your questions are honest. So, let me get this straight," she says. "You just left a woman and now you are standing in an elevator with a strange woman, and you want to fuck her? I bet you would turn around and follow me back up to my apartment. I bet you would make love with me right now, here, against this wall. You know nothing about me, and yet you're excited by the prospect of having sex with me. Morality, right and wrong, truth, honour…none of these high-minded concepts crosses your mind?"

"Lady, you don't know anything about me," he says.

The doors slide open at the main floor. Ray takes a half-step into the lobby, holds his hand over the edge and waits for the woman to move past him and good riddance to her. But the woman in the black dress does not step off the elevator and when he turns to let her know he's holding the door for her, she is not there. The elevator is empty except for a lingering scent. Maybe the scent was the only thing that was ever there. He looks around the corner and into the lobby, and then back into the empty elevator. He steps into the lobby, lets the doors slide shut. He leans against the wall between elevators and breathes, slowly, through his mouth. He isn't exactly focusing on his breathing. He's attempting to understand what just happened. He's weighing reality and finding it suspect. He wonders if he's hyperventilating. Maybe he's having an anxiety attack. There was a cousin who had these attacks all the time – what was her name? But then she wouldn't be related by blood anyway. Jesus, it was complicated being adopted. But still, what was her name? The elevator dings, the door slides open and Ray holds his breath.

An elderly woman with a dog, a black Labrador on a leash, gets off. They head toward the door. The woman does not notice him. The dog looks him over quickly and then turns away. Perhaps, he is unconscious, passed out in the hallway of the thirty-ninth floor – only dreaming about a tattooed woman in a black dress who knows his name and has no qualms about sniffing her own armpits. If the dog saw him, he must be on the ground. He is tentative about the reality he sees but at the same time, he knows he must keep moving forward – he wants to keep moving toward his car, and then across town, and finally, far away from here. He wants to make space between this place and his life.

On the way to his car, he checks his pockets for his car keys. It would be a disastrous thing to have forgotten his keys in Nancy's apartment. In his jacket pocket, he finds tickets for tonight's hockey game. He forgot he had them – a gift from a co-worker. He'd also forgotten to invite someone. The Rangers are in town, but he's pretty sure he won't be going – he wants a glass of wine, a dinner with his family. Across from his car, at the curb, he pauses. He met Nancy at a hockey game. She'd leaned over and asked him about the blue line.

"Why do they keep stopping the play at the blue line?" Her voice didn't match his expectation – it was low and husky, and shaded with a Slavic or eastern European accent.

"Seriously?" he said. He'd had two drinks already, in the club lounge, between periods. He thought this woman was goofing around, or making a statement about the pace of the game. He could not help but notice the wedding ring and its accompanying diamond, which was ostentatious and played against her simple cotton sweater and blue jeans.

"I was given these seats," she said. "I am just learning about hockey."

Nancy's seats were actually part of a divorce settlement. A Porsche, and a condo were also part of the deal. She sold the Porsche and bought a Mitsubishi. By the end of the game, two things had happened: Nancy made Ray believe he'd helped her understand the game of hockey, and she'd given him her phone number. He was also a little smitten with her. He told himself this feeling was nothing. He fell in love with expensive suits, and Swiss watches, restaurants, and random waitresses, every day. This was just one more flirtation in a long line. He'd probably never see her again.

Nancy also had his phone number. She had his business card, and she called the next day. She did not say 'hello' or 'hi, this is Nancy from the hockey game.' She assumed he'd remember her voice and got to the point. "I'm not married," she said.

"Who is this?"

"Nancy. We met last night. At the hockey game."

"Oh, yes. Hello," he said. "So you're not married. Good to know."

"Yes. I just wanted to clear that up. In case you wanted to call me, that is if you're not married. God. Maybe you're married. Are you married?"

She sounded horrified by this thought and Ray was tempted to tell her he was not married.

"I am married," he said. "Married with two daughters."

"Oh. Now I feel stupid. I should not have called. How embarrassing."

"No. Please. Don't feel stupid. It was really nice watching the game with you. It was practically innocent."

There was a long pause and Ray wondered if perhaps she'd disconnected.

"Practically innocent. Yes," she said. "Listen, can I ask you something?"

"Sure."

"How's it going?"

"How's what going?" Ray leaned back in his chair, swivelled, and looked out the window.

"Your marriage – how's it going?"

He stopped swivelling and focused on her question, which was blunt but also compelling. It was none of her business but he wanted to give her an answer. "It's fine," he said.

"My marriage was fine, too," she said. "That's why it ended. Listen, call me sometime if you'd like to have a drink."

"Sure," he said.

"To be clear. I don't want to sleep with you. I just want to know more about you. You were a good teacher. Okay. Ciao."

She disconnected.

"Bye," he said into the silence. In that moment he wanted to sleep with this woman – a year of not being touched and all his ridiculous feelings of aloneness piled up and pushed decency out of the picture.

Ray thought about his fine marriage. Surely, it was better than fine. He tried to recall the last time he had shared anything close to intimacy with Tulah. Of course he would love to have the wild exploration of a new body, a new woman who knew nothing about him – a woman with whom he shared no history. A woman who had not hurt him. A woman he hadn't hurt. She would be a clean slate. A tabula rasa.

Some sexy whisper of a voice in him said 'why not?' and he listened. Even though there was a chorus of voices singing in unison about how this was not the way to fix a marriage, he listened to the small, salacious, sexy voice instead.

....

Tulah does not sit down. She does not giggle or backtrack. She stands there and Ray calls her bluff. He places five twenties in front of her on the table. He would have liked to have folded them before placing them on the table but the new twenty-dollar bills were all plastic and security holograms and they do not fold well. Tulah takes the money and slips it into a side pocket of her purse. Ray lifts his wine glass and empties it – gulps it down. He does not wait for the waiter to pour more. He picks up the bottle, sloshes another half-glass, and takes a gulp.

"Oh, you should know – I have not washed for a week," she says. "Just like your Vikings."

Ray has been quietly obsessed – not so quiet around Tulah – with Vikings over the past few months. It began after reading a story in *The Guardian* about the remains of a Viking woman who was wearing a silver ring inscribed with the Arabic script, "for Allah." It was a mystery with no clear answers. But the speculation was delicious. The Vikings travelled as far as the Middle East and northern Africa. And there was something in the article about an emissary of the Abbasid Caliph commenting on Vikings and how they were the filthiest of all Allah's creatures because they did not wash themselves after coitus. He'd observed them as they stood up after sex and just carried on. It was a detail Ray found to be both erotic and fascinating. He's not sure why he found it to be erotic. He's not about to see a therapist about it. He'd rather simply accept it as a little quirky peccadillo and move forward. But why would Tulah do this for him? Why would she become a Viking? Ray had shared the story with her and he'd thought at the time she was not paying attention. Ray was moved by her uncleanliness.

It was likely not true about the Vikings. They were probably as clean as any other quasi-civilization in the tenth or eleventh century. In fact, some academics say, because of the close proximity of hot springs, they bathed once a week, which is far more often than most people of Medieval Europe. Ray secretly prefers the idea of filthy Vikings.

"Wait five minutes before joining me," she says, picking up her purse. He watches as she walks across the restaurant and disappears around a corner. The washrooms are downstairs. The stairs turn halfway down and at the bottom there's an atrium with a mirror and a narrow table – there are always fresh flowers on the table.

He sips his wine. He's anxious, excited, and intrigued. He's trying hard to act normal but this is not normal. It's as if the same old daily path of his life is there but now there are apparitions, and twists and dark corners. Control your breathing, he tells himself. If you can calm your breathing, you'll be fine.

He focuses on an inhalation. He focuses on an exhalation. He focuses on his next inhalation… "Okay," he says, standing and placing his napkin on the table.

There is a bouquet of yellow tulips on the table at the bottom of the stairs. Ray places his hand on door to the women's bathroom, inhales and pushes it open.

"Tulah," he hisses, before he sees her. She is leaning against the wall, which is all white subway tile, and next to her is the paper-towel dispenser. She's smiling as Ray comes in. He feels like he's in an erotic dream – a dream in which he has no control over what he's doing. She seems more than a little amused. Her smile is confident and playful. She is not second-guessing.

Yes, Ray's thinking. This is what men want. They want their lovers, their wives, their partners, to actually want to be in the room with them – a room in which, perhaps anything can happen. To engage in some sort of shared pleasure. Perfect bodies do not matter. The limited mechanics of making love do not matter. It's the simply wanting to be there with your lover.

Ray loves his wife for doing this – for pushing his understanding of desire, and for being so playful and serious at the same time.

"Okay," she says. "You paid your money." She wiggles out of her panties and pushes them into her purse. She pauses, smells her hand and smiles. She steps into the cubicle and turns around. Ray follows her in and she reaches around, pulls the door shut and locks it.

·······

He'd found a parking spot on the street, right across from her building. Ray is dizzy as he gets to his car. It's as if he just stepped off a ship and his land-legs are wobbly. He places his hand on the hood of the car and takes a couple big breaths. Nancy calls him as he is about to open the car door, and even though he is not fond of confrontation, he picks up. She's only a voice now, and discretion is still required. Discretion needs to continue. Nancy could make a mess of his life.

"What are you doing?" she says. "What the fuck do you think you're doing?"

"About what? What do you mean?" He pulls his car door open.

"Really? Did you, or did you not, just break up with me?"

"I…"

"…because nobody breaks up with me. I break up with people. I break it off. I break…"

He wants to tell her that adults don't 'break up' – only junior high school students 'break up.' Adults stop seeing each other. They drift apart. They move on. They 'don't work' anymore. They end things. They agree that it's over. But Ray can sense this is not the time to try and teach Nancy about the appropriate language around the ending of an affair.

"Nancy," he says.

"No. You don't get to do this."

"I'm sorry," he says.

"No," she says. "You can't be sorry either. This does not happen to me."

He takes a conscious breath. "Look, do you want to break up with me? Do you want me to come back up and let you break it off?"

"No. What is wrong with you?" She pauses – as if the thought crosses her mind that this may not be such a bad idea. As if she's imagining a scenario in which Ray is starting to touch her – standing behind her – his hand on her back, then her lower back, then her buttocks, and then between her legs. She will pull away, turn around and glare at him. She will ask him, *why*? Why is he doing what he's doing? Her wetness will be on his fingers, her scent, and she will say: *what's the point?* Of course, he will not have an answer. He might try to say, pleasure. Or bliss. Or desire. But he will know these words are not enough. He will shy away from the word 'love,' even if that's exactly what he feels. He will feel torn. Everything in him will say he cannot love two women at the same time – not like this. And yet he does. He will understand her question, but he will wish he didn't. He will understand there is no point. They are in stasis. He is at the limit of meaning. The pain in his eyes at this moment will give her pleasure.

"I thought…" he says into the phone. "I just thought…"

"…I wanted us to be more real and this makes you run away like a three-year-old? I wanted more, and you have a pouty tantrum. Is wanting more such a bad thing?"

"No," he says. "You absolutely deserve more. You deserve everything."

"Good. On this, we agree."

"Look," Ray says. "You had to know it would come to this eventually…"

"…I was just a distraction for you. A throw-away. And when I wanted something normal… you leave."

Yes, he wants to say. A thousand-million times yes. Because there was never any room for normal between them. This is the entire point of having an affair. Affairs are not normal – they're extraordinary, and dangerous, and secret. All these things make affairs exhilarating. Of course, Nancy distracted him from his pockets of unhappiness, from thinking about death, from knowing he was getting older by the second. She distracted him from acknowledging the idea that all of this running around and seeking peace, making money, loving, hating, empathizing and driving in automobiles was utterly meaningless. Nancy caused him to feel. His feelings for her were intense and fast. She placed him firmly in the spectrum of pleasure and desire. Sometimes, when he was in bed with Nancy he actually started to believe there could be such a thing as God, that divinity and holiness might be real. With one soft kiss, she could jolt him out of his hamster wheel of reality.

Ray never told Nancy about his dad leaving when he was five years old but it was an important part of why she didn't stand a chance. He doesn't actually know the reasons his father left but he will not do that to his kids. No matter how lovely Nancy is, he will not leave his daughters. But it's his wife too. She's growing. She's been smiling at things differently in the past few months – as if the world had become more interesting – as if there were suddenly eighteen new colours and she could see all of them. He found himself falling in love with his wife again. He wanted to focus on her, and this was not possible when he was ripped in two.

"Hello? Are you there?"

"I'd like to think that what we had was real," he says. "It just wasn't tenable."

"Tenable? Tenable? Why would you use this word?"

Because it's the right word, he thinks. "I don't know," he says.

"It's a lawyer's word, Ray. It's an asshole word. That word is a fucking asshole. God. I can't believe this. I've been so stupid."

"So was I," he says, his voice is lifeless and dull.

"What? Really, Ray? You get to walk back to your life like nothing's happened. You had me for a year and now it's done and you still have a life. How were you stupid? How could anything you've done be seen as stupid?"

"It doesn't matter. I feel stupid right now." He knows all about his own stupidity. He knew he would not leave his wife. That was never going to happen. And he knew he would not leave his daughters. And still, he pushed it to the point where he was uncomfortably, irrationally in love with Nancy.

"Where are you parked?"

"On the street," he says. "I got lucky."

Her voice is a threat. "You think it's lucky?"

"Of course it is. Parking is hell around your building. You know that."

"Good luck, bad luck, all the lucks are rolled together."

"What? What does that mean?"

"Just don't move."

"Why?"

"Because. Because I said don't move. Because I said so." Her voice is tired, but also stern and commanding.

He looks around the street. He looks at the elms arched over the boulevard and people walking – a young girl on a bike, a woman walking her dog, a man sitting against a building – his eyes closed, asleep, or in some sort of reverie.

The trees are turning already. It was cold last night. He wonders if Nancy has been making her way down to the street to find him, but the elevator always makes her phone cut out. Around the twentieth floor, cell service dropped away. She knows this. Did he hear her phone cut out? He's not sure. He thinks maybe he should start the car and leave. He'd love to go somewhere for a drink. But he stops. Surely he can give her this ridiculous bit of conversation. He will talk with her for a few minutes. Humour her, and then he will disappear into his life.

"Are you there, honey?"

This is stupid. He's not staying here. He's fine with talking but he certainly does not have to sit there in his car just because she said so. He starts the car and the stereo comes on. He turns it down to nothing and reaches across his chest to pull the seatbelt into place. He can talk with her as he drives. He wants to get the hell away from her building, her street, her condo. He wants to put her building in the rear-view mirror. He wants to start denying Nancy ever happened.

"Yes. I'm here," he says.

"Good," she says.

"Why am I here?"

Her voice becomes small and cutting. "Because I'm going to jump."

Ray turns off the car.

CHAPTER 23

Tall, ferocious and dark

"Not all who make love make marriages"
– Zhanna Petya

Nancy has fought with the darkness and the light her whole life. When she was fourteen, she filled her pockets with stones and walked into the river, just to see what that pull felt like. She stiffened against the cold shock as she walked directly into the water. The river turned her sideways and she slipped out of her coat. The current pulled her downstream and when she finally crawled out of the water, it took her two hours to walk home. Explaining to her mother that her coat was at the bottom of the river was not something she wanted to do. So she said it was stolen when she was by the river playing.

It wasn't that she wanted to die; she just wasn't sure she wanted to live. With the first tug at the weight of her coat, Nancy felt a rush of peace; a kind of relief. As if the river was whispering, 'It's okay, just let go.' Her mother would not let it go. She wanted to know who stole the coat, and why she was at the river. They were not rich and now they would have to buy a new coat and they had no extra roubles for this nonsense. Winter was coming. It was when her mother switched suddenly from frustrated and angry, to caring that Nancy broke. Her mother had paused, reframed, and asked a question. "Are you okay?" Nancy inhaled sharply at the softness of her mother's voice, and then told her everything. She told her she was in the river with stones in her pockets. She said it was because she wanted to see what it felt like. It was not that she wanted to die. It was curiosity. She begged her mother's forgiveness for losing the coat. She was sorry.

"Forget the coat," her mother said. "I am happy you are alive and in the world. You are more important than any coat."

She will never forget her mother's eyes, the brimming tears and the hollowed out sadness. Her eyes were lost in a place beyond sadness – a place so desolate that coming back was just a faded question mark. It was entirely plausible her mother's eyes would never escape this sadness.

The doctor at the clinic, who spent a distracted hour with Nancy, called it depression and prescribed antidepressants, which augmented her periods of euphoria but did little for the darkness. Nancy was abnormally gleeful and energetic for periods of time, and then she was sleeping and curled up in her bedroom for the following weeks. There was only light, and only darkness, for her. The light was never gentle. There never seemed to be dim light, twilight or dawn. It was either full-on sunlight, or 3 a.m. darkness with nary a hint of the moon. She did not tell the doctor about the sound of the wings. Nor did she tell him about the swings from energetically happy to morbidly down. He only asked her about the river and the stones in her pockets, and if she'd ever tried to kill herself before.

"I wasn't trying to die," she said, crossing her arms across her chest. "If I was trying to die, I would be dead."

"What were you trying to do?"

"I wanted to see what it felt like. That's all."

The doctor considered this. "Do you think there is more truth in one's actions, or in one's words?"

Even at fourteen years, she could recognize a leading question. "Depends on the actions," she said. "Depends on the words."

....

"Don't mess around, Nancy," Ray says. He tries to force his voice to sound normal but he has no idea what it sounds like. It's probably too relaxed. His heart is pounding and he is afraid to look up. She's joking. She must be joking. She's saying this to shock him. She wants to scare him.

"I'm not messing around. I want you to understand how serious I am about us, and about the life we could have had."

Ray tries to glance up at her building, twisting his neck to look out and up through the car window. "It's not like you to say stuff like that."

"If I wanted to be dead, I would be dead already, Ray."

"Then what's this about?"

"It's about meaning and meaningless."

"Meaningless?"

"Yes. This life. My life is meaningless. We're born, we take a few breaths, and then we die. It's pointless." She hears the sound of wings – the soft *wiff, wiff, wiff* sound, and turns quickly toward the open air beyond the balcony. It sounds as if a bird of some kind has flown over the balcony. A raven or a crow. Something big. She looks into the sky but sees nothing but grey upon grey.

"It's not pointless. It's just confusing," Ray says. "And maybe absurd."

"What?"

"Okay, life is definitely absurd, but…"

"…fuck, Ray. How is this comforting?"

"Are we having a conversation? Are we? Because absurdity and pointlessness are two completely different things."

"Why would you say this? Why would you go there? I'm depressed. I'm sad. I'm really depressed, and you're giving me a lecture on existentialism. My country produced Dostoyevsky. You think I don't recognize an existential argument when I hear one? What the fuck is wrong with you?"

"Well the line between pointlessness and absurdity is a delicate thing."

"Delicate," she says. "My brother used to call me his nezhnaya devushka. This is what he called me when I was little, his *delicate girl*."

"Your brother?"

"Yes. My older brother."

"I didn't know you had a brother," Ray says.

"I have a younger brother and sister too, twins. They are still in Kursk with my mother." She hears the wings again and this time she does not bother to look.

She thinks about her mother's kitchen and the picture of the angel Gabriel. Many of the angels were hanging in the house, including Michael, Raphael, Uriel, and Barachiel. There was an image of an angel in her bedroom that had ferocious eyes. Her mother said it was the angel of truth but she never gave that angel a name.

"Sometimes I feel as if there is an angel standing beside my bed as I am sleeping, wishing for peace, or praying for love, or just being holy. Maybe I am dreaming it. I don't know. But I will feel it so strongly that sometimes it wakes me up. And for a spilt second, as I open my eyes, I can see her standing there. For a fraction of a fragment of a second I think I can see this angel. And then I can feel all that remains of her. Do you ever get that, Ray? Do you ever feel as if someone is watching?"

"You believe in angels?"

"I believe there are many things I can't understand, yes. And many more things I can't see, or touch. Perhaps not angels, but the possibility of something intangible."

"Okay."

"My angels are not cute Hallmark card angels, Ray. They are tall, ferocious and dark. Or they are quiet and threatening and sad."

"Those kind of angels I can get behind," Ray says. The disappearing woman on the elevator. What did she say her name was? She was tall and dark, and perhaps she was ferocious.

"My mother had pictures of angels all over the house. They were beautiful and terrifying. Russians and their Orthodox Churches are crazy for angels. There's something stoic about them that matches up with the Russian soul."

She can't believe she's actually defending angels. Her mother's unquestioning belief in angels of all sorts was an irritated sore spot between them.

....

If this book were truly backwards, you would already know what happens. You would know if Nancy jumps, or not. And you might be curious to see what happens next. You would be riding the climax toward a denouement. You'd be on the downward slope. Despite the backwards conventions of structure, this narrative is not backwards. Do not try and read this book in the ascending numerical order of its chapters. Even though the numbers are counting down in a form that is perfectly backwards, the story moves from beginning to end. This flipped around order is just another lie.

....

Perhaps the Kapitán is sitting at the simple wooden table and it is warm in front of the stove. He is slurping spoonfuls of thick borscht into his mouth. Shakespeare's *Macbeth* is open on the table and he is reading as he eats. In the dacha, he reads from a collection of books he found on a bookshelf, and he chops wood. He reads Dostoevsky's *The Insulted and Injured*. He re-reads *The Master and Margarita*. He re-reads *The Sun Also Rises*. He reads Stanislaw Lem's *Solaris*. While he is reading, he limits himself to one drink a day. On the days after he finishes a book, he is drunk before noon and stays drunk until he passes out and sinks into a tossed and turned sleep. He will do this every day until he picks up a new book, and once again begins to read. While he is reading, he has hope. Between books, he is without hope. Once a week, in a neighbouring village, he buys two loaves of black bread from a bakery, provisions to make borscht, and more vodka. He had fallen into the habit of thinking about his vodka as not simply two more bottles, but rather, two more "bottles of forgetting."

The Kapitán has been AWOL for two months. He walked away from his posting without warning, and he disappeared effectively. Even if the military investigators were looking for him, which they weren't, they would find no clues. They assumed he had disappeared permanently. They assumed the Kapitán was a suicide and that his body would not be found, or it would be found and no one would care. Other men who performed the duties of informing families of the deaths of their fathers, husbands, and brothers similarly disappeared. Many backed away from the darkness of the duty. Some took their own lives. Few were able to do it for as long as the Kapitán. They assumed wrong. Anatoly was very much alive, but he was also slowly killing himself as he went through bouts of bingeing vodka followed by brief sober periods, and then bingeing again. He knew his liver was failing but he was thirsty for the bliss of not feeling anything, and dulling his memory. On most days, his thirst for numbness and forgetting outweighed his thirst for life.

There were days when he was almost happy in his isolated dacha in the woods, with his soup, the books left by the last resident, and the grey Russian days of winter. He felt as if he'd been dragging a massive weight around for years, and now that cement block was diminished. It was still there but it was less.

Two days ago it warmed up to above freezing and he built a small fire outside. He took a cup of tea and his book, and leaned against the wall of the dacha. There were chickadees in the spruce trees and

Anatoly watched them, listened to them and they made him smile. He did not think he would smile again before he died but the sound of the birds fretting in the trees, and their flying back and forth above his head, was an inexplicable joy. They were busy and loud in the forest. The cruelties and sorrows of the world did not concern the birds.

He placed another chunk of wood onto the fire and for the first time in a month, Anatoly checked his wrist for his watch, to see what time it was. It was an involuntary impulse. The watch was gone, of course. He remembered giving it to the girl. He'd bent down and put it in her hands. He was not sure if it was a gesture of kindness. It was probably something else. Something like a resignation, or a retreat, and an unspoken desire for forgiveness. It was most likely a desperate attempt to push back against the darkness. He remembered this particular girl. Her questioning eyes, her confusion, the fact she probably didn't quite understand what his being there meant. But there was something about her eyes. They were deeper and older than they should have been. It was as if she'd been through these sorts of deliveries before. As if she knew, not on the surface, but three levels down.

His father had given him the *Vostok* watch, and now the girl had it, and he hoped it would move with her through time. He had no more need for it. Except just then, because the birds had loosened something in him and he had looked for it. He had wondered about the time. The sound of the birds had caused him to come back into the stream of time after months of a routine that put him slightly outside minutes, and hours, and days.

the bird in the house

When they are finished, Tulah removes her hands from the cubicle wall and turns around. Ray can see her hands have made steamy outlines of themselves on the wooden surface of the wall. Tulah's face is flushed and her breathing is heavy. She does not pull her skirt down or refasten her bra. The downward weight of her breasts is breathtaking to Ray. He would much rather have the slope of fallen breasts than firm and perky. He knows it is an odd preference, but it is also an old preference. He has always felt this way.

"Do you still want me?" Tulah asks.

"I always want you."

"I don't mean sexually. I mean as your wife."

"Yes, I want you that way too."

"You love me?" she asks.

"Haven't stopped loving you," he says. "Ever since I started."

Tulah smiles. "When was that?"

He closes his eyes. He can smell Tulah's sex. It's a musky, sweet and dark smell. His trousers are at his feet. This was so like Tulah – to ask questions like this in odd locations, at unorthodox times – to feel vulnerable and act on that feeling – to search for assurance. "Okay," he says. "It was July 7th, 1994. About 4 a.m. It was raining. The window was open. It was the house in the flats, by the ballpark. We were sleeping on that ridiculously small bed – what was it?"

"It was a twin."

"It was so small. But I liked being that close to you. I remember the elms along the street were sad – they looked more sorrowful than majestic. You'd just finished telling me about your time in Scotland. You'd driven off the road, banged your head on the windshield, and woke up in a pub – lying on your back on top of the bar with a bunch of old Scottish buggers looking down at you. One of them was a doctor. It wasn't the story that got me. It was the small details you included.

The smell of wet wool. The dog with a leaky eye. The waitress with a stain on her apron, on her left boob. You said boob. I liked it that you said the word 'boob.' And I loved it that you stayed there in that village for two weeks…"

"…two and a half. She was lactating – the waitress. I found out later she was lactating."

"…Two-and-a-half weeks. Drinking whisky and walking the heaths in a wool sweater and rubber boots. Yeah. That's when I really started to love you. A thousand other women would have said – *I want to go home*. You stayed for the adventure and you captured Scotland."

"I was concussed."

"You made a choice."

"At the time, it seemed like the right thing to do."

"I love that picture of you."

"But it wasn't a picture, it was a story."

"I have the picture from the story."

Somebody comes into the bathroom. Tulah bites her lip, and her eyes are frantic and excited. She places her hand over his mouth. They listen as the woman pees, flushes and then leaves without washing her hands.

"Listen," Ray says. "It was the snow that sealed the deal for me. The snow falling over Scotland, and you in the window, watching it. I could imagine the dark chestnut tones of the bar behind you. The dim yellow light. The old guy leaned against the bar on his third whisky. You, sipping your drink and writing in your journal because when it snows that's what you do. You made me love Scotland and I'd never been there."

"So, just to be clear – you do love me?"

"A thousand times, yes."

……….

Later that night, in the bathtub, Tulah tries to read her book but she can't focus. She's reading a biography about the life of Claude Garamond, called *Garamondus Maximus*. The author's name is Fran Fritz, which Tulah thinks must be a pseudonym because no parent would be that cruel. She's charmed by the book because so little is known about Garamond that it's practically a book of fiction, except it's also a clever and thorough dissection of the world of letterforms and fonts. She puts the book down, which is a relief because it's 954 pages. Intriguing as it is, she can't give it proper attention. She sinks into the water. She purposely lets her memory drift toward Scotland, but this time, for herself.

She wrote in her journal, a lot. It snowed a lot. She was dizzy for the first few days. The rental car had a hefty dent in its front end and the windshield was cracked. She wasn't wearing her seatbelt and this was perplexing because she always wore her seatbelt. Something was on the road – an animal but she didn't know what it was. The patrons of the pub all had theories – from dogs, to sheep, to hares and even ghosts. Bruce MacDonald said it was a rabbit. He said there were rabbits on that stretch of the road all the time. He'd killed one the year before. Tulah had offered to buy him a whisky and he told her he didn't drink.

"I gave it up the night my son was born," he said. "I wanted to pay better attention, and couldn't do that while I was drinking."

"How old is your son?"

"He's three. Morogh – his name is Morogh. I have a daughter also. She's six months."

"What's her name?"

"We call her Fen. She was named after Keavy's grandmother – Fenella."

"Fen is a beautiful name." Tulah paused and looked at the glass of whisky on her table. It was her second and she was leaning toward a third, before noon.

Bruce smiled – his teeth were not perfectly straight. "I wasn't an alcoholic. It's not like that. I just made a choice to be present in my own life. I've nothing against those who drink a little. I'm glad of it, seeing as I make a living from it."

"Well, thank God for that."

"Trust me, I've watched you for a week now. You only drink a little. You will always only drink a little."

"Is he bugging you?" Keavy stomped her feet in the entranceway. "Leave her to her writing."

"I am not bugging anybody, wife." He moved back behind the bar and picked up a glass, and a cloth – held the glass up to the light and frowned.

"He's not bugging me," Tulah said.

"What?" The man propped against a pillar near the bar, who was sound asleep, jolted awake. He was wearing a wool cap and his beard was grey. "What happened?"

Keavy hung her coat on a hook at the front entrance. "Nothing happened, Barclay, except you woke up."

"I woke up?" He combed his hand through his hair and touched the side of his face, pulled at his beard.

"Does that surprise you?" Bruce said.

He considered this question. "At my age? Yes."

"You're not that old, ya bugger."

"I was dreaming about the giraffes..." Barclay seemed to drift back into the memory of this dream. He turned toward the window.

It was snowing. The hills and mountains were covered in white. The snow was drifting softly past the window. Tulah felt isolated and safe in the pub. It was warm and quiet while the world raged without her.

Keavy turned her attention to Tulah. "And how is that head of yours?"

"My head? I'm fine, I think."

"Good. You remember the doctor said to go easy for a week. A fine cock-a-leekie stew for lunch," Keavy said. "Chicken and leeks, carrots and rice. I think you'll like it."

"I've only been walking. Small walks."

"Another drink, then?"

"Please."

Tulah had been living on beer and Guinness stew for a week – this was her first whisky morning. She was afraid to weigh herself. There was no opportunity to check her weight in the room above the pub, but had there been a scale, she would have avoided it. The chicken and leek stew sounded like a nice change. She leaned toward Barclay. "What is the giraffe dream? Is it a good dream?"

Barclay looked at her and after an uncomfortable amount of time, he nodded. "My wife loved giraffes. I don't know why. Whenever the giraffes are in my dreams, I feel a bit closer to her. It's always a good dream."

Tulah assumed his wife had passed away, and she was wrong. Keavy told her later that night Barclay's wife – fifteen years younger than him

– was living in the south of France. She was French and the Scottish climate was too much for her, not to mention the food of Scotland. "She was a bit delicate that way," Keavy said. "And he can't let go."

The next day she could not stop thinking about Barclay. She had borrowed a sweater and one of Bruce MacDonald's rain slickers, and Keavy offered a pair of sturdy rubber boots – only a half size too big. This is what Tulah wore for her walks. She tucked a bottle of whisky into the pocket of the slicker – even though she was not entirely on board with liking whisky – and walked through the snow, and in the snow, and with snow falling all around. On that day, she thought only about Barclay and his estranged French wife and the giraffes in his dream that made him feel a bit closer to her. It broke her heart to have witnessed this sort of unmoored grief.

She has never told anyone about Barclay and his sorrow. She hasn't told another soul about the dream of the giraffes. She thinks maybe it's because she wants to keep it for herself, or that someday she will have her own dream about giraffes – though she has no idea what her giraffes would do in a dream, or what they would mean.

....

All through the next day, Tulah senses something is wrong. The girls are doing homework at the kitchen table and she is standing at the sink, looking out into the back yard. Everything is as it should be but she has a queasy feeling that something is off. This morning she burnt her toast – she hadn't noticed the setting was on high. Yesterday, she broke a heel on her favourite black pumps and two days ago, there was a sparrow in the house. She'd used the broom to shoo it toward the open door and back into the sky. The bird was fine but now she had a general feeling of anxiety, as if something were about to happen.

Last night there was the kinkiness in the bathroom at the restaurant, and that was fun, but it wasn't making love. It's not as if she didn't think about having sex with him more often. It's just, they got busy and it was difficult to make the time. Her mother would say, *Tulah, you make time for the things you want to do. You make time for the things that are important.* Tulah hopes this is not true. She hopes even if a thing is important, sometimes you truly can't find the time to do it.

If only the sparrow had not been in the house. That goddamned bird. It was a bad sign. A bird in the house meant there was death coming. Death of something. That was the saying, wasn't it? As rational as Tulah was, there was a strand of fear attached to the superstition of the bird in the house, and she wished it had not happened.

Beautiful in a subdued and quiet way

You're probably wondering about the numbering of this chapter. Twenty-one and a half? It's as if the writer had a set number of chapters in mind, and then things started to unravel. His plans went completely off the rails, and twenty-four chapters were not enough. The author's solution? These mildly inelegant half-chapters. Welcome to the first bastardized Greek Chorus, a half-chapter section of text that is neither a real chapter, nor a trivial indulgence. It is certainly not a genuine Greek Chorus. No one is singing here. No one is dancing. This is not a group of people who will comment – collectively – on the dramatic action. It's a renegade in a land of broken walls. It's an ill-fitting suit. The wrong coloured shoes. The bad haircut.

The chorus in the ancient Greek dramas sometimes offered contextual information that would help the audience follow the performance. They commented on the themes, they expressed what the main characters could not say, such as their hidden fears or secrets, or pockets of anxiety. The Greek Chorus was a touchstone for the story. Perhaps that is the goal of these Greek Choruses.

You might – because you can, on occasion, be a horny idiot – think about Greek sex when you see the term 'Greek Chorus.' It is not a massive leap to get from Greek chorus to Greek sex, and in Chapter 24, Ray's wife will make him an offer of 'Greek sex' in a restaurant. She won't call it this, but Greek sex is on Tulah's menu. One of a great many online dictionaries defines Greek sex as – "anal sex, the act of anal intercourse between a man and woman." Again, you probably know this already. There are speculations about origin of this term, the ancient Greeks and their sexual predilections, but that's not important right now.

While this may not be a genuine Greek Chorus, it is utterly and completely true. Everything you read here is true. It is all one-hundred-and-twenty percent true.

· · · · · · ·

godforsaken
1. remote, desolate
2. neglected and miserable in appearance or circumstances

· · · · · · ·

The villa near Allemond is rustic and secluded. It has a fine workshop and there is excellent wine nearby, but it is also a great deal of work. The difference between a city life with a few servants and this country life in which they do everything themselves, is astounding.

Marie Isabelle does not like it in the country. Even though their status has risen in the eyes of her friends and acquaintances because only the rich and nobility could afford a summer place, this rustic life was not for her. She could not tell her friends where she was going – only that she would be living in the country for a while. But she is a city girl, through-and-through. She wants Paris again. She misses the bustle of the markets, the cabarets and taverns, the art, and the people. She used to go to parties, banquets, and balls. Here, there are trees, a river and a tiny village. Her friends are all in Paris. She understands the need to be away from the city but she also blames Garamond for her exile. She does not dwell on it, but she could have been married to any number of men who did not have to leave Paris because they feared their associations with a degenerate publisher put their own lives in danger. Still, one morning when she is at the well drawing water, Marie Isabelle realizes there are far more positives than negatives in her life. The villa in which they are staying is dry and warm. They have chickens and they go to the market in Allemond twice a week, and they have wine. Garamond works on his typefaces but when he is with her, he is truly with her. She loves this about him. She has never felt he is looking over her shoulder at something or someone more interesting. Marie Isabelle places her unhappiness aside.

Garamond enters the room holding a piece of paper with his letter 'g' smudged into it.

"This one is balanced and elegant, and it is not in the least bit sleepy," he says. "It has the right energy." He believes his letterforms should have energy – a sort of vibrancy that invigorates the language.

And beauty. Above all, the letters that make words, that make senten-ces, that make paragraphs, that ultimately shape language and poetry, and stories – ought to be beautiful, but beautiful in a subdued and quiet way. The form of the letters should not get in the way of what is written. He hands her the sheet of paper and she looks at the letter.

"It's beautiful," she says, even though she can't see the difference between the letter 'g' of two weeks ago and this one. She thought the first 'g' he showed her was playful and bold, the same as this one. "You have improved the elegance of the letter," she says.

She looks at his face and she can see the child he was. His smile is childlike and innocent. Marie Isabelle recognizes the fact he trusts her enough to be childlike in front of her. He trusts her with his inno-cence and she does not take this trust lightly.

....

red herring
noun
1. a smoked herring.
2. something intended to divert attention from the real problem or matter at hand; a misleading clue.
3. Also called red-herring prospectus. Finance. a tentative prospectus circulated by the underwriters of a new issue of stocks or bonds that is pending approval by the US Securities and Exchange Commission: so called because the front cover of such a prospectus must carry a special notice printed in red.
4. any similar tentative financial prospectus, as one concerning a pending or proposed sale of co-operative or condominium apartments.

the sound of wings

"In the dark, all cats are grey"
— *Zhanna Petya*

And Nancy has always heard the sound of wings. This thin, wheezing sound has always been there in her life. She assumed everyone heard the sound of birds flying low and overhead, like she did. She remembers hearing the birds' wings a week before her father went to fight in the war with Afghanistan. He was teaching her to skip stones on the flat of the river. He heard it too, and stopped, and looked up. It sounded like a big bird.

"What was that, papa?" she said.

"A raven," he said. "Or a crow." But neither of them could see a raven or a crow anywhere in the sky.

But perhaps this was not a memory, but rather, a remembered story. Her father told her mother, who, years beyond, told Nancy the story.

Her mother would have blamed the sound on one of her angels. "The sound of wings is the sound of a visitation," she would say. "It is the sound of an angel watching over you." Nancy, after so many years, only thinks she remembers skipping stones with her papa. It could have been her memory of the story told to her by her mother. She remembers the air was humid and hot, and smelled of lavender. There was definitely lavender in the air. She is certain of this. There was an open field of purple rising up from the riverbank.

"Come and see this one," he said. "This is a good stone. See how flat and round? You try it." He gave her the nearly perfect stone and stood behind her, guiding her arm, showing her the motion. When she finally made her throw, it skipped three times and then was swallowed by the current, and she was thrilled.

Years beyond her father's death, Nancy's mother started to tell the story of the sound of the wings as if it was the Angel of Death that visited them on the banks of the Seym. "Death was telling your father to get ready," Nancy's mother said. "The sound of those wings was the sound of angels' wings. This is what you heard."

"Mother," Nancy said, exasperated.

"No. I am certain of this."

"Mom. This is ridiculous."

"And what did your father do when the Angel of Death appeared to him on the shore of the river? He taught his daughter to skip stones."

Nancy is not sure if her mother is pointing to a loving father, or a foolish one.

"You know dad didn't believe in angels."

"He ignored the Angel of Death and death took him a few weeks later."

"Oh my God, mother, stop it. Papa died in a stupid war, trying to save some children. There are no angels in a war. War is much too awful for angels."

"There are angels everywhere," her mother said.

Nancy could hear hurt in her mother's voice, and she let it go. "Okay, mom," she said. "Okay."

. . . .

If she really thinks about it, Nancy does not remember hearing the wings before the time she heard the sound on the banks of the Seym with her father. She does not want this memory to be the first time she heard the wings. She wants to think she remembers the wings before this. Maybe at a sixth birthday party, she was in the bathroom and the window was open and she heard that sound. Or when she was playing in the park two years before her father died – she had looked up because she'd heard the sound of wings, and there was nothing but blue. But these are not memories; they are just hopes. They're not real.

She was no longer surprised by this sound. It had become part of her life. It was so common for her that she almost rolled her eyes when she heard it just now.

. . . .

Ray is looking through the windshield at the street and the people on the sidewalk, the businesses and the trees. But he doesn't actually see anything. What the hell was he thinking? Perhaps he really was a duplicitous bastard. A woman once said that to him. After he'd broken it off with her she kept an Irish wool sweater of his and even though he loved that sweater he considered it a bargain to have traded it for a mostly smooth ending with a minimal amount of acrimony. At the time, Ray barely heard her accusation, but it stuck. Duplicitous was probably a good word for him, though he was not duplicitous with her. She was dull and dour, and he was simply tired of her.

Lately, he has been truly duplicitous. Because he has been split in two. He's been moving between hearts. He's been going to sleep with Tulah, thinking about Nancy. Making love with Nancy and thinking only about Tulah.

He is never split in two when he is with his daughters. He is whole when he is with them. His daughters are always his daughters. They are constant and delightful, even when they are grumpy. And there is no dichotomy of trees. Trees are simple and undemanding. There are simple rules with trees.

But with Tulah and Nancy, Ray has not been able to stay still. His heart has been flitting back and forth, always moving, and his heart is exhausted. It needs to land. Once he calms Nancy down, his heart will land where it's supposed to be. He will focus on his wife. He will never do this again, not to her, and not to himself.

Even an affair with a woman in a penthouse condo had become a dull creep toward the inevitable. And now, that woman is at the edge of a glass railing and she says she wants peace.

"Nancy?"

"Yes, Ray?" Nancy lights a cigarette. Ray can hear the lighter, a puffing sound, and her exhalation.

"I didn't know you smoked," he says.

"I quit a couple years ago."

"And yet you are smoking right now."

She sighs. "It is because I don't give a shit, Ray. What's a couple cigarettes?" She'd only managed to quit because of the two packages of cigarettes, in a *Ziplock* baggie in the freezer. Those packs were her escape, her parachute, and her desperate recourse. For two years, she'd resisted because in the back of her mind, she knew she could smoke any time she wanted. A cigarette was just there, under the frozen pizza and behind the cans of frozen orange juice.

"What's really going on?" Ray says.

"I'm tired," she says. "I'm tired of not being important."

"You are important…"

"…Not to you. Not anymore. Not to anyone, really."

"I'm going to come back up there…"

"…No! No. You can't come back up. I don't want you up here. Just stay where you are." But she does want him to come back up. She wants him to hold her and tell her everything is going to be fine. She wants him in her apartment, and in her bedroom and in her. She knows this about herself and she knows if she allows this to happen she will lose all power. Right now, she has power.

"You don't believe me, do you?"

He hesitates. What are the consequences of him saying he does not believe her? "I believe you are serious," he says finally. "I believe you're upset. And angry."

"You don't think I can do it, do you?"

"I think you can do anything you put your mind to."

"Good, I'm glad. Now we're making progress."

"Look, we're going to have a talk and then you're going to have a drink and go to bed."

"Do you think you have any power right now, Ray? Is that why you're telling me what I'm going to do?"

"Not about power," he says. "It was a wish."

"It sounded more like an order, and anyway, I'm already having a glass of your scotch."

"You're drinking scotch?"

"I thought I might like to taste it, other than through you."

He thinks about kissing her and a frisson twitches in his back. "And do you like the taste of it?"

"Yes. It's delicious," she says. "But it wasn't delicious at first. Only after three sips – three big sips."

His phone cuts out as another call pops up. It's Tulah's number and he declines the call.

"What was that?"

"I had another call. Another call beeped in. I'm here."

"Who was it?"

"It was work. We're in the middle of a project right now. They think I'm in a meeting."

"It was your wife, wasn't it?"

She's guessing. She couldn't know for sure. Really, it's none of her business. "It was Joe, from work," he says. "I've been trying to set up a meeting with him." He thinks about this lie. It would make no difference if she knew the truth. Wives call husbands all the time. It's normal. So why is he lying?

Tulah sends him a text message: *You must be in a meeting. Call me when you're out.*

"Shall we call your wife and have a chat? We could ask her how she feels about your being with me. We could ask her if she just called, or not."

"You know that's not going to happen."

"You mean the truth is not going to happen. Because we don't like the truth. We live in the shadows of the truth."

"You're right."

"So it was your wife?"

"No, the part about living a lie. That's true."

"I didn't say we were living a lie. I said we lived in the shadow of the truth. That's different."

CHAPTER 20

Tulah at 15

Tulah's Snow Journal
Friday, September 14, 1990 #1

The snow is falling straight down. It's heavy and wet. It makes everything innocent and new. It falls everywhere. It falls on the rich and the poor with a perfect equality. The happy and the sad. Men and women. Cats and dogs. It's so nice to walk in it – to not worry about getting my shoes wet. Because trying to avoid getting them wet would result in the same wet shoes that I have now, from just walking. To just walk and feel it touching my face and my hands is cool. I've never really thought about how much I love snow before.

I do not know if I will continue to write about snow, but I did put a number on this entry. I called it #1, but I don't know what this is.

This snow is early. Everyone is freaked out because it's barely fall and here is winter. The leaves aren't even turned yet. Not all of them anyway. Everyone is saying it won't stay but it feels cold enough that it could. It could last right into October and November and through Christmas, January, and February and all the way to the end of March. It could also be gone by the end of the week. It doesn't matter. It's here now and it's beautiful. Mom and Dad are fighting again. They're downstairs going at it. They're screaming at each other about summer vacation, and money. To fight about summer in the midst of a snowstorm is kinda funny. At least I think so.

The snow is soft. It's falling straight down but it's gentle. It muffles everything. The traffic sounds disappear. And I guess it muffles me too. I am made gentler by this falling snow. I wonder if it will always be like this.

Mr. Johnson – he's my English teacher – read a poem by this poet Rumi, called Like This. *It was beautiful. If you ever doubt my love for snow, if you ever doubt its cold complexity, if you ever doubt its soft beauty – stand in the falling snow with me, hold my hand, and look up, like this.*

....

Tulah is fifteen. She adjusts her headphones and turns the music up. She's listening to Mahler's fifth symphony, again. There's a skip around the halfway point of this record, so she'll have to get up and move the needle. She doesn't really like the music of the day. She knows it but she prefers the complexity of the '70s, R&B, jazz and folk. Classical music was new to her. This was a gift from her father, who had more than 3,000 albums of classical music and jazz. She was exploring this collection, leaping from piece to piece, randomly gathering her favourites. She'd jumped in because of the movie *Pretty Woman* and *La Traviata,* and found she liked classical music. And her father was up late one night watching a movie called *Heaven.* He did not tell her to go back to bed when she came downstairs and curled up with him on the couch. He simply put his arm around her and they watched together. There was a scene on a train, and Arvo Pärt's *Spiegel im Spiegel* was playing. Tulah fell in love with that piece of music, and Cate Blanchett's desolate face.

"Arvo Pärt is over there," her father says, pointing at the wall of albums. "Far right, one shelf down, in the middle somewhere. It's called *Spiegel im Spiegel.* Translates as – mirror in mirror."

They did not have to talk. It was something Tulah had been doing with her dad since she was ten. She would sneak downstairs and find him with a glass of scotch, watching a movie. He would always smile and make room. He was never drunk. He seemed only to be interested in sipping his drink for a few hours and reading, or watching a movie.

She's not sure if she wants to keep numbering her journal entries. It seems like a good idea but what's the point? It was a new journal, and it was the first time she'd written about snow but it was a bold stroke to put the number one there at the top of the page, as if there would be a number two, and a number three, and so on. Maybe she'll keep writing about snow. Whenever and wherever it happens, she'll write it.

This snow drew attention to itself by arriving so early.

She's done with Mahler for now. She presses play on the tape deck and Sinead O'Connor's *Nothing Compares 2 U* plays. She knows Bryan Adams's *Have You Ever Really Loved A Woman?* is next, and then Bon Jovi's *Blaze of Glory.*

Of all the songs from the '70s that she loves, she loves Janis Ian's *At Seventeen* the best. She holds this song close because her face has broken out and it seems no matter what she does, it's not going to clear up. Each pimple is a body punch to her barely emerging self-esteem. She can't imagine a boy liking her. She doesn't even like her. She is not beautiful, not like the girls who hang out at Lisa Campbell's locker between classes. Add to this, the fact Tulah is fifteen and she still does not trust her own bladder. In the past few months, she had a couple nights in which she'd woken up to a wet bed. She thought she was out of the woods with the bed-wetting, but her bladder had other ideas. She was only happy that it was not every night.

It would be devastating to be at a sleepover and have something happen, which is why she avoided sleepovers. Her mom took the blame as an overprotective parent – she was happy to be the scapegoat, the reason Tulah couldn't sleep over, the reason she was being picked up at midnight. For Tulah, her uncontrollable bladder was humbling and terrifying.

For grade 10, she pretty much keeps her head down and hopes nobody is talking about her – she wants to be grey, or beige – she hopes she's not so weird that she will draw attention and scorn. Tulah's strategy is to become almost invisible and slide through high school mostly undamaged.

Her plan works fairly well. In the first couple of months, Tulah focuses on school. She wears nothing colourful. She never raises her hand in class. She manages to develop a few friends who are equally invisible.

It was second-term language arts when the wheels of her plan fell off. In the dead of winter, Mr. Johnson saw what she was doing and told her to stop it. "Ms. Roberts? Tulah?" he said, in the third week, and in the middle of the period, actually, in the middle of a sentence. They'd been talking about Orwell's *Animal Farm*. He looked up, looked at her and tilted his head a bit – as if he'd just figured something out. "Please see me after class," he said.

She had no idea what this was about but she stayed in her seat and when everyone was gone, Mr. Johnson looked at her and smiled kindly. "You're not being honest with me, and I find that annoying."

"What? I…"

"…You are smarter than everyone in this class and yet you pretend you're average."

"I don't see how…"

"…let me finish. Last week, when I was giving my brilliant synopsis of *Animal Farm* and stopped to ask if anyone knew what literary trick Orwell was using to make his point, nobody in the room said anything. Nobody made eye contact and nobody answered. You, however, mouthed the word 'satire' as you were looking away."

"So?"

"So, you knew the answer. I think you know most of the answers to most of my questions. Sometimes it feels like you know the answers to my questions before I ask them."

"I like Orwell," she said.

"When did you read this book? When did you read *Animal Farm*?"

"Two years ago, the first time," she said.

"You're precocious," he said. "I use this word because I know you know what it means."

Tulah looked up at Mr. Johnson and smiled. She had no idea a teacher could be this direct, and honest.

⋯⋯

She starts to crawl out of the land of beige. She starts to speak up in Mr. Johnson's class, which pleases him, and in all her other classes too. Her grades, which were hovering above average, ascended to where they belonged – which was in the 'honours with distinction' range. Her face does not clear up. In fact, it gets a little worse. Her doctor says she has a new drug that is "very effective" but she's a little worried about the side effects. And, she has to be on birth control to take it. They're going to talk about it in a couple months. In early December, she realizes she hasn't had a bad night – her parents call the nights she wets the bed, 'the bad nights' – for months. She starts to get invitations to parties from a different group of friends. Not the nerds. Not the indescribable group of boys who play a complex card game that is so convoluted it's absurd. And not the pretty-pretty girls. But rather, the reasonably good-looking kids who realized being cool in high school was less important than being smart. These were the kids who valued the idea of being intelligent. To them, smart was cool.

Then there was the awful night of the talk. The talk is sad and painful. One night, about a week before Christmas, her parents sit Tulah and her sister, Alesha, down and tell them they'd tried everything but they could not seem to work out a way to live with each other. Things were going to change.

Alesha stood up. "Try fucking harder," she said and then ran down the hall to her room. The sound of a slamming door, and then silence. Her parents looked at her and waited. Tulah knew. She knew two years ago. She was not entirely surprised by this announcement. She'd noticed when her parents stopped touching. And they no longer kissed in the morning. And the presents they gave each other were less romantic and more utilitarian. Her mom gave her dad a toaster for his birthday. He gave her an espresso maker – Italian and expensive and more for himself than for her.

Inside she was a swirling storm of emotion. Her brain could not reconcile her parents not together. This was her mom and dad. They were there, together, for her entire life. It was as if she was falling down in slow motion. She couldn't stop falling and she couldn't speed it up. She just had to live with that falling feeling. She didn't understand. Even though the signs and symptoms were neatly lined up, she could not make it stay in one place. She wanted to step away, into a world she understood, a world in which the water was calm and warm. She wanted to scream and freak out and run away, but her sister had already grabbed that set of reactions. Instead, she gave her parents something that made both their mouths fall open.

"Okay," Tulah said. "I believe you tried. Now what?"

CHAPTER 19

"My brother is big"

"God gives to those who get up early"
— *Zhanna Petya*

After her father died, Nancy's brother, Slava, went away and a few months later the money started to arrive. The first Wednesday of every month, a package containing a bundle of roubles would be delivered. It was a time of great opportunity in Russia. The Soviet Union was breaking apart and new alliances were being formed. New forms of corruption were being organized inside the guise of *glasnost* and *perestroika*. For three years the money came from cities in Russia: Moscow, Saint Petersburg, and Kazan, and then Moscow again. The fourth year, the money was wired from New York.

Their mother knew, of course, but she would not speak about it. Her son was working in America. He was successful enough to send a little money each month. He was a good boy. Her friends knew better than to ask what exactly Slava was doing in America. Working in New York was the end of the conversation, not the beginning. As the monthly deposits grew in size, Zhanna Petya knew her son was moving up in the ranks of the Russian Bratva. When they talked on the phone, her first question for him was always, "Are you safe?" And he would answer: "I am surrounded by trusted and loyal men. Yes. I am safe."

By the time Nancy told her brother about the hockey player, Slava had been in New York for five years. She needed his approval before she would agree to leave with Dmitri. It took Slava a week to get back to her. "He's a good boy," he said. "A good family. If you need anything, you call me, and I will arrange it." She does not know what kind of a check he performed but she trusts her brother. "And when Dmitri has money, you tell him to call me. I have some investment funds that are low risk, and high reward."

She talked with her brother every week and Slava never failed to answer a call from his sister. Not once in nine years had she been forced to leave a message, or hang up because there was no answer. Nor had his phone ever been answered by someone other than him.

"Hallo, Nensi," he would say. "It is good to hear from you. How are you?" He never used her North-Americanized name. He preferred the name she grew up with.

"So, I am coming to America. Dmitri has signed with the Montréal Canadiens."

"You know that Montréal is in Canada, right?"

"Of course," she said. But she didn't know. She'd assumed it was in the United States. She hadn't really thought about it. All Dmitri's other options – Chicago, New York, and Florida – were clearly American.

"When do you leave?"

"Three weeks, Slava. They want Dmitri at training camp."

"I am happy for you, Nensi. You will like Montréal. It is not as old as Kursk, but it is much older than the rest of the country. Now, tell me about the twins, and how is our mother? How is she dealing with your leaving?"

Nancy fills him in. The twins are in the ninth grade. Their mother is stoic about Nancy's leaving. She is fretting but accepting. She would have preferred that Nancy and Dmitri were married before going on this adventure, but she sighed and offered one of her nuggets of wisdom – "Not all who make love make marriages," she said.

Nancy lasts two years with Dmitri. He is driven to be the best National Hockey League hockey player he can be and his hard work comes with the reward of a hefty contract. When Montréal is eliminated from the playoffs in the spring of the second year, Dmitri eliminates Nancy from his life.

They were at a restaurant on St. Catherine Street.

"I think we are done," he said.

But Nancy was not about to make it easy on him. She knew this was coming. They hadn't made love in months and he was rarely home, except to sleep. And the other hockey wives had turned cold and distant on her a couple months back, as if they knew something she didn't. "But I've just started my meal," she said. "Are you not feeling well?"

Dmitri was confused and flustered. He reached for his water glass. "I mean…"

"…you mean? You mean you are finished with something other than the meal?" Nancy crossed her arms and waited.

"Yes," he said. "Yes. I mean I…"

"Are you breaking up with me?"

"No," he said. "Yes. I suppose…"

"…No. You're not," she said. "I am breaking up with you. I can't say that I'm not disappointed. I am disappointed. But you're still a child, Dmitri. I have hope for you but the likelihood of your growing up in my lifetime is slim."

"So you're not upset?"

"If I am breaking up with you, why would I be upset?"

Later that night, Nancy called Slava.

"You will come and stay with me," he said. "I have more room than I need. I have a place I am not using, if you want it."

"It's for the best, Slava," she said. "It was my idea."

"Okay," he said. "Does he owe you anything? I will send someone to collect what he owes you."

When Nancy starts to cry, Slava's voice becomes a growl. "Did he hurt you?"

"Just my heart," she said.

. . . .

"My brother is big," Nancy says. "In New York, he is big."

"Big? What do you mean big? He's a big man? Or is he famous?"

"I mean, connected."

"Connected?"

"Yes. The Bratva, the Brotherhood, you know?"

Ray sits up straight. Is she saying what he thinks she's saying? "The Russian mafia?"

"That is a coarse name. That is not my brother. That is criminals… Slava is not a criminal. He is a businessman. He is a businessman with the Brotherhood."

"Slava?"

"Short for…Václav. It was his lawyer who negotiated with my ex-husband."

Ray thinks about the generous deal Nancy got after three years of marriage. He can imagine the kind of negotiation it might have been. There was the advantage of a public attempt to strangle her but still, Ray can see a pit-bull lawyer with a Russian accent basically telling all involved how it was going to be – end of story. He wonders if the ex-husband is still alive. He wonders if he will still be alive in a week, or two weeks, or a month. "Jesus, you're just telling me this now?"

"Telling what? Slava says not to talk about it and so I don't talk about it. And what difference would it have made to anything?"

"My brother disappeared a few months after my dad died," she says. "And then the money started coming – enough roubles to support the family.

We would get a phone call at Christmas and for birthdays, but nothing beyond these calls. He would not say what he was doing, or even where he was in the world. But he never forgot a birthday. And the money kept coming. Family is important to Slava."

Nancy takes a sip of her whisky. She thinks of it as her whisky now. She misses her dad. Her dad did not drink whisky. Like most Russians, he enjoyed his vodka. Right now, she misses him. And yesterday, and last week, she missed him. Her life is scattered with landmines of missing and she inadvertently steps on them all the time. She thinks about what it would be like to curl up with him on the couch and watch TV, or read, or just talk for a while. She tries to remember his face from her own memory, beyond the three pictures she keeps. She remembers the Kapitán's face better than her father's. The Kapitán's face was narrow and sad – he had tried to be stern and strictly military but he had failed. He was weary. More than simple weariness – he was deeply weary of the world. The *Vostok* military watch, which she wears every day, is a constant reminder of his kindness, and obliquely, it is a memory of her father.

....

If he lies to her in order to prevent her from harming herself, is it morally wrong? Ray thinks his answer is no – in this situation, with him sitting in his car at the bottom of her building, and her teetering up there, it is not morally wrong to lie. He should, and will, say anything to prevent her from killing herself. In fact, he should fabricate and elaborate. He should augment and twist and speak of love. He should admit to any absurdity. If she wants him to say something embarrassing, or true, or awful, he should say it.

Ray realizes, at this point in his life, he is morally absurd. He has been loving two women and really, nothing should stay the same. It should all change, but he won't let it. He's going to work with his wife – he wants to do that. And he wants Nancy to carry on – to get up in the morning and take a breath, and to keep moving forward, without him.

The Vintner

Well of course, the author of this book knows exactly what was said at 2:36 p.m., March 4, 1536, in the village of Allemond, France, in a small tavern, as two men – one a vintner and winemaker, and the other, the father of the Garamond font – try to figure out if they can trust each other.

. . . .

Maurice Gauguin likes Garamond instantly. He studies him as Garamond takes gulping slurps of the wine, a delicate Gamay noir, and grins with appreciation. He appears to be ravenous for the wine, as if he can't drink it fast enough. As if he does not care if he spills or drips. As if he is exceedingly thirsty.

"This wine is beautiful," Garamond says. "The acidity is prominent but the fruit is also strong. What is this called?"

"This wine is the Gamay," Gauguin says. He smiles. It makes him happy when someone truly appreciates his wine. "It is a robust grape but also a difficult grape."

Garamond leans back in his chair and looks at Monsieur Gauguin, who moves around the room with the assistance of a cane. Gauguin is a small man with intense, curious eyes. He has been wiping tables and arranging chairs as they talk. Just now he is making small adjustments to the fire in the hearth. Above the rough wooden mantle, there is a bearskin hung flat against the wall.

"How is it difficult?" Garamond says.

The vintner approaches the table, pauses as if he is wondering if this is a good idea, then sits down across from Garamond. "These grapes come into bud and flower earlier than most. It is as if they are eager to be in the glass. But sometimes these flowers are so early that a late frost will damage them. This will diminish the harvest. This is a difficulty. Add to this, its shallow roots, and the fact the soil must be just the right mix of granite and limestone in order to make the grapes exquisite. By good fortune, the land in these mountains is the right kind of soil. So perhaps, Monsieur, the soil is not a difficulty. It is, perhaps, a point of understanding. Once the grapes are on the vine, they are so thick that they must be thinned in order to assure the best fruit." Gauguin stops. "Ah, Monsieur Garamond, all grapes require love. Love and hard work."

"Good fortune? Not by the grace of God?"

"Pardon?"

"You said the soil was by good fortune. A curious choice of words."

"Are these two things not the same? Good fortune is the grace of God, and the grace of God is good fortune. The wine does not care. The wine is still the same."

Gauguin tells him about the bad years following the plague, when workers were hard to find, and the amount of cultivation dropped. During these times, the amounts of wine produced shrank substantially. But there was always something. The vineyard was too small for the Church, which controlled most of the wine production in France by way of its vast system of monasteries, and its monks, who became experts.

Gamay grapes have always grown abundantly on the Gauguin land and in the past twenty years, wine production had been slowly increasing.

"My congratulations, Monsieur. It is a delicious thing you have created."

Gauguin watches as Garamond takes another swig. The man has been in the Allemond valley for less than a month and already he looks as if he belongs. His clothing is simple and he wears no jewellery, save for a gold ring on his left hand. A rustic leather baldric across his chest secures a dagger and he carries a short sword, which is a good idea since the villa in which he is living is some distance from the village.

"You have taken up residence in the Loys Durand villa," Gauguin says. "Are you settled?"

"Yes," Garamond says. "We are settled. My wife and I have come from Lyon."

The vintner knows Garamond and his wife have come from Paris, but he does not begrudge him this lie. Trust has not been earned and perhaps his privacy is important.

"You have everything you need?"

"I thought so," Garamond says. "Until I tasted this wine. Can you send someone with a dozen bottles?"

"I will bring it myself," Gauguin says. "Is twelve bottles enough?" He assumes Garamond is well financed.

Garamond smiles. "Better make it two dozen. Now, tell me about your family. How long have you been making this wine? And how have you avoided the Church."

The vintner tells him about the Gauguin family and the Gamay vines. He talks about the successes and failures of the past twenty years. He goes through the weather of each year, and the resulting quality of the wine. He talks about the acidity caused by the early harvests, and the sweetness caused by the late harvests. When he talks about his wife, he is adrift, as if he only half understands his own capacity for love. When he speaks about the soil he squeezes the air, as if his hands are in the dirt – as if he can feel it.

Gauguin pours more wine into Garamond's glass. "Now, can you say why you and your wife have come to live in our little valley?

There is something about the passionate manner in which this man speaks about his family, and about grapes, and the soil that causes Garamond to trust him.

"My master, from many years ago has been implicated, and he has been executed."

"Implicated?" Gauguin says. "I don't follow."

"In the Affair of the Placards. He was accused of Lutheranism. And while it is true that I am not longer his apprentice, I believe they will be coming for me."

Gauguin nods. He thinks about what 'coming for me' could mean, as it was joined together with the word execution. He does not think he would like it if someone with the power to execute were coming for him. "Why would they be coming for you?"

"Because I am a typesetter, a punch cutter, and it was my typeface that was used on the placards. Because it is not a good time to be anything but devoutly Catholic. And because it is not a good time to be suspected of being anything but devoutly Catholic."

"Oh," Gauguin says. "I see."

"Yes. And even though this letter form has been sold to many publishers across France, Germany, and even in Switzerland, it may as well have been an image of my face on the placards. This is the reason I am here with you, Monsieur Gauguin, in your village, far away from Paris."

"In hiding," Gauguin whispers.

"Yes. In hiding."

"But you did not create the placard."

"No. It was a publisher in Switzerland. I doubt this detail would be taken into account. The Church sees what it wants, hears what it wants, and kills what it wants. The King gets what he wants."

Gauguin wants to ask him if he is, in fact, a Huguenot, a Protestant, but this is not something he would expect anybody in France to admit, especially not to someone he has just met. And he certainly would not expect such a confession in a public place. Especially not now, with the Roman Catholic Church on a rampage directed at the Huguenots. It would be confessing heresy. Then there is the matter of whether or not to believe him when he says he did not play a role in the publication of the brochure. Gauguin is not an ardent advocate of the Church, in that he sees the priests spreading fear, and getting fat and rich, while the little he does know of the Bible does not support the idea of fat, wealthy priests. There is a discontinuity for him. He would not frown on a man who was involved in the Affair of the Placards.

Garamond looks at Gauguin. He can see the questions floating in the air. "I am a punch cutter, a typesetter, and perhaps someday, a publisher," he says, finally. "I am a wine-lover. And I am a man who loves his wife. I try to leave religion, God, and holiness to the bishops and the priests. I am not qualified to be holy. I am only devout." He pauses and drinks more wine. "I am very devout."

Gauguin smiles. He is missing a tooth on the upper left side of his mouth. "I too am a man who loves his wife, and wine. And I too am devout. I would say that I am enthusiastically devout."

Gauguin glances quickly around the empty room and assures himself that they are alone. "Between you and I and this wine, the Church in Allemond is small, so God mostly lives in the grapes. And in the mountains. And the water. And in the soil."

"The blood of Christ," Garamond says, raising his glass.

"Yes, the blood of Christ."

"Do you ever become concerned about the possibility of the Church hearing you?"

"No, Monsieur. This does not worry me. I worry more about my wife than I do the Roman Catholic Church. She is a strong woman who fears God and loves the Church. And she is not afraid to share her mind. Have you met Natalii? She also fears that under this devout surface, my soul is in peril. She worries about my holiness, about my unholiness."

Garamond thinks he heard a hard disdain in Gauguin's voice as he spoke of the Church. "I have not had the pleasure of meeting Natalii," he says.

"Once you meet her you, you will know. She is formidable."

"To women and wine and unholiness, then," Garamond says, standing and raising his mug. "And by wine, I am including the God of the Roman Catholic Church."

Gauguin stands and drinks. When he sits down he begins to worry. He plays with the handle of his cane, the shaft of which conceals a rapier. "Who is it that will be coming for you, Monsieur?"

"The King's men. Men from the Parlement de Paris and the thugs from the Faculty of Theology."

"Are you certain these men will be coming here?"

"It is not *if*. It is *when*. It is only a matter of time before I am accused of Lutheranism. Or of being a heretic. Or both."

Gauguin stands up, a little unsteadily, and places his right hand on his heart. "Then you shall have protection. I swear it. I and all the people of Allemond shall protect you."

The men agree that Garamond will be called by a different name, except when they are alone.

"I shall call you Monsieur Emile Durand, to honour the villa in which you have made your home," Gauguin says. "To everyone in the village you will be called Monsieur Durand. It is a protection."

Even though he and Marie Isabelle have become false Durands, Garamond never inquires as to the whereabouts of the original Durands. He assumes they were victims of the plague. Their benefactor, a publisher in Geneva, had arranged the villa, and they didn't ask questions.

....

Sometimes a lie will pull hard to the left, like a flat tire on the freeway, and then it is completely out of control. You know it's going to fly off the rails the second it's out of your mouth. It's usually some almost-innocent stretch of the truth, and someone pushes back, your bluff is called, and then you're spinning around in circles on an icy mountain highway, a cliff on one side and a wall of granite on the other. Or, in a split second, you are standing naked in the middle of a room and everyone is judging – there's a bright light on every wrinkle, imperfection and inadequacy. Or one of your past professors from university is standing outside your building downtown with a megaphone, shouting to all that pass, telling everyone you're a fraud, announcing to the world that you have no idea what you're doing.

This lie that flies off the rails was so innocuous it was just barely a lie. You didn't even give it a second thought, and yet, when you started to speak, everything slipped out of control. Claude Garamond and his wife, and their sixteenth century road trip, are a lie just like that.

....

A week later, Garamond is in the village to pick up more wine and Natalii is talking about Spanish soldiers crossing the border into France.

"Spain has invaded us, Monsieur," she says, shaking her head.

Garamond shrugs. "There is always a war somewhere, Madame. Thankfully, there is also wine." He nods toward her – a sort of salute.

"You do not take an interest in the conflicts?" Natalii is not judging, rather, she is curious. "It is France, Monsieur. It is your country."

Garamond looks at her. Her smock is not modest, in that it is low-cut and too tight for her chest. He does not mind this immodesty. Her eyes are playful and interested. Her skin is pale. Her hair is the colour of fall grass; she has braided it and pulled it to the side so it rests in front of her shoulder. She wears a necklace – a silver chain with a medallion – one of the saints.

"My dear Natalii," he says. "I am very interested in the wars of men. But war is a playground for kings and queens. It is a lust for power, and a lust for celebrity. It is often an ideological argument, a religious argument – a different way of being, a different religion, a different god, a different way of thinking. And many people die as a result of these differences."

"This is true, Monsieur. Many people die as a result of the wars and campaigns."

"And to what end?"

"I do not know, Monsieur. So that France remains France?"

He is grateful that she did not suggest honour or glory, or advancement. "And when will it be enough? Does a mother in Italy love her children any less than a mother in France? Does a father look upon his daughter with less love in Spain than in Italy or Briton?"

"Parents love their children the same everywhere, Monsieur Garamond. I cannot imagine it being other than this."

Garamond nods approvingly. "And yet we applaud as our young men pick up arms and march to war," he says. "We talk about courage and honour, and we applaud. Do you not find this to be an absurdity, Madame?"

"With God on our side, we can withstand anything, conquer any army," she says.

"Ah, yes. God. Do you think perhaps our enemies believe exactly the same thing? Do you think that is a possibility, Madame?"

"But Monsieur, God is on our side."

"Is the English God different than ours?"

"The English God speaks English, Monsieur. Everyone knows this. And this God is a Protestant. This is not the true God."

"Spain and Italy?"

"The Spanish God! The Italian God!" She is exasperated.

"But regardless of the language spoken, are not all Christian Gods the same God?"

Natalii shakes her head. "No, no, no. God stands with France," she says. "God speaks French, Monsieur. It has always been so."

He looks at her and realizes she believes this. She believes God is on the side of France and with God there, France cannot fail. He wants to tell her that God does not line up and go into battle. God does not risk his life. God does not die horribly. But to what end? This is Gauguin's wife. She is the vintner's wife and she is lovely in her own way.

Garamond thanks her, and carries six bottles in a canvas sack slung over his shoulder as he walks toward the river crossing. The seventh bottle is shoved deep into his jacket pocket. Occasionally, the bottles in the sack clink together – a sharp and delicate sound that pleases him. He limps a little as he walks – a reminder of a broken leg when he was ten. The leg never healed properly and his limp kept him from the military. He opens the seventh bottle and drinks from it once he is across the river.

....

There are sixty-four occurrences of the word "wine" in this book. That's a lot. Too much wine, perhaps. Way too many references for some. It's as if all anybody does in this book is drink wine. Here's an interesting tidbit: In the 1500s, the people of France drank a heck of a lot of wine. In France, wine was more popular than water. Why? Because wine was safer. That's right; Christian Europe emerged from the Middle Ages and staggered into the Renaissance as a heavy-drinking culture that was afraid of what diseases might be in their water.

At the end of the day – and apparently early in the day, and in the middle of the day, as well – if you could afford wine, or beer, that was what you drank instead of water.

CHAPTER 18

Tulah at 17

Tulah's Snow Journal
Wednesday, December 2, 1992 #34

This is a dusty snow. As if the snow has been cranked through a flour sifter. Looking across the city, it's as if there's smoke in the air. The snow on the ground is powdery as it accumulates. Grandma Frannie told me once that the Inuit had hundreds of names for snow, a hundred ways of looking at snow. I looked it up. Most credible sources say it's no more than a dozen or so, but one of the articles I found said the Inuit word for a fine snow is "kanevvluk" and that the Inuit dialect has at least fifty-three, including "matsaaruti," for wet snow that can be used to ice a sleigh's runners, and "pukak," for the crystalline powder snow that looks like salt. I like the lie better than the reality. I love the lie that there are hundreds of Inuit terms for snow. Why not? Why wouldn't there be hundreds of ways to look at snow? Hundreds of ways to name it? They lived with snow and their lives depended on defining it. It's logical. Maybe this is why the rumours exist.

....

Tulah and her sister are staying with their dad, at his condo, which is downtown. Alesha has gone to a movie and Tulah has been listening to Whitney Houston's *I Will Always Love You*, over and over. It's a boy named Colten, at school and she believes he doesn't know she exists. She knows about him though. She talked with him once in grade 9, and she has written his name down on numerous sheets of paper, on the inside covers of binders, and once, on her arm.

Her dad knocks, softly, and comes into her room. His hair is sticking up at an odd angle at the back and his shirt is only half-tucked in. His hair never sticks up. It's always just so. She wonders what he's been doing. "I've got some bad news," he says. "Grandma Frannie died. I just got off the phone." His voice is cracked and uncontained, and at the same time, it's soft, as if this softness will make the message less awful.

"What? She died?"

"She was sick for the past few years, and tonight she passed away."

"But I just talked with her on Saturday. I talked with her two days ago… she was fine. She was fine."

"I'm sorry, Tulah. She had a massive heart attack and they couldn't…" He sits on the bed with her and she slips her hand into his.

Save her, Tulah thinks. *They couldn't save her.*

Tulah does not think about the fact her father has lost his mother. She is trying to reconcile her grandma's voice just days ago with the idea that today this voice is gone forever. She leans into her father's chest and wraps her arms around him. They sit for a long time and let the silence fill the room without questioning it.

"I feel sad," Tulah says. "But I don't know what else to feel. I don't understand how she can be gone now, when I just talked to her."

"You can feel whatever you want," her dad says. "You can take all the time you want to sort this out. No school for you tomorrow, unless you really want to go."

Tulah can see the snow falling past her bedroom window and she wants to go out in it. She wants to say goodbye to her grandmother in the snow.

The funeral is delayed because there are people coming from Zurich, and a sister from London. Sorrow lurks in them and around them. It becomes a liquid they have to push through in order to do anything and it slows them down. Tulah's mom is coming to the funeral. The designations of divorce are placed aside for death. Tulah and her sister like it that they will be a whole family for the funeral.

She does not go to school for the remainder of the week and because of her absence, Colten calls. He wonders if she's okay and she tells him the truth – she is not okay about her grandmother – but she is happy he called. Colten tries to cheer her up by telling her about one of their classmates, Brendan, who lost his trunks in the pool at a swim meet. They came off when he made a turn-around, but he kept swimming. He won the race and had to stay in the water until his coach brought him a towel. Colten thought it was hilarious. Tulah thought it was courageous.

....

When Tulah was ten, she used to spend weekends with her grandmother, in her house near the river. Everyone in the family called her Grandma Frannie. On one of these weekends, they made a fire in the downstairs fireplace, steeped some tea and watched the snow. "People are always complaining about the snow," her grandmother said. "And with good reason – it makes it difficult to drive, slower for sure, and people have to shovel it, and it's usually cold when it snows. But snow can always make you feel better. Snow has a magic but you have to invite it. You have to make room for snow inside of you."

"How do you do that?" Tulah said, thinking Grandma Frannie had made up a new game and they were about to play it.

"You touch it as it's falling. Or you let it touch you. You open yourself to it and only then can you understand the magic."

Then it is a Saturday afternoon in February and they are standing in the back yard of her Grandma Frannie's house with the snow falling like feathers. They see the deer – three hazy ghosts, standing at the edge of her property, toward the river. Tulah and Frannie have made a deal with each other to be silent until they are back in the house and tea has been made. They are just going to look at things and not say anything. Frannie has been watching the deer for a while, but she lets Tulah nudge her and point at them – so the deer become her granddaughter's discovery.

At the river's edge they find the path and after twenty minutes, Tulah is cold. They are not moving fast enough to generate their own warmth. They stop at a place where a dog, or coyote, has crossed the trail and its tracks cut into the new snow. Chickadees are chirping in the pines and far back in the woods a raven is scratching the air with its caw. Tulah looks up at her grandmother, who nods and beckons with her head to go home.

Tulah breathes her tea – a spicy chai with milk and honey. She takes a sip. "Do you think the deer thought we were ghosts?"

The grandmother recognizes the question as a penetrating one. Her granddaughter did not have to say the deer looked like ghosts through the snow. She was already down a layer, wondering what they may have looked like to the deer. This makes her happy.

....

The last time Tulah saw her grandmother there was the persistent cough. She coughed, a lot. She said it was a cold, and Tulah had believed her. They'd gone to see the movie *Unforgiven,* and the elevators in the theatre were being repaired. Her grandmother had struggled with the climb – she'd stopped twice to catch her breath.

"It's this damned cold," she said. "I'll be fine in a minute."

Tulah puts this together after midnight, after talking with her sister about it. Grandma Frannie kept her illness to herself.

....

A few months after the funeral, Tulah's dad tells her he's dating someone in his building.

"The woman in 31-A," he says. "She's a doctor." Her father acts like it's a big deal, as if two years after the divorce, he's not allowed to have a normal life and so he treads carefully.

"Good," Tulah says. "Is she coming for dinner tomorrow?"

Her father steps back, astonished. He's holding a head of lettuce. "I, I hadn't thought about inviting her. You're okay with that?"

"Dad. You deserve to be happy. Mom's dated like ten guys since you divorced."

....

Two years later, the doctor from 31-A and Tulah's father are in France on vacation and decide to get married. With a week's warning, they want Tulah and Alesha to come but Alesha is at a yoga retreat on Vancouver Island, so it's just Tulah. She does not hesitate and her dad arranges a first-class ticket to Paris. There are a dozen people from all parts of the planet gathered in a cathedral in Mâcon, near the river. The ceremony includes the mass, and the dinner afterwards is rustic but delightful. They are in a café somewhere near the river and it is stifling hot, even at 10 p.m., it is hot. Tulah is moved by the ceremony, and by the simplicity of the reception. Her father and the doctor dance to *The Way You Look Tonight* and there is a joyful lightness to the evening that makes Tulah smile pretty much all night. Two days later, she is back at school and it all feels like a dream. Her dad and his new wife decide to split their time between Mâcon and a modest place in Phoenix, Arizona.

CHAPTER 17

Enough

"You needn't be afraid of a barking dog,
but you should be afraid of a silent dog"
– *Zhanna Petya*

.Right now, Nancy would like one of her mother's angels to come and rescue her. She needs a sensible, no-bullshit kind of angel, an angel who will tell her the truth, no matter how much it hurts. Because she can't see it right now. Her mother would know which angel would be the appropriate one for hopelessness, for someone who needs to hear the truth.

Nancy wishes for her mother's kitchen, the wooden table, scratched and dented. The smell of cabbage soup. The warmth. She wants her mother's voice. She wants the twins, with their talk of school and books, and coming assignments, and boys, and girls, and friends. She wants to hear about their teachers. And she wants her mother to finally talk about Mr. Petrov, the man who runs the bookstore across from *Killfish Discount Bar* on St. Petersburg Street. He is a widower and there is no question in Nancy's mind that her mother is smitten. She visits the bookstore every Thursday and buys books, with Mr. Petrov's assistance.

She knows she wants a lot of things, but she would settle for an angel or two.

When she was younger, she wrote a poem about the archangel Michael. Writing poems was one of her ways of dealing with her excess of energy. When she was in her frenetic, happy highs, she had more energy than she could use, and in order to not go mad, she worked on her poems. Her plan was to create a suite of poems. Nancy's poem about the archangel Michael was epic length. It rambled on for close to forty pages. In it, she explored a love affair between the angel Michael and a woman named Nathalie. They argued over soup. They fought about sex, because the angel Michael had no genitals and Nathalie believed it was by choice. She thought the angel could have genitals if he really wanted them. When Nancy goes back and starts to read this poem, she cringes. It's such young writing.

Perhaps someday she will write about an angel standing on the balcony with her. The angel will have all this grey sky behind it. "Hang up the phone," she will say. Nancy almost always imagines angels as female, or at least as effeminate males. She thinks all Buddhas, except the laughing Buddhas, are female too.

"But I need this final conversation. I need…"

"Hang up the fucking phone," the angel says. "End the call. Drop the phone in the toilet. Take a hammer and smash it. Disconnect."

"Okay," she says. She holds the phone out in front of her with her finger hovering above the red button. But she can't press the button. Her hand starts to shake and she gently places the phone on the kitchen table. She looks at the angel with tears in her eyes. "Why?" she says.

The angel smiles. "Why do you want to continue?"

"So I know in my heart, and my gut, and my brain that it's over."

"Okay," the angel says. "And what combination of words would help you to know this?"

The angel is right, of course. There are only uttered words and sentences remaining. She is beyond the truth of action. "I don't think I like you very much," Nancy says.

"I'm not here to be liked. In fact, I'm not here to be seen or heard. I don't know how you can see me, or hear me." The angel will begin to flap its enormous wings. It will create such a wind that anything without significant weight will move. The corner of one of the rugs lifts. A lampshade twists away from the volume of the wind. The angel appears to have more than two wings. It's beating the air so crazily it seems as if it has multiple sets of wings. For Nancy, the sound is the thing that is disconcerting. The fwah, fwah, fwah sound of the wings is so intensely close and loud. And this flapping seems panicky, as if this angel is frightened. As if it truly does not want to be there on the deck with her. As if it is torn between staying put and flying away.

The angel calms down and Nancy smiles at her. "This is nothing," she says. "I've heard the sound of wings all my life."

....

Nancy is leaning over the railing, looking down. His car is a tiny blue toy on the street, and Ray is an ant leaning against the car. 'Tiny Blue Car' would be a good title for one of her poems, she thinks. "You can leave, Ray," she says. "You owe me nothing. You can get in your car and drive away, and never look back."

He could go home and that would be it. The news doesn't report suicides, unless you're famous. Jump or no jump, it's over. He walks around the back of his car, opens the car door and slips inside. He places his hands at ten and two on the steering wheel and squeezes. But callous is not who he is. Self-centred, shallow, unfaithful, and lying, but not callous. He needs to know she is fine before he drives away. He wants to hold the delusion that she is okay – like a good black cat purring in his lap.

"What are you doing, Ray?"

"I'm plugging my phone in. I'm almost out of battery. I thought you said I could drive away." His battery is at sixty-three percent. He does not need to plug his phone in.

"You can. I just don't want you to."

"I'm not going to."

"Good."

They are silent. He listens as she takes a drink of something.

"Are you still drinking scotch?"

"Yes," she says. "I'm drinking your scotch."

"It's not my scotch."

"No," she says. "It's not yours anymore."

"It was sweet of you to buy it," he says.

"Scotch cuts through the shit doesn't it, Ray? I mean, maybe this is my last drink..."

"...stop it or I'm coming up..."

"...No. You're not. I don't want you here. You don't belong here anymore. I don't want to have to explain this to you again. Honestly, you're like a fucking child."

"So what are we talking about?"

"Me. My unhappiness. I don't know if you've noticed or not, but I'm depressed, Ray. And even though you weren't mine, you were entertaining. You were distracting. And now I don't have you."

"It doesn't have to be the end. We can talk every now and then."

"Like friends? Really? You think we can go there?"

"We can try."

"No, it will never be enough. Not for me, and not for you. It has to be everything. It has to be all."

"But it was never 'all'."

"No, but it was enough. For a while, it was enough."

....

"That's enough." Ray is shouting at the man in the cab of the backhoe. He points at the gaping hole beside the elm. "That's deep enough. Stop!"

The man in the backhoe halts the movement of the bucket in midair, but he does not look to Ray – he looks at the Transportation foreman, who is standing behind Ray.

Ray turns around. "Look Joe," he says. "You're going to kill this tree. If you go any deeper you're going to cut through those roots. You've already damaged them."

"New sidewalks gotta go in," Joe says. "I have a schedule. All the sidewalks in this neighbourhood have to be lowered, re-graded and they all get rounded curbs."

"It's seventy, maybe eighty years old, Joe. Can't you build a smaller sidewalk?"

"There's only one way to build a sidewalk. It's gotta have a gravel bed. And for that, I have to dig, and it has to be flat. The engineers were here yesterday. Talk to them."

"I will."

Ray walks over to where the backhoe bucket is stopped. "These roots are called buttress roots and there are delicate feeder roots attached. This tree is fifteen metres and it probably weighs ten tonnes. If you cut through those roots you risk killing it."

Joe smiles. He does not want to come up with a different way to do his job. He is not interested in trees. He doesn't get paid enough to care about trees. He works with concrete.

"Do you like trees, Joe?"

"I never really think about them," he says.

"Do you have trees in your back yard?"

"What? Yes. There are trees in my yard."

"Would you miss them if they were suddenly not there?"

"I don't know. I guess so."

Ray sighs. "Here's what I need you to do, Joe. I need you to stop this section of your work right now. I will write a stop-work order so you can show your boss, and then I'll try and straighten this out."

"You want me to stop work?"

"I want you to go work somewhere else – away from any trees – while we sort this out."

"Because of a tree?"

"Yes. Because of this eighty-year-old elm. Because most of its roots are within a couple feet of the ground and that's where you're digging."

"The engineers aren't going to like this. They say it has to be flat for this sidewalk. We have to make it lower at the corner so wheel-chairs can..."

"...fuck the engineers, Joe. And fuck the handicapped. Don't you think this tree is more important than wheelchair accessibility?" He looks at Joe, who has still not moved. "Let the handicapped roll, or walk, or move on the other side of the goddamned street."

Joe has already moved on. He is thinking it is almost time for a mid-morning coffee break, and a cigarette. He could really use a smoke.

....

"I don't think it was," Ray says.

"You don't think it was what?"

"Enough," he says. "For months I was torn in two by my feelings for you. It wasn't enough. It was never enough."

"It was something other than nothing."

"Yes. It was something," he says. Ray looks out through the front window. The tree nearest to his car is a Green Ash. These trees are drought and alkali resistant. They grow quickly and they turn a pale, creamy yellow colour in the fall. This tree is tinged with yellow – it's ready to turn. And once it turns, it doesn't last long.

"I don't want to talk about us anymore. Can we talk about some-thing else?" She's fidgety – she can't decide what to do with her hands. She doesn't know if she wants to stay seated, or stand up and walk around. Despite her aversion to all things Afghan, there are three extravagant Afghan rugs in her condo – two in the living room and one outside on the balcony. She likes having these carpets because she doesn't care about them. And the more she doesn't care, the more durable they seem. They are stained, weather-worn and compressed, and still, they are beautiful.

"I think it's going to snow today," he says.

....

Once, two months after Ray starts meeting Nancy in her condo, she comes to the door and says she just wants to talk. She does not say, 'we need to talk.' She has watched enough television to know the clichéd overtones of this phrase. She says she would like it if they just talked.

"Okay," Ray says. "What would you like to talk about?"

"Everything," Nancy says. "But mostly us. I want to know this is more than just sex."

"You want to talk about how this isn't just about sex while you're wearing that?" She is wearing a black bra and matching panties.

"It's how I dress in my own home. I always dress like this."

They sit at the kitchen table. Nancy makes coffee in silence. She puts a kettle on to boil and grinds beans. She pulls two mugs and the press from the cupboard and places them on the counter. Ray could sit and enjoy her company, watch her moving around the kitchen and not say a thing. Nancy does not like the quiet gaps. She wants something in there. Inane, or profound, or whimsical – she does not like silence.

Nancy turns around and looks at him. "We make love, right?" Her face is serious and concerned – furrows between her eyes. She barely blinks.

If Ray were honest, he'd probably say he wasn't sure if it was making love or fumbling around in a field of desire. The whole thing was so part-time, he did not trust his own feelings. He used to think love came from a limitless well, and there was plenty for everybody in his life. He does not believe this now. His feelings for Nancy are diminished because she is an extra woman and there is only so much of this particular kind of love. All his feelings for her were sliced in two. All of them except desire. Desire was not diminished. Ray doesn't really care what she calls it – making love, screwing, copulating, coitus, intercourse, having sex…it doesn't matter to him. But he senses she wants to know he thinks it was making love. He realizes Nancy is still waiting for an answer, so he gives her a hopeful one.

"We make love," he says. "I wish we were making love right now."

"If you're a good boy, you may get your wish," she says.

"How, exactly, can I be good?"

The kettle starts to whistle and she lets it go. It grows to a steady, piercing scream. She observes the billowing steam as if it's a new thing. As if the frantic whistling does not exist.

"When you get there, I'll let you know. Tell me how you feel about me right now."

Irritated, he thinks. Impatient. And a little frightened. The ice of this conversation is thin. "I adore you," he says.

Nancy presses the plunger and pours the coffee. She wants him to tell her he's dropping his wife and starting a new life with her. She does not want to admit she is the clichéd mistress. This idea disgusts her. She has friends who have slept with married men and it always ended badly. So she has decided not to define what is going on between her and Ray. She'll leave it open-ended and she will try not to invest too much of her heart. She wants him to say he loves her. Maybe he is saying it when he is inside her. But she wants to hear him say it.

"So you think being flippant is going to get you somewhere?"

"But I do adore you."

She is suddenly exhausted. "Come and make love to me," she says inside a sigh.

"No. Let's finish our coffee. Tell me what you did today."

"I'm sorry? You want to talk? Instead of making love, you want to talk?" He is inviting her to be normal and now she is not sure she wants it. She wants normal but she knows this sort of temporary normal will disappear and then it will hurt. She's afraid she might fall into the hole of this *normal* and the sides will be slippery, and it will be impossible to climb back out.

In the elevator, Ray will circle around and remember she said 'come and make love to me,' not 'come and make love with me.' As if lovemaking is having something done to you, not doing something together. This bothers him. But English is a second language for Nancy. He's probably overthinking it.

....

For Ray, sex with Nancy was all lust and abandoned constraints, but once he was done, he found he quickly lost interest in her. And a wave of guilt would wash through him. There was no time to drift in the aftermath of delight. He would instantly be fighting his guilt, pushing it back.

He always made sure she was taken care of and he loved making her happy in this way, but he really didn't care. He would have preferred it if she'd leaned up and said something like "That was really nice but you probably want to go now, so you should." While she was all doe-eyed and needy, and wanting to cuddle, he was wishing to be anywhere but with her. It helped when they drank before sex, or during sex, and it definitely helped Ray if they drank after sex. Only when he was away from Nancy, moving through the rituals of daily life, did thoughts of love enter his mind. These flirtations with the idea of love were suspect in his mind, because they never came when he was with her. How can you only love someone when you are away from them?

CHAPTER 16

Tulah at 20

Tulah's Snow Journal
Friday, November 3, 1995 #79(a)

It's a wet snow, but it won't last. It has a 'best before morning' stamp. This makes it more beautiful than the kind of snow that falls and stays around for a whole winter. It's not for sure, but this snow probably won't last past noon tomorrow... I've just made tea – I do not know how old these tea bags are but the tea smells okay. Am I a horrible person for coming up here with Robert? Even though I know it's not going to last? Well, I don't know that for sure but I have this feeling in my gut that it's not him. There's someone out there who is going to be phenomenal. Not true love. Not that. But a big love. The kind of love that will be unshakeable. Better, unstoppable. It will be like an avalanche. Once it starts, you're going to wind up at the bottom of the mountain. Maybe that's a dumb metaphor. If you're swept up in an avalanche, you usually die. Is it stupid and romantic to think this way? Probably. I give myself permission to think about the quality of love. I give myself permission to ponder, ruminate, question the quality of love. I give myself permission to love. I give myself permission. I stop myself there. Everything else is stupid. I do not dream of frilly weddings or expensive, gossamer wedding dresses. I'm no princess. I want no fairy tale. I dream about a kind of massive, mysterious love. Robert is not that love. He's nice but I'm not feeling it. I had to see, though, so I could be sure. And I love the mountains. Maybe I will marry the mountains.

．．．．．．．

She wants to be standing naked in this snow. They are staying at a cabin up a twisting road on the side of a mountain, a few kilometres outside of Nelson, British Columbia. The cabin belongs to a friend of her mother's. It is off the grid. There's a generator somewhere out back and a chain of solar panels on the roof that power the lights, and they have been using the fireplace to keep the cabin warm. The cabin is small enough that the fireplace is enough. There's a cook stove in the kitchen but lighting two fires would have been overkill. The black-velvet picture of Elvis above the mantle has to be a joke. The rest of the cabin is decorated with a measure of good taste – the colours work, the furniture is classically comfortable, and the art on the walls consists of obscure prints from Modigliani, Picasso and Chagall. Tulah is drawn to the Chagall instantly. A little white card under this print reads – *The Poet with the Birds, 1911.* Tulah decides she loves Marc Chagall. She will seek out his art – see if the rest of it moves her this much. The beauty of this print stands in sharp contrast to the velvet Elvis and it was probably meant to.

The curious thing is, she doesn't wake Robert and tell him she is about to go outside and stand naked in the snow. He likely would have wanted to join her but she lets him sleep. She leaves him alone because it was a long drive up to the cabin and he'd earned a good sleep. She would bet a thousand dollars that Robert would not have come up with the idea to go naked out into the snow. He would not have thought of it himself. He wasn't creative that way. Maybe that's the real reason. And maybe it's also because he was going in for his Bachelor of Commerce and Tulah didn't know what to make of that choice.

Is it weird to want to stand on the veranda naked? If it's weird, then she's okay with that. Even if it's completely bat-shit crazy, she's fine with it.

Just after midnight, Tulah steps out onto the deck. She stops thinking about the reasons she's doing it, and the reasons she's doing it alone, and she opens herself to the snow.

On the deck the silence is shocking. It is deathly quiet at first, but it transforms into a kind of negative silence – as if sound is being withdrawn by the snow. As if each flake of snow gathers sound and silently sends it to ground. She feels small on the deck, with the light from the kitchen behind her and nothing but mountains and pine and the steady snow in front.

Tulah makes a deal with herself to stay there on the deck until she's too cold. She will push beyond discomfort. When her feet are burning cold she will go inside.

Will you marry me, mountains? she thinks.

Tulah's Snow Journal
November 3, 1995 #79(b)

Still snowing. It's 4 a.m. and it's coming down hard and fast. It's socked in and it seems endless.

....

Her footprints are covered. There's a foot of snow covering the spot where she was standing. She still thinks of it as a foot or twelve inches, not, about thirty centimetres. Robert is still asleep. When he wakes up, she probably won't tell him about her whimsy. She thinks she might want to keep it for herself.

She does not feel tired. Tulah peeks into the second bedroom, which is the main bedroom. There are white sheets covering the bed and the furniture. The woman who owns the cabin is in Arizona and only stays at this cabin in the summer months. There are three large windows along the down-mountain wall that probably make for an incredible view. The curtains are a sheer periwinkle colour. A dresser against the wall at the foot of the bed does not have a sheet over it. Tulah entertains her own curiosity. She pulls the top drawer out to find neatly stacked sheets. The second drawer is socks and a few T-shirts. The third drawer is all lingerie, silk stockings and panties and garters. Tulah pokes around in the lingerie. She can't help herself. She thinks it may be high-quality stuff. The tags seem expensive – *Guia La Bruna, Fox and Rose,* and two bras tagged *Christies,* and *made in Italy.* Underneath a lacy cream-coloured corset there are sex toys. Several small whips and an assortment of dildos in all sizes and colours. There are a couple metal contraptions that Tulah can't identify. She's intrigued by the contents of this drawer. She knows about sex toys, of course – her mother had a dildo and children all snoop through drawers – but she's never gone through the awkwardness of walking into a shop and buying one.

She picks up a cream-coloured dildo. It has a squishy feel to it – it's soft and firm at the same time. She wraps her fingers around it. Tulah hears a sound in the main room – it sounds like something has dropped. She squeaks – fumbles with the rubbery dildo and drops it onto the floor. It makes a soft thumping sound. She stands still and waits. Nothing. She tiptoes into the main room and there is only the fire crackling and she can feel the heat. Something must have shifted in the stove. She pours a drink. They brought vodka and beer. She's drinking vodka. It's after four in the morning. She pours another drink. When she is finished her second drink, Tulah stands up and decides she's a little bit drunk but she's also a little bit aroused. Just looking at the sex toys has started a slow burn inside her. The cabin is quiet except for the fire. She's going to play. She will steal the batteries from the flashlight in the kitchen and she will see. She's going to put on some expensive lingerie – she's going to wear a stranger's lingerie and see what happens.

Tulah's Snow Journal
November 3, 1995 #79(c)

I was so wrong about this snow. It's not bloody ephemeral. It's a constant. It's 5:30 a.m. and I have not slept yet. I should. We're supposed to ski today. I'd rather find a spa and get a massage. I'm starting to wonder if we'll be able to get out of this cabin. We could always ski down the road to the main highway but what then? I need to sleep, but I really should record this experience. The toys in the bedroom drawer, standing naked in the snow, and, did I mention the lingerie and toys in the drawer? I'm going to have one more drink and then bed. I don't mind drinking alone, especially on nights like this when it's a steady snow. The snow is with me so I am not alone. Tonight, I discovered I really, really like the feel of lingerie on my skin. I love lingerie. I felt so sexy. I will acknowledge the fact I was wearing someone else's lingerie – someone else's underwear – and this could have played a part in my level of excitement. And the toys. The toys were someone else's toys. And whoa!!! I can't say that I am going to go and buy my own toys, but I will certainly look at investing in some good lingerie when I get home. I love the way it makes me feel. I had no idea about lingerie.

It's as if this snow is in a hurry to reach the ground – it's still falling hard and heavy and constantly. On the deck, I thought I could smell pine scent, but maybe I wanted to smell pine. Is there a word for the smell of freshly fallen snow? I know there's a word for the smell just after it rains. It's petrichor, which is a noun. And that is the extent of my knowledge about rain. I only know this word because of Mr. Johnson. Why did he believe

*in me? What did he see in me? He caused me to believe in me. He's the
reason I'm going into teaching. But what's the word for new snow smell?
There ought to be a word for the scent of new-fallen snow. I should invent
one – mash some Latin and Inuit words together, but I am too tired to
think. Okay, I really have to sleep.*

....

Tulah slips into bed. The crinkling sound of the down quilt, the cool
sheets, the dim blue light. Robert rolls toward her. He does not open
his eyes.

"You okay?" he says, his voice low, and dark, and barely awake.

"Just had to pee," she says. "It's still snowing."

He grunts and she listens to his breathing as he sinks back
into sleep.

the Second Circle

"As long as the sun shines, one does not ask for the moon."
– Zhanna Petya

In August, Nancy picks up a call when she is pushing a shopping cart through the parking lot of a grocery store. It is early morning for her mother and 8 p.m. for Nancy. "Listen to this," her mother says. "In July 1984, Russian cosmonauts aboard the Soviet space station Salyut 7 reported seeing angels hovering just outside the space station."

Her mother goes on to paraphrase the newspaper article:

Some chalked this up to fatigue, as they had been in space for 155 days already. At first, according to Commander Oleg Atkov and cosmonauts Vladmir Solovyov and Leonid Kizim, the space station was completely bathed in an other-worldly orange light. This light appeared to come from outside the space station and moved through the walls into the craft. For a short period of time, this orange light was so bright it blinded the crew. When their vision returned, they all began looking for the source of the light. They worried about a possible explosion, as fires had occurred before on the space station, but what the crew found was more incomprehensible than the orange light. All three cosmonauts said they saw angels hovering inside the orange cloud, just outside the space station.

"They told ground control they were humanoid in appearance – their faces and bodies looked human," Nancy's mother said, "but they had wings and dazzling bright halos. The beings kept pace with the space station for ten minutes before vanishing."

"Wings and halos?" Nancy says. "This is ridiculous."

"Yes, angels have wings and halos. And it is in the newspaper, Nensi."

"Those cosmonauts were breathing too much carbon monoxide. They must have been impaired. Nobody knows what that kind of prolonged weightlessness does to the brain."

"All three, Nensi. All three saw the same seven angels. Angels! When the angels looked at the men in the space station, they smiled. The angels smiled! The cosmonauts said the angels had wonderful smiles – smiles of joy, of ecstasy. They said no human could have smiled like that."

"Mom," Nancy says. "What kind of newspaper are you reading?"

"They all said they felt a great loss when the angels disappeared. It says that, here in the article. They were devastated when the angels went away."

Nancy has just finished placing the last of her groceries into the back of her car. She pulls down on the hatch door and because Mitsubishi did not begin to think about the difficulty of this hatch and the torque required to close it, Nancy breaks a nail. She's standing behind the SUV with the hatch wide open, and she is looking at the broken nail. She bites off the ragged remainder and pulls with both hands on the hatch and finally pushes it shut.

"Jesus, Mom. Enough about angels already. Tell me how you are."

"Things are good," her mother says. She pauses and Nancy can so clearly envision her sitting at the kitchen table nodding. "I have not heard from Slava in a month. When you talk with him next, you tell him to call his mother."

....

"I was fine being the mistress, you know."

"You were what?" Ray watches as a dog, a skinny German Shepherd that looks like a coyote, trots along the sidewalk away from his car. There's a wild scruffiness to the dog that makes Ray think it really is a coyote. Even though it's moving in a straight line, it seems as if it's tilted sideways.

"I was fine being the mistress." Her words are slurred, as if she's drunk and trying too hard to not sound drunk.

He's losing patience with her. He doesn't care if she was fine. He doesn't care if she was a well-adjusted mistress. "Look," he says. "Why am I sitting here?"

Nancy takes a breath and can feel her anger. "I was just an amusement ride for you, wasn't I? Something for you to climb up on and fuck every now and then."

"That's not how it was," he says.

"I was a roller-coaster, or some other ride at the fair. You got your thrill and then you got off and carried on."

"I don't understand where this is coming from."

"It's coming from the fact it's true."

"I never thought of you like that." Ray knows if he'd been serious about Nancy, he would not have continued to treat her like a mistress.

....

He looks at the elms along the street. One of them is in trouble. It was a dry year. Rain was sporadic and not enough. A gust of wind bends the trees and a flurry of leaves is scattered across the road.

Ray's job as an arborist was not the original career he'd pursued. Ray had his law degree. He was practising in a well-respected firm. Being a lawyer was what he thought he wanted. However, on the fourth month of the second year of articling with the law firm of *Brice, Jones & Farnsworth*, Ray woke up at 4 a.m. with chest pains. This was the beginning of his realization that law was not for him. At the hospital, the doctors were surprised by Ray's blood pressure but his heart was fine. For now. They said it was a panic attack. A breakdown of everything that protects us from being overwhelmed by anxiety. He needed to move more. He needed to find a way to cope with stress. But Ray knew the slow build of twitchy unhappiness from his work as a lawyer was killing him. It wasn't the stress and it wasn't the hours – it was being completely aware of his unhappiness. There was a stench around the entire occupation that started to stick to his skin. Even the most benign fields of law contained a sleaziness factor. The so-called "heart incident" was an epiphany for Ray. The occupation of lawyer was killing him. He was one of two stars among the eight articling lawyers with the firm but he was ready to turn away. It was not easy, but he knew he was ready.

He'd spent four summers and a year out of high school working at his uncle's greenhouse and he was drawn to the memory of that joyful time. Ray's training was not formal, but it was extensive.

He got a job with the city's Parks department. It was hard work, and they kept trying to promote him into positions where he no longer actually worked on trees – but rather, managed other people who worked with trees. Ray kept refusing these promotions. But, two weeks ago, he accepted a promotion with conditions of freedom. He managed a team, he was in the field as much as he wanted, and he got a hefty raise.

It was easier to say what he did now. *Arborist* was easier on his conscience than *lawyer*. It was an additional syllable but it was easier to say. He smiles at the memory of a woman at a party who asked him what he did and he told her, except she heard *abortionist*. "You actually tell people that?" Her face was a squished horror of revulsion. "What, you don't like trees?" Ray said. But she was already gone.

....

"I want you back, Ray," Nancy says. "Even though you are a prick, I want you back. Even though you're mostly an asshole, I want things to be the same as they were."

Ray is not sure what she just said, or for how long she's been talking. "What?"

"What do you mean – what? I think I've been quite clear."

"You want me back," he says.

"Yes. I want all of you, but I'll take what I can get."

"Why?"

"Because I love you. Love is about compromise. It's about bending. It's about taking what you can get."

"I'm sorry?"

"I'm talking about love."

"I don't think that's love, Nancy."

"I accept you as you are," she says.

"You don't even know me."

She leans forward and pours another drink. "I know you cheat on your wife. And I know your cock really well."

"Yes, I know you do, but that's not exactly me. It's a body part."

Ray looks at his parking receipt, and halfway down the block he can see a uniformed woman checking the windshields of cars. His parking slip is good for six more minutes. "Any chance we can finish up in the next six minutes?"

"No," she says. "I'm getting to know you before I go."

"Go where?"

"To bed, Ray. Out dancing. Out on a date. Somewhere other than this conversation. You know. Go."

"I need to buy more time."

"You're not going to buy more time by being short and grumpy with me, Ray."

"That's not what I...Just hold on," he says. He places the phone on the passenger seat and shoulder-checks to see that no cars are coming. He swings the car door open. At the machine, he buys another hour of parking.

He sits back down behind the wheel and sighs heavily. He nods his acknowledgement to Dante's *Divine Comedy* – because he is clearly in the Inferno. He is inside the Second Circle of Hell, guilty of lust, of surrendering to the desire for fleshy pleasure and most definitely adultery. The winds are blowing and there is no peace. There is no Virgil to guide him out of this hell. Ray is alone and will have to push forward on his own. He picks up the phone. "You there?" he says.

....

It was as if Ray and Nancy were floating and helpless in the ocean and their conversation was rising and falling with three-metre swells. Sometimes they could see the jagged land, all brown and emerald green, and sometimes, it was all blue-grey water in every direction.

CHAPTER 14

Tulah meets Ray

Tulah's Snow Journal
Thursday, January 22, 1998 #140

It's snowing – fluffy, like down. It seems to hesitate, as if it's confused about where it's going. There was a moment today, up on the Beehive above Lake Agnes, when the snow was actually falling up! A breeze was pushing it up the mountain and the snow was rising up all around us. It was confusing at first and then it was amazing. And I mean 'amazing.' It was verging on unbelievable. Grandma Frannie would have loved that snow. It was way beyond magic. I thought I was going to lose my mind. Brenda and Justine were stunned into silence, which is something. Brenda asked me if the snow was falling up. 'Yeah,' I said. 'It is.' It was like some movie where gravity stops and everything floats. For a few seconds everything is magic. The Inuit call this snow priyakli. *That is, if you can believe anything on the internet. Anyway,* priyakli *is snow that looks like it's falling upward.*

We're studying poetry at school right now – all the forms of poetry. Eventually, I will have to teach a poetry unit to my students. I found out last week that I love Haiku. Not sure I could ever write one that is any good, but I really enjoy reading them and thinking about them. This one is from a Japanese poet named Basho.

> *This snowy morning:*
> *cries of the crow I despise*
> *(ah, but so beautiful!)*

See? The snow makes everything beautiful!

I'm in a room by myself. Sandi backed out at the last second so I'm stuck paying for this double room. I have two beds. I have choices. It's okay. I also have a lake view. Okay, I have a lake view across a parking lot and it's partially blocked by a massive chateau but still, it's a lake view.

....

Tulah is staying with a couple girlfriends at a small hotel near Lake Louise called Deer Lodge. The Chateau Lake Louise imposes itself at the end of the lake and her hotel is a couple hundred metres down the road from the Chateau. She is excited about being in the mountains. She and two girlfriends were going to ski up behind Mt. Fairview but the avalanche warnings spooked them and eventually chased them into the communal hot tub on top of their hotel. Brenda is majoring in psychology and Justine is a junior writer with a communications company and is now back at university, adding a degree to her experience. They take a couple bottles of wine and some plastic beer cups to the tub and stay there all afternoon. It's not swanky by a long shot but Tulah has learned that the astounding moments in life are hardly ever swanky – those moments come when you are open to adventure, when you open yourself to life, and playfulness. It snows on and off all afternoon and they watch as the mountains appear, and disappear.

Later that night, they are at the *Walliser Stube*, one of the bars in the Chateau Lake Louise. It is a dark, narrow room with chandeliers that were made from the interwoven antlers of deer and elk. They are drinking a bottle of wine – the cheapest wine on the menu because they are all students. Men have already hit on her friends, they've had drinks sent over three times. They wind up sitting with a group of accountants from a firm that is on a leadership retreat at the Chateau.

For the most part, the accountants get nowhere with the women. Brenda wants to stay and see what happens with one of them but her friends scoop her up and put her to bed. She is a compliant drunk. Once they have Brenda tucked in, Justine announces she's done as well. Tulah says goodnight and crosses the hall to her room. The snow is falling past her window – twisting through the hotel lights and the street lights in the parking lot. Even though she is exhausted, she bundles up and heads for the lake. It's a ten-minute walk and soon she is at the edge of the lake, with the surrounding mountains looming, the Chateau behind her, and the snow everywhere. The Chateau seems as if it's huge from where she's standing, but she knows looking down from the Beehive above Lake Agnes, it is a speck of trivial civilization compared to the surrounding mountains. Just now, with the cold seeping into her bones and the snow coming down harder than before, the Chateau, with its warm yellow light, is a comfort. The quiet is astounding. It aches through her and she feels the aloneness of standing on the hard shore of a frozen lake with snow falling. It's as if the snow steals any uttered sound and she can see only as far as the lights from the Chateau. The mountains are only an assumption. When the cold starts to penetrate she decides to cut through the Chateau on her way back. She can warm up and then make the walk to her hotel.

There is a man vacuuming near the entrance and he does not see her as she climbs the stairs to the upper lobby. She hears the music and at first, she thinks it's a radio, or a stereo in a back room. She keeps walking toward the music and discovers it's the sound of a piano and there's a pure melancholy to this music that draws her in. She hesitates at the door to the ballroom. Someone is playing a piano inside. Tulah is tired and cold, and certainly not in the mood for romance. She still has to walk through the snow back to her hotel. But she is curious about this melody.

An hour before Tulah's walk to the lake, Ray found the piano in the corner, at the back of an empty ballroom. He was looking for a way through – a way to get outside and find a quiet spot to have a drink; a place out of the snow where he could sit for a while. The piano, covered by a dusty quilted cover almost stopped him from playing but it wasn't secured. He pushed the cover out of the way and sat down. He had three bottles of beer that the bartender had slipped him. Ray offered to pay her for the beer but she wanted nothing. "They fell and broke," she said, winking. She passed him the bottles and he slipped them into his jacket pockets. She was flirting. He had the money. It was as if this bartender was looking for an opportunity to be kind, or flirtatious and he was it.

The piano, a Steinway that was surprisingly in tune, was a joy to play. There was such a clarity to the notes. It sang in the room but was not so crisp that the sound cut. It was full and well rounded. It was neither crystal clear, nor muddy.

It's dark in the room. The snow falling through the hotel floodlights and then sneaking through the windows creates a dim veil of something resembling light. He does not need much light to play the piano. He has no idea what he's doing. Except a riff on the blues – a sort of bastard blues and there are no wrong notes tonight. He has pre-forgiven himself for any wrong notes, and there's no order to what he plays. It's just whatever he feels. Ray was playing with a bass line – trying to get his left hand to go unconscious so his right could fool around. He was not much of a piano player at all, but he loved the sound of a piano – the thousands upon thousands of potential combinations, and melodies, and harmonies.

He loses track of time. The music allows him to drift and so he is lost inside a Bm9 when the light swings into the room, and then disappears. He knows someone has come in, or someone has opened the door and decided not to come in. He doesn't care. He's not performing. This is for him. Until this moment, he believed he was alone and this is exactly what he will continue to believe, until there's a voice, or a face, or both. He hopes whoever it is decides he's terrible, and leaves as quietly as they entered. Or, if it's security come to tell him to stop, well, there's nothing he can do about that.

Tulah sits in the darkened room, listens, and drifts. She thinks about her grandmother, and the snow. The snow has become something other than what it is and it is because of her grandmother. It's a duet of joy and missing. After twenty minutes, she approaches the piano and Ray stops playing. It's too weird for him to keep playing with this woman standing there looking at him – waiting for something. She is wearing a grey tuque and a full-length shearling coat that is too old for her and yet, she makes it work.

"Who are you?" she says.

"I'm Ray," Ray says, smiling.

"Tulah," she says. "I'm, I'm sorry I interrupted, it's just, it was beautiful. What you were playing was beautiful."

"It's just a riff on the blues," he says. "It's nothing."

"Well, it sounded a bit more than nothing." She hopes she isn't gushing as much as she thinks she is.

Ray looks at her. She's wearing what looks like pyjama bottoms under her coat.

"That's an interesting fashion statement."

She giggles. She'd forgotten about the pyjamas. "Just doing my bit to start a trend, you know."

"Ninja turtles?"

"Like I said, it's not a trend yet, but soon. I can feel it's going to catch on."

Ray decides he likes this woman. She's quick and pretty. "Hey, I have a couple beers, if you'd like a drink. They're probably warm."

"Yeah, I would love a drink."

"Oh, yeah? Okay." He hands her a bottle and she twists the cap.

"What should we drink to?" she says.

"To the snow," he says, as if she is foolish for thinking a toast could be about any other thing. He holds up his bottle. "It's everywhere and it's beautiful and it can't be avoided."

"That's a perfect toast," she says.

"I come from a long line of toasters. Bread has always feared me."

"What? Oh, bread. Oh, God that's bad." She scrunches her face.

"Years from now, when I'm telling the story of how we met to our kids, your utter confusion over my dumb joke will be one of the highlights."

"Children?"

"Yes. You remember the future don't you? A boy and two girls. Ned, Hannah and Ruth."

"Hannah is born first," she says. "Ned and Ruth are the twins."

"Twins. Ouch."

"Child birth is painful. Always," she says.

"Twins, though."

"Well, they don't come out at the same time."

"I know that," he says. "I've seen kittens being born."

"Where did Ned get his name? I can never remember."

"Uncle Ned. My mom's brother. When I was a kid, he made promises about things, and he never broke a promise."

Time compresses and becomes a small blue thing with both of them inside. They sit near the piano and talk. They share themselves. He is pre-law, she is in Education. She has a sister named Alesha and her parents are divorced. He is an only child who was adopted. She loves Thai food. He was a vegetarian for a year because of a woman. She had a friend who died in a plane crash over the South China Sea. They share the absurdities of their lives, though they do not think of these details as absurd – they think they are the fascinating bits. She has always wanted to sing opera. He has a friend who is a singer in New York. He's been to Europe three times to visit an aunt in Zurich. She's been to Hawaii.

At around 4 a.m., Tulah is exhausted. "I like this," she says. "I like you. You should come up to my room. We can keep talking... and see."

Ray smiles. "I would love to accept that offer. But I like you enough that I want to take baby steps. Is that corny?"

"No. That's not corny." She stops. "Oh God, I've come off as a floozy."

"Forget about judging yourself. I projected us into the future, with kids and the last time I checked, you can't buy a baby – you have to make them. You have to have fleshy union. You know, coitus?"

"No, I've been too forward. I stepped over a line. It's because I've been drinking."

He giggles a little bit. "I'm not judging. It's a really tempting offer. I'm just saying I'd like to go slow with you, because this has been, well, it's been brilliant."

"So, what would be the next slow step?"

"A goodnight kiss, a hug and a promise of more – breakfast maybe?" he says.

She leans in quickly and kisses him hard, but lets it soften, and it becomes a fine kiss. It becomes the kind of kiss that doesn't want to end, the kind that ends up in only one place. She pulls away and takes ownership of her own desire.

Ray yields. Her scent is faint, but heady and unforgettable. Sometimes there is surrender inside a kiss, a softening of the idea of self. He realizes he can easily imagine a future with this woman. He wants more of her. He wants to devour.

It is still snowing as he walks her to her hotel. They are walking side-by-side along a dimly lit path and Tulah reaches across space and takes his hand in hers. She encloses his hand in her mittened hand and squeezes. She will remember how right this felt. She will never forget it. And he will remember feeling utterly smitten in that moment – as if his life was completely out of control and it was okay.

At the door, he hugs her. He holds her. She wants to kiss again but he smiles and shakes his head. She watches as he turns and starts his walk back to the Chateau. He has perhaps taken a dozen steps before Tulah stops him.

"Wait," she says. "I'm available. I just thought you should know."

"What?"

"I'm available. I'm not involved with anybody else. I'm not married or anything."

"Oh," he says. "Good. I'm also available. My heart is unencumbered."

"Good," she says. "I'm glad we cleared that up."

"Me too."

They look at each other through the falling snow. It's as if they don't want this to end, as if tomorrow is not certain. "Did you know that cranes mate for life?"

"What?"

"Cranes. They mate for life. It's true. It was on the National Geographic channel. It was all about Sandhill cranes and how they mate for life."

"Okay," he says. "Good to know. Are you going to be okay getting to your room? Or do you need a crane?"

"100 percent fine. No problemo."

Oh my god, she thinks. Shut the fuck up. You sound like an idiot.

She watches as he disappears into the snow. He becomes a ghost and then he vanishes. When Tulah puts her head on the pillow, she's dizzy and she can't decide if it's the booze she consumed or the man. Or both. She glances at the clock on her bedside table and realizes she has promised to go skiing in a few hours. She starts to drift off but her eyes pop open. He didn't ask about whether or not she was married, or with someone. She brought it up. As if he didn't care, or maybe he was just as tired as she was. He said his heart was un-something. Unencumbered? Who says stuff like that? She heard 'free.' Maybe he trusted that if she were married or involved she would not have tried to sleep with him. That's too much trust, she thinks. She doesn't deserve that much trust.

. . . .

"Ms. Roberts?" It is one of the young, overly polite men at the front desk. "This was left for you," he says, handing her a folded piece of paper. Tulah stops and recognizes the excitement in her chest. His note reads: *I had to leave. A family thing. I want to keep learning to know you. Cranes are beautiful, and mildly illogical birds, aren't they?* This is followed by a couple phone numbers and an email address.

Tulah tells Brenda and Justine she had a late night and asks if they would mind not skiing. They are not disappointed. They are sitting in the window of the dining room looking at Mt Fairview, though it is hardly a fair view of the mountain. It's still snowing and the mountain is a ghost that drifts in and out of existence behind a veil of hazy white.

Brenda is confused. "What do you mean you had a late night? You went to bed same time we did."

"Well, you had a late night and I had a very late night."

Justine is trying to figure out the shading of this statement. "But you went to your room."

"Yes. I went to my room."

"And?"

"And you would have been waking up in some accountant's room if it wasn't for us," Tulah says. "We saved you from Bruce the accountant."

"You're changing the subject. What happened last night?"

"Nothing. I met a guy."

"You met a guy?" Justine says.

"Yes, a guy."

Justine places her mimosa on the table and turns toward Tulah. "Where? Was he walking around in your room? Was he hiding in the bathroom?"

"I went for a walk. It was snowing and I wanted to be out in it. I cut through the Chateau on the way back and he was there."

"In the lobby?" Brenda says.

"No, he was playing a piano, in a ballroom, in the dark."

Their waitress is approaching the table with a bottle of prosecco wrapped in a napkin, hoping to top-up their mimosas.

"Bring a new bottle," Brenda says to the waitress. "Please." She looks at Tulah. "Go on."

....

She does not call him. She emails a pithy "missed you at breakfast" and they go back and forth a bit. She's swamped at school and he's taking care of an ailing mother, which impresses Tulah. The mother was the reason he went home early from the mountains. They set a date to meet for wine in three weeks. Despite the fact nothing happened between them sexually, apart from a bit of kissing, they're both feeling a bit sheepish about their night in the mountains.

Two weeks later, she runs into him at a book launch in an Irish pub. Brenda's boyfriend, Brad, has published his first novel, a book written in second person about vampires living on a space station, and Ray shows up with two women.

"Oh God, that's him," Tulah says to Brenda. Ray is across the room, holding a drink, his arm around a tall, slender brunette with severe bangs and a slightly shorter blonde woman in a skimpy black dress, her arm in his. He's laughing about something. He sees Tulah and smiles as if he is delighted.

"Who?"

Tulah hisses. "The piano guy. The kiss. The snow. The mountains."

Brenda squints. "He's not at all how I imagined him. He's tall. He's with someone. He's with two someones."

"I can see he's with someone. I'm not blind…"

"…He's coming over." Brenda turns and slips into the crowd.

"Let me see," Ray says, "The last time we met, it was snowing and you could hear the German howitzers at the edge of the city."

Tulah tries hard not to be amused, but she knows he's riffing on *Casablanca*.

"You remembered, how lovely," she says. "But, of course, that was the night the Germans marched into Paris."

"Not an easy night to forget."

"No," she says.

"I remember almost every detail," he says. "The Germans wore grey, you wore blue."

She shakes her head at him. "How are you, really?"

"I'm good," he says.

"Really? Because if you're Rick from *Casablanca* and I'm Ilsa, then you're not good at all. You're actually damaged beyond compare. And we don't wind up together."

"Shit. Is that what happens at the end of *Casablanca*?"

"You didn't know?"

"I always fall asleep before the end. You mean Rick and Ilsa…"

"…Nope. Doesn't happen. But they'll always have Paris."

"I'm happy to see you," he says.

"I noticed you brought two dates. That's impressive."

"Dates? Oh, yeah. They're together. I came with them. They're models – both of them. They're a couple. Want an introduction? They're lovely."

"Maybe later."

"Hey, does this meeting – which is great, by the way – in any way interfere with our planned date next week? Because I'll cancel the jet."

"What?"

"The jet," he says. "I'll cancel it."

"Oh, we'll see how this night goes," she says. He's joking about having arranged a jet, she thinks. He must be joking.

"No pressure then."

"None whatsoever."

The MC blurts a 'testing-one, two, three' and then starts a long and rambling introduction of the novelist. They stand side-by-side, sipping their drinks and Tulah wants to slip her hand into his. She wants touch. She wants more than this standing and listening. She moves her forefinger slightly in the direction of his hand – more a soft twitch than anything. Ray smiles and pushes back with his hand. They listen to the author read a passage from his book. He thanks everyone and then Ray's dates find him and pull him to the far corner of the room. Brenda finds Tulah and starts to ask her a thousand questions about Ray, and about her feelings for him, and what did she think of Brad's reading, and wasn't Brad a wonderful writer.

Tulah is in a stall peeing, and she's weighing her options. She's supposed to go with Brenda and Brad, and a gaggle of other friends, to some bistro on 8th Street. She's afraid Brad will corner her and ask her for her honest opinion of the book and she'll say something stupid. Brenda had given Tulah an advance reading copy of the book a month ago and she'd breezed through it. She thought the idea was brilliant but it wasn't well executed. There were jagged edges of missing logic and that was usually fatal for a book. Would she have stopped reading it if she didn't know Brad? Probably. She was afraid she'd have a couple more drinks and then all of this would come spilling out – Brad would be hurt, Brenda would be angry, and she'd be deeply embarrassed.

She could go back into the pub and look for Ray. This would be a slightly safer course but also dangerous because she wants to sleep with him and she's not ready for that tonight. Her pubic hair has gone mad, her legs are bristly and she feels bloated.

She decides she will feign a headache and go home and watch guilty pleasure TV – something mind-numbing and stupid.

....

Ray did not have an airplane booked for their date, as he'd threatened, and she never expected it. She thought it was lovely and whimsical. Instead of flying somewhere, they went to a concert in a church, a string quartet. Béla Bartók, Schubert, and Górecki were on the program and afterwards, they go for dinner. He made her laugh. And she could make him laugh. This is important to Tulah.

Five weeks after that date they take a leap of faith on their affections. They fly to France, to Nice, for a one-week vacation. Neither of them had much money but they made it work. Ray's summer job was at his uncle's greenhouse, and his uncle said, "Go. Go be young and in love in the south of France." Tulah had been hired by a construction firm as a 'traffic girl'. She would be holding a 'slow' sign for most of the summer, and that road project didn't start until the first week of July. They fly last minute, looking for the best deal and they luck out. They find heavily discounted tickets for a flight that leaves at 2:30 a.m. Ray suggested Nice because on one of their dates Tulah mentioned she loved Marc Chagall and there was a Chagall museum in Nice.

They had planned to stay at a hostel but when they arrive, they find a dozen hotels that are inexpensive and fine. They book a room in the Garden Hotel and walk every day. They visit the *Musée National Marc Chagall* four times. They look at Chagall's paintings, and his windows, and they are silent. They make a deal not to speak until they each have a glass of wine in a café, and only then do they bang their perceptions together. Only then do they talk about what they saw and felt.

On a Thursday, they buy wine and walk back to their hotel. They hold hands as they walk and it feels as natural as if they'd been holding hands for forty years. Ray does not think about the future – he is only interested in how it feels to hold hands with a beautiful woman, on a sunny day, in the south of France. Tulah wonders if they will always be able to hold hands like this, and if it will always feel this pure.

They sit in the courtyard of the Garden Hotel, in the bright 2 p.m. sun. The courtyard is an enclosed sanctuary with the hotel on three sides and high stone wall protecting it from the cacophony of Nice. Ray removes one of the bottles of wine from his bag and sets it on the table beside his journal and a book. He brought Bulgakov's *The Master and Margarita* with him because it was a book he'd skipped in his English 303 class and he'd been intrigued by the discussion. It was a catch-up read.

"I'll see if I can find a corkscrew and glasses," he says. But before he can stand up, the maître d'hôtel, a man named François Houle, appears with two glasses. "Monsieur," he says. "Please, allow me." He looks at the wine, a *Château de la Terriere Brouilly,* without judgement, and proceeds to open it for them. Ray had picked the bottle off the shelf because he liked the heft of the word *brouilly.* And, it was inexpensive.

When the maître d' first appeared, Tulah thought they were going to be told they couldn't drink their own wine in the garden. She thought they'd broken some rule. She thought they would have to buy their wine from the hotel. But he seems delighted that they are there in the bright garden sharing a bottle. As if it's natural to do so. He unfurls the umbrella beside their table so there is the option of shade and then he disappears – he ducks back into the hotel.

Tulah drops her sunglasses from her hairline into place, and smiles. "Chagall and his blues," she says. "Those blues are so deep and rich, I get lost when I look at that colour."

"And those five paintings with that amazing red colour."

"The *Song of Songs* cycle – those were for his wife."

Tulah has decided she will smoke cigarettes on this trip, just a few, scattered throughout the day, and not out of desperation, but rather in concert with a desire for elegance. She loves the look and feel of a woman sneaking a cigarette. She thinks she looks European when she smokes and this pleases her. She does not admit any of this to Ray.

She limits her smoking because she loves the head rush of a first cigarette and does not want to abuse this feeling. Of course, she knows how terrible smoking is – the damage it does, but there is something reckless and romantic about it too. This moment seems like a good time to be elegant, so she takes out the package of *Gauloises Blondes* and pulls out a cigarette.

The maître d', once again, shows up as if by magic, with a lighter. As she has seen in movies, Tulah touches his hand as she lights her cigarette.

He glances at the book on the table. "I can see Monsieur is a reader of distinction. Has Monsieur read Michel Houellebecq's *Les Particules élémentaires*. It is an extraordinary book. I would recommend it…how is it in English? *Vigoureusement.*"

"Vigorously," Tulah says, pleased with the recovered remnants of her high school French.

"*Oui*, vigorously."

"*Merci*," Ray says, as he flips open his journal and scratches the name of the book onto the page.

The maître d' watches Ray write. "*Non*," he says. "Please allow me." He takes the pen and writes out the name of the book. "This book will bring you pleasure. Though, I do not know if it is translated."

He pours a little more wine into each of their glasses and when he is gone, Tulah smokes quietly for a while. A French police car passes the hotel with its donkey-braying siren, a sparrow pecks the ground a few metres away, and she takes a sip of her wine. "The air is yellow here," she says. "It's like we're inside a Chagall painting – with those muted yellows of his – you know? The yellows that are bold and quiet at the same time."

"If this was a Chagall painting, we would need a blue horse, or a red horse," Ray says.

"And our hands," she says. "Our hands would have to be deformed – our fingers would look like bloated sausages."

"Yes. His hands are horrible but it doesn't matter because there is so much desire."

Tulah giggles. "And we would have to be naked and embraced in a corner somewhere – barely noticeable."

"Like a beautiful afterthought," Ray says. "And there must be flowers, and birds."

"Lots of flowers," she says. "And perhaps I should only have one breast."

"Well, one breast is more than enough, but, in theory, two are more fun."

"Do you really think so?"

"Yes," Ray says, lifting the bottle from the table. "Here, have some more wine and then perhaps we can retire to our room and investigate this theory."

....

They have been dating for a year and have just started to talk about living together. They're spending a lot of time together, and rarely sleep alone. In September, Ray has to be in Sacramento for a Cybersecurity and Data Privacy Law Conference, so they go together and add an extra week at the end, to explore the area. Ray attends the conference and Tulah catches up on her reading. After the conference, they wind up in the Lime Kiln Valley, looking for Zinfandel wine.

On their first night staying in a bed and breakfast attached to a vineyard, Ray and Tulah wander away from the guesthouse and find themselves near the staff dormitory. Jesús Patiño is playing a guitar and his girlfriend, María Guadalupe, is singing. There are perhaps twenty people around a fire, listening. The song is honest and melancholy, and when it ends, they move closer to the fire because they want more. The Mexicans offer them wine, and beer, and stilted conversation. They try to meet in the middle between English and Spanish so neither language is fully spoken. At midnight there are only a few workers left because they start early in the morning and it's backbreaking work.

Each night after this, Ray and Tulah show up at the fire to listen to the music and talk. Some of the workers are less than thrilled about this invasion of their private time, but they seem to relax when Ray tells them he is putting himself through school by working as a gardener.

The third night at the fire, a man named Juan gets down on both knees and proposes to his girlfriend, Gabriela, who bursts into tears and knocks Juan over with her enthusiasm. Ray and Tulah are included in the celebration. They dance and sing, and are happy for the newly engaged couple.

Later, in bed, Tulah turns to Ray. "I love it that we were there tonight, but what if she'd said no, or that she needed time?"

"It's risky," Ray says. "That sort of love is always risky. It's jumping from a high place and learning how to fly on the way down."

"It would have been a bummer. A big bummer." She has been drinking and she is over-pronouncing her 'b's.

"It's about taking a leap of faith. It's worth the risk."

"But I wouldn't want a public proposal," she says. "Not that I think there's one coming. But I think I would prefer a private proposal because then, the answer can be completely honest." She is talking with her hands and pointing at him.

"Duly noted," Ray says.

"And no big weddings. No, no, no. Small and dimple – simple. I want to wear a black cocktail dress."

"No saying yes to an obscenely frilly and poofy dress?"

"Nope. Little black dress," she says. "That's it. And nice shoes. But that's it. Really expensive nice shoes."

....

The next day, at a restaurant in Sonora, Ray asks her. He doesn't get down on one knee, because he's a good listener. He tries to be low-key about it, so it doesn't get blown out of proportion, so it doesn't draw attention. But Tulah is beyond delighted. She jumps up and is standing in the aisle, shouting "yes, yes, yes" and by the time she is finished, the whole restaurant knows and Ray suspects people on the street know. The manager sends over a bottle of champagne.

"So much for private and honest," he says.

"Oh, to hell with private, and anyway, I am honest. This makes me happy. I'm ecstatic."

"So you don't need a ring, because I can take this back. I thought maybe..." He's digging around in his trouser pockets.

"What?"

"This." He places the box on the table and Tulah rips the ribbon off. She looks inside at a diamond and sapphire ring.

"My God, Ray," she says. "It's beyond beautiful."

The manager comes and sits down with them. Tulah slips the ring onto her finger and goes on a tour of the restaurant to show anyone and everyone. She goes into the kitchen to show the chef and out into the back alley to show their waitress, Bunny, who is taking her break with a cigarette and talking on her phone. Bunny disconnects. She is excited for Tulah, and they come back inside as Ray is opening the second bottle of champagne. Ray watches Bunny as she drinks her champagne. Even though she's smiling, there's sadness in her eyes.

. . . .

That night, after Ray and Tulah share the news with the Mexicans, Jesús Patiño and his fiancée, María Guadalupe, kiss and hug them repeatedly. They are happy and insist the engaged couple join them at the fire to celebrate. Ray and Tulah drink a good deal of tequila, and beer, and more tequila. Afterwards, in bed, their heads are spinning as they talk about when they might get married.

"My schedule is open," Ray says. "After the massive hangover I'm anticipating, my schedule is open."

"Tomorrow afternoon then," Tulah says. Her voice is resolute and fast.

"What?" He's not sure if she's serious.

"I'm not a big fan of long engagements." Tulah is thinking about her girlfriend, Beth, who has been engaged for fourteen years, and counting.

"I see. You don't like to fool around, do you?"

"Too quick for you?" She pouts as if this is a comment on the quantity of love or the quality of his love.

"A little surprising. I mean I was really thinking of a longer engagement." Tulah's face drops. Ray smiles and continues. "I was kinda hoping for the day after tomorrow."

Ray was actually thinking maybe a year down the road, which would have left them loads of time to plan for a simple, elegant and small wedding.

"Well," Tulah says, "Marriage is all about compromise, so the day after tomorrow is fine for me. Maybe we can arrange for a minister when we go into town to shop for my little black dress."

It turns out the manager of the Lime Kiln Valley vineyard, California, knows a lot of the right people – she arranges everything, including wedding rings and a wedding dinner on the crush pad. Pastor Bob, and his wife Clarice, from Sonora, perform the ceremony, and Jesús and María act as witnesses. Pastor Bob is not the first choice, but rather the first available on short notice. He's more Buddhist than anything else. He ends with "To say the words love and compassion is easy. But to accept that love and compassion are built upon patience and perseverance is not easy. Your marriage will be firm and lasting if you remember this."

They gather on the crush pad, with massive oak barrels stacked six high behind them. Jesús plays his guitar and sings a song called *Te Amo* as Tulah makes her entrance. María Guadalupe cries through the entire service – she weeps, softly, and Ray and Tulah are not certain if these are tears of sadness or joy.

the pungent, spicy scent from her armpits

Honestly, do you really care how Ray and Tulah meet? Because you're about to experience that story. Or, if you're reading this book backwards – and you know you are – you have just finished reading the story of how they met. Meeting in the darkened ballroom of a hotel in the mountains as snow is falling is a fine story. Add in the grand piano and the minor chords and it's a very good story. You're usually hesitant to ask about other peoples' how-we-met stories. You're afraid of a dreadfully bad story, during which you'll force yourself to smile and nod. And whoever is telling the bad story will look at you and know you're faking. They'll see through your lie. You believe all how-we-met stories ought to be amazing because you believe falling in love is akin to having your heads bashed together – it's violent and irrational and marvellous. That four-letter word can rip things apart. It's like ploughing a field. Like falling off the roof of a house. Like a punch to the stomach. Even if half the story is pure fabrication, it ought to be brilliant.

Attraction is weird. Apart from the physical, for Tulah, it was the fact Ray heard her when she said she loved Chagall, and he remembered. That was the tipping point for her. For Ray, it was Tulah's boldness and her willingness to play. She could be playful in the checkout of a grocery store, or sitting in front of a mirror putting on her makeup, and she was more sexually playful than any woman he knew.

....

Ray and Tulah send Christmas cards to Jesús Patiño and his wife María every year, without fail. Jesús manages a hotel resort near Tulum. They have four kids.

....

Perhaps you are wondering about the possibility of some background, or summary information that could be offered up here. Well, when

Tulah was thirty-two years old and Ray was thirty-four, there was a period of time spanning twenty-three months in which they didn't have sex once. Not even a breathless kiss. There was a litany of excuses. Tulah was having her periods. Ray's beard was too scratchy. They were both too tired. One of them had a cold. The girls were restless, or not sleeping well, or sick.

There were a few failed attempts, and eventually, it started to feel like too much work. They forgave themselves. They fumed silently. They resented each other – each blaming the other for getting old, or losing interest, or drifting into complacency. They forgave each other. They sighed, rolled over and went to sleep.

One night, well into the drought, they were in bed and Ray started to caress Tulah – moving his hand along her leg, and hip, and waist. He wasn't really thinking. It seemed like a natural thing. He wanted to touch her. The impulse surprised him. The girls were in bed. He was just touching, seeing what might happen. Something sexual, or not. It was an open-ended caress because he remembered how good it felt to be touched. He could feel her body respond – she moved ever so slightly toward his touch. But when he brushed her inner thigh with his fingertips, Tulah pulled away. She stared at him. "It's late. And your fingers are so cold. Why do you always do that?" She covered up and moved away. "I have an early staff meeting," she said.

He was thinking – *so that's it*? It's all ruined? One step off the invisible line of Tulah's perfect flight path and it's over? God, it used to be so much easier. Whatever it was about to become was done. Ray wasn't even sure he wanted to make love. He was only feeling around and now, he felt beyond stupid. Was he too eager? Probably. But it had been a year since he'd touched a woman like this. He felt like he had no idea how to touch his wife. If there was a manual that outlined, step-by-step, how to make love with Tulah, he'd misplaced his, or not read the revised edition. Each attempted loving was a stumble into the land of *wrong*. It was a minefield of mistaken choices. It was disheartening. A long time ago, he thought he was a pretty decent lover. Maybe he was delusional. Maybe he really was a daft, blundering moron and he has always been an incompetent lover.

A couple weeks later, Tulah crawled on top of him and tried to put him inside her. She was shocked when he wasn't instantly ready and asked Ray why he didn't find her attractive anymore. She'd gained a little weight but he'd always said it was fine. He was not obsessed with skinny women. He liked curves. But maybe it wasn't fine anymore. She was upset.

Ray felt like she was just trying to fuck him so it wouldn't be over a year without sex and this did not feel good. He wanted her to want to be with him. This felt like she was fulfilling some wifely duty. As if she was obligated. It was bizarre.

"You owe me nothing," he said. "This doesn't feel right. Do this because you want to do it, not because you feel you have to."

"I do want to," she said. "You're not turned on. You don't find me attractive."

Jesus, women are stupid, he thought. "I'm not sixteen," he said. "I actually need foreplay too." Ray got out of bed. He shut the bedroom door and checked on the girls. Sarah was two years old, and Patience was three. They were both sound sleepers. He went down the hall and poured a substantial portion of whisky into a squat glass. He flipped through his albums and found Miles Davis's *Sketches of Spain*. He slid open the veranda windows and the rain smell pushed into the room. He sat on the couch and even though the Miles Davis wasn't working, he felt so beaten down, he just let it play. Tulah did not follow him down the hall and into the living room. She cocooned inside her own aloneness.

Tulah was aware that she was depressed. Ray had no clue about his state of mind. He knew something was wrong. He would not have called it depression. He would have called it a lull. He did not like feeling so far away from Tulah but he was starting to get used to it – it was becoming the norm. He worried that perhaps in a day or two – perhaps in a month, or a year, or twenty minutes, he wouldn't be able, or wouldn't have the desire to make love anymore. As much as Ray tried to convince himself it was okay to not make love, not touch, not be touched – it was after midnight and he was sitting alone, drinking whisky, and listening to a scratchy Miles Davis record that was decidedly not the right music.

....

petrichor
noun
[PET-ri-kuhr]
A pleasant smell that frequently accompanies the first rain after a long
period of warm, dry weather.

....

Maybe you're worried about Claude Garamond and his work with the
Garamond font. You might be wondering, if there was a promise to not
include him as a character, why does he keep popping up? What possible insights would another scene with old Claude Garamond provide?
It's 1536, the first of March, and Garamond is working on a typeface that
will be used to set the text of a book called *Paraphrasis in Elegantiarum
Libros Laurentii Vallae,* by a writer named Erasmus. It will be his first
step toward a fully realized Garamond font.

He is in bed with his wife and his eyes are so tired he can barely
keep them open. Even though it is remarkably dark in the room, there
is a bit of the moon in the sky and there are stars. He can just barely
see the line of his wife's body. He can see the moon on her skin. And
he can smell her – the pungent, spicy scent from her armpits and a soft
musty scent of a faded perfume. He is sure she can smell him too and
prays it is not too much. He did not go to the river to wash up after
his work in the studio and it was a hot day.

"You're working too hard," Marie Isabelle says. "I'm worried about you."

Garamond ignores her and begins to trace the outline of her hip
and her waist. He traces the curve of her breast with his fingertips,
and she grunts – just one involuntary grunt, and he knows she is fine
with this touching.

She is exhausted but at the same time she wants to be defined in
space. She wants the pleasure. She purposely places aside the fact there
is something wrong with three of the chickens, and that there is money
owing to the vintner, and the butcher, and the baker. Her mother is
not well – she is struggling to walk and she has fallen down a dozen
times in the past months. And she gets news of Paris that is a month
old, sometimes more. But this is the man she loves and Marie Isabelle
believes in the importance of their marriage.

Garamond knows he is working too hard. He knows this and when he started to touch her he was not really touching her body – he was tracing the curve of an imagined letter *z* – lower case and italics – which will eventually surprise and delight even the most liberal and adventurous publishing houses. He noticed the curve of her hip and was immediately tracing the swirl of a letter. It was going to be astounding and certainly unique. When it is fully developed, the italics of this new font will not only mimic the beauty of handwriting, it will carve out a new way of seeing this letter. Garamond had almost removed himself from their bed and rushed off to his studio to sketch the line of the space between his wife's breasts into the *z*. But she grunted and this snapped him away from fonts and letterforms – it brought him to skin, and scent, and pleasure. It brought him to her. He knew that grunt was the beginning of surrender. He loved her for this grunt and for all her grunts and moans.

When they are spent, Marie Isabelle looks at Garamond. "Where are the snows of yesteryear?" she says.

He is across the room pouring two glasses of wine. "What did you say? Where are the snows of yesteryear? What? Where did you get that?"

"A poem, Claude – a poem by François Villon."

"Villon, the scoundrel?"

"Is he a scoundrel?"

"Yes, of course, he is. But how have you come to be reading his ballad?"

"It was on your desk, Claude. The title captured me – *Ballad of the Ladies of Bygone Times*. And then, of course, that line. That line that tells us life is short. It yells at us, Claude, that death will take away all of whatever we have of beauty or power." She takes a long, slow sip of her wine.

He looks at his wife – the freckles on her face and shoulders, her dark hair, braided and pulled back behind one ear – the escaped strands across her face. Her eyes, a pale blue and always looking around the room – never missing anything. He is not surprised by her intelligence and insight, or her passion. He knows he is lucky to have this woman in his life – it was amazing luck to have been pushed together with Marie Isabelle – an arrangement between her grandmother and his parents, introductions and not-so-subtle encouragements. And in the end there were expectations that a marriage would take place. He does not make a great deal of money – but the prospects around printing and publishing is growing quickly, and his new fonts, which by necessity, are getting smaller and smaller because books are getting smaller, will sell across Europe. He knows the italics will sell, he tells himself. Well, he hopes the italics will sell. He sighs. He has no idea if the italics will sell. He wants to give her a better life than this remote and borrowed house. Better than feeding chickens and milking cows. Better than the linen smocks and wool dresses – she deserves silk and velvet, and better wine. They both deserved better wine.

Tomorrow, he decides, he will get Marie Isabelle up on horseback. He will teach her to ride because someday she may have to ride. Someday, there will be no time for carriages. Garamond has arranged for the vintner to warn them about strangers asking questions and they should be ready to flee at a moment's notice. The vintner has given Garamond directions to a hut in the mountains where they can live should that day come.

Marie Isabelle notices Garamond looking at her. "Come and kiss me again," she says. "And again, and again. Kiss me right now – not with tomorrow or yesterday in your head. Kiss me now."

....

You know humans are eroded by life. Morals, principles and beliefs are mangled and contorted just by living. At least, these things are assaulted. But Ray and Tulah are relatively privileged. Do the privileged get bashed around by life too? Of course, they do. No matter if you are dirt poor or obscenely wealthy, it's all going to end in death – it's going to end badly. And what sort of journey has Nancy been on? How did she wind up threatening suicide on the balcony of the thirty-ninth floor of a high-rise?

You might begin to wonder about the certainty of this so-called Greek-Chorus section. Is there truth here? Is there anything resembling veracity here? Would you lie to yourself? Do people lie to themselves? Yes. People lie to themselves all the time. Maybe you are at work right now. It might be that you work in a tall office tower and you just went down for coffee and a walk around the block. You have been reading about sitting and how unhealthy it is to sit for long periods of time, so you've been trying to fight this with intermittent walks. On 102 Street, a woman waiting at a bus stop is dressed in a tiger suit – a cheap Halloween onesie – she has headphones on, and is singing Madonna's *Like a Virgin*, loudly and out of tune. A woman in a niqab walks by, her body a mystery, the screen across her eyes revealing nothing human. You can't imagine this is a choice. On the corner, there are two stiffly smiling people – a man and a woman – standing with a couple signs and a small table with a stack of Bibles. You acknowledge their dedication. But they might also be the poster children for the idea of lying to yourself. Surely there is an active delusion inside this faith, inside any faith. The Madonna-singing woman in the tiger suit tells herself she can sing. The woman in the niqab tells herself this cloistered prison is her choice, and that she is devout. The Christians pushing Bibles on the corner tell themselves they're doing God's work. It's all nonsense, and yet, it comforts, and on some inexplicable level, it works.

Aristotle said the Greek Chorus ought to be regarded as one of the actors. You might find this to be an interesting notion. If you were an actor in this narrative, where would you occur? Where would you be? Could you see yourself as a waitress or a waiter in the *Café Americana*, watching a man, sitting in his car, having a long conversation with someone – only attempting to read his expressions and body language to guess at what's going on. Maybe you happen to glance out your window and see Nancy standing on her balcony on the thirty-ninth floor of the building across the Avenue, and you watch as she is embroiled in a long phone conversation. Perhaps you're a monk living in the sixteenth century, in the south of France because Claude Garamond is the most likeable character in this book and that's where you want to live.

....

You should probably know this about Ray – he soared through law school and landed a job articling with Brice, Jones & Farnsworth, where he learned about zealously defending his clients first hand. No matter how repugnant the client, no matter how guilty, no matter how unrepentant, Ray was in there – defending zealously. The drug dealer who recruited underage kids from high schools with incentives of the latest electronic gadgets because they could not yet be charged as adults. The slum landlords. Ray put his blinders on and defended them as best he could. He pushed justice hard – made it stand up on its hind legs and jump through hoops. If he got a sleazy drug dealer freed, it was because the wheels of justice were working and justice had prevailed. He looked for loopholes. He sped up proceedings, or slowed them down, if it helped his client. He leveraged time and information to his client's advantage. His ethics were front and centre always – and it seemed they were bruised and redefined every day. Despite the daily assault on his principles, Ray was an associate in a growing firm, with a clear path toward becoming partner.

But the Basa case tipped him over. It was the case that caused him to question everything about the law.

Brice, Jones & Farnsworth were defending a man named Abdul momit Basa, who was driving home from a party around 5 a.m. one Saturday morning and lost control on a corner – hit and killed a woman named Caroline Franks, who jogged along that street every morning at about the same time. Basa didn't even know he'd run into Caroline Franks. He said he didn't see her. He crawled out of his Mercedes-Benz E-Class, which had eventually banged into a large oak, called for a taxi and went home to sleep. In the boardroom of the law firm of Brice, Jones & Farnsworth, with the doors closed, Basa admitted he'd been drinking and doing cocaine with about twenty people at a house party, right up until the time he crawled into his car. He also told his lawyers that he'd been with a woman who was not his wife.

The firm played the race card. Basa was Muslim and devout Muslims do not drink. They would keep him off the stand – he would never have to answer that question. They revealed that he was with his mistress and that his marriage was in tatters but that he and his wife were working on it. The prosecution brought witness after witness to say Basa had been drinking but not one witness could say they'd seen the pour – they just saw him drinking, *something*. The cocaine was ingested in the bathroom. So only the mistress could testify to that and she was unreliable, showed up for her deposition drunk, or stoned, or both. Ray was told to dig around in her past, to find something they could use, and he did. He found a drug conviction, an abandoned kid, a year-long stay in a mental institution, and two tries at rehab. The mistress was a mess and the firm of Brice, Jones & Farnsworth made sure everyone in the courtroom knew about her mess. At the end of her testimony, she was unsure about the cocaine and everyone in the courtroom was unsure about her.

It wasn't the description of Caroline Franks that ruined Ray, it was the look on her husband's face. It was not hatred, and it was not anger – it was devastation, disbelief and anguish. It was as if all of what was going on around him – the courthouse, the judge, the lawyers – all these things were part of an awful dream. He was withdrawn, and dispossessed, and yet, some part of him had to be there. Some part of him had to know the details of his own loss. Ray could not shake away the image of this man's face, his slumped posture, his eyes that saw but also did not see. Abdul momit Basa's wife was also in the courtroom. She sat behind the bench and never spoke. When Ray looked at her he saw her hopeless resignation. As if she understood the outcome of the trial would not affect her life in the least. Ray was attracted to Abdul momit Basa's wife. Her hijab, her silence and her desperate sorrow were all captivating to Ray. He has always been attracted to sad women. When he met Tulah, she was sad. Something about the snow and her grandmother.

Basa was found not guilty of criminally negligent homicide. It was raining that morning – not a heavy rain, but enough to make the roads slick. And while it appeared Basa's car did not even start to try to stop, this was inconclusive because it was raining. It was ruled an accident, and accidents do happen. Abdul momit Basa walked out of the courtroom a free man. He walked past Caroline Franks's broken husband without glancing in his direction. He walked out of the courthouse, smiling and relieved – his wife ten paces behind. He crawled into a new black Mercedes without looking back. His wife joined him in the car with all of her sadness in tow and she silently pulled the door shut. Ray wondered if Basa would have behaved differently if he'd killed a man with his automobile.

Standing in the doorway of the courtroom, Ray thought about Tulah. He could imagine her going for an early morning run – which

she occasionally did. He did not have to imagine Abdul momit Basa
– he had a clear picture of this man's indifference, his money, and his
amoral privilege. Ray's first impulse was violence. He wanted to do
something to make sure the gargantuan asshole, Abdul momit Basa,
would never hurt anyone again. It pleased him to think about hurting
Basa but he was fundamentally not a violent man. Caroline Franks's
husband ought to know the truth. Instead of violence, Ray opted for
truth. At some point in the future, he would deliver that truth to the
husband. It would likely be sooner than later. Ray was not naïve. He
knew justice was slippery. There were lawyers in his firm who could
easily rationalize Basa's vigorous defence as a fully functioning legal
system, as an example of an ill-prepared, inept, and inexperienced prosecution. The prosecuting attorneys did not ask themselves why Basa
didn't testify. There were a thousand rationalizations but the Basa case,
for Ray, was so far from the idea of decency, it made his decision easy.
Ray would turn his back on the law. He would work with trees. Trees
don't lie. They hold secrets but they don't lie.

....

Antoine Augereau was working on a book when the Roman Catholic
Church came knocking on his door. It was, as far as Garamond could
tell, a love letter to the elms of Paris. The book, titled *Ulmus*, was delivered to Garamond by Antoine's solicitor ten days after his execution.
There was no note, just the unbound pages, printed on high-quality
paper, rolled into a tube and wrapped in leather. The letterforms were
very close to Robert Estienne's typefaces and Garamond was intrigued
by the weightless fluidity of the letters.

"I was to deliver this to you." The solicitor paused and looked hard
at Garamond, who was studying the letterforms and noticing the generous margins. "He said you'd know what to do with it."

Garamond had no idea what to do with it, except read it, so this is
what he did. Half way through, he realized the book was more about
light than elms. The way elms held light. The light through the elms.
The light under the elms. Sometimes, Augereau would revisit the same
tree a dozen times, at various times of the day, and during different
seasons. Often, he would study the same tree for a day, and report the

nuances of light. These unbound pages remained a treasured secret for Garamond. He took possession of the manuscript – both physically and spiritually – and kept it private. Its typography was eloquent and surrounded by space – its words filled with longing and melancholy. There was magic in the meshing of eloquence and story and he wanted desperately to understand it.

CHAPTER 13

Strangled

"Not everyone who has a cowl on is a monk"
— *Zhanna Petya*

Sometimes Nancy imagines one of her mother's angels is leaning in and listening to the rolling chaos in her mind. She and the angel will be standing in the middle of a vast, tawny meadow. The cold nights of fall will have begun to work their magic and the trees will be turning. The breeze through the dull brown grasses is the sound of the ocean. It is the sound of a mother hushing a baby, and it is the muffled sound of wings.

This imagined angel is always wearing a fur coat with a high, folded-over collar. The fur will brush Nancy's face and it will tickle. She won't see it at first. She will reach up and scratch the side of her face and then she will know. She imagines the angel's forehead against hers and the angel is breathing slow, focused and receptive. The angel takes every thought and feeling Nancy can muster. It eavesdrops on her desires and regrets, and every shallow impulse, but it never gives anything back. It is a one-way relationship. It is unrequited.

Nancy steps back and the angel lifts its head. Its wings are massive. Its face is soft and feminine. It is at least a foot taller than her and there is a sword hanging from its belt.

"What good are you?" Nancy will want to ask.

The angel hesitates, turns around, looks for someone else in the meadow. It turns back to face her. Its wings create a bit of a breeze. "I am watching over you," the angel will say. "I am guarding you."

"Guarding me? All you do is listen? You stand around with your sympathy and sadness vibrating on high, and you listen? What good is your compassion if there is no action attached to it?"

"I am guarding you."

"What are you guarding me from?"

"From every malevolence. From all the things you know nothing about. From the details of lunacy. From the disorder of darkness."

"Oh, I know the darkness," Nancy will say. "Where are you when I hear the wings? Where are you when I am deep in the darkness?"

The angel will smile, as if to say, you're too stupid to understand, but I love you anyway. It will lean down toward Nancy as if to kiss her on the side of her face but Nancy reaches up with her hand and guides the angel's lips toward her own. She kisses and holds the angel in that kiss. The angel's wings flutter and pull at the air. They fluster the grasses in the meadow. And still, Nancy continues to kiss. She is holding the angel's head with both her hands now. She wants this useless creature to know her pain, to feel it, to comprehend the idea of want and need and desire. She is offering the tangible, everything she knows of corporal and tactile pleasure. The angel lifts ever-so-slightly from the ground and Nancy is pulled upward. Her right arm reaches around the angel's neck and shoulder. Her feet slip from her shoes and they fall askew into the grassy meadow. Nancy smells cinnamon and nutmeg. She smells clean sheets. She smells sickly sweet and cold and bitter. Her feet kick at the air and still she kisses. She kisses with her tongue and her lips, and in her mind she is touching this angel. She is moving her fingers and hands in and out of delight. She is teasing with her tongue in a thousand folds. She is tasting the fetid and the sweet and everything in between, and she is not judging. She is grinding herself into this angel's pelvis, pushing through nothing, and sensuality, and pleasure, and directly through pain and back to pleasure. She is ecstatic and naked on top of the angel, thrusting her sex, or inviting the thrust of sex, she can't tell anymore. She has moved beyond her tipping point, she has lost control and she is devoured by her own pleasure.

When Nancy stops kissing the angel, she can feel the grass tickling her bare feet. They land back in the grassy meadow. The angel steps back, its eyes wide and frightened. It positions itself sideways and reaches for its sword.

"What was that?" it asks.

Nancy is bent over and she is pushing her toes into one of her pumps. "That was proof that you don't know anything," she says. "You may listen but you know nothing."

．．．．．．．

The disorder of darkness? This idea didn't stop you? It didn't make you wonder? How in the hell can darkness be disordered? Darkness is a blank wall. Darkness is nothingness. Darkness is the absence of light. Unless there is something in the darkness that can fall out of order. But how would you know this?

．．．．．．．

"Are you hungry?" Nancy says. "I'm hungry."

"No," Ray says. "I'm not hungry." He looks up the street at the businesses across from her building. He never noticed the café on the corner before – it has an angled entrance like *Les Deux Magots* in Paris, with the sweeping awning across the front. It's *Café Americana*, and it has a patio on both sides of its main door and the patio is pulled in tight against the building. Next to the *Café Americana* is a place called the *Salad Shoppe* – a chain of some kind. Then a dry cleaner, a cellphone store, and something that looks like a massage parlour called *Classy Business*. At the end of the row there is a small Thai restaurant called *Numchok Wilai Thai Cuisine*.

"Ever been to that Thai restaurant at the end of the block?"

"My ex-husband tried to kill me in that restaurant." Her voice is level and matter-of-fact.

"You mean he wanted to kill you. You mean you had an argument. Right?"

"No, I mean he tried to kill me. It was the best Thai food I'd ever tasted. It was so good. And then I was sprawled on top of it and couldn't breathe. He was strangling me and there was food everywhere. I think I blacked out. I must have blacked out. There are bits I don't remember."

"So your marriage wasn't fine?"

"What?"

"When you called the day after the hockey game, I told you my marriage was fine and you said your marriage was just fine too and that's why it ended." He remembers this conversation because it tipped him over. It caused him to question, and doubt.

"That was a clever thing to say wasn't it?"

"So why did your husband try to kill you in a Thai restaurant."

"The usual…you know? Husbands and wives fight sometimes. And sometimes, things get out of hand."

"Okay, for the record, strangling your wife is not the usual. But you already know this. And why have I never heard about this before?"

"It's not something I like to talk about. And anyway, you and I don't have those kinds of conversations."

"Okay. Let me ask you a direct question. Why do you think your husband tried to kill you?"

"He was using me to shelter money, and my name was standing as the only contact for a couple numbered companies. I felt he was taking advantage of me. I felt used."

"Okay."

"So I transferred most of the money into my own account in the Cayman Islands, for safe-keeping." She pauses, takes a breath. "And he took offence."

"You have a bank account in the Cayman Islands?"

"I have two accounts in the Cayman Islands and one in Luxembourg. I told him over dinner. He didn't like it."

"So how much did you transfer?" Ray realizes he's likely pushing it but he had no idea about this side of her. "You don't have to answer if you don't want to. I'm just curious. Probably too curious."

"Nine hundred and sixty," she says.

"Your husband tried to kill you over a thousand bucks?" There's no way a guy tosses his wife onto a table and tries to kill her for a thousand dollars. There must be something else. Ray is thinking the guy was just a controlling asshole. It had to be something other than that paltry amount of money.

She giggles. "Thousand," she says. "Nine hundred and sixty thousand."

He tries to grasp that number, and what it might mean to have it and then lose it. "Did you…did you have to give that money back?"

"What money?"

"The money you transferred?"

"What money?" she says. "The money that was in my bank account? The money I wasn't supposed to know about? That money?"

Ray has the impulse to check his bank accounts, to make sure his paltry investments are still there. "So what happened after the restaurant?"

"A couple things. First, I had a difficult time convincing the police that my husband and I were role playing – that we liked kinky sex and this was part of our thing. I saved his ass. They really wanted to put him in jail."

"And second?"

"He moved out and I called my brother in New York," she says. "I'm going to eat a banana."

"What?"

"I'm going to eat a banana. If you want to go to the café and eat something, you can. But keep talking to me."

Ray looks at the café and shrugs. He can get a drink there, and maybe something to eat. He would certainly like a drink.

....

He sits under the awning, close to the windows and his waitress is young. She is wearing a tight black dress and heels. Ray notices all the waitresses at *Café Americana* are wearing tight black dresses and heels. He asks for a glass of pinot noir and she does not hesitate to tell him what they have by the glass, and to point out her favourite. Ray orders a nine-ounce glass.

"Is she cute?" Nancy asks.

"She's hideously ugly," Ray says.

"So, gorgeous then."

Ray thinks the waitress has lovely curves, and her eyes are curious and kind. She is not so young that this job is just an inconvenient stop on the way to some better place. There was nobody else sitting on the patio and this emptiness makes it beautiful because it's filled with potential. Ray decides this café could use some blankets for the chairs. When he was in Zurich a few years ago, Ray noticed there were neatly folded blankets on the chairs at the outside tables of the cafés and restaurants – and people used them. The blankets folded over each chair made the cafés welcoming.

"You should order some food," Nancy says. "You have to eat."

"And once I've had a bite to eat, and finished my wine, I have to go."

"No, you don't."

"Yes, I do. I can't keep this up indefinitely."

"Did you say I can't keep up this infidelity?"

"No. That's not..." Ray wonders if she's threatening now.

Ray sighs. "Yes, I've been unfaithful. You haven't been unfaithful to anybody. I actually don't need to be reminded about my less-than-up-standing character."

The curvy waitress looks over at him from behind the bar and he holds up his wine glass – nods for another.

A woman carrying a black poodle walks by the café. A man with a large backpack rides by on a bicycle. A woman wearing a sweater that falls to her ankles drags two children by their stick arms down the sidewalk. She is in a hurry; her children are not. Ray gets a different view of the street from where he is sitting. He can see the line of elms and the way the elevation rises up toward the west. The trees blur the idea of perspective – they meld together in a mass of green and pending yellow.

....

Seven weeks ago, Ray met with the engineers about the elms on a different street. It was a 7:30 a.m. meeting. He did not like morning meetings and he was a bit grumpy about this one

Ray sat alone on one side of a boardroom table. On the other side, there were three engineers. Adam Farnsworth was the executive director – the buck stopped with him. He was a bald, short man with thick-framed glasses who loved to get down to business. He was intolerant of long, imprecise meetings. He wore the title of engineer, and the iron ring of that calling, with pride – and he had a reputation as a curious and passionate problem solver.

"I'm not just talking about this one project," Ray said. "I'm looking for a solution for every project."

"What you're asking is not feasible." It was one of the junior engineers, a new guy named Charlie Masterson who brought the biggest pile of paper to the meeting – as if there was an award for the person with the biggest pile of paper on the table in front of them. Charlie was young and intense and fashionable in his checked shirt, skinny tie and narrow trousers, and this made him unlike any engineer Ray knew.

"It needs to be feasible," Ray said. "I'm looking for a solution to a problem. This city needs to build sidewalks in mature neighbourhoods without killing the trees that line those sidewalks."

Charlie picked up a binder. "We adhere to the guidelines…"

"…I've read your guidelines."

"You read the guidelines?" Charlie said. He either doesn't believe Ray, or he's impressed.

"Well, let me see. That binder you're waving around the room is the *Sidewalk Design, Construction and Maintenance Manual – a best practice for sustainable municipal infrastructure,* by the National Association of Construction Engineers. Those guidelines talk about attractive and functional sidewalks that promote the benefits of walking and that decrease our reliance on automobiles. They talk about designing sidewalks for the mobility and visually impaired. They talk about strollers, and bicycles, and construction recommendations. Space recommendations. Concrete specs. Asphalt specs. The guide tells you how to build a great sidewalk but it never mentions the value and beauty of an eighty-year-old tree."

Charlie looked at his boss, Adam Farnsworth, who was nodding silently.

"We do our best to save as many trees as we can," Charlie said.

"I know you do, but I think we can do better. The guidelines don't acknowledge mature neighbourhoods with mature trees and that's a problem. There's a thing called the protected root zone and your sidewalks – the way they're designed now – infringe on that zone, every single time."

"There's no other way to build a proper sidewalk…we have to dig."

"Look, right now, the way we replace sidewalks in mature neighbourhoods is like performing a surgery where the operation goes perfectly but the patient dies."

"What?"

"I'm asking for you to build a brilliant sidewalk and save the trees that line that sidewalk. I think we need to consider the bigger picture when it comes to neighbourhoods. An eighty-year-old elm is worth more than a perfectly constructed sidewalk."

"What?"

"Trees. They're not mentioned in the guidelines. Not one mention of trees. I'm thinking it was an oversight."

"Adam?" Charlie said. "If we don't do this right, we'll be back in ten years replacing sidewalks. Maybe less than ten years."

Adam played with the ring on his pinky finger, twirling it back and forth.

Ray smiled. "I didn't say it was going to be easy."

"At this moment, you're asking for something impossible. And impossible is always expensive. We haven't even run the numbers. Have you considered the cost?"

"Look Charlie, I don't need an answer right now. I just want you to take it to a couple meetings and see if you can solve the problem." Ray paused, remembering it was easier to catch flies with honey than with vinegar. "You're the best engineers in the city," he said, "if not the country. And I need your help."

"We'll look at it again," Charlie said. "That's all I can say."

"Before you go, I have something for you. It's a report on the benefits of mature trees. It talks a lot about the fact that the shade from urban street trees can add as much as sixty percent to the life of asphalt. Something to do with reduced daily heating and cooling." Ray handed each of the engineers a copy of the report.

The engineers stood up and so did Ray. He shook their hands as they left the room. Ray honestly did not know if he made an impression. Adam Farnsworth was the one he needed to convince and he was silent during the meeting.

Ray was alone in the conference room. He stood in the window and looked down. He has always liked the view from the forty-second floor. There are some mornings when he comes in and the sunrise is there in his window. Nine times out of ten, Ray would swirl his chair around and look at it. It was his meditation on morning light. Even though there might be a few executive assistants stomping into work in their runners and dresses, they knew not to bother him. No one came to his door with a good morning until mid-morning and by then he'd be getting ready to go out on one of the trucks with a crew to work with trees.

....

Ray decides he can do this – he can convince Nancy to go to bed and wake up in the morning, and then, to keep moving forward. He is realistic and reasonable about it and he knows he can convince her that it's logical to stay alive. "Let me tell you something," Ray says. "There is nothing pretty about what you're talking about. There's a horrifying, terrifying, ugly fall and then a splat, like someone dropping a sack of potatoes."

"Why are you...what are you doing?"

"I want you to understand that thirty-nine stories is a long time."

"I know where I am, Ray. Why are you telling me this? Why are you ruining this for me?"

"Because there is nothing beautiful about death and death is what you're talking about."

"I don't care. I won't care."

"I just want you to understand that this is an ugly business you're contemplating."

"I know what I'm doing," she says.

"Good, because I'm going to leave soon."

Nancy is quiet and Ray is hoping her silence is a tacit approval, or at least, understanding.

"Did you eat your banana?"

"Yes. I ate a banana. Are you going to eat something?"

"No. Just wine for me."

"Don't you think you should have something to eat? When was the last time you ate?"

"I don't want any food." Even he can hear the hard edge to his voice. He is not in the mood to be mothered.

"I think it will snow today, later, tonight," she says.

"And now we're talking about the weather?"

"Well it's better than being morbid and disgusting."

"Nancy, I did not tell you it would be a good idea to jump off your balcony."

"So? What does that mean?"

"It means that if anyone is morbid here, it's the woman in the mirror."

"I love it when it's snowing," she says.

"Hmmm," he says. It's more a grunt than anything. He can't believe his good fortune – two women in his life who love the snow.

"What does that mean?"

"What?"

"That sound you just made. That grunt."

"Nothing. I was just acknowledging your love of the snow."

"But I don't love the snow. I only love it when it's snowing."

CHAPTER 12

Tulah at 29

Tulah's Snow Journal
Monday, March 22, 2004 #267

I'm watching it through a hospital window and it's blowing sideways. It's slanted and hard...I don't want this baby to be born into snow like this. The snow started after we got to the hospital, and I insisted that Ray take me out into it because I had to feel it on my face before she was born. The nurses looked at us like we were crazy. Ray told them I loved snow. It's true. I do love the snow. One of the nurses asked how far apart my contractions were and I think I yelled at her, 'They're not my contractions! They're just contractions! They don't belong to me! Now, I'm going out into the snow, for a minute. I'll be right back.' The nurse insisted on coming with us. 'Fine,' I said. 'Put on a coat. It's snowing!'

Outside the main door of the women's pavilion, with a nurse and Ray, the snow changed. It was as if God inhaled and then exhaled slowly. The snow was falling down steadily. It was gentle and kind. As if someone was listening to the inside of my head. Of course we all looked up.

I asked the nurse what her name was.

She looked at me. 'Frances Marie,' she said.

I closed my eyes for a few seconds. I thought about Grandma Frannie. Her face in the snow. The taste of her tea. The feel of her hand in mine. Then I got whacked by another contraction — like a jolt of electricity through my body. It was one massive spasm. I think I moaned. I couldn't help it. Frances Marie's face switched from a kind of wonder-filled bliss, to all business and I was wheeled into the hospital and the birthing show began.

I do not remember the pain. I have words to describe it, but the pain itself is not a real memory. It was painful, but the actual pain? Nothing.

....

Patience Marie is born at 3:15 a.m. on the fourth floor of the Holy Trinity Hospital on Spadina Avenue. Around thirty-six weeks, they discovered she was turned around in the birth canal so they performed an external cephalic version, which applies pressure to the abdomen and manually manipulates the baby into a head-down position. It worked and though there was a risk of the baby rotating back into a breech position, Patience stayed put.

Tulah wanted to do it without drugs and that's exactly what happened. She and Ray breathed together, and she squeezed his hand until he couldn't feel it anymore. They played Van Morrison's *Astral Weeks,* over and over.

Patience came into the world and Ray felt a jolt of protectiveness for his daughter. He was not expecting this protectiveness to be as intense as it was. It extended not just for his daughter, but for all daughters. All girls, and young women and women in general. He could feel an instinct to shelter and protect slip into place.

The baby is settled beside them in a crib and they are exhausted. Ray crawls onto the bed beside Tulah and they both drift off. At some point, a nurse brings a warm blue blanket and covers Ray. She is so gentle. He feels it but can't will himself to wake up and say thank you. The gratefulness he feels for the blanket gets melded together with his gratefulness for Tulah, and a healthy baby daughter and the murky subconsciousness pulling him down into sleep.

In the morning, Ray kisses Tulah's forehead. He kisses his daughter and walks three blocks through virgin snow to a Starbucks. The air is wet-grey and cool, and he is happy making the first imprints in the snow. On his way back, he can see a rabbit has crossed his path. He wonders if this is lucky – a sign of some kind. He decides it's a good thing.

"Can we make one of her names – Frannie?"

"Patience Marie Frannie Roberts-Daniels?"

"Too much?"

"A little, I think. But we can go back to the drawing board with the name."

"No," Tulah says. "I love Patience Marie."

When Tulah drifts into sleep, Ray picks Patience up and holds her against his chest. He wants her to feel his breathing – the rhythm of his life, something. She is swaddled and sleeping, and after a while he starts to sing – a low and soft rendition of *Itsy Bitsy Spider.*

·······

Sarah was born about a year later, on April 16th. The sky was the colour of zinc and it was raining. On the way to the hospital, the windshield wipers working as hard as they could, Tulah wondered about precipitation and giving birth, and how she and her babies fit with snow and rain. They get out of the car and the rain smell is a heady balm.

They played William Byrd's *Mass for Four Voices* throughout the labour. It was if they were walking in a dream, or through a dream. The music made it feel holy. When Sarah was safely delivered, and the cord cut, Tulah burst into laughter. She laughed and cried and it threatened to be an incontrollable laughter. A nurse whose name was Grace brought her a cup of chamomile tea and she calmed down until she was just crying.

Ray tried to sing *Itsy Bitsy Spider* to Sarah. He thought it would be a nice tradition, a common thread between sisters, but it just woke her up. He walked with Sarah. He took her on a walk through the hospital corridors at 2 a.m., and this movement calmed her.

The next day, they were home and their family was one more.

CHAPTER II

Yellow Flowers

"Onion treats seven ailments"
– *Zhanna Petya*

Two months into their affair, Ray brings Nancy flowers. He thinks the gift of flowers is a simple thing. He finds a bouquet of yellow freesia at a sidewalk vendor and Nancy seems pleased, at first, but then she unwraps them. Her initial delight turns to anger.

She drops the bouquet on the counter as if it is a rotten fish and steps back. "You bought yellow flowers," she says.

"Yes. Freesia. They smell amazing."

"These are yellow flowers," she says. "Yellow is for funerals."

"What?"

"In Russia, yellow flowers are only for funerals." Then she is bent over and counting the stems and when she stands up straight, she is shaking with anger. "Ten," she says. "There's an even number, Ray. Even numbers of flowers are for the dead. You must never give flowers in even numbers, unless someone has died."

"I am so sorry. I didn't know."

"Go home, Ray. It's ruined. No one is dead here but you have behaved as if someone is dead." Nancy bursts into Russian and Ray has no idea what she's saying. He can't quite figure out if she's serious. It would be an amazing prank, but there's something shaky and crazy in her voice. Her voice is all edge and danger.

"I am so sorry…"

"…You could not know, unless you went to a Russian florist. But it does not matter. The insult is done and this is all ruined." She steps open the garbage pail, dumps the flowers, and lets the lid slam down. "It is insulting to give flowers like this. You must leave now." She's thinking that if she were truly important to him, he would have known about the yellow flowers. He could have asked questions, or looked it up. Only an imbecile would give an even number of yellow flowers to a Russian woman as a romantic gesture. To buy flowers without thinking beyond the fact they smell good is uncaring and stupid.

Ray steps backwards into the hallway and Nancy shuts the door. He stands in the hallway, looking at the door. He looks at the brass plate with the number 3903 on it. He wonders if perhaps she is looking through the peephole at him.

He's confused. What's ruined? This moment? Everything? She said it was all ruined. Does that mean they're done with each other? Because of yellow flowers? The bile of anger rises in his chest. This is irrational and illogical. The flowers were a gift and she'd rejected this gift based on a cultural transgression he could not be expected to know. In the elevator, he's pissed off.

Nancy is sitting on the floor, her back against the door, sobbing. She is back in time, at her father's funeral. The soldiers in their drab, green uniforms and Russian military fur ushanka hats. The funeral march was plodding and dark and minor keyed. And there were yellow flowers everywhere. Nancy was standing beside herself, watching her body be still. This means her papa is not going to catch her anymore. He will not be there to catch her at the back entrance. This means they will no longer skip stones by the river. She is holding two flowers. One of the soldiers gave her these flowers and they were both yellow.

．．．．．．．

"Tell me how you ended up like this, Ray. How are you able to do this? The lies. The hundreds of dishonesties. The stolen time. All of it."

"You mean, how can I do this to myself?"

"Is that what I meant? I thought I meant lying to your wife, sneaking around and being despicable, living this falsity. Is falsity a word?"

"I feel like you were asking about me, about what I was doing to myself."

"So you think the promises you made in your wedding ceremony were meaningless? Do you even remember what it's like to be truthful?"

Ray thinks about Lime Kiln Valley and the Mexican pickers. He can see Pastor Bob's face, Jesús playing his guitar and that woman

– Jesús's fiancée – who wouldn't stop crying. He remembers the dry purity of the air and he remembers Tulah's body in her little black dress. He remembers that night as she wriggled out of her dress – and let it slip to a puddle of black fabric at her feet. Kissing Tulah wiped away the world. When they kissed it was as if the world pulled back and let their kissing fill new space. His world was just Tulah's needy mouth. Just her skin. Just her quickened breath.

He waits for Nancy to say something and then there is an explosion on the road beside his car. The sound of glass breaking and shards of glass hitting the metal car door like frozen rain on a tin roof. Ray stops breathing. It's not her, he thinks. Please, please, please let that not be her.

All his mind will allow is that she has jumped and hit a car and the spray of glass is from the impact. Ray takes a breath, and places his hand on the door handle. He looks back and around through the windows and can't see anything out of place. People are walking on the sidewalk. There's a woman with five dogs on leashes yanking her down the sidewalk. A bike courier wearing shorts – his satchel across his back. A mom with a baby strapped to her chest. Everything is as it should be.

If that was not the sound of a body, what was it? He brings the phone back to his ear.

"Nancy?"

Silence.

"Nancy?"

"Did you get that?" she says.

"What the hell!? What did you do?"

"I really wanted that to land on your car."

"What was it?"

"That was the last of the good scotch glasses – the chunky expensive ones. Do I have your attention now?"

A wave of relief moves through him. "Jesus Christ, Nancy. You could have killed someone." He takes a full breath and he notices his breathing is shaky. Darkness looms up in the back of his mind – a chorus is chanting the mantra – *This is not going to end well, this is not going to end well.* As if the outcome of this conversation is a given. As if there's nothing he can do. It will all come back to that hockey game where they met and flirted. It will come back to the first time he kissed Nancy, and the first time he made love with her. He will fixate on all those tipping-point decisions. These flash-points of memory will be terrible and they will reverberate in him.

She speaks slowly. "Do I have your attention?"

"For Christ's sake, Nancy. Yes. Stop being so dramatic."

"So, tell me, how are you able to do this?" She really does wonder how he manages to push his life aside, for her.

"She doesn't know," he says. "That's how I can do it. It's between you and me. Tulah doesn't know."

Nancy cringes at the sound of Ray's wife's name. It's an involuntary twinge in the middle of her back.

"I'm sorry, Nancy."

"Don't be sorry. Just leave your wife and be with me. That will solve everything." She has never been so blunt, but what does she have to lose?

"I have kids. I have daughters. If you had kids you would understand..."

Nancy could have had a daughter, or a son. She was pregnant once, with the investment banker's baby, and she had a miscarriage. It was a year after they were married and she still did not know about the papers he was having her sign every month. She was lost after the miscarriage. She did not know if she wanted to try again to have a baby. She felt betrayed by her own body and devastated by the loss. She sunk into a darkness that was so deep, she didn't recognize herself. She lived at the edge of taking her own life. She thought about it every day, first thing in the morning, and last thing at night. She wrote lists of all the different ways she could imagine to kill herself. She thought about it at noon, and mid-morning and mid-afternoon. Her doctor prescribed *Lexapro*, which seemed to help her mood. And then *Ambien*, because she started to not be able to sleep.

If her child had been born, and she had stayed with her husband, she likely would not have had this affair with Ray. Of course, this is a ridiculous speculation. Her life would have been different and she and Ray likely would not have met. She was surprised at her own behaviour when she kept pursuing Ray even after he told her he was married. She completely disregarded the wife. She negated his children. She just didn't care. It shocked her, at first, but after a few months, she became accustomed to it. She acclimatized. It was a cold, delicate game of denial and artifice.

Not for the first time in this conversation, Ray is astounded, shocked that he has landed here, in a car on 4th Avenue talking with a woman thirty-nine stories above him who has threatened to jump. He somehow moved so far away from Tulah. Did they stop talking? Did they stop being husband and wife? To say it's because sex with his wife was a mine field of disappointment and frustration was only part of the picture. There was a growing contempt that seemed to be accepted – the swept-under comments that were mean but were also unacknowledged. They both did it. It was the unspoken territory under their civility. Inside this unspoken territory there was the ongoing question of marriage and sex. If the sex dries up, is the marriage invalid? Or do things change and you have to learn to deal with it? Surely, love is more than fleshy union. He tells himself to stop being so shallow. But then, he hasn't given up on sex. He's had Nancy for the past year.

"I won't make any trouble, Ray," Nancy says. "I'll go away like a good mistress. You don't have to worry. But you changed the rules of your marriage, Ray. And then you weren't honest about it."

"What?"

"You broke the rules. Of your marriage. Marriages have rules."

"You'd be surprised the things a marriage can withstand."

"You mean secrets piled on top of secrets piled on top of lies?"

"Yes." He thinks about the word mendacity. He thinks about the speech Big Daddy delivers in *Cat on a Hot Tin Roof*, in which he uses the word "mendacity." Ray had looked it up.

....

"Ray?"

"I'm here. Yes. I'm here." His back hurts from sitting in the car for so long.

"I'm sorry your marriage is flawed."

"It's not that simple," Ray says. "And anyway, all marriages are flawed. And besides, why do I have to have a reason?"

"I'm curious, that's all. I want to understand this. I want to know why you fool around on your wife. Is it just the sex?"

"No. It's more complicated than I can say, but I think I'm okay with no sex."

"You think you're okay? You're okay masturbating your way toward death?"

"Yes. That's what I tell myself. I'm okay not having sex. And the more I tell myself this, the more it becomes true. It's like how when you tell a really good lie, and if you keep telling it, it starts to become true."

"So you're not okay with a sexless marriage."

"Would you be okay?"

"I'm just sleeping with a married guy. Why are you sleeping with a Russian woman?"

Ray thinks about curiosity. He wants to believe it's because he is curious about women – he is curious about all women. He wants to know their smells and sounds and the smoothness of their skin. He loves to discover what they look like at dusk, or in the middle of night by candlelight. He wants to experience the scents, the moans and the smallest intimacies. He wants to lean back against the headboard with a glass of wine and watch them get dressed, or undressed. He wants to discover their scars, and creases.

"I'm curious about women," he says. "It's a bit of an unquenchable curiosity..."

"...and I am a woman so I qualify for your curiosity? I have a vagina so you were curious about me."

"Yes," he says. "You also have a mind, and an imagination, and a personality..."

"...Okay, okay, that's honest," she says. "A little bit appalling, but honest."

"You came after me," Ray says. "You called me the day after the hockey game. You reminded me that my marriage was only fine."

"Guilty," she says. "Guilty as charged." She raises her glass in a small toast to Ray's truth.

....

Ray looks at the hazy reflected image of himself in his car window. He's not sure about the question of why he wound up with a mistress but he is certain that he really enjoys making love. He wonders if this desire to give pleasure, this need for touch, and tenderness, is such a bad thing, or if it's wrong. Because it doesn't feel wrong. It feels horribly off course but it does not feel wrong.

10½

Milaya

What? Did you think there would be anything resembling a straight line in this book? Don't you want to know what really happened to Anatoly? You remember the Kapitán, don't you? The soldier who delivered the news of Nancy's father's death? The one who gave her that watch? As if the watch was some sort of compensation for her father.

....

After three months of reading, drinking, and barely eating, the Kapitán sits at the wooden table and starts to write a letter to the girl. He knows she will likely not get it, but perhaps with what he remembers, and what he writes, someone will find the letter and figure out how to deliver it to the right girl. He remembers the name of her father, barely. And Kursk is not a big city. Perhaps the letter will find its way to the child.

It is snowing, hard, and it is bitterly cold. Twice he has tried to walk to the village for food but turned back because the snow was too deep and he did not have the proper boots or a winter coat to make such a journey. Not even a kilometre from the dacha, he could feel the cold burrowing into his bones and he did not have the energy to fight it, so he turned around.

Anatoly is warm, as fire wood is abundant and stacked along the sheltered wall of the dacha, but this is a small consolation against his hunger.

He looks at the paper on the table and wonders if perhaps he could eat it. But he is not so desperate. Not yet. He has plenty of water, and he is using it to dilute the vodka, which goes straight to his head anyway.

Milaya, he writes, because he does not know her name. He stops. He does not know if she was a 'sweet girl.' She could have been a shit of a horrid little girl. She only looked like a sweet girl. He shakes his head. He leaves 'Milaya' and carries on.

Milaya. Hello. My name is Anatoly. You will probably not remember me, as there was a lot to process when I met you, but I am the one who gave you the wrist watch you are (hopefully) wearing. It does not matter if you don't remember me. I am not offended by this. I have a forgettable face. I am also the one who brought the news about your father. I am so sorry, milaya. I know it makes no sense that your father would go away to Afghanistan to fight in a war about nothing and for nothing but the hazy sense of an insecure ideology. A senseless war in which so many men, women and children died. I know, milaya, this does not make you feel any better about your father's death. All war is senseless. All war is barbaric. No one ever wins a war. Once a country goes to war, even if they win the war, they've lost the war. But you do not need lectures about the futility of war. You know this first-hand.

I am writing you because I know some things about your father that you should also know. I had the opportunity to read his entire record before arriving on your doorstep. I have to tell you, your father was not a good soldier. He did not follow orders. You were not told that your father was reprimanded two times. In the short time he was in Afghanistan, he was written up two times for disobeying orders and going out of his way to rescue civilians. The first time, he saved two boys and their mother. They were too terrified to move, despite loud warnings in many languages that the building in which they were hiding was about to be destroyed. The second time, he went into a house where he found a small girl, and her grandmother who could not walk by herself. The house had not been cleared. The commanders thought the sound of a crying girl could have been a trap. Nobody wanted to go inside and find out if it was a trap, or not. His commander wanted to throw grenades first and ask questions later. But your father stood up and walked toward the sound of the crying girl. He went in and his comrades held. They waited to throw their grenades. They waited for him to come out, or to be killed. The commander was not pleased about this.

The third time, well, you know what happened the third time.

Here is my theory on the matter. I think your father was saving you, little one. He was at war but he kept saving you. I think he kept asking himself what he would want to happen if this was his little girl, or boy, or mother, or wife and then he acted accordingly. He acted without fear and with a single purpose. He did not think, 'this is the enemy.' He thought, 'this is my family.' Some part of him recognized these people as his human family and in the middle of a bloody war, he acted out of love.

Anatoly's stomach growls. He looks out the window at the falling snow and the cool grey light. Tomorrow, he will have to get to the village despite his inadequate footwear, and lack of a winter coat, and despite his waning energy for such a trip. If he does not eat soon, he will not have the strength to try to get to the village.

He places the pen on the page. He can't finish the letter today. He is too distracted by his empty stomach.

CHAPTER 10

The Lover

The whole city has been waiting for this. No one likes a brown Christmas. Or a green Christmas. But the way we're rushing pell-mell toward burning as much fossil fuel as we can, as quickly as we can, it's just a matter of time before snow becomes a rare and wondrous thing. This morning, there were people up and down the block sitting on their front steps drinking coffee and reading, or smoking, or just talking. It was +6C and overcast — everyone looking up and wondering if maybe tonight it will come. Around 4 p.m., the temperature starts to fall. It's not a dive, it's more like a sigh, and suddenly, you could see your breath. Around 7 p.m., it starts to snow. A sprinkle. A few flakes first, twirling through the cool air, then a few more, then a steady fall. The first flakes melt into the ground but after an hour, the snow is too much and it starts to accumulate...

....

When Tulah is thirty-two years old, her lover gives her lingerie for Christmas, which is stupid because if she wears it in front of Ray, she'll be forced to lie. She could. It's not that she couldn't lie. It's just that lingerie was one step over the line. It's a lie that would be complex and it would carry the threat of unravelling. It would be a repugnant lie. The lingerie was a sensual, sexual, intimate gift. The Lover's intentions were fine, but his instincts were faulty. If she took this lingerie into her everyday life, it would be an unforgiveable intrusion. It was too much. Lingerie had implications she could not reconcile.

She meets him in a Holiday Inn near the airport, three days before Christmas. Her mother is watching the girls and Tulah tells everyone she is doing last-minute Christmas shopping. It is their seventh time together. Tulah had promised herself it would be okay – she could absolutely acknowledge it as a horrible mistake if she met him only three times at most, then four, then six. Now it was no longer possible to think of her behaviour as a mistake. She was doing this on purpose, because she wanted it. She was ashamed and excited and insatiable.

The third time they met was at the Hilton, uptown. He ordered a bottle of Grey Goose vodka and they drank shots sitting and looking out across the city skyline. He'd asked her about her husband and Tulah thought it was over. If they made the husband real, how could they possibly go on?

"He's a good father," she said. "And a decent human being."

The Lover poured her another shot of vodka. "Is he mean to you ever?"

"Mean? No. But, don't all marriages get a little mean as they age?"

"Perhaps. But he doesn't beat you, does he? He's not cruel?"

"Why are we talking about my husband? I don't want to talk about my husband. Let's pretend there is no husband."

"I was curious about why you were here, with me, in this hotel. I think I need a reason."

Tulah takes a breath. "I'm here because I feel broken. I feel lost and really fucking alone sometimes." The tears stream down her cheeks. "It has nothing to do with my husband."

"I'm sorry." He pulls her toward him and she rests her head on his chest. "I am sorry."

....

This was not just lingerie. It was La Perla – Italian and expensive. A grey-blue body-suit that played with shadows and lace. It was stunning and she did not want to know what it cost. She wore it for him. She tried to tell herself the lingerie made her feel sexy, but that wasn't it – meeting an almost stranger in hotel room for sex made her feel sexy. For a little while, she was not a mother to two daughters. Nor was she a wife. She was nothing but passion and desire. She was something uncontained and wild. The Lover told her he expected nothing and this lack of expectation burst the bounds of possibility. It seemed they both showed up because they wanted to and that was everything.

The Lover has a flight to New York at 6 p.m. He turns in the doorway. His eyes are grey in this light. His face softens as he smiles and then he is gone. Tulah does not get out of bed. She feels horrible and alone. She closes her eyes and begins to regret this betrayal. The fact she's lying to everyone – her mother, her kids, Ray's mother, Ray. Everyone she cares about. And why? Because she feels she needs a couple hours of pleasure from an uncomplicated man. Because when she is with The Lover, she could reinvent herself – she could be someone new – and sometimes she yearned to be someone new. But it was never a full meal. The Lover was thorough and generous, but it was never enough. There was an elemental part missing. There was no past, and certainly no future. It's not that Tulah wanted to live in the past or in the future, but she liked the potential of them in the room with her. It was comforting. In fact, these hotel meetings always left her feeling emptier and more alone than she could imagine, and ultimately, stranded inside a world she wanted no part of.

"I will not do this again," she says into the empty room. "I will never do this again." This is the same mantra she has spoken the past six times. It has become her perpetual assurance – if she says it, she will be with The Lover again. It has become the opposite of the meaning of the words that form it.

She raids the mini-bar and makes herself a double gin and tonic. The Lover puts these rooms on his corporate card. He would insist she help herself. She has one sip and pours the drink down the drain. She does not want to be drunk, or even tipsy. In the shower, she lets the temperature become hotter than comfortable – to the point of being painfully hot. She wants to scald away any trace of him. She is disgusted with herself and at the same time, she is thinking about the next time. She does not hesitate to embrace the delusion that there is something fulfilling yet to be discovered with The Lover. She stands in the shower until her skin is red and tingling.

Tulah is afraid that some part of her believes she and Ray are at the end of their marriage and that she has lost all hope. She used to know what romantic love was, she could tap into it and easily understand it. Now? It was as if someone was speaking Farsi. She knows how to love her daughters but beyond this love, she is lost. Marriage was a promise against this behaviour but sometimes the boundaries of marriage needed to be tested and it was best to do this behind closed doors. Tulah smiles. She knows this is bullshit. It's a bullshit rationalization but it almost makes her feel better.

She stuffs the lingerie into a plastic bag and slips it into a garbage can in the lobby of the hotel. As she leaves the hotel, she sighs, and shivers, and mourns the lingerie and how it made her feel. But she knows she cannot carry the lingerie forward into her life.

After the girls are in bed, Tulah has another shower. She scrubs herself hard. She soaps and re-soaps, and when she emerges she does not dry off, but jumps into bed and starts to kiss Ray. She kisses his lips, and neck and chest and belly, and she moves him into her mouth. His book falls to the floor and she begins to please him. Ray wants to touch her – he moves his hand around her buttocks, but she tells him *no*. She wants to give him pleasure. This is a one-way street. She needs this. "Be still. Let me do this," she says. Tulah is thorough, and driven, and when Ray is spent, she is happy. She feels close again. It's a frail closeness but it soothes her. She has created a bond, a sanctuary of hope. They have mixed together physically and this is a good thing. They watch TV for a while and Ray falls asleep before her. She turns the TV off. She feels such an overwhelming guilt and it threatens to drag her into darkness. But it is Christmas and the girls are bubbling with excitement. She will smile and be joyous, for them, and she will bubble with excitement, for them. She spoons herself into Ray, finds the place where they fit. Her breathing shudders and she hopes he does not notice. She leans up, touches the top of the clock radio to check that the alarm is set to the correct time, and then turns the radio on and starts to listen to an interview about global warming. She is quickly asleep.

She does not think she is dreaming. It is not that sort of dream. She is on an airplane and she is giving blowjobs to everyone. She keeps her seatbelt on and men come to 6C and line up and wait. The flight attendant announces the woman in seat 6C is giving blowjobs and she's really good. She warns that if the captain puts the seatbelt sign on, everyone will have to move back to their seats and buckle up. Tulah does not look at the faces of the men and she is unable to move her arms. It's as if her arms are paralyzed. She is happy the men are unnamed, and unknown. Everything is simple, except her jaw is tired. After a while, she starts to feel that she might be dreaming. She wonders if these men are all the men she has ever slept with. She wants to look up but she can't. The airplane goes through some turbulence but the line-up of men who are waiting does not decrease. The seatbelt sign goes on but the men in the aisle ignore it. She wonders how long the flight is. She wonders where the airplane is going. She does not remember booking a flight. Tulah has to pee and she begins to worry that she will not be able to get out of her seat and down the aisle in time. She has too much work to do. But she really has to pee.

When she wakes up, she is on the verge of peeing. She hops out of bed and tiptoes quickly into the bathroom. Sitting on the toilet, she remembers her dream. She is relieved it was not real and at the same time, fascinated by her own subconscious.

....

Merry Christmas to you, too. Ray curls on his side. Tulah has surprised him. She wouldn't let him touch her – not this time, and it was amazing. They were both relaxed and it was the perfect antidote to the insanity of Christmas. They've found presents for the girls, their family, and a few friends. They know where the family is going to gather for Christmas dinner. Christmas cards were mailed out weeks ago. And now, if it would only snow.

Tulah tucks herself behind him, fits her body into his and pulls herself tight. She shivers and Ray wonders what it is that is reverberating in her, but lets it go.

....

Lauren Smith storms into the office on a Tuesday morning and demands to see the principal. She has a kid in one of Tulah's classes and she has grave concerns. Tulah knows that every couple years, she'll lose a student or two after her first class, and there were always complaints from parents and sometimes students, who were offended by her insensitivity – by her intolerance and close-mindedness when it came to the idea of creation. Sometimes there were demands that she be fired because of her refusal to acknowledge creation in her science class. Tulah enjoyed these conflicts. She loved the meetings with the principal, the school board, and the indignant parents. Lauren Smith was threatening legal action and demanded a meeting. Tulah was in the middle of her class when she got the call from Principal Hartman.

"In the beginning God created the heaven and the earth," Lauren Smith said. The little sausage-roll curl of hair on her forehead bobbed up and down as she spoke. Tulah found this distracting. "It's in the Bible. God *created* the heavens and the earth."

Behind Lauren Smith, Principal Hartman closed his eyes and tried to even out his breathing.

I wish God would come and create some common sense in this woman right about now, Tulah thought. "That's a beautiful story," she said.

"It's not just a story." Lauren Smith said. "It's our faith. It's what the Bible says. And as a taxpayer, I have a right to insist that it be taught in this school."

"I agree with you," Tulah said. "In fact, it should be taught in every school."

"Oh? I didn't know…" Lauren Smith said, pleased but hesitant. "I'm happy we see eye-to-eye on this…"

"…but not in a science class," Tulah said. "It's theology, not biology. Those are two different things."

"But we *believe* in creation. We believe God created the heavens and the Earth. I want my child to learn about creation."

"Here it comes," Principal Hartman said, quietly.

Tulah wanted to tell this woman the fact she believed in something did not make it true. She stopped herself. She pulled back her gorge. She surprised Principal Hartman. "Well, I don't know what to say. There's some pretty sound evidence to support the idea of evolution. And we're pretty certain Homo Sapiens have been roaming around this planet for at least two hundred thousand years."

"If you're saying gays have been around for two hundred thousand years, well…"

"…Homo sapiens. Not homosexuals. Homo sapiens are humans."

"So you're saying I got gay blood in me?"

"What? No…that's not…That's absurd."

"Look, we believe in creation and I do not think it's too much to ask that creation theory be taught."

"But I teach biology. Biology is a science." She was not condescending. She really believed she could educate.

Lauren Smith turned her back on Tulah and looked directly at Principal Hartman. "This woman thinks we're all homosexuals. I want my son out of this, this person's class."

"Of course, you do, Ms. Smith," the principal said.

Tulah wanted the discussion – the opportunity to teach beyond her students. It would not be so pleasant if her principal wasn't so supportive. Principal Hartman had her back. There was always the option to take Mr. Rubinski's religion course in period six, and of course, Ms. Bergman's science class. Ms. Bergman included a robust discussion of creation in her class. She included it as an alternate theory – she gave it merit.

Every few months Susan Bergman invited Tulah and Ray for dinner and every few months, Tulah declined.

Ray was willing to take a chance on Susan Bergman. He was curious about the potential conversation. "Why don't we go for dinner, just once? Maybe they're really nice."

"Well," Tulah said, "Susan Bergman is an idiot. No matter how nice they are, this simple fact won't change."

"It's one faith-based disagreement. It's nothing."

"It's science, Ray."

"You can't judge a person based on their take on evolution."

"Why not?"

Sometimes, Tulah was more stubborn than Ray thought possible.

....

Ray's mom has cataracts and she needs Ray to drive her to her doctor. The operation to remove her cataracts is in two weeks. He takes the morning off work and picks her up. He watches as she pecks her way, carefully, delicately down the front steps. She is slower now, he thinks.

In the car, he remembers the last time she had struggled with the seatbelt, so he fastens it for her. He clicks her into her seat.

They are downtown, stopped in traffic and Ray's mom turns her body to look at him. She shifts in her seat so that she does not have to turn her neck. As if turning her neck is a difficulty. "Have you ever thought about finding your birth mom?" she says. "I'm not going to live forever, and I believe she loved you."

"I've got one mom," Ray says.

"You would not hurt my feelings if you…"

"…I've got a mom," Ray says.

"But I'm just saying…"

"…I know what you're saying," he says. "I'm just not built that way. I'm curious about the world, but not so much about this. It was enough that there was a letter. I know giving me up was difficult, and it was about love."

"That's all you need?"

"Well, I have you, mom."

"Yes, you do," she says.

CHAPTER 9

Evelyn McHale

"Success and rest don't sleep together"
— *Zhanna Petya*

Imagine a small girl living in an apartment in Kursk, in 1985. Every day her father comes home from work and every day she waits. She is perhaps four years old. At the back entrance there are three steps, and every day the girl leaps from these steps into her papa's arms, and he never fails to catch her. Sometimes he is distracted by life, and hard days at work, and he is caught off guard by his jumping daughter, but it always makes him happy to catch her. She always makes him smile.

Nancy will not remember this when she grows up. It will be the memory of a story told to her by her mother. She will wish it was her own memory, because she can only imagine the feeling of safety in this ritual. To trust this much is incomprehensible to her.

....

"Ray?"

"Yes."

"Do you remember that picture of the woman who jumped off the Empire State Building? The one where she looked like she was asleep on that car? It was like the top of the car made a nest around her body."

"Yes, I remember."

"She looked so peaceful. I'd like to be that peaceful. I love that picture."

Ray knows this picture well. A paragraph in *Life* magazine and the poignant photograph. Her name was Evelyn McHale, and it was May 1, 1947. She jumped from the observation deck of the Empire State Building. She was wearing a red dress – at least modern colour images of the black and white photo made it red. The picture haunted Ray, as it was both captivating and horrifying. Evelyn McHale was an attractive woman who was still clutching her pearl necklace when her body carved out a crumpled metal nest in the top of a car after falling for eighty-six floors. Her feet and ankles were mesmerizing. Her ankles were crossed, as if she was relaxed and at peace – as if she was resting for a while and accidentally fell asleep. This was the mystery of the photo for him. Death and sleep were confused in the moment of this picture. No one knew why she jumped. She was getting married in June, to a guy named Barry. The note she left up top said she didn't think she would make a very good wife – she was too much like her mother and her once-and-future husband would be better off without her. Why would she write: 'Tell my father, I have too many of my mother's tendencies'? What was wrong with her mother? What the hell happened to Evelyn McHale? To everyone in her life, up until that morning, she'd seemed happy.

Eventually, Ray found a pretty good reproduction of the picture, framed it and hung it in his office. It was only half morbid. He made a point of remembering her name. For some reason, Ray could not bear the thought that Evelyn McHale would be forgotten. Even though she wanted to be forgotten, he could not. He knew he was likely not the only person in the world to have been smitten with some sort of feeling for this woman. He understood this and did not care.

"She was dead, too," Ray says. "Yes, she was peaceful looking, but she was also dead. The thing you should know, the thing you can't see in that picture, is that her insides were basically liquefied when she landed. When they tried to move her, everything fell apart. That's not so pretty, is it?" Ray is not entirely certain about this, but it sounds true.

Ray hopes the picture in his office was not an omen of some sort – a bad omen pointing toward this moment.

No, she's playing with him, torturing him – that's all. She will not kill herself over him. She's smarter than that. Ray thinks about his own life – the moments of beauty and grief, sadness and joy – all the things that have given meaning, all the proofs against pointlessness. The birth of the girls. A dinner with a stranger in Macon, France – a woman who told stories about her grandmother meeting Ernest Hemingway in Africa. Sharing a bottle of 1979 *Volnay* with a climbing buddy at the base of Mt. Robson – lugging that bottle up there, along with all the climbing gear – taking the first sip and knowing the extra weight of that glass bottle was worth it. Sitting through the rehearsal of Mahler's *Symphony of a Thousand* in New York, at Carnegie Hall. And he remembers being so deeply moved by a Picasso sketch in an art gallery in Luzern, Switzerland – that he'd changed his flight so he could stay an extra week and visit it a few more times. It was a girl with a narrow face, downcast eyes, and an unsettling sadness. He can still close his eyes and see her.

"Ray!" she says.

"What?"

"What are you doing down there? I asked you a question."

"I'm here. Your voice cut out. I don't know why. What did you ask?"

"I asked you if you would mind coming to my funeral."

"There isn't going to be a funeral, because you're not going to do anything stupid. You're upset, that's all. It's okay to feel sad. It's okay to feel really, really sad. I'm not offering advice but feel whatever you need to feel and then tomorrow morning, move forward. Take a breath and move into the day."

"Hypothetically speaking. If I die before you, would you come?"

"Of course, but that's not going to happen."

He wonders if there is some way he can call the police – tell them he's got this woman on the line who is talking about killing herself and he's worried. But he has only one phone and she is listening to everything he says. He could write a note and pass it to someone on the street, but first he will try to get her to back away from the railing. But what if the police want to interview him, or afterwards, come and talk to him at the house? What if they call him at home? What if one of the cops is virtuous about marriage and decides to 'accidentally' make things right? What if this cop wants to tip the scales back toward truth? Because he will have to explain why and how he is on the phone with Nancy. He will have to use words like *affair* and *mistress* and *married*.

"What is this really about, Nancy? You know I can't stay here all day…"

"…yes you can. You'll stay there for as long as I want you to." Her voice is uplifting and pleasant, which makes it ominous.

....

At the edge of the balcony Nancy looks out over the city. The grey sky is reflected back at her in a thousand cold windows. It's cool enough to snow, maybe. She tests the air to see if she can see her breath. She takes another drink of Ray's goddamned whisky. She thinks about falling through space. She ponders her intention to jump – or rather, fall off the edge. Thirty-nine stories. She will climb over and tuck her toes between the deck and the bottom of the railing. She imagines letting go, falling backward through the air – her stomach fluttering. She will say goodbye to Ray and drop the phone on the balcony floor, and she will let go. After this, nothing she does, or thinks, or feels will matter. Nothing she does matters now. No difference. Hanging on, or letting go. It's the same thing.

"Dasvidaniya," she will whisper, "dasvidaniya."

Once she is falling through space, she will look for acceptance. She will claw her way through fear and find resignation. "Okay," she will say to herself. "Khorosho." Once she has accepted the inevitable, anything will be possible. She can see herself falling through space – a ragdoll tossed into the air. And the wind. The sound of the wind is amazing. And then she is flipping around and simply flying away from her life. Her clothing will dissolve into particles and the air around her will transform into strong wings and she will fly away. Matter will be transformed. She and the air will be the same thing. She will transcend. Somewhere in California, there is a forest that will accept the broken, and the broken-hearted. She will know this in her bones. She will not understand how she came to know it, but it will not matter. Sitting in the high branches of an ancient sequoia near the ocean, she will heal. Sequoias are good for healing and this one is over 3,000 years old. It knows about healing. She will not remember the years that brought her to be in need of healing. Time will not behave in the sequoia forest. Mostly, it will not exist. It will barely tick. The world is irrelevant here. Only breathing is important. After forty years, or thirty months, or perhaps twenty seconds, Nancy will come down from the sequoia and find herself in a small town in Oregon, where she will find work in a daycare. The children in the daycare will love her and she will love them more. She'll rent a flat above a used bookstore. The owner, a large man named Buddy, who owns two albino Dobermans, also runs a small grow-op in the garage behind the bookstore. One day, after Nancy has lived in the town for almost two years, she will meet a seriously happy man named James Finkelstein, who is a lawyer, and she will fall in love with him. The first thing James Finkelstein says to her will be delightfully odd: "It's about time you came down from that sequoia. I've been waiting for you."

She will smile. "Why would you say something like this?"

"Sequoias are ancient and sacred," he will say. "There's something sacred about you."

"But not too ancient, I hope."

He will stick out his hand. "James Finkelstein."

Nancy will recognize the opportunity to reinvent herself in that moment.

"Zhanna," she'll say. This is her mother's name. "I am Zhanna."

They will have four children – two girls, two boys. It will be the right time, and the right man. She will give birth with a midwife named Sunshine. Only the fourth baby will need more than a midwife – he will be born in St. Joseph Hospital, in Eureka. Nancy will be happy in Oregon. She will grow to love the rain and the colour green. She will wake up every morning and laugh.

At the edge of the balcony, Nancy wipes the tears from her face. She loves this imagined life in Oregon – it makes her happy, and sad. She is only sad about it because she knows how desperately far away it is. It is such a far-flung dream.

She has probably never seen a sequoia tree but she thinks she would like to see one. It's difficult to fathom a tree that is thousands of years old – a tree that was alive when Jesus was traipsing around the deserts of Galilee taking about love and peace, and heavenly kingdoms. She shakes the balcony railing with one hand. It does not budge.

....

In mid-May, Ray arrived at work with a question. "Listen," he said to an elm tree on Euclid Avenue. "I know you probably know nothing about love, about romance, about women, but you have seventy years, maybe a few more, of watching, so perhaps you know a little about human behaviour." Ray closed his eyes and felt the sway of the bucket. He could easily imagine the tree wanting to tell him about a car that stopped at its base a week ago – a man and woman having a horrible argument on their way to a party. The man is furious. The woman is indignant and stubborn. She has an accent – Polish, or Russian, or Hungarian – the tree can't be sure. They are screaming at each other when the woman gets out of the car – even though it's blocks to the party at their friends' house, and she's not exactly sure which house it is, she's done with this argument. The man drives away. The woman walks to the party. When she gets close to where she thinks the house is, she stops and listens for music, or people talking. She hears music. The tree doesn't know that the woman will drink to get drunk at the party. An hour beyond this argument, she is staggering drunk. Nor does the tree know the man goes home and listens to one of his wife's favourite albums – The Dave Brubeck Quartet's *Time Out*. He plays the album. He turns the lights out and drifts. He gets up to flip the record over and keeps repeating this pattern until he falls asleep, the record plays through, the needle lifts and gently moves to its off position.

Ray shook his head. He opened his eyes and looked up into the high, sweeping branches and breathed. "Listen, tree, do you think it's possible for a man to love two women at the same time? I mean, of course the women will be different and this difference will colour the love, but still, do you think this is possible?"

The tree said nothing.

"Not that I am considering this," Ray added. "We're just talking. And I'm only curious."

....

A delivery truck pulls up beside Ray's car and stops. It seems it's going to stay there. The driver gets out and walks around the front.

"Hold on," Ray says into the phone.

He lowers his window. The driver is intense and talks quickly. "Do you need to get out, sir?"

"I don't want to hold on," Nancy says. "What's going on? What are you doing?" Nancy gets up and walks out onto the balcony. She leans over and sees the top of the truck, a grey rectangle.

"Eventually," Ray says to the driver. "How long are you going to be?"

"We'll need an hour, maybe a bit more."

"That's fine," Ray says. There are no advertisements on the truck, which is a dull grey colour. They could be delivering anything. This conversation could not possibly go any longer than an hour but if he has to sit and wait for a bit, it's fine.

The driver moves on, looking for any other cars with people in them.

"Who are you talking to?"

"There's a truck blocking me in. I was talking to the driver. He called me 'sir.'"

"So?"

"So, I'm not a 'sir.' I'm just a guy. Old people are 'sir.' Elton John is a 'sir.'"

"Maybe you are old to him. Anyway, he was being respectful. Just take it and don't over-think. Jesus Christ, you over-think things. What are they delivering?"

"I don't know. Maybe someone is moving into your building. Maybe someone is getting new furniture. Do you want me to ask?"

"No. I don't care."

"I'd like to think they're moving a grand piano."

"I said I don't care…"

"And yet you asked. You said – *What are they delivering?*"

"I know what I said, but I really don't care. I was just filling space." She's trying to keep her voice calm and controlled but Ray is pushing her.

"Maybe I should ask. Because it would be beautiful if they were moving a grand piano. There's something romantic and nostalgic and delightful about the rigmarole around moving a piano. You know. The fat guys standing around scratching themselves and looking at the piano suspended from a rope and pulleys – you know, a block and tackle…"

She is confused by the term 'block and tackle.' She does not know what it means but she will not ask him. "…I said I don't care."

"Are you sure? Because it's no problem."

"No. I do not care."

"I'm just saying it would be really quite wonderful if it was a piano…"

She is silent for perhaps ten seconds. As he is about to ask if she's still there she comes back. "What are you doing, Ray?"

"What do you mean?"

"You're fucking with me. Why? Why would you do that? Do you really think now is the right time to throw stones at this Russian bear? I mean, timing-wise, do you really think this is a good time for that?"

He stops. Because this makes him nervous. Because they really have nothing more to say to each other. Because this is beyond pointless. He could go on. He is way beyond regretting answering her call.

"Well? Are you going to keep irritating the bear? Because, I'm telling you, Ray, that's how people get killed."

"Okay," Ray says. "No more talk about pianos."

Ray hears shouting behind the truck and somebody down the block is laying on their car horn. Traffic is down to one lane and this must be causing problems. All he keeps thinking about is a world context and none of it is cheerful. He wants to remind her there are people suffering all over the world – and most of this suffering has to do with war, injustice, poverty, religious fundamentalism, violence. There are sick people who want to be alive – who desperately want to be alive. Ray takes a big breath.

"Nancy, I want to tell you something and I want you to listen carefully."

"Will it cheer me up?"

"Just listen, okay?"

"Okay."

"So here's the thing. I really think you should grow the fuck up. I'm sorry I hurt you but grow up. Get up tomorrow morning and shake this off. And move on with your life."

"Do you think jumping off my balcony is grown up?"

"No. It's stupid."

"I think it's very grown up. I think it's mature and sophisticated." She takes a deep breath, holds, and then exhales. "I'm sad, Ray, and alone. I feel so alone. I can't grow up out of this sadness. It's massive. And I can't stop feeling alone because I am alone."

She starts to cry. Her tears are so sudden they surprise her.

"I liked you better when you were talking nonsense about pianos. I don't like it when you yell at me."

She sees the angel standing on the balcony, its back to her, looking at the city. She is not surprised by this. If someone had been in the room watching her, they would not have known she was shocked. Her heart was beating fast, and her face was flushed a little. Other than this, she appears unmoved by the angel. As if she sees angels all the time. She wants to ignore this angel. She wants to treat it like a train that is coming down the tracks toward her but will, at the last minute, veer off onto a different track. She wants to pretend it's not standing out there because of her. Or, if it's here because of her, it's just going to listen. It's a grey-coloured angel. It seems to be dressed all in grey, and in the overcast day, its skin appears to be grey too. Its shoes are black and pointed. Its wings are massive, extending a metre above its head and its bottom feathers brushing the balcony deck. They are almost not there, as if they exist in more than one place at the same time. They fade in and out of focus and at their most corporeal, they are translucent. Nancy looks away from the angel. She's not ready for angels.

8½

Rosencrantz and Guildenstern

You might be wondering about Patience and Sarah. Are you? Are you wondering why they're not more front and centre? Well, it's not their story. They are basically Rosencrantz and Guildenstern in Shakespeare's *Hamlet*. Wandering around in the background as Tulah and Ray try to sort things out. You might be thinking – Rosencrantz and Guildenstern? Huh? Is this a tragedy? Do you think the girls die? You remember a lot of people died in *Hamlet*. Rosencrantz and Guildenstern definitely died in Hamlet. But the girls? No. No. No. Who would kill off a couple of sweet girls like this? Patience and Sarah do not die. They're fine.

They have the usual childhood illnesses, colds and flus and so on.

But in the context of a book called *This Is All A Lie* you would have to say yes, both girls die when lightning strikes a tree in the back yard. They run out to see if the tree is okay, and it falls on them and kills them both. Nudge-nudge, wink-wink.

Perhaps you're starting the see how exhausting this continual lying thing is. Honestly, it's a full-time job. But it's not all lies is it? You can start to see what's true, can't you? And if you live with a lie long enough, it can start to be true. But seeing the truth inside a lie is different from the delusional, unconditional acceptance of a lie.

You can rest easy about Patience and Sarah – they're fine. They're alive at the end of the book, or the beginning – or both if you'd prefer. Their parents are constant, which is what kids want. They have boundaries and they are well loved. You don't have to worry about the girls.

Anyway, why would you want the heaviness of children running around? Children need, and need, and need some more. They are weight, and responsibility, and worry. This is not to say Ray and Tulah don't worry about their kids. They do, and not just when they're ill. They take all their responsibilities as parents seriously. They worry about the girls in school – Tulah knows first-hand the savage cruelty of eighth-grade girls. They worry about the planet – about a planet overheating and the consequences of disappearing ice caps. There are days when Ray worries about lions, elephants and certain whales, and how his girls might never see one of these creatures in the wild. And dating. Ray can't even being to think about his girls dating.

....

coquetry
noun (pl) -ries
1. flirtation

....

Here are some facts for you – so you have a better picture but not a bloated one. Patience Marie was born in 2004 and Sarah January followed about a year later. Both were born in the Holy Trinity Hospital on Spadina Avenue. Tulah opted for natural births for both girls and followed through on that promise. Patience was born to the sound of Miles Davis – the soundtrack from a 1958 Louis Malle film called *Ascenseur pour l'échafaud*. Sarah was born to the less-than-half-an-octave vocal range range of Leonard Cohen. Ray thinks he remembers hearing "Dance Me to the End of Love."

Wait. Wait a second. Way back in Chapter 12, Patience was born to a soundtrack of Van Morrison's *Astral Weeks,* and Sarah's birth had William Byrd's *Mass for Four Voices* playing. So, which one is true? The answer is, yes. If you're thinking that at this point, it doesn't matter what music was playing, well, you're catching on.

....

In 2015, Patience is eleven years old. Sarah is ten. Sarah still wets the bed. Her bladder has to catch up to the rest of her body, that's all. That's what her doctor said. There are pills now that let her go to sleepovers without too much anxiety. They work. Tulah and Ray are still anxious – did she remember to take her pills? Did some kid ask her what the pills are for? What did she say?

And Patience has been hiding the fact she can't see as well as she'd like, or needs. Just in the past few months, she has noticed things that once were sharp, are now a bit blurry. She worries that glasses will make her look nerdy – that she won't be popular anymore. She gets headaches because she's been squinting so much.

Tulah noticed her daughter squinting and asked her about it. Patience shrugged it off as being tired but Tulah suspects she will need glasses.

....

Claude Garamond probably could have used glasses. He was continually squinting at his letters and despite having a glass that allowed for the fine work of punch cutting, he had frequent headaches. This afternoon, he is sitting on a rock with his feet in the river. It is so hot he could not work any longer. The new letters will have to wait until this horrible heat has eased. He couldn't stay in the studio beyond noon. Marie Isabelle has gone back to the house to get a bottle of wine, some bread and cheese.

She brings two bottles. One, Garamond opens and the other, he wedges between the rocks in the cool flow of the water.

He loves it that she is quiet with him. He has been with women who do not stop talking. His first wife, who died of a fever, was lovely, but talked continually. At least it seemed so in his memory. Marie Isabelle measures her conversation and leaves the silences alone.

Yesterday, they saw troops on the road, headed toward Italy. Garamond had asked them where they were going but the soldiers were silent – either they didn't know, or they knew and weren't saying.

A week ago, with Garamond at ease in his favourite chair in the small tavern in the village, he looked up at Gauguin and envied him for the simplicity of his life. He grows grapes and then turns those grapes into wine. Then he sells the wine in his tavern and to the villagers. Garamond does not underestimate the work. He knows from their conversations that Gauguin works hard and long. But still, there is a simplicity that the punch cutter craves. There are days when his struggle with the letterforms feels overwhelming. He is constantly seeking perfection and presence, and at the same time, submission to the written word. The font should not matter. The font should disappear. It should get out of the way and let the poem, or story, or message come forward unhindered, always. It is a surrender of ego to make these letters so they are both elegantly beautiful, and almost invisible. And the family of the letterforms must appear to be related. There's got to be consistency and unity, or it won't work.

Marie Isabelle looks at her husband. He is lost in a reverie, stunned by the heat, and something is adrift in him. "Is this dappled?" she says, looking up into high branches that sway in the soft breezes above the river. She wants to bring him back from wherever he is in his mind.

She knows it's dappled. She knows and yet she unfurls that word as if she wants to gently nudge him into seeing it – she wants him to notice the sun through the high branches, and what it does to the ground and the water in the river. She wants him to see that it is magic. She also wants to quietly remind him to see her.

"*Oui*," Garamond says. "*Elle est tachetée.*"

She curls into him and they are quiet. The trees hush and the river lulls. But Garamond's mind is racing. He wants to tell Marie Isabelle he is sorry they had to leave Paris, her friends and her family. He wants to apologize for the danger they are in. And he wants to ask her if she would have married him had it not been arranged and massaged into being. He wants to ask about her attraction.

"I want to ask you a question."

"Mmmm," she says.

"I am wondering about your attraction. I am wondering if we would be together if it was not arranged. I ask this because I have put you in danger, and this must anger you. Are you angry with me? Were you attracted to me?"

She leans up and looks at his face, the creases on his forehead and the anxiousness in his eyes. "I am not angry," she says. "And if I was not attracted to you, I would not be with you. If I did not feel love for you, we would not be married."

"You would disobey your grandmother?"

"In a heartbeat."

"So you love me freely, with no regrets?"

"I love you freely, Claude. With all my heart. I have regrets, but not about marrying you."

"What are your regrets?"

"Another time, Claude. Let's enjoy this day."

"I am sorry I took you from Paris."

"I know, Claude. I know."

....

Good lord! You're probably asking yourself – will this incessant dipping into the world of Claude Garamond ever stop? Maybe you're wondering about how much of his story is a lie. Well, Garamond married twice – first, to a woman named Guillemette Gaultier, and after her death, to Ysabeau Le Fevre. The name Ysabeau is Medieval French and it is a variant of the name Isabelle. Beyond an insufficient family tree on a French website, there's not much information about Ysabeau. So, her question about whether or not the forest bottom is dappled, is a big, bald-faced lie. But you'd like to believe it's true, and maybe that's enough. It could have been true. It could have happened.

Listen, do you think old Claude Garamond was attracted to the vintner's wife, Natalii? The woman was nowhere near as beautiful as Marie Isabelle but there was a resigned playfulness to her that Garamond enjoyed. He looked at her as is if she were a blank canvas – she was all beautiful, busty potential. He enjoyed talking with Natalii a great deal.

And Natalii was intrigued by this man who talked about printing presses and books, wars and love, and then waited for her to voice her opinion. He listened in a way that made her feel attractive. It was as if what she had to say was important. She suspected Monsieur Garamond was interested in her sexually. She did not question this attraction. She did not want to know what it was about her that pulled at Garamond. Instead, she accepted it and held her head a little higher – she looked at him with admiration and flirtatious disdain. After all, she was a married woman.

....

Around this time, Martin Luther wrote his *Ninety-Five Theses on the Power and Efficacy of Godness Power* – it sounds better in Latin – and nailed them to the door of All Saints' Church in Wittenberg, Germany. Historians say he never actually nailed his ninety-five theses to the door of that church – that it's just a myth – but it's a hell of a story. He started a revolution, also known as the Reformation. Why was he able to do this? Because people had Bibles and they could read for themselves what was in the Bible. Why did they have Bibles? Because of Gutenberg's printing press, mechanical movable type and a booming publishing business. Who worked as a punch cutter in Paris? Claude Garamond. It all leads back to Garamond.

Maybe you're curious about the Latin – *Disputatio pro declaratione virtutis indulgentiarum.*

....

"And when will we go back to Paris, Claude?" Marie Isabelle says one morning. The birds started singing before the sunrise and this reminded her of where she was, which was not Paris, and she is grumpy. She is a long way from Paris and she is itching to see her friends, to catch up on the gossip. As much as she loves her husband and loves his company, she wants different company – she wants her friends. She is bored in the country. Even though it is a lot of work to make a life, to tend the chickens, and prepare meals and do the washing, she is bored. It is starting to be the same thing every single day.

"I do not know, my dear," Garamond says. "Our days in Paris may be over…"

Marie Isabelle reads him. She watches his hands and surmises he is uncomfortable about this conversation. She looks at his eyes, and finds he will not meet her eyes with his. He's hiding something. "What are you not telling me?"

"We're safe here."

"What do you mean we're safe here?" she says. "What have you heard, Claude?"

He sighs. "There were some men. They came to our house in Paris seven weeks ago. I got word of this two days ago – a letter arrived at the vintner's, by way of Geneva, Lyon, and then Dijon, and then Grenoble."

"What men?" She is wondering why this letter travelled in circles before coming to them.

"Men with many questions, none of which were answered."

"Are we in danger?"

"In Paris, perhaps. Here? No."

"But how can that be, Claude? Either we are in danger, or we are not in danger. There is no middle."

"We are safe here because nobody knows where we are," he says. "And in the village, we are known as Monsieur Emile Durand and his lovely wife, Madame Claire Durand."

"And you have been so insistent that I learn how to ride because we are completely safe?"

"That is just a precaution," Garamond says. "It's good to have developed this skill. In case some day we both need to ride."

"You mean run," she says.

"You have mastered the horse," he says. "This pleases me."

She looks at him as if he has just said something ridiculous. "This is what I live for. Each moment of my day, I devise new ways to please you. It is the sole purpose of my life."

They stand at the edge of the corral and look at the horses. They are restless and Garamond wonders if there is a bear in the woods, or a wolf. He reaches into his pocket and brings out an apple, which he breaks in two. Two of the horses come toward them, pushing their soft noses through the boards and Garamond holds out the apple halves in the flat of his hand to each horse. He and Marie Isabelle rub them, give them attention, in silence. Finally, Garamond looks at his wife. "It was my typeface used on the placards," he says.

"Oh, Claude."

"They will suspect I had something to do with the placards. They are probably looking for me right now."

"*Merde*," she says. "Double *merde*. This is the King, and the Roman Catholic Church. This is the Protestant Reformation. This is a dangerous thing."

"I am aware," he says.

"Should we leave France, Claude? Has it come to that?"

"No. I do not think so. But we must be ready to leave quickly, and in the meantime, we have Monsieur Gauguin's protection. And Switzerland is not too far away."

"We are our own country now, Claude," she says.

He likes the idea of being a country accountable to only them-selves. "And what is the religion in our country?"

"I think we have no religion," she says.

"What about God?"

She wants to say that God can kiss her ass but she restrains her-self. "God can go elsewhere. He is not welcome in our country. All the trouble that God brings is not wanted, or needed."

"I like our country more and more," Garamond says.

....

About six years ago, this happened. But then you already know this.

Tulah is sitting in front of the mirror, naked – her towel in a heap on the floor. She is about to apply a little makeup and blow-dry her hair. "Jesus, Ray. How long have you been thinking about this?"

He has come to her with his idea of quitting law and becoming an arborist. They are getting ready for work. Ray is in their bedroom, looking for socks.

"I know it's a huge deal but I'm not happy there."

"Happy? There?"

"Yes," Ray says. "I am not happy there. I'm just not happy about what this job is taking."

"Taking? What do you mean, taking?"

"Okay, maybe it's about what I am required to give. And I give it freely because the money that comes back is pretty good right now, and has the potential to be substantial."

She looks into the mirror at the reflection of Ray in his underwear. He is holding a small compact ball of a pair of socks.

"There's a sleaziness that cannot be avoided," he says. "A sort of built-in corruption. It's a machine that begins to erode the soul. I know I sound like a yoga teacher named Butterfly, but I feel I am becoming a little less each day."

"You're becoming a little less?"

"Less human," he says. "Less moral. Less decent." He's wearing trousers now, and looking for a shirt.

"Have you thought about applying at a different firm?"

"Yes, of course, but I'm with the best firm in the city right now. It's the law – we're not suited for each other."

"I'm a bit shocked. No, I'm a lot shocked. You worked so hard and you're a really good lawyer." She wants to scream – *You're just figuring this out now? You couldn't have discovered this aversion to the law in your first year of law school?*

"I wanted you to know that I was thinking about this, that's all."

"That's a hell of a bomb you just exploded in our life. You know the entire world is in a recession right now, right?"

"I know. I'm sorry."

As shallow as it sounds rattling around in her own head, Tulah had been counting on the money. It was going to allow them to travel, and have a new car every now and then and maybe some time off work for her. They would have no debt and they would have savings. All this was about to change.

"You want to quit law and work with trees?"

"I was thinking about trees, yes. It's something I know and love. I've been offered a job with the city."

What does he mean, offered a job? To be offered a job, people have to know you're available. Tulah realizes he has already decided, and it was not something he came to lightly. He knows the ramifications of this decision. She was there on the nights when the Basa case was being tried. She saw him suffer through that nightmarish case. At the end of the day it comes down to being moral, it's a matter of being able to live with yourself. It's a matter of looking in the mirror and not cringing. "Trees make you happy?"

"Yes, working as an arborist. Working with trees makes me happy."

She thinks about the years of law school, years of studying, and struggling to give him space so he could study, and then when he got hired Tulah thought they were good to go. There was supposed to be a pay-off. "I want you to be happy, Ray, but..."

"I know. I just don't think I can do it anymore."

Tulah stands up and turns around. Ray is picking a necktie. Then it dawns on her. There was the anxiety issue a while back.

"Your anxiety attack. Is that what's driving this?"

"That was just a symptom," he says. "Look, I promise we'll be okay. I promise. No matter what." Ray suspects she doesn't believe it's going to be okay. He knows it's going to take some work to get her to understand. He's not sure leaving the law over something as intangible as happiness is the right thing to do. Maybe a good person would step up and do the hard thing, sacrifice his happiness for the happiness of his family. Maybe this sacrifice is a way he can act honourably.

Ray goes to bed that night with Abdul momit Basa's smug face floating around in his brain, and Caroline Franks's husband's face, and Tulah's disappointed face, and trees – he thinks a lot about the simplicity of trees. He's not sure he can take the job with the city and not ruin something with Tulah. Her life was ticking away on a clear path and now he was about to change direction. Ray decides he needs Tulah to be okay about this move. He sits up in bed at around 2 a.m. and looks around the room. He looks at Tulah's back. He looks at the pillow on the floor. The light in the back lane throws the shadow of the Venetian blinds against the wall. He gets out of bed and pads down the hallway, fills the kettle, and makes tea. Tulah must be involved in this decision, he decides at around 5 a.m. If she's not okay with it, he needs a new plan.

....

The woman who stormed into Tulah's school demanding the theory of creation be included in her kid's science class creates a bit of a media storm. She yips and yaps. She comes across as a caring and concerned mom, who just wants her child to have a full and proper education. Parents, she argues, should have a say in their kids' education. She wants to make education great again. She blogs on her *Christian Wives* website and then there is a reporter on the front step wanting to talk with Tulah. Apparently, Lauren Smith has a robust following on social media.

Tulah parks out front, grabs her bag and the reporter approaches on the sidewalk.

"I was wondering if I could ask you some questions on school curriculum," she says. "For a story I'm working on." Her smile is disarming and shy.

Tulah pauses, takes a breath. "Sure," she says, shifting her bag to her other hand.

"Okay," the reporter says. "I have just a few questions. Do you think parents should have the right to influence, or even set, school curriculum?"

"That's a hell of a start," Tulah says.

The reporter is a narrow-framed, dark-haired woman with an incredibly smooth complexion. She is fashionable in her trousers and blouse, and Tulah can't help but notice her nails. They're French nails and they are immaculate.

Tulah leans back against the doorframe and smiles. "All curricula? Or one part in particular?"

"Let's start with all curricula," the reporter says.

"Okay. No. Parents alone should not have the right to set curricula. Most people are not qualified to design a curriculum."

"Including you?"

"Yes. Including me. A group of students, parents, business people, community members and subject-area experts should do it together. In fact, I believe that's how it's done."

"Okay. What about designing curricula around creation theory and the theory of evolution?"

"You mean the story of creation and the theory of evolution, right?"

"Okay," the reporter says, but Tulah can see she is not okay – she has no clue about why a scientific theory differs from a story about creation.

"All creation stories should be taught," Tulah says. She looks at the reporter, who doesn't seem to be writing much down in her notebook.

"You teach a science class, right?"

"Yes."

"Do you teach the theory of Intelligent Design in your class?"

Tulah smiles. "I do not teach my students about creation. Intelligent design is a synonym for creation, but then, I think you already know this. Look, this is not a Christian charter school. That's why creation is not taught in science class." She considers explaining the difference between a scientific theory – an idea that has been tested and proven and is generally accepted – and the word theory in everyday usage – a 'guess,' or 'assumption.' Tulah is about to start to explain but she has begun to suspect this woman is not a reporter. It's her nails. Her nails are long and perfect. Tulah knew a reporter once and her nails were never maintained. Long nails like this woman's were not good for typing. "I think all the creation stories should be taught in a religion class or a theology class, so…"

"…but you won't teach your students about creation theory."

"Was that a question or a statement?"

"A question."

Tulah sighs. This woman is definitely not a reporter. "Why? Because creation isn't a scientific theory. It's the same reason I don't teach them Hansel and Gretel, or Snow White, or Goldilocks."

The so-called reporter steps back and looks hard at Tulah. "You're comparing the Bible to a nursery rhyme?"

Tulah opens the door and steps inside. "Yes, I am. Give my regards to Ms. Smith and her cult," she says.

"Wait," the woman says. "If everything started with the Big Bang, what was going on before that?"

"Certainly not an elderly man with a white beard, plotting human existence on a chalkboard. There are things we can't know…" She stops. "Oh why bother." Tulah shuts the door. She lets herself slide to the floor, her back against the door and when she looks up at Ray, there are tears in her eyes. "It's the twenty-first century," she says. "And we can't seem to escape these barbaric, backward superstitions. We're still a bunch of ignorant monkeys grunting in the jungle, looking into the night sky, completely filled with fear."

"I'm sorry," Ray says.

"What's wrong with us?"

"Us?"

"Yes. Human beings."

"What happened out there? What did she do?"

"She's not a reporter. She's some sort of fundamentalist church woman inflicting her beliefs by asking idiotic questions."

Ray helps her up and hands her a glass of wine. He is angry that Tulah has been hurt – and he feels protective.

"She should leave," he says. His voice is a growl as he strains to get a look at her through the window.

"She's harmless and pathetic. It's just…it's so disheartening."

"You're not alone, you know."

"I know that."

"I have to get the girls," Ray says. He scoops his car keys from the table at the front entrance. "They stayed late at school for an audition. There's more wine on the counter."

The woman is standing on the sidewalk, halfway to the curb. She's on her phone and when she sees Ray she moves toward him, and follows along, getting closer with each step.

His first impulse is to ignore her. "We're done here," Ray says.

"But I have just a couple more questions for your wife."

"Can't always get what we want, can we?" he says.

"What is your wife afraid of? I just have a few more questions."

Ray stops, turns and looks hard at the alleged reporter. She takes two quick steps back, almost falls. "No," he says. "You have dogma, and canon, and some sort of idiotic faith."

"Are you accusing me..."

"...of being a superstitious idiot who would probably like nothing better than for us to march right back into the Dark Ages? Yes, I am."

"These are innocent questions. The public has a right to know. I just want to know what your wife has against Christianity. Why is she attacking the Christian faith?"

"What did you just say?" Ray's voice is barely above a growl.

"I..." She takes another backwards step.

"You said you were a reporter. A reporter with what publication?"

She hesitates. "I was talking to your wife."

"What newspaper do you work for? What media?"

"I was talking with your..."

"...You're not a goddamned reporter. You're some sort of mental fucking defective. You should try thinking for yourself."

"I'm with the *Herald*," she says, quickly.

"The *Herald* what? We don't have a *Herald*. Show me your ID."

"I don't have to show you my ID."

"Fine, you're not a reporter. You can talk it over with the police when they get here."

"You called the police?"

"No, I didn't call the police," Ray says. The woman looks relieved. "My Christian-hating wife called the police. She told them you have a gun."

Ray smiles at the incredible timing of a distant siren. It comes at the perfect moment and it makes it quite dramatic as he gets into his car and drives away. He glances back and can see the woman hustling down the street toward her car.

....

Somewhere in the middle of all this, after children, and before affairs, and in the midst of abandoned intimacy, Ray follows Tulah into the lingerie section of a large department store, which is a labyrinth at the butt end of a massive shopping mall. He finds himself standing and looking at racks of nylons, and leggings and tables filled with colourful panties. There's a bin of umbrellas next to a table of panties, and Ray does not question this. In this store, umbrellas are apparently feminine. And everybody knows that when women think about panties, they also think about umbrellas. Tulah is one aisle over leafing through piles of lacy panties and she stops on a bronzy brown pair. She holds them up in the air and tilts her head. Buying panties is not something they have ever discussed. Tulah knows what she likes and Ray has never developed an opinion about panties other than he believes white lingerie is the sexiest colour for lingerie. Tulah has never asked for his opinion. She turns to look at him and smiles. There is such a soft ease in her smile. In this moment, Ray loves his wife. As she is elbow-deep in panties, he adores her. He wants to spend a hundred years figuring out ways to make her smile just like this.

"These are nice," she says, holding them up for him.

"I'll fight you for them," he says.

"What?"

"I'll fight you for them."

Tulah is confused, but when Ray pulls an umbrella from the rack, and holds it up, she figures it out.

"You think you're that good, do you?" She steps toward the rack and pulls out a purple umbrella.

"En guard," she says, thrusting the pointy end toward Ray.

Tulah thrusts first and Ray parries it aside. He pushes his sword toward her heart and she glances it away then twirls and catches him on his left arm. He deflects her umbrella downward and raises his to just under her chin. Tulah backs away, raises her sword, her eyes fierce and engaged.

A dark-haired woman with a name tag is standing at the edge of the section and she appears to be uncertain, hesitant.

Tulah does not lower her sword. "Do you give up?"

"You can have them," Ray says. "This time."

CHAPTER 8

Meeting The Lover

Tulah's Snow Journal
Tuesday, June 6, 2008 #388

The snow feels new, as if it's a first snow in the fall. As if we skipped summer altogether. It is wet and heavy, and beautiful. The weather came from the east and that always means something weird. It's not unheard-of, but it is strange for it to snow in June. Traffic has stopped and it is so quiet. Every now and then you can hear clumps of snow thumping to the ground, and sometimes, the sound of tree branches breaking under the weight. There are branches down across the city. Some neighbourhoods have lost power. I've decided not to worry about my pots. They were on sale. It's too late to run out there and cover them up. Anyway, I read somewhere that marigolds are resilient little bastards. Not sure about potato vines, and begonias. And the violas I think are not going to do well with this snow cover.

The birds in the trees grin and bear – they must be freaked out. Most people have removed winter tires. Summer tires and all-season tires are useless in this. I can hear tires spinning all over the neighbourhood – people stuck on the side streets. The city waits for the bruised snow clouds to pass and June to force itself into existence.

....

There are still swatches of snow on the ground, but it's mostly gone. There's a story Tulah read once about a snow storm and a bush that usually blossoms in the spring – she can't recall the kind of bush it was. This bush was budding and about to burst into bloom but a cold snap arrived and the buds died – they disappeared. A few weeks later, the weather warmed up and the buds appeared again. A monk noticed these appearing and disappearing buds and asked the questions – what has happened to those unborn buds? Were the new buds the same as the old ones? It was a story about manifesting and not manifesting. The monk decided the buds were not the same and they were not different.

When conditions are sufficient they manifest and when conditions are not they go into hiding. Things wait until the moment is right to manifest. This barely recalled story seems appropriate today because the apple tree in the back yard had just come into bloom before the snow came.

Tulah steps out onto the back deck, which needs to be stained this summer, and looks at her potted plants, and at the apple tree. She takes a sip of coffee and wonders what the tree will do now. Will there be no apples? A few apples? Or will it send out blossoms again?

In the shower, she shaves her legs and does her best to curtail her pubic hair with a dull razor. She writes 'razors' on her shopping list, underneath 'AA batteries.' She's going to meet The Lover at a hotel downtown. He's here for two nights. She's meeting him at 10 a.m. for coffee. Teachers never get to call in sick. At least not at this school. The night before, Tulah pulls up lesson plans, arranges for a substitute and briefs her substitute by email. She drops the girls with her mom for the day.

In the café, she sits at a corner table near the window. She likes the way the trunks of the trees along the boulevard turn black when they're wet. It's been drizzling, on and off, all morning.

A blonde woman sitting at a table near the bar has placed her glasses on the table next to her cappuccino, and she is reading a book. She is alone at the table but Tulah thinks the woman is lonely. There's something about her posture that seems defeated and isolated.

Outside, a couple hug and kiss and seem genuinely pleased to see each other. The man is wearing a grey tuque. The woman has an umbrella but it is unopened. They come inside and sit at a booth along the far wall. They have to ask for the booth and the waitress seems irritated by this request.

....

Tulah remembers the first time she met The Lover. It was a year ago in a bar at the airport. She was going to visit her sister in Chicago. He was flying to some country in South America. He'd dropped a book beside her table and she noticed. It was a book of Zen koans. She had no idea what a koan was, but it sounded exotic. She scooped the book from the floor, handed it to him, and he smiled his gratitude.

"I'm always losing this book," he said. "It's like it doesn't want to be with me. It keeps jumping ship." She can't place his accent. It makes his 'b's bigger than normal but she can't place it.

"Do you think books have that sort of willpower?"

"No. They only have power."

"Is this a good book?"

"Third time it's fallen out of my bag. I've been reading it for three years. It's not the kind of book to read in order. You just open it up..." He handed her the book and she followed his instructions. "Open it up, and flip until you feel like you should stop. Then read that koan."

Tulah stopped on a koan called: "If You Love, Love Openly." It was about a group of twenty monks and one nun. The monks and the nun, whose name was Eshun, were practising meditation with a Zen master. Even though her head was shaved and her dress plain, Eshun was quite pretty and several of the monks secretly fell in love with her. One of them wrote her a love letter, asking her to meet with him in private. Eshun did not reply but the following day the Zen master gave a lecture to the group, and when it was over, Eshun stood up. She turned toward the monk who had written to her and said, 'If you really love me so much, come and embrace me now.'

"I don't know what to think," Tulah said.

"Don't think. Just live with it for a while. See what comes."

They had drinks. They had more drinks and then they rebooked flights, rearranged schedules, and wound up in a hotel at the airport.

The Lover opened another bottle of champagne and filled her glass.

Tulah was curled between his legs. They fell into each other and lost track of themselves. It was constant and exhausting. They devoured each other, and the champagne. And then more champagne. She took possession of him because he was so willingly hers. He surrendered and it was as if everything he was became part of her being. She had a penis and testicles, and her arms were covered by tattoos – her right arm a snarling bear, and her left, a haloed Mary – the mother of Jesus, holding a haloed baby Jesus. These tattoos stopped just above his wrists; when he wore a suit there were no visible tattoos.

She knew this sudden sexual joining with The Lover was not public and it would never be public. It was not the open embrace Eshun was demanding of her smitten monk. It was all about secrets and deception and lies.

A little after 3 a.m. he leaned up in the bed. "I am a little in love with you, Eshun."

"That was fast," Tulah said. But it was what she was feeling too. And his voice was her voice anyway, so she was saying it to herself. "And this is insane. You know that, right?"

"Do you think love can be slowed down?" The Lover asked. "Do you think it sticks to a schedule? Do you think it behaves like a good brown dog?"

"No," Tulah said. "Of course, not."

"You know that love is insane, always. It's a mad dog. It's a form of insanity."

"Good. I have a steady supply of insanity. I get it from Mexico. I have a guy who sells it to me in a baggie."

"Yes? What's his name?"

"Jesús," Tulah said. "His name is Jesús."

The Lover brushed her thigh with his fingertips and Tulah shivered. He nibbled her neck, and she let her legs fall open like a sigh. "Jesus," she said. "Jesus, Mary, Joseph and the donkey."

....

For a while, Tulah becomes more sexual. She enjoys her body. She meets The Lover, sporadically and with little difficulty. She arranges time because it feels good to indulge this desire. She does not question its importance. She does not want to think about what it means to have a lover. For a few hours, they are everything and anything to each other, and then she goes back to her life. And he goes back to his life.

Tulah finds that she wants Ray while this is going on. She salivates when she thinks about making love with him. The walls to their lovemaking disappear. She no longer cares about anything but pleasure – giving it, and receiving it. She feels closer to Ray, happy with him, happy with their life.

Tulah does not think about The Lover. She does not yearn. She does not crave more of him. She denies him. She creates a complex and delusional room, and she only goes there minutes before, during, and scant minutes after meeting The Lover. Beyond their liaisons, she denies all thoughts about him, every memory, and even his name. Someone will say his name – not naming The Lover, but rather, someone with the same name as his, and Tulah will be surprised. The utterance of his name will shock her because she will remember his body, her pleasure, and it comes too quickly for her to deny. It gets past her defences. She will lose her way in the conversation. People will ask her if she's okay.

....

The Lover shows up, ten minutes late.

"Traffic," he says. "Everything is backed up. They're pruning trees at the end of the block and half the road is blocked."

"The snow brought down a lot of branches," she says.

"Hell of a thing."

"Yes. God's way of making the trees stronger."

"Do the trees really get stronger?"

"This is what I understand," she says.

"Part of God's plan?"

"A consequence of weather."

"Not God?"

"It's just an idiomatic quirk. It's just the weather," she says.

They have a glass of wine. He seems distracted. He can't seem to look at her and Tulah asks if he's okay.

"It's been a long week," he says.

"It's Tuesday," Tulah says, giggling a little.

"Work is difficult right now." He stops. "But we don't talk about stuff like this. Tell me something you care about right now. Tell me about what you're reading. Let's have another glass of wine."

They swing into a banter that is serious but avoids anything resembling the routines of their daily lives. But she senses something is wrong. This meeting has none of the joyful dance. It seems forced and prodded. As if this affair, which is supposed to be an escape from the reality of their lives into something only about pleasure and bliss, has become an obligation. They make love in his hotel room with afternoon light slanted through the windows. It seems as if they've just begun when

The Lover stops and rolls to his side and looks at her. "Do you know what Chaucer called this?"

"My vagina?" she says. She's confused.

"Yes. In his *Canterbury Tales* he called it *la belle chose*. It means the *pretty thing*, or the *lovely thing*."

"Why are you telling me this?"

"I don't know. I just remembered it and thought you ought to know, if you didn't already know."

"I didn't know," she says. "But my *belle chose* would like some attention just now."

Afterward, she does not feel weightless – like the times before this one – but rather, weighed down. She looks at The Lover. He is dressing, slowly, as if he is deep in thought. He picks up his coat, kisses her on the cheek and pauses. He sits at the end of the bed.

"Do you ever feel depressed?"

"Depressed? Yes. Sometimes."

"What do you do about it?"

"Are you depressed, my dear? I'm sorry. I thought something was off. I've been thoughtless."

"No. I'm fine. I'm just tired. I was wondering about you."

"Oh. Well, yes. Sometimes I get depressed." She wonders why he's asking.

"And how do you handle it?"

"I count my blessings. I drink a glass of champagne that I can barely afford. I watch my daughters sleep. I get up in the morning and smile and breathe and move forward."

"Does this happen often?"

Tulah smiles. "Do you mind me asking why you're curious about this?"

"I just wondered. I have a sister…I have a sister who struggles with darkness."

"Darkness? Darkness is not what I'd call my depression. I have periods of time when grey is everything. Nothing is defined. Everything is dull and grey. Which is different than darkness, I think."

"Yes. Darkness is more serious. A bigger thing."

"Is your sister okay?"

"Most of the time. It comes and goes."

"I didn't know you had a sister..."

"I have to get going," he says, standing up.

When he is gone, Tulah looks at the shadows on the wall. She thinks about the lightness of a shadow – she would like to be a shadow of something beautiful – comprised of the absence of light, the negative of mass, the ephemeral shape of something solid.

....

They put the girls to bed and meet on the front deck. It's cool and humid. The snow has dragged the temperature down and even though it's mostly melted, it's still chilly. Tulah puts on a khaki green jacket and Ray finds a grey sweater at the back entrance – it's grey and ripped at its armpits but he can't bear to throw it out.

"I do not understand this woman," Tulah says. "She won't let it go. I mean school is done for the year. You'd think she'd give it a rest."

Ray smiles. He has no idea what she's talking about.

Tulah can see his confusion. "That woman who wants creation taught in a science class," she says.

"Oh, her," Ray says. "What's she doing, besides being irrelevant?"

"She's presenting at the next School Board meeting. They're giving her ten minutes."

"And?"

"And it's horrifying. This woman is going to spew her bullshit, flawed logic as fact and it will sound sane, because she's just a caring mom. And more importantly, she will make it seem harmless."

"And if she breaks it down to the unanswerable question of what was there before the Big Bang?"

"She won't. For her, it was God. It was all God. Everything is God. God is the way and the answer to everything. This makes me want to drink. What do we have?"

"There's a bottle of pinot-something in the fridge but I can't remember how long it's been there."

CHAPTER 7

Anxious

"It is better to be slapped by the truth than kissed by a lie"
— *Zhanna Petya*

When Nancy was in the throes of sex, she was able to forget almost everything. The wings never came when she was making love and this was a good reason for her to take lovers. In coitus, the darkness pulled back and left her alone. Her husband's need to have sex every day, no matter what, was in the beginning, a balm. There were no wings in that first year. But the monotony of his need began to wear thin for her. She was required to be there, her legs spread, or her ass in the air. She was required to be ready and to act willing. Even if she was sick, he would insist on fucking her. Soon, she was hearing the wings every day. Sometimes she heard the wings twice in one day, and she began to dread sex. She began to manufacture escapes. She found ways to remove herself from the house. A visit to New York to see her brother, or a yoga retreat in Mexico, always timed to happen at the busiest time of year for her husband; anything to get out of the house.

Slava did not come to her wedding. He was away on business. The company was expanding into South America and Slava was living, temporarily, in Venezuela. He called from Valencia and asked her if she was sure about this banker.

"Yes, Slava," Nancy said. "He's a good man."

"How do you know he is a good man?"

"I know it has only been a few months," she said, "but he makes me happy."

Slava met the banker only once. He'd checked on him and found nothing out of line. He came from a decent family that had roots in Virginia, and he'd studied business at Stanford. His reputation within the banking community was spotless. He had no criminal record, but there had been some murmurings about an investigation into associations with an off-shore bank. The investigation died before the rumours could coagulate. The banker was clean but there was something about him that Slava didn't like. There was an arrogance in the way he held himself and this rubbed him the wrong way. It was as if the banker cared too much about the way he looked.

"If at some point in the future, he stops making you happy, you will talk to me about it, right?" Slava said.

"Don't worry, brother," she said. "He's one of the good ones."

"I am sorry to have to miss the wedding."

"Venezuela is a long trip," she said. "It's a small wedding anyway."

"I'm sending a present."

"You don't have to do that."

"It's done. A man named Vladimir will drop off an envelope at the gallery tomorrow. You can use it on your honeymoon. He looks a bit scary but he has the disposition of a kitten. Is that the right word? Disposition? Meaning his character, or personality?"

"Disposition is a good word," Nancy said.

"I still struggle to tell a joke in English. It's a horrible language for jokes. In Russian, I can be funny. In English, I am not so funny."

"Your English is perfect to me," she said.

"Listen, I must go now. I just wanted to say congratulations, dear Nensi. I am happy for you."

"Thank you, Slava. When will you be home?"

"A few months, perhaps a little longer. Anytime you want to talk, you know how to reach me."

They honeymooned in Hawaii, on the Island of Maui, and for the first months Nancy was in the light. Around month seven she crashed and wanted to hide. She could feel it coming and as much as she wanted to stop it, it always came.

"I'm too depressed for sex," she said. "I'm just really down right now."

"Nonsense," the banker said. "Nobody is ever that depressed."

"I am. I feel sad right now."

"Do you want a drink?"

"No. I just want to be left alone," she said.

"Are you my wife?"

"Yes, of course I'm your wife." She smiled, trying to bring a lightness to the conversation. "But it's okay to take a break every now and then, right?"

"Yes, of course, but once you start it could become habitual and that would ruin our marriage. You don't want to ruin our marriage, do you? You don't want to be unhappy, do you? Of course, you don't."

"No. I don't want to ruin anything. I just feel sad right now."

He rolled her over onto her stomach. "It's okay," he said. "Relax and you will feel better. I promise."

But it was not better. As he was pushing himself into her, she heard the flapping sound of wings. For the following months, the banker prodded her to have sex each day. He insisted, for the sake of their marriage. Once a week, he sent flowers to her at work and each night he demanded sex. He was upfront about the potential undoing of their marriage if they didn't have sex every day. He believed it and he wanted her to believe it too. Nancy moaned in all the right places and groaned in the appropriate moments and their life moved forward. Even when her darkness ended, the pall of the previous months hung over her and it was never again making love – it had become a release of endorphins. Or exercise. Or a distasteful job. She could not tell her brother about her sex life. He was her brother. And besides, he would not have understood that sometimes you have to do things that might not feel good – that even if you were not in the mood, it was fine to make your husband happy. Slava would want to do something; he would insist on trying to make a correction. Apart from the pigeon at school, she had never seen evidence of his protection, but she'd heard enough that she had no doubt about his capacity for violence, and she trusted his protection was always there if she needed it.

Nancy knew, intellectually, she should just say *no*, and only *yes* when she felt like it, but she was a little afraid of the banker's reaction. He was so passionate about their marriage and the idea that it hung by the fragile thread of their daily intercourse. She considered this a weakness in herself, a flaw and she hated herself for it. But she could not muster a denial; she just let him do whatever he wanted.

....

Two months ago, Nancy was with her girlfriend, Sofia, at a café that was altogether too trendy for both of them, but in a convenient location. They steered their indifference through farmer-friendly coffee beans and a locally grown vegan menu, and found a window table. Sofia is normally well put together. She will come for coffee as if she is about to walk a runway in Paris. But today she has pulled her hair back into a ponytail and she is not wearing makeup. She told Nancy she'd looked on the floor for a sweatshirt that wasn't too wrinkled and smelled okay, pulled on a pair of jeans and runners.

"I sprayed some perfume," Sofia said, smiling. "It's the time difference between London and here. I wind up working in the middle of the night. I'm fine at 3 a.m. but I'm a wreck during the day. I can barely make breakfast and drive Emily to school."

Nancy knew Sofia was involved in some kinky cam stuff that was relatively lucrative and most of her clients were overseas. She had worked hard to develop a solid list of regulars. And she worked even harder to keep this life separate from her daughter.

Beyond London and 3 a.m., Nancy does not remember much of the conversation with Sofia. They shared a bottle of prosecco and Sofia told her about a client who lived in a place called Shiraz, in Iran, who wanted her to dress in a burka and talk dirty. Just talk. Not touch herself. Not play with dildos. Just talk.

It was the couple in the corner that distracted Nancy – they held hands across the table and looked at each other as if the café, the city, and the world were irrelevant. Nancy watched them as a melancholy envy expanded in her chest. She wanted what they had. She wanted that sort of magic, even if it didn't last. She recognized it as corny and romantic but this did not matter. She wanted that out-of-time craziness with someone and when she thought about who she would want to sit across from her, she gasped.

"What's wrong?"

"I'm in love with Ray," Nancy said, her voice low and lifeless.

"The married guy?"

Nancy nodded, slowly. This realization took the wind out of her. Why not the gorgeous man who leads her spin class, or the man with the beard who is often at the *Select* – the one who drinks a bottle of wine by himself over the course of the night? Or why not any number of other men in her life? Why did her mind go to Ray? She thought she was doing such a good job of stopping it at sex.

Nancy looked at the couple, who were still holding hands and talking. She had to get out of the café. She asked the waiter to add two flutes of champagne to her bill and to deliver these drinks to the lovers after she was gone.

....

"I think we should call your wife," she says. "We can call her together. Wouldn't that be fun?"

Ray says nothing.

"Don't you want to see how things will play out? I do. I mean, what if she doesn't care that you've been banging some Russian woman? Wouldn't that be a pleasant surprise? Then we could carry on being together. We could start again."

"Do you know one woman on the planet who would be okay with this?"

Nancy pauses. She tries to put herself in Ray's wife's position. *She's married to a decent guy. They have two kids, and a house in the suburbs. They are happy, happy, happy and then along comes another woman who not only fucks her husband but wants to take him from her.* Nancy can feel the anger in her gut, and a raging possessiveness.

"Rules always have exceptions."

"What does that mean?"

"It means, I still think we should see what happens. Let's call Tuna."

Ray hesitates. Did she do that on purpose? Has he ever mentioned his wife by name? Or has she always been 'my wife.' "Tulah," he says. "It's Tulah."

"Really, Ray. That's a name for a cat. That's what you call your cat." She mimics calling a cat – "Here, Tulah. Come on, pussy! Here, Tulah."

"That's hilarious," Ray says. Something deep inside of him believed her when she said she was going to jump. There was a hard determination, and a resignation in her voice that was utterly believable – as if the string of her voice was pulled taut. He believed her but he did not want to believe her.

"Tell me why you just ran away."

"I didn't run away. I walked. And then there was the elevator ride…"

"Stop being a literal prick…You know what I mean."

Ray glances at the building across the sidewalk. He looks up. The sky is grey and greyer and it's reflected silver-grey in the building's windows. It feels like snow.

"Honestly? The idea of leaving my family was never on the table."

"You might have told me that up front."

"Yes, I should have."

"So then why were you with me for so long? I thought…" But she does not want to say what she thought. She thought they were moving closer and closer to something real. She feels stupid again, for the twentieth time in the past hour.

"I thought things would change. I thought I would change. I didn't."

Her voice sounds distant and stretched out. "Well, that's something, Ray. That's something."

"What are you doing up there? You sound funny. Please tell me you're sitting on the couch with a drink."

"Look up, Ray."

"What do you mean, look up?"

"I mean look up. I see the top of your car. You should see me. I can see you. At least I think it's your car."

Ray steps out of his car and moves around the front to the sidewalk. He looks up and barely sees her leaned out over the balcony railing, waving both arms.

"Can you see me?"

"Yes," he says. "I can see you."

"Watch this."

Ray watches as she swings a leg over and then the other, and she sits with her legs dangling. That railing is four inches and she's perched like a bird. She's holding the phone in one hand and holding the rail with the other.

"Come on, Nancy. Can you please not do that?"

"Why not? This makes me feel alive."

"You're making me feel alive too. But not in a good way."

"Good. I want you to feel alive."

"What are you doing, Nancy?"

"Flirting," she says. "Whoa…" She slips. The phone clacks to the balcony deck and skitters across the floor. She twists off the narrow edge of the railing and smacks face-first into the glass. She hangs from the railing, her feet flailing, searching frantically for a hold – a hold that is not the empty space of falling to her death. Both hands on the railing above her head, she needs a purchase for her feet. She knows she will not be able to pull herself up without a foothold. She does not have the strength in her arms. Her right foot finds a lip, one toe in a crack, and this is enough. She pushes up and finds the ledge with her left foot. Then she is standing with both feet on the ledge, hands glued to the railing, facing the open mouth of her apartment. She stops to find her place, to catch her breath, to realize she is not falling. Her back is to the grey city and she is fine. She focuses on the balcony, the cool metal of the railing, the glass.

Nancy is afraid to move. She's a frozen gargoyle, all terror and fear. Her heart is pounding hard. It was a good slip, she thinks. She fights the voices that want her to go sit in the middle of her living room – away from this precipice, and not move for three years. She blocks those voices. She should stay in the place that makes her afraid. Nothing good will come by avoiding the things that make us anxious. "I'm anxious now," she says. "Really, really anxious. Astoundingly anxious. Stupendously anxious." She starts to giggle, then calms down and focuses.

The glass is cold on the fronts of her legs. She takes a deep breath. One leg up and over, and finally her whole body over. She listens to the voices that are shouting for her to have a drink. She glances at the phone, thinks about picking it up, but she needs to take care of her fear. Her fear wants her to sit in the middle of the room and not move. Her fear wants her to stop breathing. Her fear wants to pour a hefty drink.

She grabs the first bottle on the bar. It's the whisky that used to be Ray's and she pours a good portion into a wine glass. She gulps it and the warmth sinks through the middle of her body.

She walks toward the edge and picks up the phone. "Hi," she says.

"Jesus Christ, what the fuck are you doing up there? You have to promise not to do that sort of thing again. My heart stopped."

"Did it really?"

"No. It's a saying. It's an idiom. Are you okay?"

"That was exciting, wasn't it? I'm feeling alive now," she says. "I'm also having a drink."

"Good." He wishes he could have another drink, or two, or three.

"Ray?"

"Yes," he says.

"Do you think that woman who jumped from the Empire State Building died from fright before she landed on the roof of the car? Do you think it's possible to be scared to death?"

Ray wonders if Evelyn McHale was alive in her crumpled car roof nest. Did she have time to cross her ankles and clutch the pearl necklace before she died?

"Ray?"

"I don't know."

"You don't know if it's possible?"

"I suppose it's possible."

"Then I hope that's what happens to me."

"Stop talking like that. If you want me to stay and keep talking with you, I need you to stop talking about dying, about jumping."

"But you're the reason I haven't jumped yet, Ray. You're doing such a good job of keeping me company."

"Okay, I'm done. You know what? Fuck you, if you want to die. Go ahead." He gets into his car, yanks the door shut, and pushes the start button, hard. He tosses the phone onto the passenger's seat but he can't leave.

"Goddamn it," he says. He crosses his arms and stares through the windshield at the blue *Lexus* hatchback in front on his car. A 'baby on board' sticker beneath the rear window. And a stylized fish symbol. As if a 'baby on board' sticker will change everything – as if other drivers will see the sticker and immediately slow down, they will want to give space to the car transporting a baby. It's bullshit. Tulah's mom had tried to get him to put a sticker like this on his car when the girls were born and he had summarily rejected it as nonsense.

He looks at the phone. She's not saying anything – there is no tinny thread of her voice. It's as if she's waiting. He glances at her building, twists and leans back and looks for her. She's not there. Fear jolts up from his stomach. Ray wants to leave. He wants to hang up and drive away from this woman but he can't. The threat of Nancy jumping, and the fact she holds the secret of them means he will stay until she tells him he can leave.

....

Joe's crew is only following the rules. They dig the old sidewalks up and trench a new foundation. In the course of their digging, they tear away all the primary roots on the west side of a dozen mature elms. They don't stop after three trees. They stick to their work plan. They follow the plan to the letter and the plan does not mention trees so they don't concern themselves with trees. At the end of the day, as a courtesy, they decide to call the tree guys. They're feeding tree roots into the wood-chipper when Ray arrives. They've already poured in the gravel bed and they've got a little packing machine going in the trench.

He doesn't remember throwing the shovel. He picks it up in a rage and throws it hard at the first truck he sees. It flies end-over-end and hits the windshield with a sharp crack. Later on, they'll say he could have killed someone.

"Did we, or did we not, have a conversation about the root-systems of elms?"

Joe is standing beside his truck, with a couple guys from his crew. The shovel handle is sticking straight out of the windshield. There's a guy in the driver's seat and one kneeling on the hood trying to figure out if they should try to pull it all the way through, or push it back out.

"These guys are witnesses. They saw you throw the shovel," Joe says.

"Witnesses?" Ray is shouting, crazy loud. "Witness this. I threw a shovel at this prick's truck. The shovel is a penalty for being the stupidest dumb fuck employed by the city."

Joe starts to move at Ray and his boys hold him back, barely.

"Nobody talks to me like that," Joe says. "Who the fuck do you think you are?" Joe is frothing. Ray has never actually seen anybody froth at the mouth before.

"I'm a guy trying to do his job, just like you Joe."

"You're nothing like me, college boy," Joe says.

"Really? I have a couple degrees and you don't, so you take that as permission to be stupid? Is that how your world works?"

"You're going to pay for this." He points at his windshield.

Ray is barely contained. He wants to throw another shovel. But his brain has come back and he knows that he needs Joe to appear more out of control than him. "Well, of course I am, Joe. And you're probably going to keep your job, regardless of the fact that you're the dumbest tree-killing fuck I know."

Again, Joe's boys grab him as he lunges at Ray. Ray doesn't flinch. He'd welcome the pain of a punch or two – and the opportunity to land a couple himself. He turns his back on Joe and looks at Arturo and Hank, bearded, steely-eyed guys from his truck who have protectively gathered at Ray's back. He hadn't realized they were there and feels grateful, and oddly moved by their support.

"Well," he says to them. "Let's weigh the damage."

....

Ray picks the girls up from school and he is exhausted. He's worn thin by a long, long day, and also by the prospect of being hauled into his director's office in the morning. He makes breakfast for supper – bacon and eggs, cereal, and toast. The girls watch an hour of television, and then both Patience and Sarah want a bedtime story. Patience wants the story about the bear and the strawberry and Sarah wants the Tom Waits story about the little boy sitting on the overturned bucket in a world where everything is dead and everyone has died. Ray has told her more than once that the Tom Waits story is a spoof of what bedtime stories are supposed to be – it is, in fact, the opposite of a bedtime story. But she loves it. She wanted to know what a spoof was and after Ray told her, and then reassured her it was not like bullying, she thought the story was even better.

Ray honestly wants the girls just to go to sleep with no stories, but Tulah isn't home yet. He takes a breath. And another. He tells himself the girls won't always want to be with him, let alone listen to him read a story. They're going to turn into teenagers who do all their own reading, and who will want to hang out with friends instead of their parents. He knows this in his gut and he dreads it. Already, he has fading memories of holding them in the middle of the night and singing them back to sleep. Even though he is beyond exhausted, he is pre-missing his daughters. He makes a mug of tea, the King Cole tea that he can only find at one grocery store in the city, and reads the story of the big bear and the strawberry. Then he fakes his way through the Tom Waits story – he is astounded at how dark, and hopeless it is, and how much his daughter enjoys it.

When Tulah gets home, Ray is almost done the bottle of wine he opened after the girls were asleep.

"Hi honey," he says. "There's a little wine left."

"Rough day?" She smells bacon and wonders if she's imagining it.

"Lost some trees today – a stand of a dozen seventy-year-olds. They probably won't survive because I am ineffect-ial, insigacent…because I suck. I suck at my job."

"What happened?" Tulah pours herself a glass of wine and sits down next to Ray.

"I threw a shovel," he says.

"Okay," she says. "That's not so bad."

"I threw a shovel through the windshield of a truck. I threw a shovel right through a fucking windshield. But I had back-up so it's okay. S'okay. Everything's s'okay. My backups had beards. And they were big, big, big."

"Oh, Ray," she says, pouring the remainder of the wine into a glass for herself. "Start at the beginning."

CHAPTER 6

The Lover turns her down

Tulah's Snow Journal
Tuesday, November 23, 2008 #399

This snow is not beautiful! It just makes me feel weary, worn-down and flat. What the hell happened to me? This is yet another snowstorm and it's not even December. Enough already! It seems like it hasn't stopped snowing since early October. It doesn't snow in Mexico and a sandy beach with someone to bring the margaritas seems like a great idea right now...

At yoga last night, Gerta showed us a meditation. "This is the Sa Ta Na Ma mantra," she said. "Sa is the beginning, the totality of everything that was and everything that will be. It is the birth. Ta is life, existence and creativity. Na is death, the change and the transformation of consciousness. Ma is rebirth. It is the regeneration that allows us to experience the idea of the infinite." I think I may have rolled my eyes. I love Gerta. She's a gentle, intuitive teacher. But this was too much.

Christ was I wrong. She showed us the finger movements – Sa is thumb to forefinger, Ta is thumb to middle finger. Na is thumb to ring finger and Ma is thumb to pinky finger. We sat in silence, going through the finger movements of the mantra. We sat for eleven minutes and I broke. At the end of the meditation I was sobbing and I did not know why, or how. It was a gush of emotion from some hidden alcove. It shocked me. Gerta acknowledged that this could happen. She made it easy for me to be where I was. She accepted it and understood it, and then guarded my space. And this made me break a little harder.

The snow. The snow. If I were to define this snow, I would simply call it morning snow. I couldn't sleep. I was up at 5:30 a.m. and I saw the snow as it fell through the street lights. Morning snow is really no different than any other snow, except for the way it makes you feel, because it's morning. And the light is distinctly hopeful in the morning – even light that is subdued by snow and cloud. I saw the snow and felt hopeful. Maybe it's because when it snows, the temperature rises a little. Maybe it's about innocence – the snow covers everything and we begin again. Today, I will perform Sa Ta Na Ma for eleven minutes and see if I can come out the other side focused and calm, and clear. And hopefully not bawling my eyes out. Ha!

....

She is sitting at a Starbucks near Hamilton Square. The windows are fogged. It is not as romantic as she imagines a Paris café might be, but the fogged windows create a hazy comfort, a feeling that this café is cloistered and safe. The snow is a steady, unrelenting thing, and watching snow fall past a café window is always magic.

She watches him as he crosses the street and pauses by a large tree that has been wrapped in lights. Ray would know what kind of tree it is. To Tulah, it is just another massive tree in a boulevard of other massive trees. The lights are blurred and diffused by the snow. The Lover is wearing a black leather jacket and a navy blue scarf in a tight loop around his neck. He needs a haircut. He's wearing a faded Mets baseball cap that is frayed around the edges. It is the third time she has seen him wearing this hat. "It was my dad's team, and it became our family's team," he said, when she asked about it. "We are all about hopeless causes."

The Lover stomps his feet at the doorway. He sits down and does not look at her. He is twitchy and holds his coffee mug as if it's a shield – a barrier against what's to come. Tulah can see something is wrong.

He takes a breath and exhales. "I can't do this anymore," he says. "I feel ripped up inside. I have an ulcer. I can't…"

"…Because I'm married? Is that it?"

"No. Because I am." He half smiles. He has decided this is a good story. It is a believable story that will make for a clean break. Because she knows what it is like to deceive, she will not chase after him. She will let him go.

She tells herself to breathe but she can't seem to find her breath. Tulah had always assumed he was not married. He didn't wear a ring. He just didn't seem married. She'd never asked because it wasn't any of her business. He never talked about his wife. Of course, he didn't talk about his wife.

The Lover sees Tulah looking at his hands. "We don't believe in rings," he says. "It's not something we believe in."

"You have a wife." Tulah takes quick, inadequate breaths.

"Yes." He stands. "I'm so sorry. I have to go."

She sits and pretends to read for an hour, as her breathing returns to normal. She feels rejected and hurt. He'd become a sanctuary for her and she thought she was the only one with the key. Apparently, she was wrong. Someone else had a key and they were there first, tucked into his bed, reading a book and sipping herbal tea.

Did The Lover's wife know about her? This question swirls in her mind. Did she know anything? If they don't believe in wedding rings, are there other marriage customs to which they don't subscribe? All of these questions are moot. He's gone. She'll likely never see him again.

. . . .

A few weeks later, Tulah and Ray decide they will make weekly dates for sex. Tulah had read an article in a magazine that recommended this make-a-date-for-sex strategy and they decide it will be a great way to spark themselves back into having a sex life. They always feel better after sex, no matter how awkward, no matter how stilted or incomplete. They decide that every Friday, no matter how tired or busy they are, they will drop the kids with Ray's mom for the night, and have sex. They won't call it anything. They'll just have sex, make love, fuck – it doesn't matter, they just want to be physical with each other.

"If it's on our calendar, it's more likely to happen," Tulah says. "And it'll be something we can look forward to. You know, anticipation as foreplay. It can just be about us, our pleasure."

They do it for two weeks before it falls apart. The third week, Tulah is angry about something and she locks the bedroom door before Ray is in there. He hears her shut the door, and he can see the light is out. He tests the handle, gently, so she won't know that he knows the door is locked, and then he sleeps on the couch. They never go back to weekly sex. The locked door reverberates in Ray. He goes into the calendar on their phones and deletes the appointments. He knows it's immature and pouty. He realizes this as he is doing it, but he's hurt and he wants Tulah to know he's hurt. By locking the bedroom door, she was telling

Ray that her anger about something neither of them will remember in a couple days was more important than the continuation of them.

Two nights later, Ray and Tulah sit down to watch a movie together with the girls. The girls usually sprawl on the floor or on the chaise, with Tulah and Ray stretched out on the couch, which was weathered, chestnut-coloured leather. On this night, Ray and Sarah curl up on the chaise – he makes a point of asking her to come and sit with him – Patience and Tulah take the couch.

"This is different," Patience says.

"Change is as good as a rest," Ray says. He takes his hurt feelings and resentment, and makes a conscious decision to carry them forward. In time, they will fade away to almost nothing, but even *almost nothing* is a fragment of a thing still not forgotten.

They fall back into the pattern of excuses, and resentment, and unspoken blame – and it all leads to a solid wall of sexual indifference.

. . . .

Tulah was pissed off. She was beyond angry and she thought retreating to their bedroom and locking him out would be better than saying something she regretted – something she would not be able to take back. They'd met for drinks after work and Ray was flirtatious with the waitress. It was supposed to be their night – their special night. The girls were with Tulah's mom, they had the night to themselves, and he decides this is the perfect time to flirt with their server. He should have been focused on her – he should have been moving the conversation toward something resembling foreplay with Tulah. The romance should have been directed at her, not the server, a woman barely mid-twenties and barely dressed. And it didn't help that this woman touched Ray on his shoulder, and then on his hand. She was flirting back. Ray had no idea he was pissing Tulah off with each charming quip, with each playful comment. The fact he had no idea what was wrong pissed her off too. Her anger was compounded by his ignorance about what she was angry about.

. . . .

After The Lover leaves, Tulah is bombarded by a shockwave of emotions – she's angry, disappointed, relieved and sad. Her emotions are so unsettled, halfway home, she wonders about the wisdom of driving. She pulls over to the side of the road and stops. She sits and stares out the windshield as the snow falls steadily through her view. Every couple minutes she flicks the windshield wiper to clear away the snow. There's music playing, a vacuous female pop singer named after a Starbucks coffee who sounds like a dozen other vacuous female pop singers. It's not loud, or soft enough to be annoying. She would not say she is listening to the music, but it's nice that it's there.

By the time she gets to her mom's house, Tulah has had enough of the snow. The roads are sluggish, and driving is slippery and slow. She'd like a couple years without snow. She wants nothing to do with it. She wants to hide from it.

Someone is stuck near the corner to her mom's street. As she drives by, she can see Mrs. Bowerman, who is well into her seventies and lives two doors down from her mother's, standing beside the stuck car. She's standing beside her car trying to wave someone down. She looks helpless and frail. Mrs. Bowerman used to call her mother to complain about Tulah crossing her lawn, instead of taking the long way – sticking to the sidewalk – when she was delivering fliers. Tulah's flier route was a miserable, short-lived job made less pleasant by Mrs. Bowerman's constant barrage of complaints. Tulah couldn't understand what grass was for, if not to walk on. Mrs. Bowerman used to call her 'girl.' 'Your girl walked across my grass again,' she'd say. 'That girl is going to make a path – she'll kill my grass.' So Tulah wouldn't do it for a few weeks, then, she'd risk it – she'd skip quickly across the grass, and sure enough, Mrs. Bowerman would be banging on her living room window, shouting "Girl! Girl! I see you, Girl!"

Tulah honks, twice. "Fuck you, Mrs. Bowerman," she says, smiling and waving as she drives by. She drives slowly enough that the old woman can see who she is.

Her mother is surprised. She thought she had her granddaughters for the whole day.

"Plans changed," Tulah says. She looks at the girls. "We're going to do something fun."

"Will there be cookies? And milk?" Patience is pouting. She is not happy that she's going to miss afternoon snacks with her grandma.

Tulah's mother stops her in the hallway. "Is everything all right?"

"Yes, mom. Everything is peachy."

In the car, Tulah asks the girls what they want to do.

"I want to go to the zoo," Patience says.

"I want to see Santa," Sarah says. "Santa! Santa! Santa!"

"The zoo is closed for the winter," Tulah says. "We can see Santa some other time. Let's do something really fun."

"Santa is fun," Sarah says.

"Yes, but let's save him for another time, okay?"

Traffic is slow. The snow is coming down harder now and Tulah drives aimlessly. She finds herself on 127th Street, heading north. She is not focused. She should be concentrating on her driving and the roads but she keeps drifting to The Lover and his wife. "What the fuck?" she whispers.

She pulls into the parking lot for the Bronx Bowling Lanes and stops near the front door. There are two large women in tight clothing huddled close to the building, smoking.

Bowling will be fun, Tulah thinks. She wants to throw the ball down the lane and knock things down. There's a violence to bowling that matches her mood. She wants to smash the pins with the ball. She wants to pulverize the pins with her ball. She turns around, looks at the girls and sighs. Bowling is a bad idea. Her girls are too young. She's not thinking straight. Bowling is not a game for a three- and four-year-old.

Tulah starts the car. "Santa it is," she says, and the girls cheer. Patience starts to sing *Jingle Bells* and her sister joins her.

"You sing too, mommy," Sarah says.

Tulah points her car in the direction of South Point Shopping Mall, and sings along with her daughters, who are excited and happy in their car seats.

....

There have been many times in her life when Tulah wished she could have a conversation with her sister, or to meet for a glass of wine, or a cup of coffee, or a meal. But Alesha has been living in northern India, in Dharamsala, for the past fifteen years. She went there to study yoga for a couple months and found the people, and the mountains, and the yoga suited her. She got a job in a hotel. She picked up enough Hindi and Tibetan to make her a valuable employee.

"This life suits me," she said after five years. "There are mountains in my eyes every morning."

"Have you become a Buddhist?"

"Not yet. One of the men I work with talks non-stop about it. But I have not been swayed. I am no religion, but if I had to choose, it would be Buddhism."

Tulah gets lengthy letters from Alesha three times a year, and occasionally, a phone call when Alesha is on duty at the hotel. The twelve-hour time difference was a problem, as one of them would always be tired. Each letter begins the same, with a description of the mountains, the cedar tree outside her window, the weather, and the way the clouds look. The last ten years she has been teaching yoga in one of the hotel spas, and she does massages for a steady list of clients in her house. Tulah had seen pictures of this house and it would be a stretch to call it a cabin. It was at best a lovely hut. Tulah has long ago come to a kind of peace about the way her sister started her letters. After all, she lives at the edge of the Himalayas in the same vicinity as the Dalai Lama. Of course it's beautiful, and it ought to be in every letter.

Now is one of the times Tulah wished Alesha had her own phone, or that she was just down the block, or across town; anything but in a lovely hut on the side of a mountain in some distant time zone. She thinks she could share this irrational heartache with her sister. She could share the story of The Lover with her sister and her sister would listen without judgement. None of Tulah's friends would understand. They all adored Ray. Alesha would get it, but she had effectively removed herself from this life, from her nieces, and their mother, and all the details of Tulah. There were mornings when Tulah woke up angry about this removal and moved through her day feeling resentful toward her sister. She loved and missed Alesha but her love was a constant mix of hard-fought understanding and bitterness.

People used to ask about Alesha and Tulah's stock answer was – *She's in India. She studies yoga and she's peaceful; she's peaceful and nimble.*

Mortal sin

There were no cafés in Paris in the 1500s. If you were to travel back in time to 1502 Paris, you would not be able to find a café, or a cup of coffee. Coffee was coming but it would be a few years. Can you imagine a world without coffee? Someone at a dinner party once asked you when you would like to live, if you could pick any time in human history. You said you'd like it to be a year that is after the invention of soap and antibiotics, which was a clever answer, verging on wise. But it was not really in the spirit of the question. Your real answer would likely be 1500, in the middle of the Renaissance. It's just, there was so much going on. Columbus was accidentally finding land between Europe and China. The Protestant Reformation was happening. The printing press. Michelangelo. Galileo. Shakespeare was coming. *On the Revolution of Heavenly Bodies* by Nicolaus Copernicus was published – purporting his theory that the earth revolves around the sun. And coffee. The idea of coffee comes into the English language in the 1580s by way of the Dutch *koffie*, which came from the Turkish *kahve*, which came from the Arabic *qahwah*.

If you look up the word *qahwah*, you might find a description of a particular type of Arabic coffee drink that contains coffee, crushed cardamom, cloves, saffron, and rose water. You might even stumble upon directions for preparing this coffee.

．．．．．．．

Claude Garamond and his lovely wife, Marie Isabelle, knew nothing about coffee. And Vikings knew nothing about coffee. You probably feel sorry for Claude Garamond and Marie Isabelle, and for those imagined Vikings too. You love coffee and they have no idea – no clue what they're missing.

Look, don't worry too much about the fine people of France in the sixteenth century. They may not have had coffee yet, but they had wine and they drank a lot of it. Most of Europe staggered into the Renaissance in a drunken stupor. Wine was a cure for almost everything, in many regions it was considered a food group, and it was the preferred beverage over water. People didn't trust water. They trusted wine.

....

Claude Garamond is watching his wife. She is standing naked in the open doorway looking out at the rain and the forest beyond. Eloise, the maidservant from Allemond, comes only every other day and today is not one of those days. They feel this is their sacred space and they can be naked wherever they wish, and whenever they please – though, the maidservant does complicate this freedom.

Garamond brings his full attention to his wife. He likes the way the colour of her skin contrasts the dark green of the forest that rises up behind her. He likes it that he can only see what the doorframe allows – what is beyond these limits is a mystery. The light in the sky is a translucent grey – it glows grey. She stands there for a long time, just looking and breathing. Her body is shaped like a violin, or a cello. Her curves are luxurious and long. He wonders if she has stopped in the doorway for him, or for herself. She could not know how lovely she looks because she is not watching herself from the bed, so perhaps she is pausing for herself. Maybe she thought she would give him the gift of her behind. Garamond decides it does not matter why she is beautiful in the doorway, it only matters that she is.

She takes a couple steps beyond the overhang of the roof, into the yard, and squats. She lets her water mix with the rain. It has been raining all day and all of the previous night. There was a respite around sunrise, but then it began again. Even though it is August, the humidity of the rain causes it to feel chilly. It is after noon and they have a fire going to take the damp away. Marie Isabelle crawls back into bed and snuggles closer to Garamond. She has come to a place in herself where she no longer craves the commotion of Paris. She is fine and happy here in this dwelling near the village of Allemond. They have become friends with the vintner and his wife, Natalii, and the two couples sit down for a meal each Friday – they drink wine and talk and there is always laughter.

Marie Isabelle wiggles herself closer to Garamond. This is not the life she imagined but it has become a life she loves. This is a sanctuary she has come to cherish – the nuances of light along the forest bottom, the patterns of bird song, the vagaries of light on the river. They have many books – both published and yet-to-be published – and good wine, and friends. Garamond works on his type designs each day. New manuscripts arrive weekly for consideration and it is Marie Isabelle who reads these books first. She gives her opinion and Garamond listens. She suspects her husband could be a publisher soon. When she is not reading, Marie Isabelle wanders through the woods and talks with Eloise who is a fine cook and does most of the cleaning.

....

Marie Isabelle and Eloise have just crossed the river and they are sitting down to dry their feet and legs before stepping back into their shoes and stockings. It is a warm spring day. The snow has retreated to the high places in the mountains and there is new green in the forests.

"There is a boy in the village," Eloise says. "He is the son of the butcher." She stops and regards the flow of the water in the river.

"You like this boy?"

"Yes," the maidservant says. "I like him." She blushes and will not lift her gaze from the river.

Marie Isabelle watches the girl as she dries her feet. She projects innocence. She looks at the world as if she is a newborn chick just hatched from the egg. Everything is wonderful and nothing is dangerous. She knows nothing of the world. She knows nothing about beauty, even though she has it. The girl has long black hair, loosely braided and pulled to the side and she dresses plainly except for a silver ring on her right forefinger.

"We are both women, are we not?" She recognizes this is a stretch as Eloise has just turned fifteen.

"*Oui*, Madame."

"Then it is safe to assume a certain familiarity about the nuances of the female spirit."

"*Oui*, Madame."

"And we understand each other, as women do, about the interplay of the flesh? We can talk freely and openly about the fleshy affairs between men and women?"

"I think so, Madame."

They begin to walk toward the forest along the path that will take them to the Durand residence. The air becomes cooler immediately as they move under the trees and out of the sun.

"Perhaps, even between women this is imprudent, but have you been in union with this butcher's son?"

"You mean fornication and such? Yes, we did," Eloise says, grinning. But she is quickly embarrassed and there is fear in her eyes. "Last month. It was only one time, Madame. With God as my witness, it was only one time."

"Oh," Marie Isabelle says. She was not expecting the conversation to veer so abruptly toward the bawdy. It is not that she is prudish. She is surprised by the candour of this girl.

"I know it is a sin. I know God will punish me but it felt so good, Madame. How is it that something that feels so good can be a sin? I know the sin of fornication is a grave one but fornication should not feel so heavenly. If it is not heavenly then why does it feel that way? Oh, Madame, I fear even this conversation is a sin…"

"Stop," Marie Isabelle says. "Everybody sins."

"Surely not his Holiness the Pope."

"Yes, even the Pope. Even his Holiness Paul the Third. All human beings."

"You and Monsieur Garamond?"

"Yes. Of course, we carry our sins."

"I doubt this very much, Madame."

"Look, forget about the sinning for a moment. What about you? Do you love this butcher's son?"

"Love?"

"Yes, you know? When breathing becomes difficult because he is in the room. When you think about him, always. When you feel as if you are home any time you are with him?"

"But I live on the edge of the village and he lives in the centre of the village. Our homes are far apart."

"No. I was speaking about a spiritual home – you know, when you feel safe and protected and at ease."

"Oh, Madame, the church is very small and the priest is only there two days a week."

Marie Isabelle sighs. It is hopeless with this girl.

Eloise pouts. "It is unforgiveable to fornicate outside of wedlock."

Marie Isabelle stops walking. "Unforgiveable? I doubt God cares," she says.

"But fornication is a mortal sin, is it not?"

"And the two shall become one flesh. So they are no longer two but one flesh."

"What is that?"

"That's the Bible. Jesus said that, actually."

"Jesus Christ?" The girl crosses herself with great enthusiasm.

"Yes. Jesus Christ."

"Did Jesus really say this? He encouraged the two to become one? How do you know Jesus said this?"

"Because I've read the Bible."

Eloise looks at Marie Isabelle as if she is a miracle. "You read?"

"Yes. I read. I can teach you, if you want. Then you can read the Bible for yourself and you will not have to rely on the priest to tell you what's in it."

They walk for perhaps 100 feet in silence. Eloise, with tears in her eyes, looks at Marie Isabelle. "I should like that very much, Madame."

"Good," Marie Isabelle says. "We will begin next week."

....

Four days later Marie Isabelle finds the girl curled into a ball in the corner of the pantry, sobbing. "The priest says I will surely go to hell for this mortal sin. I have committed a mortal sin! I must never have sex again or I will go to hell for eternity. I do not want to go to hell, Madame. Not even for one day."

"Have you performed the acts of the penitent?"

"Yes, Madame."

"You made your confession, you have embraced your contrition, and you have performed some sort of penance?"

"Yes, Madame."

"And I trust you will find some way to make amends?"

"Yes, Madame, but I am worried about my contrition."

"What are you worried about?"

"I am worried that I am not sorry. Part of me is not sorry at all. Only the god-fearing part of me is sorry. I do not know how to change this, Madame."

Marie Isabelle is frustrated by this aspect of the church. She has often wondered if human beings could be moral without God's direction. If people were left alone, what would happen? If we were ignorant of the presence of God, what would happen? It is as if the Church, with all its parental rules and laws, treats people like children, and there is never any growing up. She does not dare speak these thoughts out loud, but surely she can't be the only one having them.

She looks at Eloise, who is tortured with fears of going to hell because she did something natural that felt good. She would like to offer absolution to this poor girl, but for some reason, only men can do this. Men invested with the power of God. Marie Isabelle would like to tell the priest in Allemond to go to hell.

"Say the words of contrition," Marie Isabelle says. "Even if these words are not entirely true. Keep saying these words until they are true."

"Lie to the Church? I do not know if I can do this."

That priest is just a man, Marie Isabelle thinks. He shits and pisses, and has urges like any other man. "Yes. Say the words you wish to be true, take the absolution from this priest, then go home and have a good sleep."

Eloise stops crying but Marie Isabelle can see she is thinking things over. The girl is conflicted and unsure. This older woman has counselled her to lie to a priest, which is a lie to the Church, which is a lie to God, which is yet another mortal sin.

CHAPTER 5

...an outfit for falling off a building

"A wolf's legs feed him."
– Zhanna Petya

The wings were such a common thing in her life she hardly looked up anymore. She would hear the flapping sound and shrug, and carry on. It was as if she was walking through thick mud. When the darkness came, she could barely lift her feet and she was always exhausted. She would remember her father and skipping stones on the banks of the Seym. She would remember the Kapitán. She would remember how everything in her life was slightly less after the Kapitán walked away. And she would remember waking up one morning a month after her father's funeral service and finding a note from Slava. He promised in his note that if she was ever in trouble, he would come, he would be there. He told her that even though he called her his *delicate flower*, he believed she was the strongest of them all.

A literature teacher at her school convinced Nancy to try her hand and heart at poetry, and she found it was a fine way to cope with her frenzied energy and hyper-emotional periods. She could also dive into the darkness with her poetry. She coped better when her darkness was captured on the page. She could focus and obsess about poetry, about words and phrases, and not think about death, or the sound of the wings. She could contain her emotions. The teacher pointed to Anna Akhmatova, Sylvia Plath, and Yevtushenko, and Nancy read everything she could find from these poets. She pushed beyond these recommendations to discover other poets.

At sixteen, Nancy became sexually active. She was sexually hyperactive. She was having intercourse with her math teacher, and a freshman college student from the Kursk State University, and with any boy who showed interest. She slept with a second cousin from Saint Petersburg and a classmate named Sonia. Her appetite for sex, while she was in her euphoric periods, was voracious. Inside the darkness, she wanted nothing to do with it.

When Nancy was nine years old, she made the mistake of telling one of her friends she heard the sound of wings but never saw the birds that made the sound. She assumed everyone heard wings and nobody talked about it. She thought it was normal. It turned out Nancy's friend was not much of a friend, and she told the story to anyone who would listen. Pretty soon, Nancy had acquired the nickname Spooky and she was teased incessantly. One lunch hour, a bunch of boys caught a pigeon and they were chasing Nancy around the yard. The pigeon, held by its feet, was flapping and frantic. A group of perhaps ten boys and girls were following the boys, chanting "Spooky, Spooky, Spooky..." The boy who was holding the bird was named Alexei. Nancy was not afraid of the pigeon or the boy; she was embarrassed, she felt betrayed by the girl, and she was angry that something so personal was out in the open. It was so horribly out of context. They all thought she was weird and she didn't want to be weird in the eyes of her schoolmates. And she worried that perhaps she really was weird. Not weird in a quirky, charming way, but in a bad way – in a way that shone a light on the fact you were damaged and possibly dangerous. She tried to ignore them but the yard was enclosed so there was no place to hide. She was on the verge of bolting for home, but then there would be phone calls to her mother and what had started as sharing a private thing would become massively public. Slava was not a big boy. He was two grades ahead of Nancy but about the same height. He was wiry. His hair was black and long, and he wore thick, black-framed glasses. It was as if he appeared out of thin air. He stood in front of the group and with a soft, pleading voice, said, "Stop. Please. Stop."

"Fuck you," Alexei said, looking over top of Slava's head at Nancy. "Your sister is Spooky. Spooky. Spoo..."

Slava punched Alexei in the throat, fast and hard, and Alexei was down on the ground, clutching his throat and coughing – trying to get a full breath. Slava looked at the pigeon. Its legs had been tied together and it was flopping around on the grass. One of its wings looked wrong, damaged in some way. He picked up the bird and looked at the crowd of kids who were gathered around. They were no longer chanting. Slava scanned slowly from face to face as he twisted the pigeon's neck until it stopped moving. He dropped the bird on the ground next to Alexei. "Anybody else?" he said.

The next week, the girl who had proven to be not much of a friend fell down a flight of stairs between classes and broke her leg. Nancy was not sorry about this accident but she wondered if Slava knew anything about the girl's fall. She did not know where he was when it happened and she did not ask. Nancy was never teased again.

The last time she saw Slava he had new tattoos on his arms and wrists. He was still wiry and lean. She had asked him if he remembered the day the soldier came and told them of their father's death.

"I was fishing," he said. "I remember I pulled too many fish from the river that day. I had to stop. They were biting everything. You always have to leave some fish for the river."

He smiled at the memory and for a few seconds he was no longer a big man with the Brotherhood. He was just Slava, her brother, who resembled their father when he smiled.

"You have his name and you have his smile," she said. "You looked like our father, Slava, just now."

"I regret not being there for you and our mother on that day."

"You were there afterwards. You supported us when we were lost."

....

"Now, you must tell me a story, Ray. As long as I can hear your voice, I am fine. Your voice lets me keep breathing. I want to keep hearing your voice. But I don't know what will happen when we stop talking. I honestly don't know."

"This is bullshit. I'm not going to sit in my car and wait for you to do something stupid..."

"...You can't come up here. I don't want you up here. And you must not leave. Not until we have an understanding."

"What do you mean? What kind of understanding?"

"We need to understand each other."

"I understand you," he says.

"No, you don't. You haven't even scratched the surface of me." He doesn't know about the wings, she thinks. He has no idea what it's like to live with the wings.

"We've made love dozens of times. I think I know you quite well."

"You know a little about my body. And it was seventy-four times, Ray. But it was all silliness. A trick of light across a shoulder blade. A scent of something simultaneously spicy and sweet and squalid. A pocket of lust. A frail thing, suspended in time. I do not exist there. I am beyond there in a place where you refused to go. Now tell me a story."

"I don't know any..."

"...just tell me a fucking story, Ray."

....

He grasps at whatever is there in his brain. Vikings. He starts with the ring. What is the story of the ring? The woman's remains were found in Sweden. It speaks to a range of activity – the Vikings were in the Middle East. They went that far. But what were they doing there? *The Guardian* story talked about an emissary of the Abbasid Caliph whose name was Ahmad ibn Fadlan. This writer was disgusted by the apparent lack of Viking hygiene. '*They are the foulest of all Allah's creatures*,' Fadlan wrote in the tenth century. '*They do not clean themselves after excreting or urinating or wash themselves when in a state of ritual impurity after coitus and do not even wash their hands after eating.*'

"This was only one man's observation," Ray says. "But I can imagine the Vikings were not popular in the seaports of Europe. So perhaps this observation was tainted by hatred."

"Go on," Nancy says.

"It's a love story," he says. "It's the bitter end of a love story..."

Maybe Nancy closes her eyes as she listens. She leans back and starts to see the story Ray is concocting. She can see a couple making love in tall grass near the ocean. The grass flows in waves. The ocean flows in waves. In the distance is a large house with a grassy roof and low clay walls. The house melds with the hilly landscape. At first glance it appears to be another hill but there are people coming and going through sturdy doorways, and there's smoke rising from a chimney at one end. It's as if these people did not want their houses to be seen from the ocean.

The lovers uncouple. Ingemar pulls away, he rolls over and looks up at the sky. Embla frowns. This does not make her happy. It was nice to have Ingemar back from the south, but she's not ready for another child, and this felt as if it was the right timing. There's a softness inside her that screams fertility. She was wetter than usual. And now she was filled with his seed. She stands up. She was making soup and it needs to be watched.

Ingemar picks up his clothing and looks for Embla. She is already back at the fire with three other women who are all shorter than her. "I am going to the hot water," he says, and he strides off toward the hot spring.

"Of course, you are," Embla says, after he is gone. The women around the fire giggle. Ingemar is famous for his daily visits to the hot springs, where he floats and is quiet in the steaming water. He says it helps to heal his wounds. No one complains. Ingemar is a skilled negotiator and because of those skills, they will often avoid battle. The Vikings are not only courageous, savage fighters – they are pragmatic. They will arrive in a harbour with sixty or more ships and it will be Ingemar who goes ashore alone. He negotiates a payment so the warriors in the harbour do not have to invade. He ransoms the village so things don't have to get messy.

When Ingemar lowers himself into the hot water, he thinks about Eira. He loves Embla and their son but he desires Eira, a Chieftain's daughter from Ribe, which is up the coast. When he looked at Eira and she looked back, her eyes were filled with such a ferocious lust that he would be off balance, unable to speak, or think. He was pulled by her need. Her eyes troubled him. Even now, after spending himself on Embla and soaking in the hot water, he is aroused.

"Yet another unfaithful man? Really, Ray?"

"It's the story, not me," Ray says.

"You're telling the story and I recognize it. You make adultery sound so goddamned romantic. It's not, you know. Oh, maybe for you it is, but not for me. For the other woman it's not much fun at all."

"Do you want me to stop?"

"No. Keep going. But I'm pouring another drink first." She places the phone on the coffee table.

Ray can hear her clanking around with the ice, and pulling the cork, and the glug-glug sound.

On the street where Ray is parked, traffic has backed up. Maybe there's an accident up the road. The two west-bound lanes are stopped and the truck beside his car hasn't moved in five minutes. A couple car horns sound behind – impatient toots and longer blasts of *What the Hell is Going on?* He couldn't leave right now if he wanted.

....

"So, this Viking woman, this Eira from Ribe – does she look like me?"

"It doesn't matter," Ray says. "Because nothing happens."

"What do you mean, nothing happens? What the hell kind of a story is that?"

"Ingemar is devoted to his wife. He is attracted to Eira but he made a promise to his wife and he keeps his promises."

"Jesus Christ, sweetheart. If you're going to tell a story at least make the characters do what they would really do. I don't think that's true. It doesn't sound true – this virtuous Viking."

"Ingemar is a decent man," Ray says. "But this does not mean he doesn't suffer. He is tempted and he chooses to do nothing. Do you know the German word, *Sehnsucht*? It means a longing for some thing that cannot be expressed. Is there a word like that in Russian?"

"We have *toska*. *Toska* is a sick-to-your-stomach yearning – a kind of intense love-sickness."

"So this is what Ingemar chooses to do. He loves his wife and he suffers *toska*."

"He's an idiot," Nancy says. "Life is too short for this sort of *toska* suffering. Life was even shorter back then. He should have fucked Eira from Ribe."

"But there's something beautiful about denying. About choosing faithfulness over indulgence."

"You're so romantic it hurts my fucking head."

"I'm not romantic."

"But that's a romantic idea – that sacrifice is honourable, that denying desire is the preferred high road…It's bullshit, Ray. It's not realistic. And it's not beautiful. In reality, people lust and they act on it, or they regret not acting on it."

"I have a question for you. It's not about Vikings but it is a good one."

"Okay," she says.

"What if you were the wife? What if you were Embla?"

Nancy is silent and Ray waits. The sounds of traffic – he hears a siren and then it's picked up by Nancy's phone. The sound in the phone is delayed, as it has to travel up thirty-nine floors, as it bounces off buildings.

"If I was the wife, there would be no straying."

"But what if there was?" Ray says. "How would you feel if you were Embla? Hypothetically."

"I don't like this question. Ask something else."

"You don't like this question?"

"No. Ask something else."

"Ask something else? Like what?"

"Why do you keep repeating things like a fucking parrot? Why are we even talking about this? This is not a good story, Ray. I will tell you a good story. This story is about shoes. Once upon a time, there was a Russian woman who would buy shoes and name them after her ex-lovers. I'm going to buy a pair of shoes and name them after you. There's a pair of Steigers I've had my eye on for quite a while. They will be my Rays."

"Why would you do that?"

"So that every time I wear them, I know I am walking all over you. That you are beneath me."

"That's clever."

"No, not clever. Juvenile, actually, but pleasing. It pleases me to think about it."

Nancy giggles, as if everything is fine.

"But this is pure silliness, isn't it? If today is my last day, there will be no shoes. No Steigers. No Rays."

"I think the Steigers are a good reason to hang around until tomorrow."

"Do you, Ray?"

"Yes. I'll even buy. I'll buy the Steigers for you."

"Do you think I need your money, Ray? Your generosity? Your pity?"

"No. I think you have plenty of money. I don't know why I said that."

"You can help me with one thing."

"What's that?"

"I need to decide if I should be dressed or not. I mean, I won't survive the fall so any concept of vanity is ridiculous. If I am going to be dressed I will need your help to pick out something appropriate."

"Very funny."

"I'm serious. I have a fine collection of lingerie, as you know. In fact, I'm going to put some of it on now. Dying is a serious business, Ray. And one should dress appropriately."

"I'm not interested in your death. I want nothing to do with it."

"Why not? Help me find an outfit for falling off a building. Maybe we can Google – what to wear when jumping off a building – and see what comes up."

"You think this is funny?"

"But isn't that something you love? You know, to sit on the bed propped against the headboard with a glass of something and watch me get dressed? And watch me get undressed? You used to love doing that. You did it with me, surely this is something you do with your wife too."

"Well, a woman getting dressed is a woman at her most vulnerable, and her most beautiful."

"You really believe that, don't you? And what about when a woman gets undressed?"

"That's a different thing entirely."

"How so?"

"One is unintentional, the other, if she knows she's being watched, is intentional." Ray remembers going to see strippers when he was younger and being mostly unaffected by what they were doing on stage. On stage was fake, and plastic, and cold. It was when they were done their so-called dancing, and the lights were no longer on them – and as they started to get dressed a kind of erotic magic happened. When the women started to pull on dresses, or tops, or pants, and wrapped themselves in robes, he was aroused. These moments after the dance were vulnerable. For Ray, these moments were erotic.

A woman in a large, white SUV pulls up beside Ray's car and the window lowers. She toots her horn. He lowers his window. She leans over the passenger's seat. "Are you leaving?"

"No," Ray says.

"It's just, I've been around the block five times and you're still there, and…"

"…and?"

"And nothing," she says.

"Tell her there's a parkade at the end of the block," Nancy says.

"There's a parkade at the end of the block," he says.

"I know," the woman says. "It's just this is a really great spot. And I've been circling for almost an hour now."

"Tell her to fuck off," Nancy says.

"What?"

"Do it or I'll drop something on her fucking car." Nancy stands up and looks around her living room. She spots a heavy crystal vase she'd never liked – an expensive wedding present from her marriage. She crosses the room and picks it up, measures it for flight, imagines it falling toward the street.

Ray looks at the woman's vehicle. It's a Cadillac Escalade – massive and gaudy. And expensive. Eighty thousand dollars, at least, the last he checked. One of his guys had accidentally dropped a rather large branch on an Escalade three weeks ago and Ray had looked up the price of a new one.

"Tell the nice lady to fuck off, Ray. You have five seconds."

The Escalade's window is up and the woman is back behind the steering wheel already.

"Fuck off," he says to the white wall of her vehicle.

"Louder."

"Really?" Ray raises his window.

"Yes, really." She is standing at the railing, holding the vase shakily, with one hand.

"Fuck off," he says again, louder than before.

"Good boy," Nancy says. "I could get used to this, Ray. You know, having all the power." Nancy leans out over the railing and watches the small, white rectangle move slowly down the block.

"I don't like it when you talk to strange women," she says.

"So I noticed. But in her defence, how could she possibly know I was talking with you?"

"I could tell by her voice that she was interested in more than a parking spot."

There are times in Ray's life when he will be in the middle of a conversation and realize the person he's talking with has just said something so incredibly ridiculous it will verge on the concept of insanity. This is one of those times. But then, this entire thing has been on the border of insane.

"So, I think the black lace, La Perla stockings and wide suspender belt – you know the lacy one? What do you think? You always leaned toward the white for some reason. I used to think men liked black lingerie the best, but you ruined that assumption."

"Shut up."

"That's nice."

"Shut up," he says.

"But if I shut up, then what will we have, Ray? All we have are our voices. I talk and you listen. You talk and I listen – well, I half-listen because I don't give a fuck anymore."

"If you don't care anymore, then why are you keeping me here?"

"I'm not keeping you here," she says.

"Yes you are. You threaten to jump if I leave. You keep talking about dying. You keep talking about jumping…"

"…we all have to die eventually," she says. "And today is a good day to die."

Black Elk. From *Black Elk Speaks*, Ray thinks. He read the book in university. It's a quote from Black Elk. She probably doesn't know she's paraphrasing Black Elk.

"Today is not a good day to die," Ray says.

"Do you fear death?"

"I fear your death," he says.

"I'm not keeping you here, Ray – you are. Your guilt. Your sorrow. Your fucked-up sense of honour. That's why you're sitting there."

"Maybe," he says.

Ray closes his eyes. He can hear the wind moving in the leaves of the elms – the hushing sound that could be the ocean. He envies the wind. It moves through the upper branches and beyond. It is barely concerned with gravity. It touches what it wants to touch, when it wants – and then it's gone. It moves beyond here.

....

Ray's not certain but he thinks this is the longest he's ever been on the phone with anyone. His voice is scratched and dry, and his head is pounding – a throbbing sort of pain at the temples. He really wants this to end gently, with kindness, with compassion. His mind whirls with all the possible scenarios. One of those is Nancy insisting on more of the Viking story.

He tries to imagine what would happen next. Perhaps Ingmar gives the ring to Eira from Ribe. So Eira is the woman who was wearing the ring and she was the one they found in 1904, buried in the Viking grave fields at Birka, west of Stockholm. Ingmar gave her the silver ring with the glass stone. He kept it in the folded envelope of a chart for four years, keeping the chart hidden, waiting for an opportunity.

He'd tried to trade for it in Constantinople but the man didn't want to let it go. It was a pink-violet coloured stone that reminded Ingmar of Eira's lips. Eventually, the man, a silversmith, decided the ring was not worth his life and so it became Ingmar's. It became his constant companion – a reminder of Eira and everything he felt for her.

By the time Ingmar gets around to giving Eira the ring, she's married and has two children. Ingmar returned home from the southern lands and his new daughter was already two years old, and his son, eleven. He had not seen his daughter, whose name was Sassa.

Ingmar stops in Ribe first because he is delivering silk from Persia. Ribe is famous for its hot springs and this is where Ingmar goes once he has concluded his business. He is at the hot springs, already in the water, when Eira arrives. She drops her dress and slips silently into the water before she sees him.

"Where is your husband?" he says.

"Who's there?" She sinks down into the water until just her head is exposed and squints into the mist. "I thought I was alone."

"You look well." He wants to hold her face in his hands and kiss her, and not stop kissing her. He saw only the hazy ghost of her as she entered the water through the rising steam. Her black hair woven into a single cord and reaching down her back. Her breasts more lovely than he could imagine – heavy and round.

"Ingmar?"

"Yes," he says.

She inhales quickly and it makes a sound. Eira is embarrassed by this inhalation – she is irritated that her heart was so easily uncovered. "Are you well?" she says, bringing as much cool dignity to her voice as she can muster. "Are you whole?"

"It was a long journey. But yes, I am well and whole." He had new scars but these were insignificant – the wounds had healed months ago.

She moves closer to the sound of his voice – at least, she moves in the direction of where she thinks his voice might be coming.

"In truth," she says, "I have birthed two children and my body is more than I would like."

They are silent except for the sound of the water.

"He went west," Eira says. "To Iceland and beyond."

"Who? Who went west?"

"My husband."

"Yes. He is a good man. A brave man. So I have heard…"

Her voice is whisper. "He's not you," she says. Her hands find him and they are kissing. Her lips are soft and Ingmar is lost. They explore each other, hands searching and caressing, discovering what they can't have in the slow-motion water. They do not stop kissing. They are innocent and surprised by each other's bodies. They are aroused and excited, and at the same time, they both understand it is a dangerous and forbidden country they've entered. It starts to snow and still, they are kissing. They create a new world in the hot water, with the swirling steam and falling snow – a world in which they are the only two inhabitants. A world in which all they feel is protected by the slow water. When they stop kissing, Eira's face is raw from his beard, and she is crying softly. "Tell me about the east," she says. "Please. Tell me anything. Everything."

They are embraced in the pool, the snow falling steadily, the moon a soft, hazy thing, and it is so quiet. They wait inside the silence. If he speaks, the spell will be finished and they will be on their way out of the cocoon. If she speaks – if she again asks for something from him, it will be over. She does not try to make it work in her head – because it can't work. She has children with a good man. She is a wife. She is the daughter of a chieftain. Eira keeps her mind on the feel of being with him, the water and the snow pin-pricking her face. Ingmar does not let his mind venture forward either. Tomorrow, he tells himself, will take care of itself. Tomorrow, he will sail home to his family. This is different than tomorrow. He wants to make love with this woman but if he does this thing, tomorrow he will wake up and trim his beard and his reflection in the washing bowl will not be the reflection of an honourable man.

"In Persia," he says. "Women wear veils. They are hidden and mysterious."

The next morning before boarding his ship, he sends Eira the ring. He folds it into a chart. A servant delivers the chart and Eira discovers the ring. She slips it onto her finger. She will never remove the ring from her finger. Her husband will think it was a gift from her father. She will see Ingmar only one more time and by then he will be an old man.

. . . .

Ray picks Adam Farnsworth up in front of his house just after 4:30 a.m. Adam stows his briefcase in the back seat and puts his seatbelt on.

"I'm not sure why we're up this early," he says. "I don't know what you expect to show me..."

"Trust me, Adam." Ray hands him a chrome go-cup of coffee.

They listen to the radio. There's a story about a new dinosaur discovered in Alberta, an Ornithomimus that had feathers like an ostrich. After the dinosaur story, there's a news report about a missing airplane – somewhere in the Indian Ocean, they lost an airplane full of people. When they arrive at Crescent Avenue, the light is just seeping into the sky. The sky is a reserved pale blue – a graduated band of pink at the horizon.

"How the hell do you lose an entire airplane?" Adam says.

"We're here," Ray says, pulling over and killing the engine.

"Now what," Adam says.

"Now we go for a walk."

Adam gets out of the car and looks up at a canopy of elm boughs. The light is subdued.

"Is this why we're here?"

"The map is not the territory, Adam. We can talk about trees and the beauty of trees until we are blue in the face. You have to see them, and smell, and feel what it's like under these trees. You have to experience the ground underneath to really know them. You have to experience this light." Ray sips his coffee and Adam does the same.

They walk along Crescent. They walk on the crumbling sidewalk under the massive elms and when the trees end, they cross the street and walk back toward the car. Ray doesn't say anything. He lets the trees make their own argument.

Back in the car, Adam doesn't say anything – not right away. He taps out something on his iPad and slips it back into his briefcase.

"You let me know what you need," he says. "We'll find a way to make it work. I just sent you a reminder to send me a schematic of your average elm tree and its root system."

"Thank you, Adam."

"You're right that trees aren't mentioned in the guidelines for building sidewalks," Adam says. "They ought to be."

"Is there a way we make that happen?"

"I don't see why not. Just show us where your protected root zone is and we'll stay away from it."

"You seem really sure about this," Ray says. "I know the way this bureaucracy works. It's slow to change and in the next year, we're about to build a lot of sidewalks."

"And re-build," Adam says, smiling.

When Adam smiles, Ray sees the nine-year-old – it's a kid's smile, mischievous and playful. "Well, I wrote the guidelines," he says. "So amending them shouldn't be a problem."

....

Ray opens his eyes. He has no intention of sharing this with Nancy. She seems to be reading her own overlaid version of the story anyway. Perhaps it's stupid to think that his Vikings did nothing but kiss and touch each other in that hot spring. Perhaps this flirtation with lust is worse than if they'd made love. Now, there is an unfinished thing; a perfect, challenging, unflinching, and unfinished thing.

It's been hours. He's been talking with Nancy for hours. It's time to end it. He needs a good ending to their conversation – an ending that will allow him to sleep – an ending that will allow him to look in the mirror in the morning and not cringe.

....

In March, the Kapitán is sitting outside the dacha with a book and a cup of tea when a bird that is smaller than a crow but looks like a crow lands three feet away from him, on the handle of a broken wheelbarrow. He hears it before he sees it. The sound of its wings scares him. He looks up and all around at the sky and then finds the bird. It's a jackdaw. He identifies it later that day by looking in the Audubon book called *The Bird Species of Russia*, which is one of the books on the shelf inside. In addition to this jackdaw, there are hooded crows, robins, nuthatches, Siberian tits and a tawny owl living in the forest around the dacha. He is not entirely certain about the owl. It could be a boreal owl. He only saw it once, in dim light. He starts to carry the bird book with him anytime he goes outside.

The jackdaw sits and watches Anatoly, as if it's waiting for him to do something. This bird, while related to crows, is greyish in colour and does not have the oily black sheen of crows or ravens. Anatoly's first impulse is to shoo it away. But there is something off about it. It has one blue eye, and one green. This can't be normal. It has to be a genetic glitch. He decides that if this odd-looking bird can tolerate his company, he will reciprocate. He pulls a small chunk of bread from the piece in his pocket and tosses it toward the bird. The jackdaw looks at the bread in the grass, then at Anatoly but doesn't move.

"Don't you like bread?"

The bird tilts its head, as if it's trying to understand.

"It's good bread," he says. "Are you not hungry, bird?"

The jackdaw continues to watch Anatoly, and only when he gets up to go inside does the bird lift into the air. Anatoly stands in the doorway, half-turned and watches as it disappears into the forest.

The jackdaw becomes a regular visitor. It comes each morning when light begins to fill the small dacha. It squeaks and caws outside Anatoly's bedroom window. The bird waits as he lights a fire and boils water for tea. With his tea sitting beside him on a stump, the steam twisting into the cool morning, Anatoly will tell the bird about the book he is reading. "Tatyana Tolstaya. Do you know this writer, bird?"

The bird seems to be listening.

"This book is called *On the Golden Porch*. It is set not too far from here, which probably explains why it is in the dacha. The woman in the book is too dominant for me. I prefer the husband, who is called Uncle Pasha. He is a clever illusion. His life on the surface is dull, filled with routine and following orders, but the depth and richness of his true life is heartening." Anatoly never forgets to put something aside for the bird, a chunk of bread, a sliver of cheese, a bit of sausage.

Some mornings, Anatoly and the jackdaw sit in silence, as if they are waiting for the sunrise. As if they are waiting for the warmth of the sun to ease them into the day.

One morning in early April, Anatoly staggered out the door and fell at the bottom of the stair. He'd finished Tolstaya's book the day before and started drinking soon after. The bird watched and waited for him to wake up, and it was there when he opened his eyes. "You are a good bird," he said. "I am glad you waited. What do you want to talk about today?"

On the morning of April 4, the jackdaw does not fuss outside Anatoly's window. It does not come. It does not caw or scratch at the window pane. There is only the delicate sound of sparrows, and tits, and nuthatches in the forest, doing what they must.

Madame Chernakov

Yup. That's right. Vikings. You know this is another broken promise, don't you? Yet another lie. You had to know this was going to happen.

....

koan
[koh-ahn]
noun, plural koans, koan. Zen.
1. a nonsensical or paradoxical question to a student for which an answer is demanded, the stress of meditation on the question often being illuminating.

....

Chapter 8. At the top. The day of the week is wrong. June 6, 2008 was not a Tuesday. It was a Friday. Does this throw all the dates and days of the week into question for you? Or maybe this confession convinces you that the author has being paying attention to these sorts of inaccurate details all along. Does it matter? Maybe it should.

....

You have a healthy distrust of people who are always announcing how much they love their wives or husbands. The ones who are repeatedly saying aloud how much they love each other, how they adore each other – how beautiful they are. You think about Queen Gertrude in Hamlet – *The lady doth protest too much, methinks*. It's as if they are trying to convince themselves – and the rest of the world – that they love this much, adore this much, or worship this much. Liars! Ray and Tulah are not like this. There has always been a cool vibe between them, even when they were living through those times when couples don't like each other, but still love.

Ray and Tulah were in Toronto one year for the Toronto International Film Festival. They stayed at the Intercontinental on Bloor. At a movie showing, one of the producers of the film they were about to watch offered up a long, drawn-out introduction, during which he mentioned how much he loved his beautiful wife three times, and how grateful he was that she supported him, and again, how much he adored her and how gorgeous she was. Ray cringed for the man – felt embarrassed for him. He does not trust people who show off their love this way. It's meaningless braggadocio.

....

absolution
noun
1. act of absolving; a freeing from blame or guilt; release from consequences, obligations, or penalties.
2. state of being absolved.
3. Roman Catholic Theology.
    a. a remission of sin or of the punishment for sin, made by a priest in the sacrament of penance on the ground of authority received from Christ.
    b. the formula declaring such remission.
3. Protestant Theology.
    a declaration or assurance of divine forgiveness to penitent believers, made after confession of sins.

....

Here's a thing you likely don't know about Ray. One morning, about a year-and-a-half ago, he woke up and realized he could imagine his daughters successful and happy in the world. Not necessarily rich or famous, but rather, happy and mostly fulfilled. He sat down at the kitchen counter with his morning coffee, and knew they were going to be okay. The future would take care of itself. They will struggle and face heartache and be disappointed in their lives, but they'll be fine. He watched them and even at ten and eleven he could see their resilience and gumption.

A week later, he's driving to work and sees a maple tree completely aflame in its fall colours – the stunning oranges and reds massed up against a grey sky. Maybe it's a trick of morning light, but Ray chokes. The tears flow down his face and by the time he gets to work, he has no idea how he feels about anyone in his life. He understands the love he has for his daughters – this is irrefutable and intrinsic but beyond this, there's a void. He feels nothing when it comes to Tulah. He does not care about trees or his job. He is removed and alone, standing in a massive hole. And he can't seem to catch his breath. He can't get a full breath.

In that moment, he knows he could easily turn to Tulah and say – *'I have no idea what I feel for you. I just don't know. I might hate you. I might love you more than ever. I do not know.'* She might be upset about this and Ray can imagine himself not caring about that too. He neither loves nor hates Tulah. He can't even say he likes her. There is just a horrible void. It's as if all the possible feelings one person could have for another are mixed together – love and hatred, lust and ambivalence, repulsion and utter joy, and more. *Good morning*, and *Go fuck yourself*, and *Did you sleep well?* are all the same thing. Everything is the same and all feeling is washed away. It's as if he's been beaten to the point where he can't feel the punches anymore. Ray sits in his car in the parking lot, numb and stunned.

His life feels like a throwaway. And yet, the patterns of his life are just there – ready and waiting for him. The hamster wheel is waiting for him to crawl aboard and start walking again, and to keep walking until he is dead.

At 9:30 a.m., Rebecca Foster, an administrative assistant in his unit who always smells faintly of patchouli, taps on Ray's window, softly. Even this gentle knock scares him. He lowers the window.

"Are you okay?" she says.

"I don't know," Ray says.

Rebecca nods as if she recognizes something. "Yeah," she says.

She walks around the front of the car and lets herself in. She sits in the passenger seat and says nothing. Ray is grateful she does not try to fill the space with small talk. She does not check her phone. She does not seem impatient. She just sits and waits. They look out the front windshield together. They look at parked cars. They watch the trees, and the sky. Eventually, Ray takes a big shaky breath, and exhales, and he tells her what he's not feeling. He tells her this lack of feeling even threatens to overtake his daughters. Just the thought of his daughters has always made him smile – if not physically, at least in his head. But this thing is eating away at that smile.

He talks about Tulah. He tells Rebecca he doesn't understand what happened, and then asks her if she knows what happened.

"I don't know," she says. "But I think you should sit down with Madame Chernakov."

"Madame what?"

"Chernakov. Madame Chernakov. It's what she likes to be called. She's a Jungian. She can help, I think. She has helped me in the past."

"Is she a fortune reader? She sounds like a fortune reader."

"No, she's a psychologist. Deeply Jungian. Mildly eccentric. You'll like her."

....

Rebecca Foster pulls whatever strings she can and Ray is sitting in Madame Chernakov's office the next morning. She is a tall blonde who is turning grey. She's letting the grey into her hair just a little – because, goddamn it, she earned it. Her hair is short and her bangs make her look younger than she likely is. When Ray shakes her hand, he recognizes a steady watchfulness in her eyes. Her eyes are fast and kind and they watch everything. He would not venture to guess as to what colour they are – somewhere between grey and blue, but maybe a speck of green too.

Her office is sparse. It's one big open space – a desk against a brick wall, and a sitting area with a couple chairs and a couch positioned on a blue-burgundy Persian rug. The floors are oak and they creak. The curtains are a blue sheer fabric and they soften everything in the room. The office is on the third floor of a brownstone on 96th Street, next to three buildings that are shuttered and derelict. Ray had to step over a sleeping man who had likely peed himself, repeatedly. In the lobby, he pushed the button for 314 and got a garbled voice that was all static, and then a buzzer.

Madame Chernakov fills a pitcher with water from a gurgling dispenser in the corner, and sets it on an end table beside the couch. "My name is Russian," she says. "But I am not. My ex-husband was Russian. My people are from Finland."

"You kept your husband's name," Ray says.

"Why not? It's a good name and I loved him."

He wonders if by 'ex' she means divorced. There's something in the way she says it that makes him think she could have meant deceased. "And you like to be called Madame Chernakov."

"Yes. It's quite off-putting isn't it? I mean, am I a Madame? Am I a woman who manages a brothel? Or just a little eccentric? Now, tell me why you're here."

Ray takes a couple breaths. He likes the directness of this woman. "It's stupid, but I think I've stopped feeling," he says. "I can't feel anything."

"That doesn't sound stupid. That sounds like a big problem, yes?"

"Yes. Well, I'd prefer to feel things. I mean, I can think about feelings, and understand the feelings I ought to have, but I have no emotions. I'm numb. Well, I cried about a goddamned maple tree yesterday."

She tilts her head and smiles. "A maple tree? Tell me about that tree."

"It was red and orange – you know. It was as if the tree was on fire. It was stunning."

"So what was it about the maple that moved you? What was it about that particular tree?"

"I don't know. I saw it and I teared up. And then I couldn't stop."

"Okay. Were there other trees around it?"

"No."

"So the beautiful maple in all its fall colours was alone?"

"Yes. It was alone. It was beautiful and alone, and it was turned already. I mean, it's only the third week in September. It's too bloody early."

Madame Chernakov wants to mention the Jane Hirshfield poem about a maple that burns for three days without stinting and then drops all its leaves, but perhaps another time. "And this was the morning you realized you had no feelings?"

"Yes. It scared me," Ray says. "It still scares me." He wants to add that he suspects he still has feelings, it's just he can't connect to them. They don't make sense. It's as if his feelings have been translated into a hybrid of Chinese and he's expected to read them.

She writes in her notebook. She lets the silence stretch into the nearly empty room. Ray notices there are no books, no bookshelves, and nothing hanging on the walls. There are what look like framed diplomas leaned against the far wall, as if she meant to hang them but lost interest in the project.

"Often, this sort of numbness is a cumulative response to things that have been hurting us – something painful has been building in you and you've not dealt with. And now, you've gone numb in order to stop the pain. Your body, mind and even your soul are telling you something needs to change. Does that make sense?"

"So this is fixable? I'll start to feel things again?"

"Do you want to feel things again?"

"Are you kidding me? Yes. I don't like this. It's frightening."

"Frightening?"

"I mean it's terrifying. This emptiness is terrifying. I don't know how else to explain it. I can't feel anything." He is lightheaded, dizzy, as if he's been only half breathing.

Madame Chernakov pours him a glass of water. She passes it to him and he takes a long drink. She leans back in her chair and picks up her notepad.

"So why is this terrifying for you?"

"Because it's not normal. Because I've felt things all my life and now it appears to be gone. I never noticed how important feelings were before. That sounds flaky."

"All this is good. But why is this absence of feeling terrifying?"

Ray would love to give Madame Chernakov what she wants but he has no idea what that is.

"Isn't it terrifying for most people to stop having feelings?"

"Yes," she says. "This is obvious. But there's something more for you. I can sense it. There's something beneath the obvious. What specifically scares you about this?"

He thinks about sitting in the car with Rebecca Foster and looking across the parking lot at the East Yard. Trees poking up above the top of the fence. Trucks coming and going in the early morning. "I guess part of it could be that I can still function as if there's nothing wrong. People don't notice and that makes me sad."

Madame Chernakov writes things down. She takes her time. As if she wants to get it right.

"Okay. We'll revisit this. Tell me about your life. You're married?"

"Yes. And we have two daughters."

"And they are how old?"

"Eight and nine."

"And your feelings for your daughters?"

"Those feelings are still there. I know my love for my daughters." But this is a lie. It is only a wish posing as the truth. He's not sure about his daughters. It's just too painful to admit these doubts in the air.

"So it's mostly your feelings for your wife?"

"Yes, but it's more than that. It's the people I work with. It's music, and art, and pretty much everything I feel strongly about. Trees. I work with trees. I used to love trees and now…I have no idea."

"What about parents? Your mother? Your father?"

"My mother? She died. About six months ago, she passed away."

"I'm sorry to hear that."

"It was sudden, unexpected, but I'm fine about it. I don't know if I've been more sad than normal. Is there a right amount of sadness?"

Madame Chernakov looks at him as if she is trying to figure out if he's serious or not. "There is no right way to grieve. No right way to be sad. No correct amount of sadness."

"I have missed her," Ray says. "In the past months, I have missed her."

"Do you mind me asking how old she was?"

"She was seventy-four."

"And how do you feel about your mother's passing?"

"I honestly don't know what I feel."

"And your father?"

"He's not in the picture. He left when I was five. I don't know why. I don't think my mother knew why either – at least she never said."

"Is it important that you know?"

Ray smiles. "Sometimes I'm curious about it, that's all. I mean, was he an alien who got called back to the mother ship? Which would make me an alien too. Which would be kinda cool. Or was he just a prick who, after five years, decided he didn't want to be a father anymore? When I was a kid, I liked to imagine he was a spy who abandoned us in order to save our lives. Or, maybe he was just a really nice gay man who made a deal with my mom so she could adopt a kid. And after five years, he just couldn't keep the charade going anymore."

She tilts her head, puzzled. "So there's a biological dad too?"

"Yes."

"What about a connection with him?"

"It's not something I've thought about."

"So there's been no contact at all?"

"Nothing."

"Do you think you're depressed right now?"

"Is depression a feeling?"

Madame Chernakov nods. "It's more a state of being."

"But mostly, someone feels depressed?"

"Yes, we feel depressed."

"Then, no. I feel nothing. That's why I'm here."

The therapist smiles. As if he's been amusing and she approves. "So you might be depressed. And we know that you are terrified about not feeling anything. You have these two overwhelming feelings – fear and perhaps sadness, but nothing else. So we will begin where there is evidence of some feeling and from there we will move forward."

At the end of the session she tells Ray to start keeping a dream journal. "Every morning you will record your dreams and you will bring them here for our sessions."

"I don't remember my dreams," he says. "Only the strange ones. And very rarely." He is doubtful. How can he write down his dreams when he barely remembers them.

"Put a journal beside the bed and in the morning when you see it, you will remember your dreams."

"Can I ask why you want me to do this?"

"Yes you can. But I think you wanted to say 'may' I ask why? – which is a different question."

"Did you just correct my grammar?"

Madame Chernakov grunts and smiles. "No charge," she says. "We look at your dreams because the subconscious is where the gold is hidden – I think the key to your missing emotions is there, in the subconscious. This is soul work. When you share a dream with me, I will always say to myself, I have no idea what this dream means, then we can begin. We will try to look at them clean."

"Okay," Ray says but he is sceptical.

She can hear the doubtfulness in his voice. "Dreams offer insight into ourselves that we are likely unaware of. That's their value."

The next morning, Ray wakes up, sees his journal, and writes down the details of his dream. He'd dreamed he was in the mountains, standing beside his car, and a bear was coming up out of the ditch beside the road. He felt safe beside the car but he could not move. The bear was massive – though he had yet to see it – and it was coming toward him but he could not move. He wanted to get back inside the car and shut the door, but he was paralyzed. As if by telling him to remember his dreams, Madame Chernakov had willed it to be true.

He starts seeing Madame Chernakov twice a week and tells no one about these sessions. Rebecca Foster knew but she was the one who got him an appointment. They always began with a dream. These talks became a refuge where he was listened to, and there was no judgement. He trusted her and she started to call Ray 'dear.' He, in turn, called her his Madame.

"Oh my dear Ray," she would say. "How are your feelings today?"

"As well as can be expected, Madame," he says.

After three months with the therapist, Ray's feelings start to shift back to normal. Not fully, but he is able to navigate his way forward. There is no longer a massive void. He starts to know what he feels about the people in his life again.

....

temenos

noun

a temple enclosure or court in ancient Greece: a sacred precinct
(Greek – a piece of land cut off and assigned as an official domain, especially to kings and chiefs, or a piece of land marked off from common uses and dedicated to a God, a sanctuary, holy grove or holy precinct)

....

"You said you were adopted?" Madame Chernakov says.

"Yes. I've always known. It wasn't some secret I stumbled across."

"Okay."

"And before you ask, I don't need to find my birth-mom. I am not an episode of Oprah. I am not some teary-eyed, middle-aged woman whose life is not complete until she finds her real mom. I know enough."

"Do you mind sharing what you know?"

"My birth-mom was alone when she had me. She took a trip to visit an aunt in Saskatchewan. She went by herself and was gone for about nine months."

"So you have relatives in Saskatchewan?"

"No. You're not getting it. There was no aunt. There was some sort of home for unwed mothers, a place run by nuns. My so-called dad was long gone by then. He probably didn't even know. Still doesn't know."

"And how do you know this? How do you know about the trip to Saskatchewan, and that your biological father was out of the picture?"

"Do we really need to go through this?"

"Humour me. It gives me a fuller picture of your life."

"There was a note. A sort of love note to an abandoned kid. You know...*I'm* giving you up out of love. I'm too young, and want a good life for you...*I'll* never forget you. *I'll* never forget you. The usual stuff birth-moms say before they disappear. Except, I noticed it's all about her. It's not, *we're* giving you up, or *we'll* never stop loving you."

"Okay. So you were adopted and then?"

"Yes. And then that dad left too."

"How old were you?"

"Five. Probably not supposed to remember that far back but I think I do remember the day he left."

"Jesus. You've certainly filled up on abandonment haven't you?"

....

When Ray meets Nancy at the hockey game, he quickly stumbles forward into her, into infidelity, into a mostly hopeless, nothing-to-lose embrace.

"There's a complication," Ray says to Madame Chernakov.

"A complication?"

"Yes. A lover."

"A lover other than your wife?"

"Yes."

"A lover your wife knows nothing about? A mistress then?"

Ray nods.

"When did this happen?"

"A month ago," he says. "Maybe a little bit more than a month."

"Do you love your wife?"

"Yes," he says. "I think we've already established this."

"And do you love this lover? This additional woman?"

Ray hesitates, then shrugs. His mouth, a tight line of resignation. He has no idea about loving Nancy.

"This is a problem," Madame Chernakov says. "This is a difficulty for you."

"It's exhausting," Ray says. "And difficult."

"Exhausting?" Madame Chernakov sits up straighter in her chair.

"Yes. I'm exhausted by it. Just thinking about it is exhausting."

"What, in particular, is exhausting?"

"The lies. I am constantly lying to myself, and everyone in my life, and when I'm not lying, I'm denying. And when I'm not denying, I'm trying to convince myself that I'm not some despicable asshole with no honour or decency."

"Do you know why you have this extra woman?"

"Why do you call her that?"

"What do you want to call her?"

"Jesus, I don't want to call her anything. I want to deny that she's real. I want to pretend I haven't done anything with her."

"Why do you think you see this woman?"

"What?"

"Just the first thing that comes to mind."

"The first thing? Sex."

"It's better? Or different?"

"No. It happens."

"Sex happens? You mean you are not having sex with your wife?"

"Once or twice a year, and honestly, it's so complicated. It's become such an ordeal that it's almost become more bother than it's worth. It's not fun anymore. It's not playful. It used to be playful."

"Okay."

"And with Nancy it's easy and lovely."

"Nancy is her name?"

"Yes."

"You'd like love-making to be this easy and lovely with your wife?"

"Yes, but I don't know how to make that happen. There's so much shit piled up. So much that we've said. And not said. It's all sitting there."

"Okay." Madame Chernakov focuses her writing. She writes and Ray waits.

"What do you feel for this extra woman?"

He's not sure how he feels about Madame calling Nancy an extra woman. There's too much honesty in it and it grates on him. "What do you mean, feel?"

"What do you feel for her? Desire? Love? Excitement?"

"I mostly think that anything is possible. When I am with her, it's as if anything could be possible. There are no walls. No barriers."

"Okay, but what do you feel?"

"Honestly, I feel excited most of the time. So desire. I think it's mostly desire."

"How do you think she feels about you?"

"Feels about me?"

"Yes. Could you make a guess?"

"She probably likes me. I suppose she thinks I'm swell."

"Swell?"

Ray looks at his therapist. She appears to be surprised and appalled. As if she was not expecting him so use the word 'swell' and having heard it, she is disgusted.

He half-smiles. "Are you judging me?"

"No. But I think you're bullshitting me. I think you do not want to consider this woman's feelings at all. You are denying her feelings. You're denying her humanity because you feel guilty."

Ray looks at the therapist, her neutral face and penetrating eyes. She's got her hand clasped around a pair of reading glasses that hang from a cord around her neck. He wants to ask her if there was a question in that bundle of pronouncements, or if she was just summing up. He doesn't want to admit to himself that Nancy is just about having sex with a pretty woman. It's certainly not about her feelings. It's not about feelings at all. He actually doesn't care about Nancy. It's nothing but sex. And that means he is an incredibly shallow, stupid person, and he does not want to think about that. He prefers the Woody Allen assertion that sex without love is a meaningless experience, but as far as meaningless experiences go it's pretty damn good. He does not want to talk about his own shallowness. Nor does he want to talk about guilt.

God damn Madame Chernakov for arriving at the truth so quickly. She's nodding at him now, as if she can see that he's figured it out – as if she knows she's right. He's not going to give her that certainty. "I think you could be right," he says. "But it would have been nice to have arrived there on my own."

"You want me to act like a therapist."

"Yes. You know, ask those gentle, probing questions and then eventually, I arrive at the truth?"

"Life is short," she says. "Break the rules and move forward."

. . . .

A month ago, Ray parked outside Madame Chernakov's building and for the first time in a year, hesitated when he thought about going inside. He wondered if he needed this session.

Madame Chernakov is intently making coffee. She is sitting at the table and there is a small white timer at her elbow. She is making a French press of coffee and she is waiting for the timer to go off, at which point she will stir the coffee, plunge the screen to the bottom of the carafe, and pour.

She looks across the room at Ray. "What are you going to do with this extra woman?"

"Madame, have I ever called her the extra woman?"

"No, you have not. But this is what she is to you. You have said you will not leave your wife, so what is it that you are doing?" The therapist smiles. "Things have to move, my dear. Things must always be moving."

"The end is near for the extra woman," Ray says. "I can feel it coming to an end."

"Do you think she will be fine with this?"

"These things always end. They don't last."

"That's not what I asked." Madame Chernakov stares at him, waits for an answer and he does not give her one.

. . . .

The first time, Ray meets Nancy in a hotel room, which she insists on arranging. He takes the afternoon off and knocks on the door of 1740. He remembers the colour of the carpet in the hallway was grey and he remembers hesitating before knocking on the door. She is wearing only a garter and stockings, which would not have worked had they been any colour other than white. It was as if she had done nothing special – this was how she always dressed. She kisses him and they fall onto the bed. She is ravenous, as if she is starving. They discover each other inside a sort of desperate flurry of kissing. There is champagne in a bucket beside the bed, which they drink, and after an hour, they order more.

Ray is not looking for it, but there is one disquieting moment that threatens to tip him over. It is the picture of a sexual shiver. It is the thing that anchors his lust to this woman. It is a thing that cannot be planned, or arranged. The sheets and blankets are all on the floor. She is slouched against the headboard, her knees pulled up, and he is opening the second bottle of champagne. His back is to her. He pops the cork, turns around and there is the perfect picture of her readiness – the slumped curve of her breasts in the late afternoon light, the way the empty champagne flute in her hand is tilted, carelessly – and the tone of her skin against the white top-sheet – all of this takes his breath. Everything going on in that moment added to the picture – the heady scent of sex in the room, the anticipation of pleasure, and more champagne. This moment is the thing he chases for the next year. It is the thing he will recall ten years in the future. It will always make him feel a little lost and it will always ache. It is ground-zero for love, or in-love-ness, lust, or desire – it doesn't matter what it's called. Perhaps it is a little like trying to describe jazz.

"Are you going to stand there like a statue or pour?" she said. "Come over here." She spoke in Russian. She was a little tipsy and happy, and she forgot for a moment where she was.

"What?" he said. "What did you say?"

"I said, you look beautiful standing over there."

"Really?"

"Yes, really."

CHAPTER 4

Tulah at 38

Sometimes snow is not beautiful. Sometimes it is just hard to be in it, and it is bitterly cold. But it is not the snow's fault. It's me who makes the snow beautiful, or ugly. It's always me. I bring my sensibilities to it. The snow is a thing. I make it lovely, or gentle, or kind. I personify it. Maybe I shouldn't.

This storm has come from the east. It's managed to stop almost everything. Power lines are down across the city. We still have power. The girls are watching a movie.

I stepped out on the back porch for a few seconds to feel it. It's a stringent cold and the snow is heavy – it was rain before it was snow, and it was above zero before it was freezing. That's why the lines are down, and why tree branches are breaking. The ice covered the branches and then a heavy wet snow.

....

It's luxurious and powerful. It is not the kind of snow that sucks the humidity from the air. Instead, it feels silky on her face – cold and silky. Tulah steps back from the snow and pours a glass of wine. She's bundled up in a down coat and scarf, sitting on the front porch and enjoying her wine. Ray is working with the power company – he's out with a city truck, trying to save as many trees as possible while the crews restore power.

Tulah has marking to do, and a lesson plan to develop for next week – she's been teaching a drama class and feels she is out of her element. Patience has a grade 4 teacher who is not a good teacher – she is unprepared, she digresses and she seems to have no inclination to get her students' knowledge level to the point where they are capable of moving forward. She seems to be just trying to get through the year. Tulah is horrified by this so-so teacher, and offended. She won't make waves but she's going to make sure Patience gets everything she needs to move forward. Also, love-making is on her mind. She is worried about love-making. It's been eight-and-a-half months since she and Ray made love, and he has stopped asking. He's stopped trying and so has she. There's scant intimacy between them and she knows this is not good. They have children. They parent. They work jobs. They come home exhausted and they sleep. She knows how much calmer she feels after they make love, how much more she feels for Ray, and yet they don't make time for it. She tries to imagine Ray with a mistress and can't fathom it.

All these things are cycling through her head, but it is snowing and this changes things. At least, it should change things. This snow that has caused power outages and broken trees, and a gridlocked city, is not kind. Tulah knows it's her who makes the snow magic and beautiful – and there will be snow that helps make that happen, and then there will be snow like this. The bad teacher, and her lack of a love life are colouring this snow. She can't push past her life to find the magic. She thinks the wine will help. She hopes the wine will make the world more beautiful.

Ray doesn't touch her anymore. He keeps to himself. She is growing accustomed to the view of his back in bed. He used to love fondling her breasts, for no reason except they felt good, and now, nothing. He used to caress her body in bed – he would move his hand along the outline of her body and then sometimes, they would make love. He doesn't do that anymore. The possibility that he has lost interest in her is real. Maybe she has failed to be interesting enough.

....

It's early April when they take Sarah to the doctor with swollen glands and an unusual lack of energy. They don't tell her that the options are mononucleosis or leukemia. They drive home with the radio tuned to satellite pop. She's eight years old, for Christ's sake. They just tell her that she's sick and they're doing some tests to find out why, or what it is. Her glands are swollen, and she's lethargic and tired.

Mono is also known as *kissing disease*, and while Sarah is appalled by this idea – because she hasn't kissed anyone expect her parents and her sister – she secretly kind of likes it. The fact she is suspected of kissing a boy will be a little thrilling for her. Her doctor will say it was likely something innocent, like a shared water fountain at school. Tylenol and rest is the extent of the treatment, and limited contact sports for a few months, which suites Sarah fine. She's a reader and she will be encouraged to read a lot more than she already does. She will spend her days lolling around the house, reading and watching TV. When she complains about feeling achy, they will give her Tylenol. All this if it's mono.

Ray and Tulah try to act normal, but they are both living in the land of 'What if?' Tulah's mom comes over and pampers Sarah. Ray and Tulah do not tell her about the options. They both try to carry on as if everything is mostly fine. But it doesn't last. Tulah arranges a few days off, and Ray only lasts a half-day at work. He's with a crew in the downtown core that is taking out trees that will be replaced. The trees are either diseased or damaged beyond repair, and Ray can't focus. One of his girls is sick and it could be bad. He can't work. He's going to drop someone out of a tree or he's going to fall out of a tree. He's distracted. He does not ask permission to go home. He just tells his crew he's taking the rest of the day – a family matter.

He and Tulah hold each other. "We will deal with whatever comes," Ray says. "And we will come through. Sarah will be fine. No matter what, she will be fine." They crawl into bed and talk until they're hoarse. They try not to get ahead. The doctors don't know anything. It's a blood test and then they'll know. Until then, it's only mono. It's kissing disease. That's all it is. They tell each other this but then they hold onto each other because they are afraid. Ray wakes up at 3 a.m. He checks on both girls and makes tea. He finds a Western on TV – a movie called *Silverado*, which is partly a Western and partly a send-up of all Westerns. At 4:15 a.m., Tulah snuggles in beside him. They watch with glazed eyes – focused but not focused, following the movie and not really seeing anything. They drift in and out of sleep until Patience wakes them up at 7:30 a.m. The alarm in their bedroom woke her up.

"Can you get Sarah up, Patience? Tell her we're making breakfast." Tulah flops over onto the couch and her cheek finds the cool leather.

Patience scurries down the hallway and in a few minutes both girls appear at the kitchen bar. Ray places bowls in front of them. He looks at Sarah. Notices the bags under her eyes. "How are you feeling?"

"About the same. But my throat is sore."

"If you want to go back to bed you can," Ray says. "Or, you can have ice cream and bananas for breakfast."

"Yes, please," Sarah says.

"Me too," Patience says.

"Me three." Tulah has joined them at the bar.

Ray drives Patience to school and Tulah tucks Sarah into their bed. She throws a load of wash into the machine and sets the timer. In the shower she thinks about how she is going to fill her day with activities so she does not constantly worry about Sarah. Because she will speculate and think about worst-case scenarios. She will worry herself into believing it's bad news. She will go online and scare herself shitless with half-facts and symptomatic medical diagnosis sites. She will allow herself to become a pathetic wreck. If she does not keep herself busy, this is what will happen. She knows this about herself.

Ray brings home three massive bottles of Orangina because he knows Sarah loves it, and she's supposed to drink a lot.

....

Nothing mattered but Sarah. For three days, as they waited to hear about the results of the blood test, nothing mattered. Making love or not making love, good teachers or bad, jobs and friends; all these things shifted toward irrelevant. These details of a life became dandelion fluff floating around in a big empty room.

They get the call on the third morning.

"It's mono," Tulah whispers after she hangs up, and they collapse into each other in tears. They hold on as a wave of relief pounds against them and through them.

....

Two weeks later, one of her kids brings it up in class and she doesn't have the heart to shut him down. She doesn't want to be hard. She has been trying to be less rigid about things. She's not up to it this morning.

"What about the creation theory?" Brad Bucknell's face is earnest and it appears he really wants an answer – he's not just poking the teacher bear with a pointy stick.

"You mean the creation story?"

Brad Bucknell has no idea. He only knows he's heard the term *creation theory* and so this is what he repeats. This is what he says he believes. There is no distinction between story and scientific theory for him. Creation is true and that's all he knows – it's all he's been told.

"We don't cover that in this class," Tulah says.

"But we believe…"

"…it's not in the curriculum, so we don't cover it," Tulah says as gently as she can. "Okay? Now, I believe we were talking about how scientific knowledge is developed and tested. How does a scientific theory differ from our everyday understanding of the idea of a theory?" Tulah looks around the room. "Anyone?"

But Brad Bucknell is not finished with her yet. He stands up and his voice booms in the room. "In the beginning God created the heavens and the earth."

Tulah sighs. "Mr. Bucknell. First of all, you raise your hand if you want to say something in my class, and secondly, this is not a Bible school. It's a science class. If you want to stand up and shout Bible verses I suggest you save it for Sunday service. Now, sit down." Her voice becomes hard and raspy.

Brad Bucknell smiles. He does not sit down. "Are you saying that God didn't create the heavens and the earth?"

"God? Well, Mr. Bucknell, not that it's any of your business, but I like to imagine a world where God does not exist. Because everything would be permitted."

"What?"

"If someone can tell me who said that – without resorting to Google, I will be very impressed." Tulah looks at Brad Bucknell's face. He's confused and a little off guard. "We were discussing the idea of scientific theory and creation is not a theory."

"Are you an atheist, Ms. Roberts?"

"My beliefs about God are irrelevant in this class Mr. Bucknell. Sit. Down."

Brad Bucknell can hear the crazy edge to Tulah's voice. Her voice has become a high-pitched razor wire. He sits down.

Tulah wants to assign her class an essay on the differences between religious doctrine and scientific theory. She wants to force feed them the understanding but she steps back and smiles.

"Jean-Paul Sartre attributes that quote about God to Dostoyevsky. 'If God did not exist, everything would be permitted.'" Tulah looks around her classroom. "Jean-Paul Sartre, anybody?"

Kyla Rubins, who always sits near the front of the class – never right at the front of the class, raises her hand. "He was a philosopher."

"That's right, he was a French philosopher, playwright, novelist, and more. Anybody want to weigh in on Dostoyevsky?"

． ． ． ． ． ．

"Why are we so wired up to know the answers to why we're here, and how we're here?" Tulah looks at Principal Hartman. They are standing in the hallway after school. "What the hell, Jerry."

"Okay, come with me." He guides her to his office, shuts the door and locks it. He unlocks the bottom file drawer, pulls out a bottle of bourbon and pours two drinks.

"I mean, this kid has an uncle over in Afghanistan fighting the Taliban. Little Brad Bucknell would be the first to agree that the Taliban are fundamentalist pecker-heads, and he has no idea that he's on his way to becoming a fundamentalist pecker-head himself." Tulah shoots back her bourbon and Principal Hartman pours her another. "Little Brad Bucknell is just a few baby steps away from stoning homosexuals in the square and insisting that women be completely covered, and all men grow beards."

"Was it that bad?"

"You should have heard this kid today. Loud and cocksure and so dense."

"I've met the parents. The nicest, sweetest couple you could imagine."

"Go figure," Tulah says.

"Salt of the Earth. I'd venture to say, enlightened."

"So what happened to their kid?"

"God works in mysterious ways."

"Thanks for this," she says, holding up her glass. "And for letting me vent. It's been a rough couple weeks. I'm overreacting. I overreacted. Poor Brad Bucknell."

"I saw him in the hallway after class. He looked no worse for wear. He was fine."

"We shall see what tomorrow brings."

"I've got your back, Tulah. You know that, right?"

....

Ray's mom dies on a Sunday morning in early February. Edith Daria Daniels gets up and dresses for church. Five years ago she became a member of the First United Pentecostal Church on Downy Avenue. She sits down at the kitchen table with her usual cup of instant coffee and a muffin. At some point, halfway through her muffin and with half a cup of coffee left, Edith exhales and everything stops. She didn't choke. She just keeled over onto the floor.

Ray finds out from her doctor that his mom had breast cancer and she had refused treatment. She did not tell her doctor this, but she was convinced God was going heal her – she believed in divine healing. She believed in the power of the faith healing at the First United Pentecostal Church. When Ray read this in her journal, his mouth fell open. His mother was a bright woman but it was apparent in her writing that she was terribly lonely.

In fact, she did not die because of the cancer. She died because she had a massive heart attack.

It's 4:30 a.m. and Ray is standing at the graveyard. The snow is a sigh in the air, as if it is falling in slow motion. His mom was put to ground yesterday afternoon and at 3:30 a.m., after trying for three hours to fall asleep, he decided to go back to the graveyard and have a chat with her. He writes a note for Tulah and drives to Speyside Cemetery. The snow starts as he turns onto the main road. He parks and starts out toward the spot where she's buried. The snow falling through the lights along the road makes the light a clearly defined thing – it only goes so far. A rabbit watches him as he walks by. It doesn't move but it's ready to move. The rabbit is hunkered down in front of a headstone for Jessie Abernethy – born December 4, 1825, died December 5, 1895. Jessie Abernethy is 'Not Forgotten.' Ray wonders who it was who was not going to forget her.

He arrives at his mother's grave and stands under the two, robustly healthy Douglas firs. He looks at the mound of dirt that is quickly being covered by the snow.

"I'm sorry you were lonely," Ray says.

You read my journal, he imagines his mother saying.

"I hope it's okay that I read it. I'd forgotten how well you write."

I have always had nice handwriting.

"You know that's not what I mean. I mean you put words together in a way that is pleasing, entertaining and often moving."

You're upset about the Pentecostals, aren't you? It was comforting. That's all it was. It was an extended family.

"I don't care about that but faith healing, mom? Really? I mean, it's superstitious insanity. You're smarter than that."

I know. I know.

"Do you? I mean the Bible is not a medical journal, mom. You had cancer and your response was something out of the Dark Ages."

I know what I had.

"I'm just saying, people recover from breast cancer all the time, and it's not because of faith healing, or prayer."

Tell me how you are.

"I'm not done with you and the Pentecostals."

It doesn't matter now. Anyway, I had a heart attack.

Ray pats his left shoulder to knock the snow off, then his right.

"You're right," he says. "Sarah has mononucleosis. She has mono but she's going to be fine."

Poor dear. You had mono when you were in grade 2.

"What? I don't remember that."

You missed six weeks of school. The kids in your class sent you get-well notes. I still have them somewhere. Well, you have them now.

"Did you at any point take me to church to get healed? You know, when I had mono?"

You don't want to let it go, do you?

"I'm fine now. I had to get that out of my system." Ray inhales the cold air and then exhales in a long stream. "I should have come around more. I should have been there for you. I didn't know you were so lonely."

Never underestimate loneliness, she says. *It's an affliction. It's a pack of barking, yipping dogs and sometimes it's difficult to control. It can even bite you when you're in a crowded room, or in bed with a lover.*

"I'm sorry...I should have noticed. I..."

He imagines no response. He does not want to forgive himself so he lets his mother's voice go silent. He leaves her with her Pentecostals, the foot-washing, the healing God, and Hallelujah, and amen.

....

After his mother's death, Ray becomes more desperate for life. He hugs the girls a little longer every night. He watches them sleep sometimes and the act of standing in the doorway becomes a long prayer for their safety and their happiness.

He and Tulah drink better wine.

He wants to make love with Tulah. He wants it to be raw and uncertain, as if they are discovering something. But he has no idea how to lean over and start kissing her. Nor does he remember how to touch her body. She is far away and he feels clumsy and stupid and inadequate. The last dozen times he tried to start to make love with Tulah, she was not interested. His mind has been telling him to stop struggling – his mind wants him to give up, to accept a marriage with no sex, that it's fine. His body just wants pleasure. He feels betrayed by this, and older than he is, and sad. He feels betrayed when in the middle of the night Tulah will reach out and hold his hand, because this is the act of a lover, and they are not lovers anymore. These vague intimacies are petty deceits and they stab at him – they mock him. Ray is stalled between decidedly doing nothing and moving blindly forward on faith.

The Summoner's Tale

They meet at the river. Monsieur Gauguin and his wife are on the far side and Garamond wades into the stream; he pushes across the river to greet them. Natalii pulls her skirts up to above her waist and the two men, Garamond and Gauguin help her across the river. Marie Isabelle sits on a rock and watches. She laughs when Natalii almost falls into the water and the two men almost fall with her. There is much splashing and finding footing on the tricky river stones and then they're safely across. Gauguin turns around and goes back into the river to fetch his bag on the far shore and he moves much quicker by himself. Once he is back with them, they walk through the forest toward the Durand villa.

Eloise has prepared a feast of roasted chicken and a mix of vegetables, including turnips, leeks, and beans. The dinner is rounded out by the addition of a smoked ham and a selection of pork sausages with a creamy peppercorn sauce. After dinner they nibble on a slab of Brie with a platter of plump Gamay grapes.

"I have a story from the English writer Chaucer," Gauguin says.

"Not Chaucer again," Natalii says. "Please, Maurice. He is a crude writer. Soon Marie Isabelle and I will be having conversations about the chickens and asking each other if our cocks are okay. Is your cock performing? Does your cock stand?"

Marie Isabelle looks at Natalii with amusement, her eyes glistening and intrigued.

"I heard this one only three weeks ago," Gauguin says. "A soldier in the tasting room shared it. He said it was one of Chaucer's but of course, there is no way to know for sure." Gauguin called the small tavern attached to the vineyard a tasting room because that's what it was used for.

"I would love to hear a story," Marie Isabelle says. "Please, Monsieur Gauguin."

"Maurice," he says. "Please call me Maurice."

"Very well, Maurice," she says. Marie Isabelle looks at Natalii. "If it is not too much of an inconvenience for you, dear Natalii. I love stories. I would love to hear a story."

"He has promised that it is a new story, so I have no more objection in me. But I warn you: once you leave the gate of the corral open, the horses will run for many, many miles and soon it will be the middle of the night and you will have forgotten that you started out trying to find the horses."

Gauguin looks at her as if he is not quite sure about how deep her insult cuts, but he lets it go. "Chaucer, in these tales, is writing about pilgrims," Gauguin says. "They are on their way to the cathedral in Canterbury, and they are all telling stories. It's a competition of sorts."

Of course, Garamond knows about Chaucer's audacious manuscript, and has read some of the tales. Though his English is not as refined as it should be, he managed to get the gist of Chaucer's work. Garamond is intrigued to see which tale Gauguin intends to share.

"There is a Summoner," Gauguin says, "and his tale involves a friar who travels from church to church, preaching and begging for payment. As soon as this friar gets his payment he moves to the next church. He would often write down the names of his benefactors on a tablet, with a promise to pray for them, but he would then erase these names as soon as he was on the road again. He is more charlatan than holy man."

Gauguin pours wine into glasses all around the table, plying his audience.

Garamond is intrigued. He has not read the Summoner's Tale. He thinks about the summoners he knew in Paris, men who worked for the church and would call people before the court for their spiritual crimes such as adultery, or heresy, or witchcraft, with the threat of excommunication always front and centre.

"This friar visits the home of a wealthy man who is sick in bed and attempts to extort money for prayers. Imagine the wickedness of such a thing. This supposed holy man, this shit of a friar tells the sick man that he has not recovered because he has not given him enough money. The friar then delivers a sermon about the dangers of anger and the importance of giving money, and at this point, the sick man reaches his limit. He tells the friar that he does indeed have something more to give him, but that he must swear to divide it evenly with all the other friars. The friar nods his head contemplatively and then solemnly he agrees to do it. So the sick man tells the friar to put his hand down his back and beneath his buttocks, where he has hidden something of great value." Gauguin starts to laugh. "Can you imagine this scene? Come, Natalii. Stand up with me. Let us make a demonstration."

Natalii shakes her head. "No, thank you, Maurice. I am comfortable where I am."

They have all been drinking wine and so Marie Isabelle stands up and pulls Natalii with her. "You tell the story, Maurice, and we will perform the actions." She smiles at the Vintner's wife. "Okay?" And Natalii nods.

"A perfect solution, my dear," Gauguin says. He plops himself down at the sturdy wooden table and takes a gulp of his wine.

Garamond is amused. He is happily drunk, but not so drunk as to be silly. The dinner sits well in his gut and the wine is a fine companion. The company is delightful.

Gauguin clears his throat. "*Put thy hand down by my back*, the sick man says. *And grope well behind. Beneath my buttocks.* And this is exactly what the friar does. He thrusts his hand into the cleft and feels around, looking for the valuable prize."

The men watch as Marie Isabelle snakes her hand under the waist line of Natalii's dress and reaches down beneath her ass, and curves into the beyond. Natalii giggles, a nervous, hesitant sound in the room. It is wet between her legs, and warm.

"And?" Marie Isabelle grunts. "And?"

Gauguin continues. "The friar is groping around down there, feeling all around the sick man's anus…"

"…Oh," Natalii says and they all recognize that it was not a voluntary utterance. All four of them start to giggle.

Marie Isabelle can feel the shiver that starts in Natalii's lower back. They share this secret.

"Just as the friar is groping all around sick man's ass, the sick man lets loose a voluptuous fart against the friar's hand."

"What?" Marie Isabelle says.

But Natalii bears down quickly and releases a fart into Marie Isabelle's hand, and they are all laughing. They can hear Eloise laughing in the pantry. Marie Isabelle leaves her hand between Natalii's cheeks and only when they stop laughing does she remove it.

It feels as if she is moving her hand slower than she ought to, as if it has its own mind, and does not want to leave this place.

When they finally calm down, Garamond pours wine for all that want wine, which is everyone. He is happily excited and he is aroused.

"You beautiful actors upon this trifle of a stage can sit down now," Gauguin says. "You were an excellent representation of the tale, and funny as funny can be, but let me tell you, there is more, and it gets better."

Natalii sits down next to Garamond, who is trying to hide his erection by pulling himself a bit closer to the table. She looks at his lap, smiles and shakes her head.

Eloise comes into the room, her eyes down and away from the possibility of any engagement. She tends the fire, making it bigger, and then retreats to the pantry.

While everyone is watching Eloise, without looking, Natalii reaches behind and places her hand on Garamond's cock, as if she has actually put her hand on his knee and the gesture is completely innocent. He does not remove her hand. He does not react at all. "Carry on, Maurice. Take us to the end," she says, squeezing.

Natalii's hand remains in Garamond's crotch, and he looks across the table at his wife, who sneaks her hand up to just beneath her nose and inhales deeply.

Gauguin, who was watching Eloise at the fire and followed her retreat, smiles at his wife's encouragement and clears his throat.

....

A week later, Gauguin and Garamond have ridden high up into the mountains as Gauguin wanted to show him the route of an escape, if it came to that. At the edge of a meadow, they dismount and lead the horses. They push across the meadow and up the mountain toward a rock wall. At the base of this wall is a small lake where they will rest the horses.

"There was something honourable in the friar," Gauguin says. "No matter how corrupt, or despicable, he could not hide from his own honour."

They have returned to their ongoing discussion of the Summoner's Tale.

"That is the real joke of this story," Garamond says. "The heart of the story is that the friar is tortured by this promise to share what he found. He made a vow and something inside him insists he must stay true to that vow, no matter how absurd, or abhorrent."

"Do you think we all possess that kind of honour?"

Garamond stops, caresses the side of his horse's face. "I do not know, my friend. I would like to think so."

....

What if you don't like it that the Kapitán died? Maybe you thought he was a decent enough man and even though drinking himself to death seemed true, you just didn't like it. You'd like to see him survive. Do you actually know anyone who has died of liver failure? Okay, even if you do know someone, do you know two people? See? It's rare. Think about the telltale signs that there may be some whopping lies in this story. What if the title of this book is true? What if the Kapitán's death is one of the big whoppers?

So on the morning of April 4, when the Jackdaw comes looking for Anatoly at the window of his dacha, he is gone, but not gone in the sense that he is dead. He is removed. He is no longer there. Maybe he woke up on the morning of April 3rd, took a deep breath and realized there was a different kind of duty; a duty to keep breathing, a duty to try and give something back. He decides to honour the gift of his life. Did he have a dream about his mother, or his sister? Did an old lover visit him in his sleep? This lover would be naked and dark and luxurious, and she would whisper the truth to Anatoly. "Forgetting is not courageous," she might say. "There is no honour in forgetting. Forgive yourself and move forward." And then she would lean in to kiss him hard; a sweaty and desperate kiss that would draw Anatoly back toward life. He would never take another drink. Sometimes he would want to drink but he would never again need a drink.

Maybe he moves to Kursk, assumes a new name and opens a bookstore across from Killfish Discount Bar on St. Petersburg Street. He starts to look for ways to make a difference. Then one day, a woman to whom he once delivered bad news walks into his bookstore, and even though he is much too old to be in love, he is smitten.

CHAPTER 3

"I feel certain that I am going mad again"

"You do not need a whip to urge on an obedient horse"
– *Zhanna Petya*

The darkness came for her again, a week ago and it was a devastating bleakness. The sound of the wings was in her dreams. It was so loud and she could not move. The sound enfolded her. She was in the middle of it. Wingtips brushed her face and the air was a mayhem of back and forth, and up and down. She startled awake, and managed to lean against the headboard but she did not get out of the bed. She wanted to go back to sleep, but she'd already slept eleven hours. She does not want to think about what the spark was. There were a few therapists over the years that wanted her to go back to the onset of the darkness and try and find the trigger. *What's the trigger?* they would ask. *What happened just before the sound of the wings?*

She and Ray had made love the day before. He'd arrived just before 3 p.m. and left at 5:20 p.m. After loving each other he'd asked her about her hometown.

"Kursk?" she said, coming out of the bathroom. "It's old. And relatively small."

"Did you live in a house?"

She looked hard at him, suspicious and unsure. He was sprawled on the bed where she left him. His cock was spent and limp, and flopped onto his leg. She'd made sure to cum. In fact, she'd orgasmed twice. It was almost too much pleasure and she felt drained by it. She was unapologetic about getting her own orgasms. She pursued this release aggressively and rarely failed. Talking about sex would have been easier than responding to these queries. His questions disturbed her. It was almost too personal. She was being asked to open up and it felt too vulnerable. It was confusing. Why was he interested in the place she grew up? Why now, and not any other time over the past year?

"It was a kind of row-house, so attached to others."

"Were you a happy kid?"

"No, Ray," she said. "For the most part, I was not happy. My father died and my brother left. My brother and I were best friends. And it was Russia before Glasnost."

"No moments of joy? No happiness?"

She sighed, closed her eyes and drew on the well of her memory. "There was one time when I went fishing with my brother and it was beautiful. And there was a teacher of literature who encouraged me to write poetry." She would not tell him about her father. Her father would not have approved of this adulterous entanglement. He would have thought it harmful to her in some way. He would have told her she is diminishing her soul. He would have been right.

"Do you still write poetry?"

"Poetry?"

"Yes. Do you still write poetry?"

She can't decide if she wants to tell him about her poems. As if writing poetry is more intimate than what they just did. As if poetry is more exposed than sex.

"Not for a long time," she said.

They went back and forth like this, and while it made Nancy uncomfortable, she had to see where it was leading. As he was getting dressed he told her he was embarrassed about how little he knew about her. These were normal, everyday questions. Her answers were the little things that lovers knew about each other.

He stopped in the doorway, the edge of the door in his hand, and turned around to look at her. It was a long look, as if he was trying desperately to remember her, the light on her face, the mess of bed behind her, the curve of her belly, the smell of sex in the room. He'd never looked at her like this before.

When he was gone Nancy reached for the remote and turned on the television. She started to flip through the channels but nothing appealed to her. Nothing stopped her. After a half-hour of flipping and trying to be interested in something, anything, she quit. She muted the television. She left it on because it was a flickering light, and that was something. She found three-day-old pizza in the fridge and warmed three slices in the microwave. She ran a bath and poured green bath salts into the bubbling water. She lit candles and slipped into the hot water. There were a dozen books piled in the window beside the tub but none of them was the right book. She could feel the darkness coming and wanted to say no. She wanted to reject the darkness before it arrived. She wanted to return it unopened. After two hours in the bath, she was still twitchy and anxious. The looming darkness was almost worse than the darkness itself.

There were so many pharmaceutical options. She'd been diagnosed properly a few years ago as a mid-level bipolar. "It's not as frightening as it sounds," the doctor had said. "It used to be called manic depressive disorder, which is a kinder term I think."

Nancy had glared at him, her face a flat and focused disapproval.

"Or, we could just go right on calling it bipolar."

The term bipolar made her think of two polar bears and that cheered her up a little.

She knew what to do. She knew there were drugs that would take the edge off. She had a lot of pills in her bathroom cabinet, *Valproate* and *Zeldox* among them, but for now, she rejected these. She decided to call her brother first. It was 9 p.m. in New York. Her brother could talk her through. He always made her feel better. He was able to even her out to the point where she was thinking straight. She punched his number and the phone rang six times. A woman answered. Her voice was hard but it was definitely a woman. And just like that, Nancy knew her bother was dead. She stopped breathing. Her heart stopped beating.

"Yes?" the woman said.

"I was…I was looking for Slava," she said, hoping against what she already knew.

"Who is this?"

"This is his sister, Nensi." Oh God, she was thinking. Make this quick. Please don't fuck around.

It sounded as if the woman was shuffling through papers. Finally, the shuffling sound stopped. "Slava was killed yesterday," she said. She switched to Russian. "Your brother is dead. I am sorry."

....

Nancy takes a breath. She exhales without thinking. She takes another breath, and in slow motion she places the phone down on the couch.

She should have asked 'how?' She should have uttered that one word, 'how?' But she could not form the word. It would not come. And what does the 'how' matter? 'What' was devastating by itself. It did not need the 'how.' He was killed. That's all she needs.

She sits and does nothing. She sinks into a paralysis. She can't comprehend what the woman on the phone has said. She is thinking only in Russian. The woman told her something she already knew, some news she does not want. She wants to reject this woman's message. It could be this woman has found Slava's phone and she is making a joke, a cruel joke. But when, in ten years, has Slava ever not answered his phone? No, she was not joking. She was telling the truth. Nancy decides she should call her mother but she's confused about what time it is in Kursk. She does not want a drink but she thinks she should have one. It's what people do. When someone...when someone...people drink when that happens to someone you love. She will call her mother tomorrow. Tomorrow is a long time from now, perhaps. And she will be more focused tomorrow. Perhaps she will never leave this room. She will sink into the couch and she will dissolve and no one will be able to find her. Police detectives will form hunches about her whereabouts. One smart detective will drop a line into the couch. The line will have a sharp hook. He will be hoping to catch her. But she will be so dissolved and small she will be able to just sit and watch the hook glide through the subatomic matter all around her.

She should stand up and pour a drink, because this is what is done. People have drinks to blunt the edges of hard realities. But she can't move. And anyway, she is already standing. She is standing inside a memory. She is fifteen years old, holding a fishing pole on the shore of the Seym with Slava. He is down on his knees, helping her with her hook. They are fishing for perch and he is fixing a minnow for her.

"Okay," Slava says, checking the hook one more time. "Throw it just at the edge of the weeds. See?" She winds up and casts the line and hook toward where Slava is pointing. She remembers the feel of the line going out, the pull of it. The tiny clicking of the fishing rod sprocket. The sound of the river, constant and unwavering. The clouds bundled grey above them. When she catches her first fish, Slava is ecstatic. He is jumping up and down and hugging her. The fish put up a fight. It ran and jumped and swerved, and Slava talked her through it. He did not even begin to grab the pole. He only encouraged. Nancy does not remember feeling happier. He loved to fish, and yet all afternoon, his one job was to help her. He baited her hook, and taught her everything he knew. She remembers he was a beautiful teacher, down on his knees in the river stones, giving her encouragement, giving her all his attention. His gear was untouched, in a pile with his coat. She pulled five fish from the river that day and they ate those fish for dinner.

....

Sometime before 4 a.m., but after 2:30 a.m., she decides she will hold this grief. She will place it in a room and shut the door, and only open it when she feels she can take it. She will grieve in pieces, in small chunks. This is her plan. This is the only way for her to survive. At around 5 a.m., she remembers Slava never called her Nancy and she decides to change her name back to Nensi. Just because and fuck all those who can't handle it.

Eventually she gets off the couch and pours herself a mug of frozen vodka. She drinks half the vodka and crawls into bed. She wonders if she will disintegrate into particles when she falls asleep. She wonders if in the morning she will be less than dust. Perhaps she will disappear into the subatomic particles of grief. *Why Slava?* she thinks, and then she is asleep.

....

"I'm so tired, Ray. I want nothing. I want nothingness." Nancy pulls the phone away from her ear and looks at it as if she doesn't quite recognize it, as if it is some artefact that has no meaning. She moves it back to her other ear and smiles. "I want to feel nothing," she says.

Ray has been using the speaker function for the past hour because the phone was getting too hot. "Stop it. Enough."

"Why? Don't you want me to be honest?" She takes another drink of scotch.

"Sure. But nothingness is overrated. It's not much fun feeling nothing. I've been to the land of no feelings and it's just grey and depressing. It's not a nice place."

"When have you ever felt nothing?"

"Before I met you. It really scared me so I got some help."

"You're joking, right? You got help? What does that mean, Ray?"

"A therapist. A psychologist."

"I didn't think you had any cracks, other than an obsessive horni-ness for slightly used Russian women."

"You think I have no cracks other than my feelings for you?" He can hear her lighting another cigarette. "Look, this is nonsense. I'm going to have to hang up, eventually. I'm going to have to go."

"So will I," Nancy says. She looks around the deck. She notices that Death is sitting and smoking in the chair across from her. He holds his cigarette funny – between his thumb and forefinger as if he is pinching it. He is a serious-looking, grey-haired man with a three-day beard. He says nothing but he watches her like a hawk as he smokes.

"Nancy?"

"Death is here, Ray," she says. "He's watching me."

Ray sighs. "Really?"

"Yes, really." She wants to ask Ray what she should do.

"What does Death look like?"

"He kind of looks like Brad Pitt...No, George Clooney. No, Brad Pitt. No..."

"...Are you drunk?"

"Probably. But still, his looks keep changing."

"How do you know it's Death?"

"I heard the wings, Ray. I have always heard the wings. All my life. And anyway, who else would it be? Should I ask? I will ask."

"Jesus Christ, Nancy."

"No, I'm pretty sure this is Death. This is not Jesus Christ."

"Really?" Ray is beyond tired and now this new wrinkle, a new twist. Nancy has wound up the winding down clock.

"Okay," she says to Death. "Just to be clear. You are Death, am I correct?"

Death tilts his head and looks at her silently, quizzically.

Nancy tries it in Russian. "Preevyet," she says. "Kak vas zavoot? Eto vashe imya smert?"

Death smiles and nods.

"Oh, my God. Death is Russian, Ray. I do not know if this is good news or bad, but Death is definitely Russian." She ponders the idea that Heaven might be like Russia, and if so, there will be line-ups, and corruption, and ugly cars. But there will also be vodka, and generosity, and stoic people who can withstand much hardship. But in Heaven, there would be no hardships, so perhaps the Russian people of Heaven would become fat and lazy.

Ray sits up straight in his seat. She sees the Angel of Death and she's having a conversation with him. This is not good news. This is a complication that threatens to extend things. He'd been hoping this conversation would fade away – that it would expire because they'd run out of things to say. "Do you think you could do something for me?" he says.

"Of course, darling. I love you. I would do anything for you. But you know, I feel certain that I am going mad again."

Mad again? What does she mean, mad again? Ray can't tell if she's drunk or engaged in some intense sarcasm. He decides to take her seriously.

"Okay, would you please take the phone with you and crawl into bed? And I will call you later to see how you are. I promise."

"Why would I do that, Ray? I have a guest. Don't you think I should offer Death some vodka? I will get the vodka from the freezer. And maybe some cheese. What goes with vodka? A little black caviar, maybe?"

"What are you doing, Nancy?"

"Me? I am having a drink with Death, Ray. What are you doing?" She is surprised that Death is not impatient. He seems dispassionate, almost uninterested – like a man in a train station who has resigned himself to waiting. While she loves the stoic Russian-ness of his demeanour, she would prefer that Death was eager, or intense. His indifference is disturbing. She would like Death to say what he is doing in her living room.

"Stop fooling around," Ray says. "I'm serious. What are you doing?"

"I am seriously having a drink with Death."

"So you're completely delusional? If you really see Death, you're in trouble. It's a serious thing."

"Perhaps," she says. "It's no matter. I want to ask you something."

Ray doesn't say anything. He's considering a mad dash across the sidewalk and into her building. She's drunk and she's probably not watching. But there was the problem of the dead zone halfway up to her floor. The phone would cut out, or the call would be dropped, and she would know.

"I need some sort of sign you've heard me and you're okay with me asking you a question."

"Yes. A question. You have a question. What's your goddamned question?"

"What's wrong with you? Why are you being mean to me?"

"I'm sorry. I'm tired. I'm exhausted. What did you want to ask me?"

"Okay. If I die before you, I want to know if you will bring flowers to my grave? I'd like flowers. Not every day. Just once a month, or whenever you feel like it. Could you do that for me?"

He sighs. "Hypothetically? Sure, I can do that for you."

"Good. But I don't like roses. And I don't like daisies. I actually don't like any flower that looks like a daisy."

"What about yellow flowers?" he says. He remembers the sting of her rejecting his yellow flowers.

"Yes, Ray. In this case, an even number of yellow flowers would be perfectly appropriate."

"But let's be clear. You're not dying today or anytime soon," he says. "So, you can send Death away. He won't be needed today." He stops. "Jesus, Nancy. Do you see what you've done? Now you've got me talking about Death like it's actually in the room with you."

"But we're just speculating, darling. We're just supposing. We're just having a little fun."

"Do you really see Death? Or are you playing around?"

"Don't you believe in angels, Ray?"

Ray's not sure how to answer. The woman in the elevator who wasn't there once they arrived at the main floor – the woman who knew his name, who knew he was having an affair – she shook something in him. Was she an angel? If that hard-edged, no-bullshit woman was his guardian angel then he was in worse shape than he imagined.

"No. I do not believe in angels."

"Not even a little?"

"Belief in something isn't by degrees," he says. "It's either yes, you believe in a thing, or no, you don't believe in that thing."

"What if you have doubts about your belief, or you are open to the idea of a new belief?

"Then you believe in a thing, and you have doubts. Or you don't believe, yet."

"I think you're being too simplistic, Ray."

Nancy looks at Death. He looks like George Clooney and he is frowning and shaking his head. He lights another cigarette.

"If you are really seeing things we should get you to a hospital. If you're actually having a break from reality then it's serious."

"Oh, you'd like that wouldn't you? You'd like to see me strapped down, wouldn't you? Helpless and sedated? Does that turn you on, Ray? That way you could walk away and not feel anything. Death says no, by the way. No hospitals. Death thinks I'm perfectly fine."

Ray can hear Nancy speaking Russian. It's muffled as if she is holding her hand over the phone's receiver. She speaks, and then waits. Then she speaks some more.

"Death says he likes me, Ray. Do you like me? Did you ever like me?"

"Can you be serious for a second? Just stop it. Stop playing around."

"Do you like me?"

"Of course I like you. I really think it would be a good idea for you to lie down…"

"…and I think I'm fine here with Death, and right now, I win. Besides, going to bed would remind me of you, and that would make me sad. The smell of you is in my bed, Ray. That's so depressing." She raises her glass to Death and he nods toward her as if he approves.

Nancy is confused. "What are you nodding about? What?"

Ray looks out the window and up the building. "Who are you really talking with?" He considers the possibility she has another phone and she is having a conversation with someone else. The thought crosses his mind that she's called her brother and a car full of Russian mafia is going to pull up beside him, pull out their guns, and that will be it.

"I told you. Death is here and he's nodding about something I've said, or done. For all I know it could be something I'm thinking."

"Death reads your mind?"

"Of course he does, darling. Don't you know anything?"

"You're drunk, Nancy."

"Yes. I am, a bit, but that doesn't mean I shouldn't be nice to Death. You should always remember your manners. Now, tell me why you like me."

"What?"

"You said you liked me before. Tell me why."

He sighs. "I could tell you you're beautiful but I think you already know that. I don't want to tell you what you already know. The most important thing was it seemed like you really wanted to be there with me. Every time."

Silence. As if she is considering his answer. And then, "Of course, I wanted to be there, Ray. Is that your wife? Does your wife not want to be there anymore? Is that it? So now what will you have?"

Ray thinks about this and decides he has a friend who used to be a lover. And he has two amazing daughters. His life is full of love, and sensation. It amuses him that he thinks about Madame Chernakov in this moment – he can see her making coffee and it pleases him that she is in his life. Even though he pays her for her attention, it has never felt like a relationship based on money. It has always felt like two old friends having a chat. She has slowly become part of his family.

Nancy is right. He's going back to a sexless, deeply flawed marriage and this is depressing. His life will play out. He and Tulah will do some sort of marriage counselling. They might go to a retreat in Arizona and learn how to touch each other again, learn how to trust each other again. They'll do some sort of lame closing-your-eyes-and-falling-backwards-into-each-other's-arms exercise. The girls will grow up and leave home. They'll get married, have kids of their own. Maybe Nancy will take up painting as a hobby, or perhaps she will try to write a book. He will retire. He will still love to work with trees so he'll putter around the yard and the neighbours' yards, offering up advice. He'll walk around the neighbourhood with a pruning saw. And then he will die. Or he will get very sick and then he will die. He will become *old*-old and be a burden on everyone in his life, and then he will die. His life is a roulette ball that has landed on the black number thirty-six and now it's just a matter of waiting for the wheel to stop spinning. And this is the way the world ends, not with a bang, but a ticking-down roulette wheel and a whimper. Between the desire and the spasm. Between potency and existence. He has become one of Eliot's *Hollow Men*. But he does not want to be a Hollow Man. He wants to grit his teeth and squeeze the extraordinary out of this life, and he wants to do it with Tulah. Because she is his first and best witness. He thinks about holding her hand – there is a particular way that they mesh their fingers together and in that meshing is a deep love. It is sometimes slippery but it's there in the DNA of that grasp.

"How am I beautiful?" Nancy says.

"What? What are you talking about?"

"You said I was beautiful. Tell me how I am beautiful."

"Jesus, Nancy. I don't see the point. Are you really that vain? I mean…"

"…I want to know," she says. "Tell me."

He sighs. "I'm not playing this game with you."

"And I am taking a walk out to the edge of the balcony."

A jolt of panic flashes through him. Jesus Christ! She's got Death in the room with her and she's going to jump. This is her clever way of telling him she's going to jump. Ray gets out of his car and looks up. He is standing on the street and fear is his only constant. Fear is his companion now and it's not going to leave. Ray sees balcony after rising balcony but no Nancy. From where he is, unless she's out there on the edge, he can't tell which balcony is hers.

....

Adam Farnsworth calls on a Friday morning. Ray stands up. He picks up the phone.

"Adam," he says. "How are you?"

"Not so good," Adam says. "It's that thing you and I talked about. It's not going to fly. My people have come up with a solution but the City Manager's office thinks it's too expensive. They balked at the price tag. They're not going to send it up. It's not happening. I'm sorry."

"Is there anything…"

"…I met with Bruce yesterday. This is an election year. Money is tight right now, and they'd rather plant new trees. You might be able to sell it to a new administration at some point in the future."

"Can we try to take it to council ourselves?"

"You're up against potholes and school lunches for poor kids. Your trees will lose every day of the week and three times on Sunday. I'm sorry, Ray."

It's done. His scheme to save trees is done. This knowledge sinks into Ray. "I appreciate everything you tried to do, Adam. Thanks for letting me know."

"Let's go for coffee sometime."

The line goes dead and Ray kicks his garbage can, hard. It flies across the office and whacks against the window. He wants to find a way around, but he can't focus right now. Samantha, his executive assistant, whose hair is always pulled back severely, knocks on the door – opens it slowly. "Everything okay?"

"Yes. Fine," Ray says. "I just got some bad news."

Samantha pulls the door shut and Ray clears his afternoon. He checks the schedule to see where his crews are. He will hang out with trees and people who love trees and to hell with everything else. On his way out, he looks at Samantha and the three stacks of files piled on her desk.

"Sam," he says. "I've cleared my calendar. I want you to take the rest of the day off. Go to a movie. Go home. Go shopping. Go for a glass of wine. I don't care."

"Mr. Daniels," she says. "I have…"

"…whatever you have, can wait. Go." He pauses in the doorway, turns around and puts a fifty dollar bill on Samantha's desk. "Go and have a really great glass of wine, on me. I insist."

…….

Ray watches as a breeze releases a mess of leaves from the elms along the street. He'd like to think the leaves have a distinct order in their falling. He entertains the whimsy that they let go when it's their turn. He imagines it's all about the mathematics of beauty – twenty-three leaves let go right now, thirty-four leaves in the next gust of wind, four leaves in the next, and so on. But of course, this sprinkling of leaves is a crazy random chaos. There is no mathematics of beauty.

A group of pigeons frightens and takes off quickly over top of Ray's car. And then he sees her. He sees the woman from the elevator, the blunt, sexy woman with the flowery tattoos; the one wearing the black cocktail dress and a grey scarf wrapped around her neck. As she walks away from his car, Ray can see the luxurious fluidity of her gait. She moves smoothly and quickly along the sidewalk and he wonders if she is cold. She must be cold without a coat. His first impulse is to get out of his car and run after her, gently touch her arm, and say: "Hey. Hi. Again. Hi, again." He imagines her smiling knowingly, as if she is mildly amused by his awkwardness, and she can read his intention, even though he is not entirely certain of his intention. She will say nothing and they will stand in the middle of the sidewalk, locked together, as mothers with children move around, old men with poodles move around, and lovers release hands – are split in two by the rocks in the middle of the stream.

He sits in his car, looking at the dull grey day and the trees along the avenue. Ray watches as the leaves on the sidewalk part to let her through. It's as if they are blown aside by a gust of meticulous wind. A swatch of bare cement is left in her wake. He wants her to pause as if she just thought of something important, turn around, and walk back to his car. He wants to watch her getting closer to him, the movement of her body, the sway of it, and her determined, curious face. He wants her to lean into the car and kiss him hard on the lips. He wants her to tell him exactly what to do. He wants to do everything she asks.

"I release you, Ray," Nancy says.

"What?"

"I release you. Go home to your wife. I'm tired of this so-called conversation. I'm tired of you. I'm going to bed and in the morning, I will...well, who cares. In the morning I'll do something that is none of your business. I'm going to dream about a life in which I never met you. I'm going to wipe you away, like a dirty countertop."

"You're okay?"

"No, I am not fucking okay, but I'm also not going to jump off this building because of you. You are charming, Ray, but underneath your skin, you're not a nice person. And when I was with you, I was not a nice person either. I was an awful person and I wallowed in this delusion. I am not blaming you. I blame me."

"I'm sorry, Nancy. I am truly sorry about this..."

"I have to tell you something, Ray. I don't want you to take this the wrong way, but I hope your daughters never meet anyone like you."

Ray inhales and holds. He pulls the phone away from his face. This flat statement stings. It takes his breath. She's right, of course. He also hopes his daughters meet someone better than him.

"Well, we're being honest, right?"

"Okay," he says.

"You sound like you're a good dad. And they sound like great kids. I hope they meet and fall in love with men who are not living inside a lie. That's all I meant." Nancy realizes she's just hurt him and she feels awful about it.

Ray's head is swirling. What if this is all a lie? Every move. Every action and every utterance of love. All lies. Big lies, little lies, white lies, black lies, and lies of omission.

"I…" Ray watches the wind move through the elms. He is drained. He wants to hide from his own life. "I hope that too," he says.

"I am not saying this to be mean. And not to hurt you. Just honest, you know?" Now she's apologizing and she has no clue why.

"Yeah, I know," he says. "I know."

"Go, Ray. Go, before I get mean again and have the urge to drop something else on you. Something bigger."

"What will you do now?"

"What do you mean? I told you. I'll go to bed and fall asleep, and wake up, and do something. In the morning, I will sit on the edge of the bed and take a breath. And then I will continue to breathe. By noon, I will have forgotten your face. By dinner time, I will be hard-pressed to recall your name."

"Death is not waiting around is he?"

"No. Death? Death isn't real, Ray. What's wrong with you? Listen, if he comes back I'll send him over to your house." She looks at the empty couch where Death was sitting. She suspects he is in the bath-room, though she does not know why. Does the Angel of Death pee? Is he in there primping? Combing his hair?

"That's nice," Ray says.

"Oh my God, did I hurt your feelings again?"

"It's just that this was never about wishing you dead. I have always wanted you to be alive and well. I want you to be happy." He looks out the window. He realizes Nancy doesn't understand the reason he has been sitting in his car for the past four hours – feels like twelve – is all about her being well, and happy, and alive. Most importantly, alive. How could she not get this?

She blinks the tears out of her eyes. This is the man she loves. Regardless of wives, or intentions, or beginnings or endings, or even the Russian-speaking Angel of Death; love is love, and she believes Ray loves her the best he can, or could. It's just it makes her so sad to think of saying goodbye. "I'm sorry. You're right. Endings are always important. There is no reason this ending should not be a good one. If Death comes back I will put him to work cleaning up this apartment, and then I will send him on his way. I promise."

Death, who looks like Ryan Gosling now, has come back into the room and he is inching his way up the far wall, watching her, his back to the wall, pushing with his feet. When he reaches the ceiling he stops and closes his eyes. He becomes the gargoyle in the room and Nancy shivers.

"That's not right," she says.

"What's not right?"

Nancy giggles. "Nothing. I think I've had too much to drink. Go home. There's nothing for you here. Not anymore. Even if you wanted to start again, there's no point."

"You're okay?"

Nancy shakes her head. She thinks this conversation has moved firmly into the realm of pathetic. "Yes, Ray. I'm perfectly fine." She does not have the courage to tell him everything she feels, everything she knows, the remainder of her story. She will hold her secrets because there's an odd comfort in holding tight to these things. Sometimes it takes too much courage to be truthful and today she does not have any of that kind of courage.

. . . .

In a penthouse apartment on Lafayette Street, in New York, a woman named Olga is packing Slava's things into cardboard boxes. Some of the boxes will be forwarded to his sister. A book, *The Habit of Rivers* by Ted Leeson, is among the items that will go to the sister. Olga picks it up and flips through its pages. The book is well used, and apparently, well loved. There are annotations in the margins throughout, all scribbled in Russian. It is, as far as Olga can tell, a book about fishing. The letter falls from the pages onto the floor. It is addressed to Mr. Slava Petya but inside it is something other than a letter to Slava. It is a letter to an unnamed girl, a *milaya,* a *sweet girl.* It is a letter that addresses the war in Afghanistan and a father who died in this war, and the love this father has for his family, but especially the girl. Olga reads the letter twice. In her second reading, she starts to weep, tears streaming unchecked down her cheeks. She is not weeping for the girl, the *sweet girl,* but rather, for herself. She remembers her own father and it ruins her heart a little.

Olga slips the letter back into the pages of the fishing book and places it into the box going to the sister. She wonders if the sister is the sweet girl in the letter, but she cannot imagine Slava holding such a thing back from his sister. She wonders what happened to the writer of the letter.

CHAPTER 2

Nancy and Tulah

Tulah's Snow Journal
Tuesday, September 22, 2015 #487

I'm breaking the rules. I'm writing this entry before it snows. I've seen enough goddamned weather to know when it's going to snow. I've paid attention to snow. I know the signs. These are snow clouds. The colour of bruised zinc. Dove grey. Massed up at the horizon in a particular way. I stopped on the back deck this morning, looked up, and sobbed. I do not know what's wrong with me. This snow, the snow that will be here soon, is breaking my heart. I can't seem to stop blubbering.

My hormones are ramped up for some reason. I'm all emotion and short on reasons why.

....

Ray is at a soccer game with the girls – the second-last game of the season. It's Patience's soccer game. Sarah usually sits in the stands and reads. She'll look up and smile when there's a goal but really, she supports her sister just by being there.

Tulah opted out of the game because she had marking to do. She'll go to the final game of the season.

The phone rings. She picks up and listens to Principal Hartman. Lauren Smith is suing him, the school and the school board. There's some sort of accusation of sexual harassment too. Apparently, Lauren Smith was not appeased. She wants all the students of Strathmore Senior High School to be taught creation, not just her kid and the children in Mr. Rubinski's period six science class. Principal Hartman has been suspended by the board – they called it a deviation from the designed curriculum, and the protocols around accusations of sexual harassment include an automatic suspension until a full investigation has been held.

"Sexual harassment? Are you serious, Jerry?"

"It's that woman and it's nonsense. I wondered at the time, why she insisted on shutting the door at our last meeting and now I know. I'm temporarily suspended. The board had no choice."

"What did she say?"

"Doesn't matter. The stink of guilt attaches itself to accusations like this. She might be smart enough to have figured this out. Look, I don't have your back anymore. You're going to have to throw the Christians a bone."

"How about a 200,000-year-old fossil of a human bone."

"You know what I mean, Tulah."

"Can we fight this?"

"Yes, of course we're going to fight it, but in the meantime I'm suspended and there will be a replacement, and they'll come after you."

"Me?"

"Yes, I suspect this is all about you. You have to promise me to go strictly by the book for the next little while."

"By the book?"

"Yes, you remember what the curriculum is, don't you? Promise me you'll stick to the guidelines. It won't kill you to mention creation in your class. And be nice about it."

"Yes, it will kill me, but I promise."

"And when you mention it, you'll steer away from sarcasm?"

"Oh, you know me."

"Humour them, Tulah. And stay away from the fringe books. Stick to the approved list of books. Just stick to the curriculum. Be spotless."

He sounds tired – his voice is strained and pulled tight.

"You okay?"

"Yes. I'll be fine," he says. "Just protect yourself, Tulah. You're on their radar. You have to stop tilting at windmills. They're not going to change."

"Pick my battles. I know."

"You'll be fine," he says.

"I still don't understand how this could happen. I mean you're suspended. What the hell is going on?"

"It's an elected school board. They're doing the right thing – by the book."

"You'll sort it out?"

"Of course," he says. "Let the dogs bark. It's a sign that we're on track."

Tulah hangs up. She feels sick to her stomach. This news about school hurts. Lauren Smith is succeeding in taking all the fun out of teaching. This is a failure of enlightenment, a personal failure against the darkness of ignorance. Tulah takes this news from Principal Hartman as a hard kick to the gut. She takes this disappointment and places it on a shelf with Ray's elms. Maybe they can cling to each other and that will be some sort of solace against these losses. They can hold each other in the dark and feel safe, and eventually they will fight again. They can be light for each other.

....

Tulah looks up from her marking and sighs. The phone is ringing again. She picks it up and says nothing. The woman hesitates before saying anything and Tulah thinks it's a machine trying to sell her something, but then a human voice jumps in. It is not some mechanical, recorded voice. And Tulah listens.

"What did you say your name was?"

"Nancy."

"Nincy?"

"No. Nancy."

Tulah is still not certain. "Okay, look, whatever your fucking name is, you should know, I am too old for jealousy. I've been there and I'm not interested anymore. What do you want?"

"Did you actually hear me? I'm sleeping with your husband."

Tulah swallows. She wills her voice to be unwavering. "So?" she says. "Good for you. I do not own him. He is not my property. If he wants to spend his sex on some twit, I don't care."

"You're not angry? Because I would be royally pissed off. I would want to rip your fucking head off if you did this to me."

Tulah *is* angry, seething. Just on principle, she's angry, but there's no way she is going to show this woman her anger. Also, this is a surprise and its immediacy stings. She's going to hold it together. "He sleeps with me, honey. He wakes up with me. He has a life with me. We have children together." Tulah pauses. She holds her breath. She says a little prayer – *please, please, please, don't say you're pregnant. That,*

I couldn't take. Dear God, she thinks. *Don't let this woman tell me she's pregnant. Please, God. Please.*

"But you're married to him."

"And?" Tulah says. She exhales.

"And when you're married…" Nancy doesn't finish. Either this woman is truly unaffected by this or she's pretending – and she's an amazing liar. There are rules in marriages, for God's sake. "You're the good wife, aren't you?"

"Well it's better than being an amusement ride, honey. Because that's all you are."

Nancy is silent. Tulah does not feel good about calling this woman an amusement ride. She knows it is hurtful but she is shocked and wounded and off balance. The words just tumbled out. But she is protective now, of her husband. This other woman is trying to hurt him, she's betraying his trust in her, and this pisses Tulah off. She is not surprised Ray had it in him to fool around on her. But the jolt of hearing this woman's voice takes her breath away. The realization that Ray actually did fool around on her shakes her to the core. But there is also a quiet voice reminding her she is not innocent. A voice that assures her that jealousy would be a meaningless waste. That she has already forgiven Ray for this, because she has no choice but forgiveness. She has no choice. She could pretend there was no Lover but that would be such a massive lie she's not sure she could live with it. She does not want a no-fly zone in her own consciousness.

"Okay," Tulah says. "Are we done here?"

"Don't you want to know how long it's been going on?"

"No…" Hang up, she tells herself. Hang the phone up now.

"…A year. I've been fucking him for a year. Thirteen months, actually. We were together yesterday." Nancy rolls to her back and looks at the ceiling. She wants a reaction from the wife. That's all. She does not care if she ruins Ray's life. She wants the wife to break. She suspects this woman doesn't know anything – that this is all a surprise. But she's not showing any sign of being surprised.

Tulah is quiet. This woman is lying about being with Ray yesterday. She knows this because they spent the day shopping, and shared a bottle of wine over dinner. They had Thai food. But the length of time this has being going on staggers her. Something lurches in her stomach. She did not know. She did not think Ray possessed that kind of craftiness. She fights the tears that want to come. In the past year they had made love three times, maybe. She did not blame him. Not entirely. They were busy having a life with two daughters, and jobs. Half the time she was exhausted, and the other half their sex felt awkward and forced.

"I don't care," Tulah says. "You think you're telling me something I didn't already know. You're dumber than I imagined."

"You don't care that I've been fucking your husband?"

Tulah can't say the word 'no.' She knows she won't be able to sell a flat denial. "If he wants to relieve himself with some bimbo, I could care less."

"Are you really that much of a heartless bitch?"

"Look, you don't sleep with him. He fucks you – that's all. I know this because I'm the one he sleeps with, wakes up with and has a life with. You're nothing but a fuck. Why don't you go try and ruin someone else's life."

Nancy does not say anything for a long time. Tulah can hear her breathing. "You two deserve each other," she says finally.

"Thank you, yes," Tulah says, as if inside a slow realization. "Yes, we do."

"I don't mean…"

Tulah puts the phone down. She's done. She does not want to hear any more. She curls into the brown leather couch and tries to sort out what she's heard, what she believes, and what she knows. She attempts to define the truth. She wants to nail the truth to the floor so she can make decisions about it. She doesn't know if she's numb, or her body is pretending to be numb, or if she's so angry she doesn't know anything at all about her own life. All the while, there's a reservoir of tears that wants to break, but she won't let it. Not until she knows what's next.

……

Patience scored a goal in the game and they came home with rosy cheeks and frozen slushy drinks. It was a cool night for a game. Ray had looked at her and asked if she was all right.

"Fine. Yes. Good. It was a peaceful night."

"Are you sure?" he says. "You look a little rattled."

"Just tired," she says. "It was a hard night of marking."

The snow starts to come down after the girls are in bed and Ray is settled with a drink on the couch. The opening scenes of some Italian film are on the screen as Tulah bundles up in her down coat, thick scarf and boots. "I'm going out for a walk," she says.

He knows better than to question Tulah and her snow. But there is something off. Her voice is almost normal but there is a quiver that changes it slightly. "Do you and your snow want some company?" he says. "I happen to love the woman who loves the snow."

Her face is sad as she looks at him. She seems at the edge of something. "I know you do, but not tonight."

Tulah is vibrating on high as she steps out into it. She is one massive undulating wave of anger and forgiveness and hurt and acceptance. She takes a moment at the top of the front walk to catch her breath.

The snow is a soft drift through streetlights. She is aware of her ritual, the pattern of paying attention to the snow but she is shaken off course by this woman's phone call. She wants to shout and scream and demand to know her husband's heart – all of it. She wants every hidden alcove, every tucked-away secret. She wants it to be over with this woman on the phone. She wants assurances and promises. She wants guarantees. She is disgusted and seething, and she knows she will do nothing but carry on. She does not want a confrontation. A confrontation will solve nothing. Tulah wants to not know about this horrible woman and Ray.

She tries again to pay attention to the snow.

When she is halfway up McVale Hill, Tulah realizes whatever was going on between Ray and the shrill woman is over. The phone call was the bitter end. It had to be. It was meant to hurt her and to hurt Ray. It was meant to hurt them, and it was desperate. That woman was trying to explode Ray's life so she could pick up the pieces, or because she is spiteful and without hope. Tulah decides she will not let their life explode, or implode. She will not let that happen. She and Ray will prevail. They will abide as a family. She will not let this ruin anything.

....

Ray remembers having an argument with Tulah one night after a party. It was five, perhaps six, years ago. She'd accused him of flirting with a woman who was blatantly coming on to him. The woman had been in an argument with her husband before the party, and she'd gotten out of the car three blocks away. Her husband had driven off in a rage, in the opposite direction. Tulah kept calling the woman, whose name was Maureen, 'that woman in the orange gunnysack.'

"She was sad, and drunk," Ray said. "She was depressed about the fight she'd had with her husband."

"That woman was a horny bitch who didn't care that you were married, or that your wife was across the room. And what was that thing she was wearing? It was like an orange sack. Hideous." There were rules of conduct at parties and flirting all night with Tulah's husband was a transgression of these rules. In fact, rule number one was, do not attempt to seduce Tulah's husband at a party.

"It was harmless flirting," he said.

"It was foreplay." Tulah slammed her wine glass down on the table and the stem broke. She gulped the remaining wine and placed the broken glass on its side on the table where it teetered back and forth. "Tell me you didn't want to sleep with her."

Ray did not hesitate. "I did not want to sleep with her. That was the furthest thing from my mind." Ray had absolutely wanted to sleep with her. The orange gunnysack woman was an attractive drunk with breasts like perfect melons. She was tall and witty, and kept touching his arm, and his hand, and his arm again. Apparently she wanted to sleep with him. They'd been talking about books. She'd started by saying she recognized the talent of Alice Munro but that she found Munro so dreadfully dull that she was unreadable. "Utterly unreadable," she'd said. Ray jumped to Munro's defence and then they were embroiled in a conversation about books, and writers.

"I like to listen to you when I know you're lying," Tulah said.

"What? Why would you say that? I'm not lying about this…"

"…It's because it's beautiful and repulsive at the same time. There should be a word for when something is simultaneously beautiful and repulsive, don't you think? A German word – like *Weltschmerz* or *Lebensmüde*."

Ray did not know what *Lebensmüde* was but he looked it up later and found that it meant you were tired of life, or *life tired*. When you or someone you know is about to do something so stupid it could kill you, or them, a German would say you are experiencing *Lebensmüde*.

"What's beautiful about knowing someone is lying to you?"

"Because people will often lie to protect you, or shield you. Or maybe they're saying something they wish were true. Or telling you something they think you want to hear. And if you know they are doing this, then, it becomes beautiful."

"And the repulsive bit?"

"By accepting a lie and pretending it is not a lie, I am also lying. I am sucked into the deception and I feel shitty about myself, and about us. One lie, allowed to live, is always fruitful and it always multiplies. This is the repulsive part that happens simultaneously with the beautiful part."

"But I am not with that woman. I am with you. I am here with you tonight as I am every night. I will be with you in the morning, as I am every morning."

"I know."

"Did I embarrass you?"

"No. Maybe you embarrassed yourself a little because she was so obviously coming on to you and you stuck around for it. Jesus, Ray, what were you thinking?"

"Lie or no lie, here I am."

"And you want me to believe the lie that you did not want to make love with that woman?"

"Yes. I want you to believe it," Ray said. "Because it's true."

"You see, if I know you are lying…"

"…which I am not."

"…if I know you're lying, and I really listen to you, I can understand the truth of the lie. I can know what it means."

"What does this one mean?"

Tulah smiled. "It means you love me. It means you love me hard and with all your heart. You love me to the point of ruin."

And just like that, they were no longer fighting.

………

Madame Chernakov's building is under renovation.

"They found asbestos," she says. "Horrifying. This room is fine, but the lobby? Not so much. They're going to make a safe tunnel through the lobby."

"What does that mean?"

"It means you may have to step through sheets of plastic and there will be workers in the lobby and hallways. They might be wearing masks."

"I don't care. We're safe here, right?"

"Yes."

"Good. Listen, I realized something last night. I was thinking about our conversations and I tried to put myself in your shoes." Ray looks at her shoes, black high heels that are probably expensive. "Not those shoes but, well, you know what I mean. I've come to the conclusion that you must think I am an ass – a genuine asshole."

"You know my role is not to judge. I listen and we sort things out."

"Seriously, though, on some level, you must find me repulsive."

"Do you want me to find you repulsive?"

"Really? We can't just have a conversation?"

Madame Chernakov shakes her head. "I am not perfect, Ray. I'm human, just like you. I make a ton of mistakes. I have regrets. I get confused in my own life."

"Well, for the record, you should know...my wife is not entirely innocent in this marriage. I want you to know something about her..."

Ray wants to see if Madame Chernakov will go where he thinks she will go, which is the culpability of each spouse in the success or failure of any marriage. But she doesn't bite. She waits.

"She had an affair a few years back," Ray says.

"Okay," the therapist says. "And how did you sort this affair out?"

"No. It wasn't like that. My guys were working outside a hotel downtown and one of them recognized her. She was going in."

"Does she know you know?"

"What good would that do?"

"Oh I don't know. It would be honest and open. It must have hurt finding out like that. How did you feel?"

"I felt, you know, loved, secure and happy..."

"...I thought we talked about sarcasm."

"Sorry. I felt shitty. Worse than shitty. I mean, we'd lost our way sexually, and she had found someone else, sexually...yeah, I felt shitty. Hurt."

"Do you think it was a one-time thing?"

"I don't know."

"You could ask her."

"Again, why? I don't want to know. It's none of my business. She didn't leave. We're still together, in the fray. That's the important bit."

"Have you forgiven her? I mean in your heart?"

"I've thought about it so much that I think I've stopped caring. I've more or less forgotten about it. Forgetting is better than forgiving. I love her."

"So, no to the idea of forgiveness?"

"It was what she needed to do, so no. No forgiveness. None required."

It hurt like hell to know Tulah was sharing her body with someone else when they made love so infrequently. He felt inadequate and insignificant and angry. His brain kept telling him that if this was what his wife needed, fine. But his heart was a mess. His heart was so hurt it couldn't comprehend. He hoped it was just a physical attraction for Tulah, and not something messier.

Madame Chernakov leans back in her chair and takes a big breath. "Oh, my dear boy, you're either incredibly enlightened, or in some sort of elaborate self-denial. Do you think this affair has anything to do with you and your extra woman?"

"You mean, was I hurt and decided to have an affair of my own, as payback?"

"Something like that, yes. Tulah's affair was some kind of tacit approval for you to fool around."

"No," he says. "I don't think I work like that." Ray thinks about his extra woman, about Nancy. Why does Madame Chernakov insist on calling her that? He misses the simplicity of their love-making but also recognises it for what it was. It lacked substance. Nancy was a blonde-haired, Russian ghost. A lusty, vanished ghost.

....

Nancy is leaning against the railing looking out at the rolling grey sky. She looks directly down and shivers – an involuntary spark up the middle of her back. The temperature is dropping. It feels like snow and she is not dressed for snow. She thinks about the full-length fox fur in the front closet – a gift from the hockey player. It would be ideal right now but she does not have the energy to fetch it.

"So long, Ray," she says. "Go home. I heard the feathers flapping again. I heard the wings. Go home."

"You're going to be fine," Ray says, willing it, hoping it, commanding it to be true.

"I already am," she says. "It's just love. It's just a silly game we girls play to entertain ourselves. I'm fine about everything." She thinks about Slava. He would have made Ray suffer a great deal. He would have hurt him. Her stomach muscles tighten with the thought of her brother. To say she misses him does a disservice to the word, and she has not even begun to think about grieving. She wants to go back to the time they were fishing by the river in Kursk. She wants to catch her first fish and in the instant her brother is excited, Nancy wants to turn off time. She wants to live for a thousand years in that moment, in which her brother is pure and happy, and she is proud and giddy with joy. Of course, she would not know a thousand years are passing because there would be no time in that moment. It would all be true and real and unadulterated by time. Time can go fuck itself.

The line goes dead. Ray starts his car, shoulder checks and pulls into traffic.

Nancy watches as the small rectangle of his car moves down the block.

"It's just love," she says.

She is standing in the doorway of her bedroom and she is more than exhausted. She looks at the bed. There are a dozen unnecessary pillows, arranged perfectly, overlapping colour-matched squares. She pushes them onto the floor. She yanks at the sheet, slips under the covers and sighs heavily as she shuts her eyes.

Escape

Maybe you met a woman on a ski hill once and as you were forced to sit with her in the lift, she told you a story about when she was on a high school band trip. The students are all staying in a gymnasium, boys on one side, girls on the other, and chaperones in the middle. One morning, one of the teachers gets up on stage early in the morning and plays the first few chords of a progression but doesn't play the final chord. He waits a few minutes and plays it again. He plays a C chord, then the F, then a G, and then leaves it alone. He didn't finish. He let the G hang in mid-air with no resolution. He keeps playing the progression and leaving that missing chord there like an itch not scratched. It is horribly unfinished. Students start to sit up in their sleeping bags and they are looking around the gym at other kids sitting up in their sleeping bags. The unfinished thing woke them and they are confused. One girl in the middle of the throng of sleeping girls stands up and screams "What the Fuck!" She storms up on stage, the teacher steps back, out of her way, and she finds the missing C-chord; the one that finishes the progression. Everyone in the gym takes a breath.

Perhaps, for the writer, the story of the Garamonds is like this unfinished chord progression. He has to finish. He has to see what that final chord feels like, and only then will he be able to take a breath.

....

The girl arrives, out of breath, with three bottles of Meursault. It is not a day that she would normally be there. It is not a wine the Garamonds would usually drink. It is an altogether unusual visit.

"These are from Monsieur Gauguin. I told him you do not partake of the white, but he insisted. I am sorry. It is what he gave me. He told me to hurry."

"Thank you, Eloise," Garamond says. He places his pen sideways on a stack of paper. He purposely slows his breathing.

"And the river is running high and so I struggled with my crossing…I am sorry it took me so long."

"Thank you for your delivery," he says. "I am sorry it was a difficult crossing. By how much time were you delayed?"

"I was turned back twice by the river." Eloise sits down on the bench, her back against the outside wall of the villa. She is panting.

"Will you and Madame be needing me today? As you know, Monsieur, this is not my day for working, and my mother will want me back."

"I think we're fine," he says. "You can go back to the village." He is uncertain about Eloise. He is uncertain about her trustworthiness. He suspects Gauguin did not tell her about the purpose of her delivery because she shows no signs of knowing. The three bottles are a signal from Gauguin that there are men in the village asking about them. He sent the maidservant with the wine but did not let her in on the secret. This may be a symptom of Gauguin's mistrust.

"You'll be okay crossing the river? Do you want me to come and make sure you get across?"

"Without the weight of the wine, it will be an easier crossing on the way back," she says. "Thank you for your offer but I will be fine."

Was it Eloise who sent word to the Faculty of Theology? But why would she do this? Perhaps Eloise is their private summoner and she is calling them to stand up and be accountable for their sins against the Church.

When he is certain she is gone, Garamond finds Marie Isabelle. She is brushing her hair in the in the morning light. She is sitting in front of a mirror, her robe puddled at her waist. Garamond stops and inhales this image of his wife. She is the perfect stillness of a high mountain lake at sunrise. He breathes the new yellow light from the window on her skin and the peace of the room, and then he throws a jagged stone into the middle of the lake.

"They have come," he says. "It's time for us to leave."

Marie Isabelle inhales sharply, turns to look at Garamond, and pauses to let this news sink in. She exhales and then she moves into action. They have bags ready to go, and provisions that are easily loaded onto packhorses. Garamond saddles the horses and ties them off to the corral. He pauses and looks around the small courtyard. He will miss this place. It has been an ideal retreat from the world and a fine place to work. They were happy here, and now they were venturing into the unknown. Gauguin had arranged a place for them, a shepherd's hut on the side of a mountain near the Swiss border. He had warned them it would be secluded and hard, but safe.

In less than an hour, they are on the road, moving away from Allemond.

....

They stop at the edge of a lake to water their horses and Marie Isabelle can't hold it in any longer. "Was it Eloise?" she says. "Was it Eloise who made another confession to the priest in the village, and included our conversation as a sin?"

Garamond, who is checking the hoof of one of the packhorses, looks up at her. "Do you think this is possible? What conversation?"

"We talked about the mortal sin of fornication."

"Has the girl committed this sin?"

"So she said. Oh, Claude, I fear I may have been too blunt. I trusted her. I wanted to trust her. I wanted to trust her decency and her intelligence and her common sense."

"It's okay," Garamond says. "We're going to be fine."

"I caused this. I am the reason we are on the run again."

"Enough." He goes to her and pulls her close. She's shaking. "If the girl did this thing, she was unaware of it. She did not know her confession would cause this."

Marie Isabelle is crying now. "But how could her confession cause anything?"

She is talking about the Seal of the Confessional. Garamond thinks about the significance of breaking this seal – if a priest reveals a sin disclosed to him in the tribunal of penance there are serious consequences. He is deposed from the priestly office and sent into the confinement of a monastery to perform a never-ending penance. It is a gravely serious matter to break the Seal of the Confessional, and yet there were men asking about them in the village. Someone talked to the Church. It could have been one of the villagers, or someone passing through who heard about a punch cutter living in the forest, or the priest, who heard a confession. Someone talked to the Church and the Church came looking.

the Tilt-O-Whirl of Us

Tulah Roberts looks at her husband, who is leaning over his coffee mug protectively. "I don't want to be your friend anymore," she says. "I don't want to be the mother of your children. And I don't want to be your life partner." It's Saturday morning. The clock on the stove reads 7:42 a.m. They are in the kitchen having coffee together. The girls are still asleep. Ray was just going to stand up and play some music but Tulah causes him to stay where he is.

It's a little early for this, he thinks. "Okay," he says. "You have my attention."

"Good."

"So what's this about? What do you want to be?"

"I want me to be more than enough for you. I want to be your wife and your lover and enough."

"Okay," Ray says carefully. "You're more than enough for me."

"No, it has to be more than just saying it."

"I mean it."

"It has to be more than you saying it and then saying you really mean it. We need a renewal," Tulah says. "I want to feel really in love with you again. Do you think that's possible?"

Ray smiles. "You feel out of love right now?

She bites her lower lip. "I don't want to sleep walk through my life, through this marriage. I want disruption and chaos and love."

"I do too."

Tulah leans forward and places her hand on his. "So, let's decide to fix it."

"Please tell me you're not considering trust exercises in some therapist's office?" He pauses. "Do you want to get married again?"

"I wasn't going there but getting re-married isn't a bad idea. We can re-write our vows. Make them suit us. Adapt them to now."

"I would marry you again. But before that, I'd like to understand us again," Ray says. "I'd like to know how we're going to move forward.

I'd like the design of it. Some of the small details like the font and the font size, and whether or not we're one column or two, but also the big picture – the theme, the vision. You know."

Tulah smiles. "We're not a corporation, Ray."

"That's not what I meant. I meant an agreement that looks backward and forward, but mostly looks at the present. Maybe it's as simple as disruption and chaos and love. Or love, respect, and honour. Or love, whimsy and playfulness. Maybe it focuses on the details of the present." He hopes a reframing of them might distil to a few basic principles and if they can work on these things, everything else will fall away.

"I like the idea of having a theme for us," Tulah says.

"The theme of us. The theme park of us."

"Yes," she says. "We have to discover new ways to connect."

"I'll meet you in the theme park of us, right next to the merry-go-round."

"The Tilt-O-Whirl," Tulah says. "I love the Tilt-O-Whirl. Meet me at the Tilt-O-Whirl of Us and you've got a date."

He'd love to suggest Madame Chernakov. She would know what to do. She could look at 'completely botched' and see a way to make it work again. She could convince Humpty Dumpty to smarten up and get his shit together.

"I'll meet you on the Tilt-O-Whirl of Us," he says. "I'll be there." Ray loves the idea of a Tilt-O-Whirl because it's a grounded carnival ride that constantly surprises. It seems innocent and tame but it can really toss you around. And there are unexpected moments when it is just delightful.

....

Ray wakes up nauseated and slips out of bed. In the bathroom, he sits on the edge of the tub and looks at the toilet. He contemplates his stomach and if he is actually going to be sick or not. He swallows, and swallows again, and then swallows again. After a few minutes of indecision, he decides no, he's not really feeling sick to his stomach.

In the kitchen, he opens the fridge and looks inside. There's a half-bottle of chardonnay in the side door and he decides this is an appropriate drink for 4:45 a.m. He fills a coffee mug with wine and steps out onto the front veranda. He places his wine down and goes back inside for a jacket. Maybe he should have made a coffee, or tea.

The chickadees are flapping and fretting in the pine, zooming in and out of the tree, having breakfast. Ray does not want to think about anything. He just wants the birds, the trees and his mug of wine. He does not want to think about Nancy. He has spent altogether too much time thinking about her in the past year. He takes a gulp of the wine. He should tell Tulah he has been distracted, and maybe a bit preoccupied, but he is not distracted anymore. Oh that's perfect. 'Distracted' as a euphemism for 'fucking around.' Beautiful. He will not tell Tulah about Nancy – not directly. He will carry that burden himself. It would solve nothing to be forthright. Tulah knows he is far from perfect. She knows they have been horribly detached. He will swallow Nancy and move forward. He will acknowledge his guilt and dishonesties, and turn toward the hard places – the places where there is work to do. He will try to forget the hellish phone conversation that threatened to never end – and he will count himself lucky that she was finally, after four hours, fine about things. He will open himself to happiness in whatever form it wants to take. He will be happy with Tulah. They will be happy again.

Ray is cold. He tries to light the deck heater – a tiny propane heater that only takes the edge of the cold away – but it won't light. The hollow metal clicking sound of the starter cuts into the morning but Ray can't get it going. He knocks the propane hose against the deck floor a couple times, in case there is a blockage, but the heater will not light. He tries to light it with a wooden match to get the smallest of flames going, to somehow draw out the propane, but there is nothing.

....

Madame Chernakov does not offer him a mug of coffee. She pours it and places the mug beside his chair without asking. Despite thinking he would not tell her about the long conversation with Nancy, he does.

"Nobody wants to be alone," she says. "We humans will put up with a lot to avoid being alone."

"Do you mean to say alone? Not lonely? Because I've always made that distinction."

"I mean alone, and lonely."

"So we will tolerate being miserable and unhappy, just so long as we are not alone?"

"Oh, my dear Ray, are you just now realizing there is no black? There is no white? It's all grey, my dear."

"So, I will be a little bit unhappy sometimes but I won't be alone?"

"We are all damaged," she says. "It's life. Do you feel okay about it being over? Are you okay?"

"Yes. It was hard. I should never have answered that call. But yeah, I'm okay."

Madame Chernakov looks away. She watches the clouds moving in the upper corner of the window. She listens to the creaking of the water pipes as they try to push heat into the building. She closes her eyes. When she opens them, she turns to face Ray. "And Tulah?"

He thinks about the kinky door Tulah opened the other day in the bathroom of that restaurant. A small shiver moves up his spine. "She wants to work on us. She wants some sort of renewal."

"Do you think this is a good idea?"

"Of course. I love her. I think anything that smashes us together is brilliant. Call it what you want…" Ray pauses and looks hard at the therapist. "But I don't want Bob and Bernice Fuckwad from Illinois who run touchy-feely couples' retreats for folks who want to rejuvenate their marriages. You see, Bob and Bernice Fuckwad from Illinois found each other on Christian Mingle Dot Com and they were featured on Oprah in 1993, and they have all the touchy-feely answers to a happy marriage. I don't want all the pat answers. I want real guidance. I want some sort of wisdom about this."

Madame Chernakov giggles. "Jesus, Ray," she says. "Sometimes you amuse me. I can recommend some therapists with integrity, and honour."

Ray thinks about bearing witness. They have been witnesses to each other's lives and sometimes when you are witnessing, you see things you wish you hadn't. But you do not look away just because it's unpleasant. You hear things you wish you hadn't. You feel ugly things and sometimes say ugly things. These are only the trees and a marriage is a forest.

....

Ray pushes the starter button on the heater and clicks it repeatedly. He taps the hose again. The heater sparks and the flame flutters a bit, but it will not stay lit. He is not going to give up. He'll keep trying until he is exhausted and even then, he'll keep trying until eventually, the spark will ignite a blue-orange ring of flame and it will hold.

*"But when a woman decides to sleep with a man,
there is no wall she will not scale, no fortress she will not destroy,
no moral consideration she will not ignore at its very root:
there is no God worth worrying about."*
– Gabriel García Márquez, *Love in the Time of Cholera*

*"But first there was life. Hidden beneath the blah, blah, blah.
It is all settled beneath the chitter chatter and the noise. Silence and sentiment.
Emotion and fear. The haggard, inconstant flashes of beauty.
And then the wretched squalor and miserable humanity.
All buried under the cover of the embarrassment of being in the world …
blah, blah, blah."*
– Jep Gambardella (from the film – *The Great Beauty*)

the cranes confined to the nest

If this really was the prologue, it might begin like this; *Tulah is alone in the kitchen, it's raining, Mozart's music is floating around the room, and Ray is still sleeping.* But surely you know by now, you're riding along the surface of the backwards skeleton of a novel. You're moving forward in time while the chapter numbers and other undisputed conventions of novels have been counting down toward something. If that little voice in your head is saying that at the end of this countdown there might be a payoff, a climax, a "damn, I honestly did not see that coming" moment, well, forget about it. That's not going to happen. This story is pretty much done. No loose ends here. Just a soft landing. There is enough hardness in the world.

....

On that morning, Tulah toasts a plain bagel and looks around the room. She's the one who wanted an open-concept home and now it has lost its appeal. She wants smaller rooms now, not this hollowed-out openness. She wants the clarity of cozy compartments and passageways from room to room. She wants rooms of different colours, not this one-tone auditorium. She does not put margarine on her bagel. She used to, but now it's a skiff of butter, or nothing. It was some story she read online that reminded her that margarine was coloured to make it look like real butter. In the same way, she does not drink Diet Coke anymore – in fact, she doesn't drink diet-anything. Whatever the sweetener is, she has decided she does not want it in her body. Every now and then, she'll have a real Coke, with real sugar. She flips open the laptop on the counter and picks some music – this morning, Mozart's *Vesperae solennes de confessore* with Kiri Te Kanawa.

The day is grey. It's drizzling and all the colours are vibrant and sharp. The grey-green junipers pop against the pewter sky. The tree trunks on the boulevard are high-contrast black, and the puddles on the street are bowls of silver. This music is a good match. She clicks on play and her hunch is confirmed. The strings caress the morning and then Kiri Te Kanawa's voice floats in the room. And of course the genius of Mozart is always there in each breath, each note, each phrase. And there is the perfect grey light in the room and the constant drizzle outside.

The girls are at a sleepover and will have to be picked up at noon. It's nice that they're only a year apart and get invited to the same birthday parties and sleep-overs. Tulah suspects at some point in the future this will change. They'll want separation, but for now, it's a good thing.

Last night, she and Ray met in the middle of the bed and held each other for a long time. They said nothing. They touched without desire or need or any sexual wanting. As if there was another level of intimacy that was beyond all that. As if they were both tired of the bullshit and wanted something true. They'd pushed through a membrane into this new land of observance where, maybe, sexual anxieties could not exist – a land where there was only beholding and no judging. They observed each other with newborn curiosity and expected nothing. At 3 a.m., when Tulah got up to pee, they were still intermingled together in the middle of the bed, still touching. When she crawled out of bed, wide-awake at 5:05 a.m., Ray was on his side, still in the middle of the bed. As if this was an end-point of something, and it was okay to be dead weight, to be adrift inside your own unconscious breathing. She sat on the toilet and felt hopeful, and she had just begun to fight for them. She felt closer to Ray this morning than she had for the past year. Ray was in their bed, not that woman's bed – and that's all that mattered. Where you go to sleep, and where you wake up, these are the most important things. The little voice in her head is squeaking – What about love? What about respect? What about kindness? Tulah ignores the little voice.

She takes her coffee mug and lets the Mozart push her down the long hallway toward the girls' rooms. She stands in the doorway of Sarah's room. It's tidy and everything has a place. Her bed is made and along the top, above the pillows, there is a line of a dozen teddy bears, placed carefully, all looking out. Patience's room is a disaster zone – blankets strewn in a pile in the middle of the bed, the fitted sheet pulled up at the corner, exposing the mattress, and a pile of books against the wall, ready to tip. Tulah picks up two empty water glasses from the dresser and pads barefoot back toward the kitchen. She hesitates outside their bedroom door and listens – she can't hear anything moving. Ray is still asleep.

She sits at the kitchen island and sips her coffee. She is too old for the myth of perfect love that lasts forever and ever, amen – the myth that is so embedded in the idea of marriage. There is no Cinderella, no Sleeping Beauty, no happily ever after. Human beings get distracted. They grow tired of their own patterns. They tire of what they have and they look around. Or they forget how to kiss. Or they forget how to start to make love. Married couples get distracted by the lives they devise – by jobs, and children, and desires. And if a husband or a wife strays, it is never a mistake. They like to say that straying is a mistake, but it never is. It is always on purpose. Tulah knows in her heart it is always a choice. She also knows that infidelity is never simple. Are you meeting in a hotel at the airport, are you looking at pornography, or are you practically leering at that executive assistant in your office? Are you flirting? Are you open to the advances of a man who accidentally drops a book beside you at the airport? How far are you willing to go? How many lies are you willing to tell? How many lies are you willing to live? How many lines are you willing to cross?

She decides she is not jealous. She must rise up and move beyond jealousy because she can't go there. She is only a little hurt, and it is a small thing to forgive a little hurt.

"We are happy," she whispers into the room. "I am happy. We are happy."

Tulah takes a big breath and when she exhales she is angry again. She thought her anger was at bay, but it was a pissed-off elephant in the room – an elephant that was confused and enraged and desperate. She grips her coffee mug – her impulse is to throw it across the room, through the window and into the grey day. She looks at the mug. Patience made this mug – it was a gift from her daughter and Tulah feels awful.

She takes a sip of her coffee, which is lukewarm. She wonders if she needs forgiveness, or if she should offer it. What about the idea of absolution? Is absolution only a Catholic thing? Because she wants to be absolved, and she wants Ray to ask for it, and neither of them is Catholic. She knows forgiveness has a power that exists beyond any concept of God, but she is unsure about absolution. She does not know anybody in her life who would be qualified to grant absolution for her sins. Maybe the Dalai Lama. She can imagine the Dalai Lama listening to her long list of sins. He will listen, his eyes brimming with compassion and then he'll lean forward and touch his forehead to hers. Maybe she will feel some sort of deep jolt of awakening – she will have touched an old, fully awakened soul. He will look at her, quizzically tilting his head. "Stop being bad," he will say. "Stop it. Practise kindness. Practise compassion." Then he will smile and step back, and Tulah will know she is absolved.

....

Ray is dreaming he is a Viking. In this dream, Nancy is wearing his ring. It is not the simple silver ring from the newspaper article – not the one that was found in the Viking grave fields near Stockholm. This ring is white gold, or platinum, and it's set with a massive diamond.

It is raining in his dream, and everything is wet. He and Nancy are on a ship at sea. The water is a murky green-grey and the sky is a study of the colour of zinc. They are sheltered below deck in a small cabin. The smell of wet wood. And chickens. And damp wool. Nancy is in bed beside him. She is scratching him with her ring – the diamond has turned under on her finger and she does not rotate it. She's trying to be gentle and loving with her touches, but Ray's body is covered in scratches, some deeper than others. The scratches turn immediately into scars. Regardless of the pain, Ray wants her to touch him – he lifts toward her touch.

She planes her hand with its jagged ring along his lower back and across his right buttock. There is an immediate welt – a striation. "Can you feel that?" she asks.

Ray looks at her. Her lips are so red. They are full and pouty and shockingly red. "Yes," he says, "I can feel that."

"Good," she says. "It's important to feel things."

She lifts her hand and begins again in a different spot.

....

Tulah picks up the phone before it rings twice. She does not check the call display – she just scoops it up and says hello on an exhalation. It's the police. The woman killed herself – a handful of sleeping pills – perhaps some vodka. They're doing an autopsy. They found Ray's number on her phone – a long conversation four days ago. There were a couple other calls after that but nothing as substantial as a four-hour-and-thirty-nine-minute conversation.

Tulah sits down. A shiver of tears. An exhausting, consuming sorrow. A jolt of breathless pain stabs through her core. She swallows hard, and then again. "Four hours and thirty-nine minutes," she says. The length of this call was almost more shocking than the fact the woman was dead. What did they talk about for almost five hours? There is an assumed intimacy in a phone call that length. She tells the police officer on the phone that she will let Ray know. She will get Ray to call back. "Yes," she says. "It's sad news."

"Did you know Ms. Petya well?"

"She was an acquaintance," Tulah says. "My husband knew her better than I did."

"Your husband is Ray Daniels?"

"Yes. I know we have different last names. I'm Roberts. Tulah Roberts." She spells her first name for the policeman. "We don't believe in hyphens," she adds. She can hear her own voice explaining their names to this policeman, and at the same time she is appalled that she is doing it.

The officer is silent, as he is trying to understand what she's talking about. As if it's beyond him somehow. What is she saying about hyphens? Finally, he clears his throat. He tells her everything. It comes out in one long stream. There was no note but there is no doubt this was a suicide. She cleaned the entire apartment, did all the laundry, folded it and put it away. She took the garbage out and dusted, everything. She vacuumed and scrubbed every surface – even the glass railing on the balcony was cleaned. Every pair of shoes in her apartment was polished. There were sixty-seven pairs of shoes, organized by colour and heel. All the dishes were done and placed in the cupboards. She was wearing a red dress and a string of white pearls. Her hand was locked on the pearls when they found her. "...Her hair was done. I mean, it looked pretty," he adds. "Her ankles were crossed and she was – I don't know if this sounds weird – but I thought she looked peaceful..."

Tulah is confused. Why is he sharing all these details about this dead woman? She does not want to know anything about this god-damned woman, and this policeman is spitting out details she will not be able to forget. Why would he notice her ankles were crossed? Why doesn't he tell his wife these things? Or a co-worker? Or his mom? Anyone but her.

"I don't know why…"

"…I am sorry. I don't mean to weigh you down with this, especially when the deceased was just an acquaintance. Please accept my apologies." He's having a hard time reconciling the discontinuities in the woman's apartment. The way everything was perfect – obsessively so – and then that one desperate act of utter chaos. A handful of pills. Well, that and the fact her nylon was ripped – the left leg. With all she did to make sure everything was in its place, why didn't she take the time to put on a pair of nylons that wasn't ripped? The policeman thinks about the empty pill containers placed neatly on the bedside table – Percocet and Ambien.

"Her nylons had a rip in them," he says, more to himself than to the woman on the phone.

"…maybe it was her only pair," Tulah says, hoping this offering will end things.

"Ah, yes, of course, that could be. I'll look into that." He can't imagine why this ripped nylon would be important. He tells himself to just let it go but little things like this nag at him. The police officer does not tell her about the white silk scarf tied to the balcony rail, or caught there somehow. This was another strange detail of this death but he was beginning to sense the deceased woman was less than an acquaintance to Tulah Roberts. He decides not to tell her about the test on the bedside table next to the pill bottles. The dead woman was probably pregnant. They won't be sure until after the autopsy but the pregnancy kit was left there on purpose – it was not hidden or discarded. It was placed just so. It seemed everything in the apartment was arranged with purpose. The dead woman looked peaceful in her bed, clutching her pearls in one hand, but the whole picture was disconcertingly familiar to him, as if he'd seen her like this before, or he'd seen this pose somewhere.

He clears his throat. "Anyway, again, I apologize for dropping this news on you so early in the morning. We just have some questions for your husband. You understand – it was a lengthy phone call. As a follow-up, we'd like to know what that call was about. You understand, Ms. Roberts. It's just routine."

"I won't forget to tell him," she says. "This is sad news. So awful..." Her voice trails away.

"You have my number? It's extension 346."

"Yes. I have it."

"I am sorry, Ms. Roberts."

"What? What did you say?"

"I'm sorry for the loss of your...of your acquaintance."

"Yes, of course. Thank you," she says.

He disconnects.

"Fuck," Tulah says, a soft whisper into the morning. She sits on the sprawling leather couch and lets her gaze be in the direction of the windows and the back yard and the snow clouds. She is not one for drinking in the morning but a shot of vodka seems like the right thing. She pulls the bottle from the freezer and slow-flows it into a water glass. She shoots it back – it's icy cold and harsh and it burns down her throat – and then she pours another.

Part of her is fine with the death of this woman – the jealous, petty part of her – the part that can so clearly imagine this woman and Ray making love. The part of her that was hurt by a year or more of secrecy and lies could care less about this woman's death. Mostly, Tulah is sad. Ray's mistress was a human being who wanted to be loved, who wanted to love and in this basic respect, she was no different than Tulah. And really, what does it matter? He's a good husband, and father, and friend. She would not want anyone else to witness her life. Oh God, this is bullshit. She knows this is bullshit. All these things are just lofty, high-road goals – they are the Buddhist way, they are the way of forgiveness. Right now, all she can think is that he is a selfish bastard, an asshole, and her husband. She was a horrible person too, but she'd stopped being like that. She was not so horrid now. She was well beyond being vile and now he has reminded her of her own sins. She does not know what to feel. Everything is swirling.

It's too soon, but she can see herself shouldering part of the blame for this woman's death. She can draw the line from an unhappy Ray being open to the idea of an affair, to him breaking the affair off, and then this woman killing herself. At the bottom of it all, was Tulah, because she played a role in Ray's unhappiness. Tulah shouldered part of the blame for not having a sex life with her husband. Her desire faded and she did nothing about it. She is baffled by her diminished sexual wanting. Perhaps she just stopped caring. And Ray went to this poor woman for sex. Tulah may as well have killed her with her own hands. She killed her. And a few days ago, she told her she was nothing more than an amusement ride. She may as well have force-fed her those pills. The police will want to question her next. The police will figure this out. They'll know it was her. Tulah can feel panic rising in her body – she can't get a full breath. She has to calm down but she can't focus on calming down. She starts to feel dizzy. She leans forward and hangs her head between her legs – and eventually she is able to get an almost-full breath. Then another. The police don't know anything. Another breath. They just have routine questions for Ray. Not her. They're not interested in her. They don't care about her and Ray's sex life. And anyway, there was the craziness in the bathroom at the restaurant a couple of days back. That was something. But the police won't care about that either.

At the bar, she pours another shot of vodka and pounds it back. In an hour or so, she will wake Ray. She will not make him a press of coffee as she usually does on weekends, and he will notice but he will say nothing. She will tell him to sit down, she will tell him what happened and he will know she knows, and this makes her sad. She grieves for all of them – for the poor dead woman, for Ray and for herself.

Perhaps she will look at him and say, "Did you love her?"

"In my own stupid way," he might say. "I cared about her in my own stupid way. What does it matter now?"

"You're right," Tulah will say. "It doesn't matter now."

But it will matter. She will stifle her anger, and in time, she might be okay with this answer. She knows she cannot judge. She cannot stand and point her finger at him and then look in the mirror with any honesty, or honour. There will be no screaming, and no hollering about this woman. Because Tulah still yearns for her lover. She yearns and yet she still feels betrayed by Ray. He snuck around. He lied. He lied, a lot. She knows the number of lies it takes to have an affair.

Perhaps, Tulah thinks, Ray will notice she is calmer than she ought to be, more accepting, less angry. This could be partly because the woman died and death has a funny way of lining up priorities. But perhaps, eventually, he will think she is not crazy angry about Nancy because she's guilty of the same thing. He might see her behaviour as a puzzle. One day next month, or two years away, or eighty-four days in the future, or a half a year down the road, Ray will lean back in his chair and smile. "So, what was his name?" he'll say. And Tulah will be relieved. She will exhale and she will tell him everything.

She thinks about cranes. She remembers seeing a television show about the Sandhill cranes and how they mate for life. They return year-after-year to the same breeding ground with the same mate. They do not define their connection and they certainly don't question it. They nest and have baby cranes. She is unsure about what a baby crane is called. A chick? She and Ray have become cranes confined to a nest. They made this defective nest and now it was theirs.

Tulah hopes Ray will be able to come to an understanding of who he is and who they are and quietly step past this Petya woman – the dead woman. Tulah shivers. The woman killed herself. She cleaned for days and then killed herself. She took a bunch of pills, crossed her ankles and clutched her pearls, and went to sleep. She wonders if this woman knew – if she was aware that she was drifting off and not coming back. Never coming back. Was there a moment of doubt – a split second in which she suddenly did not want to die?

It would be like Ray to bear this weight himself – to carry the dead woman, and any guilt he felt about her, and not say anything about it. It would not occur to him to tell Tulah everything and beg forgiveness. He would think this was cruel and selfish, and purposely hurtful. Now, this quiet journey will not be possible. He will have to come up with a different way to move forward. There will be guilt but it won't just be about having an affair with this woman – it will also be guilt about her death.

The rain is coming down steadily now. Perhaps it will turn to snow in the evening, but Tulah does not care. She no longer wants to write about snow, or even think about it. It has taken her forty years of living to arrive at a place beyond snow. She is done with winter. If it snows later on, she will have a drink and go to bed.

She would rather focus on rain. Rain is life. It makes things grow. It does not cover up. It amplifies colour and brings clarity. It makes the world more vibrant. Tulah slips out of her robe and steps out onto the veranda in her bra and panties. She shivers instantly, shocked by how cold it is. She breathes her way into it – she welcomes the rain on her skin. This morning, she needs to be exactly in this moment – dripping rain, cold and shivering, guilty, indignant, and sad.

She wants the enchantment of the rain, as if she lives in a world where it will be always raining – a world where the rain never stops. She imagines a place where the rain holds all the nutrients of sunlight. People in this world are in a state of constant renewal, a constant and steady baptism. Every time they are wet by rain, they are healed and forgiven. The rain is a salve that never ends. Nothing bad sticks to the people of this rainy world. No one will know they are innocent because everyone is innocent. There will be forbidden things, and taboos, and a list of sins, but these will be small things, and the rain will always wash away any transgressions.

She might watch a small child who is colouring a picture.

What colour is the sky? Tulah will say.

Grey, the child will say. *The sky is grey.*

And what about the stars at night?

The child will be confused. *What are stars at night? There is only rain at night. It is dark at night.*

The child will finish colouring and then start to draw thin, streaky lines across her picture.

What are you doing?

Finishing my picture, the child will say.

What are those lines? Tulah will ask.

Those lines are the rain.

What does the rain mean?

The child will look up at Tulah as if she is stupid. *It means we are all forgiven,* the child says. *It means you are forgiven.*

Tulah will step forward and lean in. *What? What did you say?*

But the child is engrossed in colouring, lost in the picture. Then the child will be inside the picture, sitting at a wooden table and colouring a picture of a child, who is colouring at a wooden table, and there is a half-naked woman leaned over the child asking questions about forgiveness and rain and the colour grey.

Tulah jerks her eyes open. A shiver tickles across her shoulder blades. The sky is so grey. She wants this rain to colour her. She wants to feel the pulsating aliveness; the violent happiness she knows is just beyond her grasp.

. . . .

IT'S TEMPTING TO KEEP GOING HERE — TO STAY TRUE TO THE GAME, THIS CONSPIRACY OF WORDS, THIS SOFT TRICKERY. But that's all done now. That about does 'er. This is not part of the narrative. Not really. There will be no sneaking in an extra scene or two with old Claude Garamond, or a heartbroken Viking. Enough. But maybe you need to know if they make it. Do Garamond and his lovely wife get away from the Church?

. . . .

Imagine this: *Marie Isabelle and Garamond arrive at the retreat high above the Tarentaise Valley. It was a difficult journey in which Garamond did a lot of looking back to make sure they were not being followed. They have fallen into new patterns in their nineteen days on the mountain, and one of these is to linger a while in bed before venturing into the day.*

It's early. They are in bed, warm and cocooned under a heavy down quilt. They can see their breath in the room. Neither of them wants to get up and make a fire. The view from the bed is all mountain peaks with striations of snow, and lush fingers of pine rising up the slopes. Below them in the valley there are a few vineyards and the beginnings of a village. In the time they have been living in this hut they have not seen another human being. It's a simple stone dwelling built into the side of the mountain, with a chicken coop, a nearby stream and a small vegetable plot. They've been living on chicken and wine since they arrived. The vintner said the place was called Planay.

Garamond regrets having to run, but when the warning came, he knew there were men asking pointed questions about them in the village, and they could not wait around to greet them. Even though Garamond would likely have been exonerated because his association with his former mentor was not substantial, there was a risk that the stench around the implication and execution of Antoine Augereau would taint a trial, if it came to that. These days when the ideas of Protestantism were challenging the doctrine and authority of the Roman Catholic Church, an implication could be a death sentence. And given Garamond's Protestant predilection it was probably best to ride out this transitioning period in seclusion. Living in isolation above the Planay Valley was a fine thing.

He knows Marie Isabelle had settled at the house near Allemond and that their life had tumbled into pleasant routines. If not entirely happy, Garamond hoped she was at least a little happy there. They had friends, and she had the maidservant, Eloise, and they had a steady supply of books. Garamond had his workshop, the hut with all his equipment, and the time to work. And now, it was disrupted again, and reorganized into patterns that were more difficult. Today he will check the snares and see if he's caught any rabbits because they will soon run out of chickens. Marie Isabelle will garden – she will harvest the root vegetables hopefully for a rabbit stew.

Later on, Garamond will chop wood for the stove and perhaps explore a nearby lake for fish. He does not know how to fish but surely it can't be too difficult. On his way to the lake, he will accidentally flush a covey of black grouse. Three of them will arc away to his right and then curve directly back overhead. They will be trying to steer him away from their nests. The sound of the wings frantically beating the air above his head will cause Garamond to duck. The wings sound closer than they are and that sound scares him. When Garamond stands up straight he will take note of where he is. He will not think the grouse are beautiful; he will think, we can eat those.

Eventually, he will start to work again. There is a spot with good light near the side door where he will set up a sturdy table and continue to refine his letterforms.

Marie Isabelle moans as she wriggles her behind into Garamond's front. She grunts a little and he notices – moves his hand to the sweaty alcove between her breasts. She thinks about sex, just for a second – she thinks about all of it, all the possibilities of the morning with her husband, in bed, under the eider-down duvet. This is her home now, not houses or villas, or cities, or villages or towns, but this feeling of belonging she has with her husband. It is the only thing of value. It is home. A shiver twitches *through the middle of her body, a tingling spasm of anticipation, and she grunts again. Garamond pulls her closer and she is happy.*

Here's the thing…it's sad about Nancy, or Nensi, but how could you possibly predict that, or prevent it, as it happens? She checked out on her own terms, and while it's kinda nice that she gets to do things her way, it's heartbreaking. Too much loss. Sometimes a person can bounce back from any loss, and sometimes a solitary loss becomes too much to bear.

Listen, you should know this about old Claude Garamond and his sixteenth century world: Maurice Gauguin was no fool. The vintner could see his wife was attracted to Garamond, and that regardless of the fact she was a god-fearing woman, something might eventually happen between them. Hell, even *he* was drawn toward Garamond's obsessive, artistic personality. Gauguin figured it was just a matter of time before Garamond and Natalii were humping like bunnies in the woods. So he sent the warning of the three bottles of Meursault, not because there were men from Paris in the village, but because he wanted to get rid of the threat of Garamond. Of course, Garamond wanted nothing to do with Natalii. He was fanatically in love with his wife. Would he tease, and push at the edges of flirtation? Yes. But to bed another women was out of the question for him. Point of honour to Claude Garamond.

Go back to near the beginning and read the "Epilogue." It ought to make perfect sense now.

"The only kind of literature that is possible today: a literature that is both critical and creative." – Italo Calvino (This is here because the author both understands it, and does not understand it.) And this quote from Calvino's Six Memos for the Next Millennium: *"Overambitious projects may be objectionable in many fields, but not in literature. Literature remains alive only if we set ourselves immeasurable goals, far beyond all hope of achievement. Only if poets and writers set themselves tasks that no one else dares imagine will literature continue to have a function,"* an idea the author embraces, but fears he may have embraced a little too wholeheartedly.

The line "I feel certain that I am going mad again," the title of Chapter 3, is from Virginia Woolf's handwritten suicide note.

Drink your eight cups of water per day. It'll do you a world of good.

The author would, in all honesty, like to acknowledge the following people: Cindy-Lou T., and M. Mackenzie T., for steadying the ship, and for being delightful, and making me laugh. Paulette Dube for her perfect encouragement. Leah Fowler for her mind and heart. The support of Gail Sobat and Geoff McMaster, and all the talented artists at *YouthWrite* – Noel, Nick, Joe, Marla, Caleb, Spyder, Shelby, Robert Jahrig, Conni Massing et al. Amazing friends – Colin, Patty, Sue, Rob. The fine literary conversations with Harding. Extraordinary editor, Lara Hinchberger. Gregg Shilliday and all the fine folks at *Great Plains Publications/Enfield & Wizenty*. And finally, my Italian muses – Italo Calvino, Alessandro Baricco and Paolo Sorrentino.